Advance Praise for *Sila's Revenge*

*"As mighty and mending as 10,000 drums! Sila's Revenge
is a global adventure with a uniting message. Jamie Bastedo
is truly at the top of his game."*
– Richard Van Camp, author of *The Lesser Blessed* and
  The Moon of Letting Go

*"This youth thriller set in a forbidding future ... picks up
where Bastedo's last novel,* On Thin Ice, *left off. Our heroine,
Ashley Anowiak, is now 18 and her informed passion for
protecting the planet has intensified ... Ashley has explosive
youthful energy and raw determination on her side, but can
she summon the collective action needed to change the climate's
future? ... A powerful voice that demands to be heard."*
– *News North*

SILA'S REVENGE

SILA'S REVENGE

JAMIE BASTEDO

Red Deer PRESS

Published by Red Deer Press
A Fitzhenry & Whiteside Company
www.reddeerpress.com

Credits
Edited by Peter Carver, Interview by Peter Carver
Cover design by Jacquie Morris and Delta Embree, Liverpool, Nova Scotia
Cover images courtesy of iStockphoto and Jacquie Morris
Author photo by Ross Burnet
Text design by Tanya Montini
Printed and bound in Canada for Red Deer Press

A Horse with No Name
Words and music by Dewey Bunnell © 1972 (Renewed) Warner Bros. Music Limited.
All rights for the Western Hemisphere controlled by WB Music Corp. All rights renewed.

I Got You (I Feel Good)
Written by James Brown. Used by permission of Fort Knox Music, Inc.

Acknowledgments
Financial support provided by the Canada Council, and the Government of Canada
through the Book Publishing Industry Development Program (BPIDP).

Canada Council   Conseil des Arts
for the Arts   du Canada

Library and Archives Canada Cataloguing in Publication
Bastedo, Jamie, 1955-
Sila's revenge / Jamie Bastedo.
ISBN 978-0-88995-422-9
I. Title.
PS8553.A82418S54 2009   jC813'.6   C2009-903058-6

United States Cataloging-in-Publication Data
Bastedo, Jamie.
Sila's revenge / Jamie Bastedo.
[256] p. : cm.
Summary: Prepared to do anything to get the world's attention on the plight of the Earth, Ashley travels from her remote Arctic community, to New York City to perform in the Dream Drummer group.
ISBN: 978-0-8899-5422-9 (pbk.)
1. Global warming – Fiction – Juvenile literature. I. Title.
[Fic] dc22 PZ7.B378Si 2009

ANCIENT FOREST™
FRIENDLY

Preserving our environment
Red Deer Press chose to print the pages of this
book on recycled paper and saved these resources[1]:

energy	water	greenhouse gases	solid waste
15 million BTUs	83,944 L	2,089 kg	611 kg

48
trees were saved
for our forests

Printed by Webcom Inc. on
Legacy TB Natural 100% post-consumer waste.

[1]Estimates were made using the Environmental Defense Paper Calculator.

FSC

Mixed Sources
Product group from well-managed
forests, controlled sources and
recycled wood or fiber

Cert no. SW-COC-002358
www.fsc.org
© 1996 Forest Stewardship Council

For Don Jossa
who befriended the feathered thing on his shoulder
called hope.

Who is Sila?

As told to Danish scholar and explorer, Dr. Knud Rasmussen, by Najagneq, a powerful Iñupiaq shaman in Nome, Alaska, 1927.

"Who is Sila?"

"Sila is a power that cannot be explained in words. She is a very strong spirit, the upholder of the universe, of the weather, in fact, all life on Earth. She is so mighty that her speech comes to us not through ordinary words but through storms, snowfall, rain showers, the tempests of the sea, all the forces that humans fear. Or she may speak through sunshine, calm seas, or innocent, playing children who understand nothing but are closest to her."

"What does she look like?"

"No one has ever seen Sila. Her dwelling place is so mysterious that she is with us and infinitely far away at the same time. The inhabitant or soul of the universe is never seen. Her voice alone is heard. All we know is that she has a gentle voice, like a humming woman, a voice so fine and so soothing that even children cannot become afraid. Only the whispering animals and deceased relatives know her language. And those people who carry the world inside, who pay attention to her messengers."

"And what does Sila say?"

"When times are good, Sila has little to say to humans. What she says is this: 'Respect life and be not afraid of the universe. We are all family.' Then she disappears into her infinite nothingness and remains away as long as people do not abuse life and have respect for their daily food and other gifts from the land and sea."

"And if they do not?"

"There will be consequences."

"What kind?"

"All we know is they will not be good."

PART 1

NANURTALIK, CANADA'S ARCTIC COAST

The world can tell us everything we want to know.
The only problem for the world is that it doesn't have a voice.
But the world's messages are there.
They are always talking to us.

– Quitsak Tarkiasuk, Inuit Elder

The world had a beginning called the Mother of All Things.
Once you have found the Mother, you can know her children.
Having known the children, hold tightly to the Mother.
Your whole life will be preserved from peril.

– Lao Tzu, *Tao Te Ching*

ECO-WARRIOR

EMPIRE OIL TRAILER
AUGUST 25TH, 11:45 PM

As I sloshed a full jerry can of stolen gas on the trailer floor, it occurred to me that this would be one expensive fire. Not for the big oil bastards. They were filthy rich. But for Dad. It was his gas I stole. Not exactly cheap up here. Nothing is, especially when every snowmobile, comic book, and cucumber is either flown in, barged in, or trucked in over a temporary ice road. How people are supposed to survive in the High Arctic is beyond me. Especially now with our climate falling apart.

But I wasn't in the mood to chew on such heavy questions. I had serious work to do.

The trick was to make sure I'd covered as much of the floor and walls as possible to get the whole trailer going up in flames. I wanted to knock this sucker clean off the map. My basic idea was to stop a southern Goliath from crushing our village.

For good measure I dumped gas on a stack of pipeline engineering plans, a row of fancy computers, and a huge box of Empire Oil PR brochures that promised economic paradise to all northerners.

A flashing red light above a computer screen caught my eye. A Webcam winked at me. I doused it with my last dribbles of gas and dove out the window I'd smashed.

It didn't take long to figure out my escape. Run for Anirniq Hill— Angel Hill—the most sacred landmark along a hundred miles of sea-coast. Where the veil between us and the spirit world was said to be paper thin. Where, according to our Elders, light-filled drum dancers, or *tuurngaq*, popped out of the rocks every Christmas and New Year's and partied. Where Empire Oil wanted to build a humongous compressor station. To pump natural gas out of our land, right past our back doors, all the way to California. So they could power their electric can openers, gobble barbecued pig's tails, and drive their Hummers to the beach while we froze in the dark.

My plan was to sit back and watch the fire show from the top of Anirniq Hill. Just me and a stone inukshuk, an audience of two.

The first rule of the eco-warrior: *Nobody gets hurt.* I hadn't seen a light in the trailer since a bunch of Empire executives dressed like lumberjacks flew back to New York after a big pipeline powwow. The event had been organized by our moneygrubbing mayor, Gordon Jacobs. The front page of *News North* showed him slapping their backs as they stepped onto their private jet.

No Empire butts would burn.

The second rule of the eco-warrior: *Don't get caught.* I'd always worked alone in this business of monkey-wrenching—pulling up stakes marking the compressor station site, dumping sand in the gas tanks of Empire bulldozers, chucking their toolboxes into the sea. Our house was empty. My parents, Gabe, and my little brother Pauloosie had taken our boat to Inniturliq for their annual shopping spree—no thrill for me. I'm allergic to shopping. And now that darkness had returned to the night sky, no matter how crazy things got once the flames took off, Ashley the Arsonist would be invisible up on Anirniq Hill. Besides, nobody climbed up there much anymore, let alone in the middle of a wet, foggy night.

I'd wait until things died down, sneak back home, and go straight to bed. I would tell no one of my perfect crime.

Except maybe Rosie and Becca. How could I not tell them?

I wasn't scared. Never once thought I'd get caught.

I was mostly just angry.

I lit a match. Then, for good measure, the whole book of matches. I tossed the little fireball through the smashed window.

There was a great whoosh of flames. Another window popped out, just like in some old war movie.

I ran like hell to the top of the hill. I shook with nervous laughter all the way, thinking: *How easy was that!*

GOODBYE JACQUES

TUULLIK PINGO
SIX WEEKS EARLIER, JULY 14TH, 4:00 PM

Why angry? I'll tell why angry.

It started a couple of years ago, one Labor Day weekend, when my best friend Rosie's house was flattened by a freak storm. Half of Nanurtalik got flooded. The graveyard busted open and skeletons rolled into the sea. The town's main fuel tank burst and the cops warned people not to smoke outside or the streets might catch fire.

A couple of months later, two classmates ended up dead, thanks to unusually thin ice on the winter road to Inniturliq. One went to the bottom of the Arctic Ocean in his pickup truck. The other was ripped apart by a starving polar bear.

Then we got hammered by a six-day blizzard, stronger and longer than any storm our Elders could remember. In the middle of it, somebody fired bullets into our house while shooting at another polar bear, driven into town by shrinking sea ice.

At my father's whaling camp, I've watched beluga meat go putrid in the sun before it had a chance to dry properly because our summers are getting too hot. I've heard hunters complain that seals and caribou, ducks and geese aren't where they're supposed to be any more because of weird changes to their migration. I've had a hundred-year-old Elder cry on my shoulder because she couldn't predict the weather anymore.

All this trouble, chewing away at our land, at our culture, caused by one thing: an Arctic climate gone crazy.

The last straw was losing Jacques.

Even in my last year of high school, when our drumming group took off and rehearsals and gigs kept me busier than ever, I stole hours on the land like a miser pinching pennies. Not hunting, not fishing, not picking berries. Not doing much of anything, really.

Maybe hanging out on the Spit, sifting its satin-smooth pebbles for polar bear bones. Tromping the sedge meadows behind Crab Bay, inspecting empty snow goose nests for downy feathers, lighter and softer than air. Sketching the funnel-shaped web of a wolf spider or a house-sized boulder dropped by a glacier. Or sitting on Anirniq Hill, eyes closed, listening to the music of my village. Two ravens nattering at each other from the top of the church bell tower, rowdy laughter bursting through the open doors of the poolhall, hunks of spring ice brushing up against the metal legs of the government pier, and underneath everything, my favorite sound, the slow heaving of the ocean, like the Earth itself was breathing. Like Sila's breath.

Jacques was the only one who ever joined me for such pointless activities. Jacques, our black Labradoodle with a rose-colored nose and spring-loaded legs. My ever-loyal buddy on the land.

It happened on a stinking hot day in mid-July. Half the town had been going around in bathing suits all week, like we lived in Florida. Rosie, Becca, and I jumped in the Arctic Ocean to cool off about ten times a day. I'd been helping Dad lead a tour to Tuullik Pingo, a mini-mountain of moss-covered ice. Of course, Jacques had to come along. The German tourists didn't mind. In fact, he always seemed to boost my tips.

We did the usual tour around the base of the pingo, then up our secret trail to the summit. A light breeze kept the bugs down. I showed them lots of tundra flowers in perfect bloom, which up here last, like, three days if you're lucky. I spotted a mother grizzly and her two cubs across the bay, chomping on a washed-up beluga carcass. Of course, the tourists went nuts, firing a thousand pictures each and spouting off in frantic German. Mom had packed an awesome box lunch with fresh-baked croissants and real Swiss chocolates. I let them think I put it together.

But, God, it was hot.

We'd usually go back to town by boat, but I told Dad I'd walk the dog home along the beach. Jacques tended to throw up in boats, which wasn't exactly good for business.

As the tour boat slowly pulled away from shore, I, an adorable young Inuk woman, standing on a deserted beach in a summer parka and seal-skin *kamiiks*, with the world's tallest pingo behind her, had become the target of their cameras. After what felt like half an hour of waving and smiling, I whistled for Jacques and started moseying down the beach.

Jacques and I were joined at the heart by some kind of invisible rubber band. Once he was out the door, Jacques would take off like a prisoner making a jailbreak. It used to worry me when he was a pup, but I soon learned that he would always bounce back. Each time, he'd nudge my leg with his muzzle then bolt off in another direction. But this time, after walking way down the beach, well beyond Jacques's normal comfort zone, he still hadn't brushed my leg. Just as I turned to whistle again, I heard a yelp from the base of the pingo.

Jacques's hind legs were boinging around as usual but the rest of him had sunk up to his chest in fresh muck. I noticed a huge slab of wet soil slumping off the pingo just above him.

I booted it down the beach, yelling his name. As the soil inched over him, a gaping wound opened behind it, revealing the white flesh

JAMIE BASTEDO

of the pingo's permafrost core. I marched straight into the spreading puddle of cold muck. Jacques almost licked my face off as I desperately clawed at the ground to free his front legs.

I managed to yank one leg out. The slab curled over us like the hide of a freshly butchered muskox. Icy mud and water slopped on our heads. One of his back legs started sinking out of sight. I looked down at my own feet. Both kamiiks were filling with mud.

Arctic quicksand.

I screamed and clawed and yanked until I heard a horrible sucking noise above me. A dark shadow swallowed us. I fell back on my ass as the car-sized slab landed squarely on Jacques.

I heard one muffled yowl, then a disgusting gurgle like a giant digesting its meal.

GOODBYE GOLIATH

ANIRNIQ HILL
AUGUST 26TH, 12:20 AM

No more Jacques. Smothered when a traditional trail used for hundreds, maybe thousands of years, collapsed on him. Killed by melting permafrost that triggered the mudslide that ate him.

Death by climate change.

Yeah, I was mad all right. I'd relived that awful day a hundred times.

At first I thought all I could do was shake my fist at the sky. Or maybe at everyone down south who was burning up fossil fuels like they'd last forever, like they didn't dump megatons of carbon in the air, like they had nothing at all to do with screwing our climate.

So, no surprise that I boiled over when the Empire Oil boys rolled into town, foisting modern-day trinkets and beads on us at a public meeting in Tuktu Hall. Imported buckets of Kentucky Fried Chicken. Chocolate cake served up on throwaway Styrofoam plates. Free ball caps, pens, and Frisbees plastered with Empire Oil's green dinosaur logo. And—oh yeah!—dumbed-down plans for a monster pipeline compressor station that would change Nanurtalik forever.

"Only as loud as your lawn mower," they'd said.

No lawns up here, fellas, I thought.

"We should add that it will be a mile away," they'd said. "Up close, the compressors sound more like a jet taking off. A small jet."

Enough plane noise up here already, thanks. How am I supposed to hear the Earth breathe?

"But you won't see the station," they'd said. "We'll hide everything behind the hill."

Our sacred hill.

What pissed me off most was the hypocrisy. Our two-faced mayor loved to wail to the media over all the evil things climate change was doing to our sea ice, our land, our livelihoods. Nanurtalik had become world famous for our collapsing streets, sinking buildings, and freak storms. But when the world's largest carbon company waltzed into town, guess who rolled out the red carpet for them? Mayor Lord Gord and his pals, of course.

Don't you get it?

No, they didn't get it. What most people got was the promise of jobs, cheaper groceries, and an annual trip to Disneyland for the kids.

Sitting in that hall, listening to the bullshit from both sides of the table, I had a sudden vision. It was small but hot, like a shooting star. I knew exactly what to do.

JAMIE BASTEDO

Burn down their damn trailer. Stop Goliath in his tracks.

What really surprised me, what got me laughing so hard I almost knocked over the inukshuk, was the huge pumpkin halo that crowned my fire. The fog off the ocean had turned to pea soup, so thick it seemed to ignite. A pillar of black smoke skewered the center of the halo, adding a nice touch to my latest work of art.

I got another surprise when the lights went out. Half of Nanurtalik fell into darkness. I figured the fire melted some wires leading to the trailer and broke the line.

Oops.

Oh well. With no glare from streetlights or windows, the show only got better.

By the time the town's lone fire truck arrived—I'm talking half an hour after I tossed the match—I could see right through the trailer. All flames.

Goodbye walls.

There was a loud thunk and a fist of sparks punched the sky.

Goodbye roof.

Three guys from the volunteer fire crew jumped out of the truck, took one look at the fire, then jumped back in. The truck zoomed backwards a few feet and parked. The guys jumped out again, leaned back against the truck hood, and folded their arms. The truck's red and orange lights gave a cool disco accent to the fog.

Little groups started showing up to have a look-see. Soon the street was lined with people warming themselves in front of my fire. I should have left them bags of marshmallows to celebrate with.

It would have made a great front page photo in the *New York Times*: *Inuit roast Empire's plans for Arctic pipeline.*

That would show those Empire bastards.

Goodbye Goliath.

It started to rain, first a little pissing, then a good August downpour.

People covered their heads and took off.

The flames died down. Nothing much left to burn, anyway.

The fire truck drove away.

I clapped my hands, slapped the inukshuk on the back, and ran for home.

My plan had worked perfectly. The eco-warrior's code was upheld.

Nobody hurt.

Nobody caught.

At least, so I thought.

THE INVITATION

AROUND THE TABLE, ASHLEY'S HOUSE
AUGUST 29TH, 4:15 PM

"*Mon Dieu*, Ash, did you say Carnegie Hall?"

"Well, yeah, Mom. Somebody down there must've stumbled on our Web site and played a few tunes. I guess they liked our shtick."

"And no surprise," Mom said. "Who else on Earth does what you do? Traditional Inuit drumming, avant-garde throat-singing, a spicy dash of fiddle."

"That would be yours truly," Gabe said, bowing so low he almost bashed his head on the kitchen counter. I shot out my hand and caught his forehead just in time.

"So anyways," I continued, "there's this fringey string quartet booked for mid-December, like, cellos and stuff, and they thought it would be cool if we—"

"Carnegie Hall?" Mom repeated.

"What's so special about—"

"It just so happens to be the most famous concert hall in the world."

Rosie twiddled an ear as if it was full of wax. "Sorry, Carole. I think my hearing's going. Gotta fix the muffler on my four-wheeler. Did you say, *in the world?*"

"Holy *crimpuff!* Without question. For my eighteenth birthday, Ash's grandparents drove me down from Montreal to New York to see Bob Dylan on the Carnegie stage."

This I could not believe. My stick-in-the-mud Irish grandfather took Mom to see the most radical folksinger ever? "Bob Dylan? Daddo took *you* to see *him?*"

"It was your Mima's idea, actually. She always had a fighting streak in her. Bit of a radical. I think that's where you get it."

Aana sniffed. "A lot from Uitajuq too, don't forget."

"*Bien sur,* Aana."

My grandmother on my dad's side called me nothing else. Uitajuq. Inuktitut for "Open-eyes." Born in an iglu a hundred years ago. The great grandmother I was named after. By Aana, in fact.

"So, who else performs there?" Rosie asked.

"Who hasn't? Like, the Beatles. I'll never forget, February 12th, 1964."

"You saw *the* Beatles?" Rosie asked.

"On TV. Playing live at Carnegie Hall. That's when Beatlemania exploded across North America."

"Beatlemania?" Gabe said. "Sounds dangerous. Break out the bug spray!"

"They were a band, Gabe," I said, "not bugs. Probably the most famous rock band ever."

"Not to mention orchestras!" Mom said. "The London Symphony, the Berlin Philharmonic, the Japanese Imperial Company. It is truly one magnificent theater. Red carpets, velvet seats. The place is five stories high with balconies to the ceiling. Holds three thousand people. Hollywood stars, fashion plates, princes, and kings. Carnegie's a royal palace for performers!" She dusted flour off her apron and gave me a big hug. "And now, the Dream Drummers, live from Nanurtalik, on the Carnegie stage. I simply can't believe it!"

I let her wallow in pride for a moment, then wriggled free.

Gabe ran for his fiddle. He raised it high, then teased out a series of joyful whoops that sounded exactly like a red-throated loon.

"I can't believe it, either," said Dad, who was fixing his chain saw on the dinner table. Again. We were the only house in Nanurtalik with a woodstove. But sand in the driftwood played hell with his chain saw. He saw it as another way to save money. With oil and gas in the ground all around us, we still had to pay through the nose to barge it here from down south. A fact he never let us forget. "Do you know how much it would cost to fly you to New York?"

"Our whole group, Dad," I said, sliding the letter from Carnegie Hall toward him.

"What?" he said, grabbing the letter and smudging it with a greasy thumb.

"They invited our whole group. Me, Rosie, Becca, Gabe. Everybody."

"All right!" Gabe cried. "New York City, here we come! It's curtain time, kids! Let's hit the stage running!"

"Not quite so fast, Gabe," Mom said as she plucked the letter from Dad's hands. "What's this include, exactly?"

"Read it yourself," I said.

"Third-last paragraph," Rosie said.

We'd read that letter to each other so many times we could recite it backwards.

Dad stared at the chain saw, his hands parked in idle, as Mom read out loud. *"We are pleased to offer your group a world debut fee of one thousand dollars plus two complimentary rooms and meal vouchers for a three-day stay at the Sheraton hotel in downtown Manhattan."* Mom turned to Dad. "How about that, eh, Moise?"

"Not bad," he said, not looking up. "But I was thinking more about getting there and back. Anything resembling air tickets in the envelope?"

"Ah, well, actually, no," I said. "But—"

"Could be a long dogsled trip." Dad looked up at the log ceiling. "Flying would probably cost you … hmm … at least fifteen hundred bucks each. Let's say two grand, to be safe. So that's maybe eight thousand bucks. Then there's taxis and—"

"Only *seven* thousand, once they pay us."

Dad slowly pushed back his Red Power ball cap. "Uh-huh. Well, it'd be a whole hell of a lot cheaper for everybody if you just sent them your demo CD. That's if you ever finish it. They can tell all those rich and famous people to close their eyes and pretend it's live. I'll even spot for the postage."

Money, money, money. That was all Dad ever talked about, especially since he lost a foot to frostbite.

"Moise!" Mom scolded. "Let her do this thing. Can you imagine? The world's your oyster once you've performed at Carnegie Hall."

"Ash-o-mania!" shouted Gabe.

"I'm allergic to oysters," Dad said.

Aana put down the kamiik she was embroidering—a red rose on snow—and carefully slipped a needle into her sealskin pincushion. She looked at her son across the table through bifocals that gave her beluga eyes.

He tried to stare down his chain saw—and lost.

Aana gently touched his hand. "Let the kids go, Moise. World needs to hear our drums. Our stories. Help keep Sila happy."

Dad yanked his hat down but let her hand lie on his.

Aana glanced at the living room window, pounded by yet another brutal rainstorm. Her round chest heaved. "Just look at all this crazy weather. *Maiksuk!* Sila's running out of patience. Let them go, Moise."

I was taken aback by Aana's support. Even in her mid-eighties, Aana had eyes as piercing as harpoons. Enough to give a polar bear a fright. I was glad to have her on our side.

Aana talked a lot about Sila, almost like an old friend. Sila, that fickle force that ruled the wind and sea and just about everything else not nailed down. One night over candlelight, after a winter gale had knocked out our power—for the tenth time that day—Aana warned of *Sila qatlunaatitut.* How if we messed things up too much, if we pushed Sila too far, she'd hit back. Hard. The next day, a throat-singing number spilled out of me, like, I mean, out of nowhere. I called it "Sila's Revenge." It became a smash hit single overnight, at least in little Nanurtalik. I hadn't seen this as a card up my sleeve but, looking at Dad's crinkled brow, I was ready to lay anything on the table.

"Aana's right, Dad. We can help spread the word down south about what's really happening up here with our screwed-up climate. How it's all connected."

Dad went back to work on his chain saw. "Costs a lot to save the world."

"We'll raise the money, Dad. Remember last Christmas? We did that gig in Inniturliq. Scraped up tickets for all four of us, *plus* you and Mom."

"That was basically a freebie from Aklak Air," he said, holding a sparkplug up to the light. "The manager owed me big after his cargo monkeys trashed a very expensive mixing board for the station. Anyways, Ash, Inniturliq and New York City are in slightly different ballparks."

Since turning eighteen, I had vowed that my penny-pinching father would never again throw a wrench in my artsy plans, whether painting, sculpting or, more recently, music. "We'll raise the bucks, Daddy-o." I squeezed his shoulders from behind and kissed his unshaven cheek. "With your help, in fact. You watch."

IGNITION

"I *knew* it!" I shouted, almost dropping my cell phone in the sand. "I just knew we could find the bucks!"

"Piece a' cake, Ash," Rosie said on the other end.

Thanks to all the free airtime Dad had given us on his radio station, we'd managed to raise two thousand dollars in just a week. The four of us had crammed into the tiny broadcast booth and cranked out all of our tunes several times over. With Mom's help, we dug out recordings of just about any pop star that had played at Carnegie Hall. Between numbers, Gabe would crack his usual Eskimo jokes or burn up his fiddle strings with everyone's favorite jigs and reels. But we were still a hell of a long way from New York.

Until Rosie got the call.

"So, who's the moneybags?" I said.

"Hey, get this. None other than your bosom buddies with the KFC and Frisbees."

"*What?* You don't mean—"

"Who else has that kinda dough? The evil empire, of course."

A shiver of anger shook my body, like I felt when busting that trailer window, sloshing gas everywhere, tossing the match.

"But ... but that's *black* money, Rosie! Oily, stinky, black money. You didn't say we'd take it."

"Well, shee-it, of course I did. It's already in the mail. Can't bite the hand that feeds you."

"Yeah, but this is, like, kind of a climate change thing we're doing and they're the ones that—"

"We're doing a *gig,* Ash, not a sermon. At freakin' Carnegie Hall! We fly to New York. Get world famous. Empire Oil collects a few green brownie points. Smells like win-win to me."

"Yeah, but—"

"Think about it, Ash. The fact that they're coughing up this money for us means you're, like, totally legit in their books."

I knew exactly what she was talking about. Even after the cops found an empty jerry can beside the trailer with ANOWIAK written all over it—how could I have been so stupid?—they figured some kid stole it from Dad's shop.

Sounded good to me. "I guess so, eh?"

"Well, duh."

I heard a faint rumble and looked beyond the curling Spit to a bank of dark clouds rolling in off the ocean. There was an eerie static in the air, like it was about to ignite.

"You still there, Ash?"

A warm rain started falling. "Yeah, yeah. It's just getting a little weird out here. Should be snowing but it feels like the Bahamas right now. Thunder, even." I pulled up the collar of my jean jacket and started walking back to town. "So what does Becca think about all this?"

"Haven't told her. You're the team captain."

I'd never asked for that role. I was an artist, not a singer. Me, a tone-deaf musical dunce, leading a drumming group. But once I discovered throat-singing—or did it discover me?—there was no turning back. Most of the numbers we did sprang out of my throat. The first time it happened, the time Uncle Jonah coaxed a song out of me with his drum, it was like releasing a bird that had been caged in my throat since the day I was born. He called it Uitajuq's song. After that, they just kept coming. The songs were deep inside of me and all I had to do was listen. It was like tuning into a frequency, a built-in radio station. Mom liked to say they came from heaven.

Whatever.

"So why did they call *you?*" I asked.

"I happened to be at your house, looking for you. We had a rehearsal. *Remember?*"

"Oh, God, sorry. I needed some air. Gotta get more organized."

"You said it, Captain. Anyways, your mom forced some of her cinnamon buns on me and that's when they called."

"Where are you now?"

"Your place. You better get your butt over here before Gabe eats the last bun."

"Yeah, I'm coming. We need to talk about this, Rosie."

"What's there to talk about? Our ship's come in. Time to climb on board."

"Call Becca. I'll be right there."

"I roger that."

As I reached for the *END* button on my cell phone, there was a deafening crack above me. I saw a flash of light shoot out of the phone. It slugged the right side of my head just above the ear. I flew backwards like I'd been hit by a bus. The next thing I knew, I was flying upwards. I looked around. I saw a body lying face down on the beach.

My body.

ROUTINE MASSACRE

It started with the scream of baby snails.

Horrible. One after another.

It was the first thing I remembered after the lightning strike. A whispered wail. I heard it somewhere in my head. The lightning knocked something loose in there. Busted open a long-locked door. Blew it right off the hinges and threw me in. I landed in some dark, echo-filled chamber in the basement of my mind.

My ears had nothing to do with it.

Still, I could *hear* those little suckers, crawling up the glass toward the light, only to get squished by Mom's thumb.

It never used to bother me much. Mass murder was part of Mom's Saturday morning housecleaning ritual. She'd hover over the fish tank, holding a coffee in one hand, squishing snails with the other.

There'd been an explosion of pesky snails in our tank. They devoured the fancy aquatic plants Mom had brought on her lap all the way from Montreal. Sometimes they carpeted the glass so bad, you could barely see the expensive kissing gouramis and silver dollar fish inside. Worst of all, for Mom at least, they crawled all over her bubbling Buddha statue—into his eyes, across his sacred belly, up his nose. Mom's answer to overpopulation was squishing them when they came within range of her probing fingers.

That Saturday morning, three days after I got fried by a lightning bolt, I didn't see any of this. I never even opened my eyes. Aana told me later that I groaned a bit while Mom did her routine massacre. After that, I blacked out again for hours.

But I know what I heard. Don't ask me how. The whispered screams of snuffed-out snails.

My first call for help from the animal world.

THE MESSAGE

ASHLEY'S HOUSE
SEPTEMBER 8TH, 3:20 PM

I'm told the first word I said, shouted, actually, while clawing my way out of the coma, was "Uitajuq!" She dragged me by the hand out of a deep, dark pit. She gave me back my dreams. And, for a few precious moments, something more, much more.

I'm standing alone on the Spit, looking over a calm sea. A full moon lights up gentle swells that reflect a million rippling stars. The smooth pebbles at my feet look like giant pearls in the moon glow.

A falling star streaks across the sky and seems to land just off the Spit before flickering out. I strain my dream ears for some sizzle or pop but hear only the soft murmur of the sea as it caresses the beach.

I detect a faint splash in the direction of the fallen star, like the sound a beluga makes when it bobs above the water to look around.

Something else falls from the sky. I hear the swoosh of wing-beats and a huge bird lands at the water's edge, so close I can hear the click of its claws as it touches down. The bird's stork-like legs and powder-puff rump tell me it's a sandhill crane. Like me, it looks out to sea where the star fell, listening.

More splashes and I notice a figure walking out of the water toward us. As it draws closer, I recognize the silhouette of a woman's traditional caribou-skin parka. The moon is behind her, igniting a halo of glistening seawater that drips from her clothing. I peer into her shadowed face but see only blackness.

Just a few paces from me, the woman turns away to face the crane. The bird withdraws its long neck and stoops low before her. A moment passes, as if some sacred message is shared between them, heart to heart. The crane spreads its wings and springs to its full height, leaping and hopping in a high-step dance. Joyful rattling cries pour from its upturned beak. The woman kneels and offers her hands to the bird. It comes to her and lays its beak in her open palms.

I feel universes away. My heart burns to know what message has passed between these two beings. As if in answer to my thoughts, the woman stands abruptly, letting moonlight fill her face. I see a young woman with Aana's mischievous smile, my father's sloping brow, and Uncle Jonah's bear-like nose. Long black braids spill from her parka in two silky loops.

Uitajuq. The long-dead woman I'm named after.

She stands, then breaks into a run straight for me—right into me—and we merge!

Everything changes, like I've flipped TV channels. My normal senses shut down as a whole new world opens up. Every pebble on the beach gains a unique personality. Each becomes a part of me, like cells in a larger body that we share. Each has a sound, like the notes of a sky-filling song that stretches around the planet. I turn to the sea. It's like I can hear the distinct hum of each water molecule. I look up. Each star pulses to its own cosmic beat.

Then I remember the crane. It stoops before me, as it did for Uitajuq, and watches expectantly. I focus hard on it and, with my new third ear, I hear a rhythmic whisper, almost like throat-singing. Something brittle *inside of me crumbles and I understand the bird's wordless message:*

Listen.

It's all alive. It's all connected. It's all intelligent.

And we are all family.

Like a flash flood through a dry riverbed, this knowledge pours through me, washing away all separateness between me and the crane, the sea, and the stars—until Uitajuq steps out of me and the sound ends.

I am devastated, feeling terribly small and alone. "Uitajuq! Uitajuq! Help me, please! Don't leave me like this! I WANT IT BACK!" She turns around and looks at me through almond-shaped eyes, brimming with kindness. She walks up to me and wraps her arms around me.

The first clue that my coma had broken was this feeling that someone had used my brain as a chopping block. I mean, for an ax, not a paring knife. The next was my stomach. It felt like I'd swallowed an insane cat that scraped my insides raw. Next came my legs. Like they'd been run over by an eighteen-wheel truck.

Piece by piece, my body gradually wired itself back together, sending one message through my nervous system: *pain.*

Given a choice, I would have retreated back into a numbing coma forever and ever, amen.

Goodbye pain.

But I had no choice.

Something much bigger than Ashley, far beyond pain, pulled me up and out of it. A new craving, to recover that deep, all-knowing connection with the Earth that Uitajuq had opened for me.

THE VISIT

I woke to the sound of Rosie's horsey laugh.

"That's one insane bird," she said.

"Shhh."

That had to be Mom.

I fought to open my eyes. They seemed crazy-glued shut.

"Well, I'll be damned."

Dad's voice.

I cracked one eye open, then the other. Candles.

Is this my funeral?

I became aware of a strange tapping noise. Something banging on the window right beside my bed.

"What the hell's *he* doing here?" Dad said. "Shoulda flown south weeks ago."

I slowly turned my face to the window.

"Ashley!" Mom cried. "Thank God!"

I felt her squeeze my hand. It felt hot and sweaty, like she'd been holding it for hours.

The daylight hurt my eyes.

"You'll be okay, darling," Mom said.

The tapping got more frantic.

I squinted, trying to focus. As my vision cleared, I thought I heard a new sound, a whispered cry that seemed to drill straight into my brain. I reached up to cover my ear. The whispers got louder, almost drowning out the tapping.

"Careful, Ash," Mom said.

My fingers slowly explored a thick bandage covering the right side of my head.

My eyes finally cleared.

The tapping sound stopped. The whispering faded.

Through the rain-streaked window I could see the unmistakable cherry cap and long brown beak of a sandhill crane, its orange, unblinking eyes locked onto mine.

Am I still dreaming?

I bolted upright.

The crane gave one rattling cry and hopped backward off the roof. I almost smashed my head against the window as I watched it dissolve into the rain.

I flopped backwards on the bed.

"*Mon Dieu*, Ash—take it easy," Mom said.

Pain reclaimed my body.

I lay there whimpering for a while until Gabe got me humming to his fiddle music. Today's medicine: "Maple Sugar," one of my favorites, and he knew it.

I cracked my eyes open to see him playing at the end of my bed.

I lifted my head and looked around my bedroom. Pillows and sleeping bags everywhere, like people had moved in for my death vigil. Gabe, Mom, Rosie, Becca, Dad. Even Aana, who hardly ever came upstairs and was now snoring in my comfy chair.

"Thanks, Gabe," I said when he stopped.

He tripped his way around the bed and groped for my arm. "Music'll save your worried soul, Ash."

"And get us on the Carnegie stage," Rosie said. "Still feel up to it, Ash?"

I had to laugh in spite of the pain in my head. "You're such a diva," I mumbled.

"What?" Rosie said.

"A diva. Always looking for the spotlight."

"Like, maybe *later*, Rosie?" Becca said, moving up beside my bed. "We can sign contracts later, baby. Let Miss Lightning Rod get her head screwed back on." She opened her arms and was about to drop into a hug when she turned to Mom. "Is this safe?"

"Gently, please," Mom said. "And don't touch the right side of her head. She's going to have a big owie there for some time."

Becca hugged me as if I was a crystal doll. "We were *so* scared, Ash." I felt tears on my unbandaged cheek.

"What's with all the candles?" I asked Mom when it was her turn. "I thought I'd died."

"You almost did, Ash. The doctor said your eyes would be sensitive for a while."

"Did he say anything about my ears? I heard this weird whispering sound when I woke up."

"No, dear. Probably just your headache."

"Yeah, probably," I said, not really believing it.

Rosie ended the hug lineup.

"I'll be okay," I told her. "Could be fun in New York."

She lifted her head and looked me square in the eye. "Even if it's Empire money?"

I'd forgotten that little detail. "Oh, yeah … Ah, what the hell. They can't own us."

"Now you're talkin', Ash!" Rosie said. "I knew you were saved for a higher purpose."

"Hah," I said, pushing her away.

Aana shuffled in behind her with a big yawn. Her thick glasses were smudged as usual but clear enough for me to see the grandmother's love in her eyes. She picked up my hand and slowly rubbed it between hers.

"You missed the bird, Aana," I said. "A big crane. Slept right through it."

She looked out the window for a long time, listening.

Everyone went quiet.

"It was the strangest thing, *Anaana*," Dad finally said. "If I'd opened the window, it would've hopped right on Ashley's bed and danced for her."

Aana stopped rubbing my hand and smiled proudly at me. "Not so strange for Uitajuq."

PART 2

NEW YORK CITY

What if a small group of these world leaders were to conclude the
principal risk to the Earth comes from the actions of the rich countries?
In order to save the planet, the group decides:
Isn't the only hope for the planet that the industrialized civilizations collapse?
Isn't it our responsibility to bring this about?

– Maurice Strong, United Nations Environment Program

We now seem to be nearing tipping points
past which truly cataclysmic damage would be inevitable.
We might stop just short of some of those tipping points
like the Road Runner screeching to a halt at the edge of a very high cliff.

– Bill McKibben, Science writer

Our responsibility as societies is to keep climate change at the level
where nature can continue to be an ally in this problem
and doesn't turn into an enemy.

– Dr. Chris Field, Climate scientist

WATCH YOUR BACK

STREET VENDOR STALL, TIMES SQUARE
DECEMBER 13TH, 4:15 PM

"Hot nuts! Hot nuts!"

Rosie's horsey laugh cut through the traffic noise. "Hey, now that sounds like fun."

"Yeah," Gabe yelled, "but what about a hot *dog*? I'm craving one somethin' fierce."

The street vendor grabbed three wrapped hot dogs from under a heat lamp and started juggling them like a pro. "We got it all right here, brother. How can I dress it for you?"

He was the blackest man I'd ever seen, at least six foot six with an oddly twisted smile. He was crammed into a dinky wheeled stall. It looked warm in there as we ducked under its flimsy tin awning to get out of the freezing drizzle.

"Dress it?" Gabe said.

"Like, ketchup and stuff," I said. "What do you want on it?"

Gabe started laughing, bending over, holding his stomach like he was going to puke. "I've waited my whole life for this moment!" he roared. "What did the Buddha say to the hot dog salesman?"

"I don't know, man," the guy said, still juggling.

"Make me *one* with everything!"

Becca groaned.

"Don't you get it, Ash?" Gabe yelled. "Don't you get it? Heard it on *Saturday Night Live*."

The vendor stopped juggling and looked at Gabe expectantly. Once he got that Gabe was blind, he turned to me.

"That's a good one, Gabe," I said. "Now, what'll it be?"

"Everything! One with everything!"

"Make that two," I said. I normally detested hot dogs. Mom called them fatal franks. But I hadn't eaten since the crappy snacks on the plane, and these dogs were steaming hot.

"Make that three," Becca said.

"Hot nuts for me, darlin'," Rosie said, leaning forward into the steam.

"Where you folks from?" the big man asked as he opened the buns and piled them high with ketchup, relish, mustard, onions, and chilies.

"The north pole," Rosie said. "Just dropped in to do a bit of Christmas shopping."

"Not 'nough elves up there?"

Rosie laughed. "Uh, yeah, that's right. Real union freaks."

"Uh-huh. First time in New York City?"

"First time in *any* city," Rosie said. "You got any advice for a herd of Eskimo nomads?"

The vendor looked at Becca's pale skin and blonde hair. "S'cuse me, but you don't look like an Eskimo."

"Actually, she's not an Eskimo," I said. "I mean, Inuk." All the traffic and noise was messing my head. "I mean, we're all from up—"

He shoved the bulging dogs at us. "Whatever," he said, folding his arms. "Alls I can say is, watch your back, sister. Never know when—"

Somebody slammed into my shoulder. A wiry guy about half the vendor's height tore past us, knocking Gabe's hot dog to the grungy sidewalk.

"Hey, what the—" Gabe shouted.

"Stop him!" screamed a fat lady all decked out in leather and jewels. "My purse!" She bumped into Becca as she stomped past and Becca's hot dog joined Gabe's in the grunge.

"Cripes!" Becca said.

More scuffling nearby. I clutched my hot dog close to my chest. A jock in spandex tights, pushing a baby stroller, doubled over like he was shot. He flung open the stroller's plastic cover, whipped out a military rifle, and sprinted past us like an Olympic runner.

"See what I mean?" the vendor said with his arms still folded like nothing had happened.

"Who the hell was *that*?" I said.

"Some hard up crack-head."

"No, I mean the guy with the stroller."

"Oh, him. Anti-terrorist spy."

"A spy."

"Uh-huh. New York's crawling with 'em. Never know where they'll pop up. S'posed to make the streets safer."

"Safer."

"Uh-huh."

"Machine guns in baby strollers," Becca said.

"Uh-huh. One of their tricks. But like I say, watch your back. If the gangstas don't get you, the spies will."

"Ooh-kay. Thanks." I passed my half-eaten hot dog to Gabe while stepping around the multicolored mess on the sidewalk.

"S'cuse me," the vendor called after us, "but ain't you gonna pay for those dogs?"

"Right," I said handing him some random bills.

"See what I mean?" he said with a crooked smile. "Wolves every-where."

SOUL MUSIC

7TH AVENUE, TIMES SQUARE
DECEMBER 13TH, 4:30 PM

"Not bad," Rosie said as we joined the river of anonymous humans pouring through Times Square. "Ten minutes on the streets of Manhattan and we see our first robbery."

"Welcome to the urban jungle," Becca said. She pressed against my shoulder like we do up north when it's forty below with an icy wind blasting our faces. For protection. Not against the weather but to fend off blaring horns, screaming sirens. Pounding jackhammers, roaring engines. Stinky trucks, belching buses. Sky-high neon signs pushing Cadillacs, candy, and Coca-Cola. Wall-to-wall zombies trapped in a fossil-fueled orgy of consumerism. The storefronts said it all. Blowout Video. Digital Dreams. Dunkin' Donuts. Girls Galore. I tucked closer to Becca, feeling like an abandoned caribou calf.

Rosie, on the other hand, was totally into it. She stuck out her chin and let out a long, soaring whistle between her teeth. "Do you believe it?" she yelled to no one in particular. "Times Square! Shopper's heaven! This place is overflowing with anything your little heart might desire."

"Like food, maybe?" Gabe said. "I'm still hungry."

Rosie pointed to a huge neon guitar hanging over the street about a block away. "How's about the Hard Rock Cafe?"

"Sounds good to me," Gabe said.

"Don't even think of it!" yelled a man in a trench coat right beside us. Gabe spun around and faced him. "What's your problem, buddy?"

The man ignored Gabe, apparently talking to himself. "It's time to cut and run, Frank. Market's going down. It's crash and burn time. Sell 'em now ... What? ... Shit, no! I'm talkin' flat-out, balls-to-the-wall sell! ... What? ... That's right, Frank. Dump every goddamned share."

The guy reached into his coat, pulled out a Blackberry, and started text messaging while still screaming at somebody named Frank. Then I noticed the tiny phone thingy tucked in his ear. He marched, head down, straight for a red light. Still staring at his Blackberry and yelling something about "hot stocks," he stepped off the curb onto the street.

"Ah, sir!" I said as my hand involuntarily shot out to grab his arm. He flashed me a searing look, like I'd pulled a knife on him, then dove ahead, slaloming through an intersection clogged with honking cars.

"Who's the guy with his balls to the wall?" Gabe asked.

"Must be some suicidal banker," Becca said.

"This town is nuts," I said, tightening my grip on Gabe's hand.

We heard more screaming on the other side of the street. It turned out to be singing.

"Whoa! I feel good, I knew that I would, now ..."

A black guy wearing a Cleveland Indians ball cap and beat-up parka sat on an overturned milk crate beating a homemade set of drums. Well, sort of drums. I'm talking plastic buckets of all shapes and sizes, a few big cans and bottles, and a bent chunk of aluminum siding. He'd made cymbals out of car hubcaps and a metal toilet seat. His drumsticks, blurred by his flying hands, looked like they were whittled from busted baseball bats. He was singing his lungs out.

"Whoa! I feel nice, like sugar and spice, I feel nice, like sugar and spice. So nice, so nice, I got you ..."

An upright bucket that once held Lego was tied to the shopping cart he used as a drum stand. I peered in to see his haul for the day: a few loose bills and a bunch of bruised bananas. I tossed in all the change I had in my pocket, maybe a buck and a half.

Gabe, always ready to jam, whipped out his harmonica and started honking along with him. They connected instantly as only musicians can, feeding riffs to each other. This hard up Manhattan street person and a blind Inuk from the Great White North. Gabe bobbed and danced around, oblivious to the passing throng. He smiled so hard he could hardly play. I felt the stress and strain of getting here fall away like old skin. I'd almost forgotten the healing power of good soul music.

"We should seriously try busking," Rosie said as we reluctantly turned our backs on Mr. Sugar and Spice. "Could make a killing in a place like this."

"Did you look in his money pot?" Becca asked. "Peanuts."

"That's an old trick," Rosie said. "Keep it almost empty and people take pity on you."

Somehow I couldn't imagine my Sila songs taking flight in Times Square where flashing billboards blocked the sky and the Earth was wrapped in a cement straitjacket.

"Whoa! I feel good!" Gabe sang, perfectly echoing the drummer's voice. He stopped abruptly, slumping his head to his chest. "No, I don't. I feel bad! I thought we were going to—"

"It's right here, Gabe." I said. "The Hard Rock Cafe." Gabe often crashed after a high like that, especially if I didn't get food into him. I was so not in the mood for one of his manic meltdowns.

Just before we got to the restaurant, it was my turn to put on the brakes. Above the crash and clatter of the street, I could feel a strange vibration coming up through my feet, a rising wave of energy that leaked through a metal grate below me.

Becca looked at me and crinkled her nose. "Cripes, Ash, what now?"

"Can't you feel that?"

"What?"

I wished I'd kept my mouth shut. Becca was no stranger to my "spells," as she called them. But the vibration climbed up my legs, shaking my whole body.

"What? What?"

Rosie snorted. "Get your shit together, sisters. It's the freakin' subway."

"Right," I said, grabbing Gabe's arm like it was him that stopped me. "Let's eat."

STOP LOOK LISTEN

HARD ROCK CAFE, TIMES SQUARE
DECEMBER 13TH, 5:00 PM

"Like, this is going to save the planet?" Becca said, "Buying a bunch of cheap plastic crap labeled *Save the Planet?*" She held up a huge mug with a beery-eyed Santa on it.

Rosie made us stop in the café's Rock Shop before heading downstairs to eat. "Hey, there's some good crap here. Check out these racy pink panties." Stamped on the bum were the words: *For the love of the Earth.* "Or here, perfect for you, Ash." Rosie handed me a pair of plastic Earth earrings spattered with blobs of green for continents, none of which I recognized.

"Uh, not quite my style."

On our way downstairs we discovered a display of four beheaded mannequins dressed in drab gray suits.

"Wow," Rosie said. "The British *invasion.*"

"Huh?" Becca said.

"Actual uniforms of the very first soldiers."

"What are you talkin'?"

"The Beatles, girl. They wore these when they stormed North America."

I remembered Mom's stories about Beatlemania. "That was, what, 1964?"

"February 12. Changed the face of rock 'n' roll forever. Bombed the hell out of American pop music."

"And they, like, launched their attack from—"

"You guessed it, Carnegie Hall. Where we party tomorrow night."

I stared at the dusty suits. My legs went limp and I had to steady myself against the glass display case. A wave of stage fright swept through me, exposing an awful truth: Tomorrow we'd perform in front of thousands of people on the most famous stage in the world.

"If these aliens could change the world from the Carnegie stage," Becca said, "why not *us*? Put throat singing on the Top 40 charts. Declare war on climate change."

"Sounds like a plan, Bexie," Gabe said. "Declare war on cheap plastic crap! Save the planet! But, like, can we *eat* first?"

"Great idea, Gabe," I said, steering him down another flight of stairs.

I knew we'd dawdled too long when Gabe broke down beside the guitar wall. Imagine, three hundred shiny electric guitars, slit in half down the neck and stuck sideways on a wall. This did not go over well with Gabe, whose fingers raced over their polished bodies even as he started bawling like a seven-year-old.

"Who could *do* this?" He sobbed. "This is a crime against music, against everything we stand for. Somebody *murdered* all these beautiful guitars. This is horrible! *Horrible!*"

We stood in a packed lineup, waiting to get into the dining bar. A circle quickly opened around us as Gabe wound up for a grand mal spaz attack.

"It's okay, Gabe," I said, sounding a lot like my mother. "They must have been factory rejects or something. Nobody could play them. Somebody's idea of art, I guess."

"It's a slaughterhouse! A guitar slaughterhouse! Somebody's gonna pay for this!"

The crowd parted to let a big brute through. He had biceps the size of soccer balls and wore a black Hard Rock T-shirt with the words *Save Water, Drink Beer* on it. I saw a bulldog look in his eye as he plowed his way straight for us.

"So much for supper," Becca muttered.

"I'll handle this," Rosie said, stepping toward the bouncer.

I yanked Gabe's hands off the guitars. His arms felt like iron bars. His whole body shook. "Gabe. *Gabe!* It's okay. We're leaving."

"Hey man, everything's cool," Rosie said to the bouncer before he could open his mouth. "Gabe's just really excited to be here and, well, he gets a little antsy if he hasn't eaten for a while. It's, like, kind of a medical thing."

The bouncer's face softened a notch. "Want me to call an ambulance?" he said in a thick Spanish accent.

"No thanks, really. He'll be okay as soon as he gets a bite in him."

The bouncer studied Gabe for a moment, who was whimpering pitifully in time with the rocking of his head. "Dis way," he said.

"Do something, Ash!" whispered Rosie. "Gabe's so uptight his ass squeaks when he walks."

As the bouncer led us away from the dining bar, I braced myself for one of two scenarios—Gabe collapsing in a heap like a toddler refusing to walk, or Gabe exploding into a violent tantrum, lashing out at anyone or anything within hitting distance.

The bouncer kept glancing over his shoulder at Gabe as he led us toward a side door marked *Staff Only*. As he swung the door open, a flood of juicy aromas hit us in the face.

Gabe straightened and flared his nose. "Now we're talkin'!" he said, cracking a weak grin.

The Hard Rock kitchen was in high gear with necktied servers running in and out, and a dozen cooks in white stovepipe hats chopping, frying, or stirring mouthwatering creations.

I knew this would be bad for Gabe, real bad. Getting a whiff of food heaven just before being thrown out onto the cold, hard street. I was about to pilfer a big fat mushroom—anything to put in his stomach—when a giant cleaver came down on it, wielded by a tall cook with a pirate's mustache. He gave me a wink, then tossed me an even bigger mushroom the size of an apple.

"Thanks," I said sheepishly.

He closed his eyes for a second and held a finger to his lips.

I got the picture and shoved the mushroom into my jacket. This might just save us all from disaster.

The bouncer whipped open another door. I expected a blast of clammy New York winter. Instead, what greeted us was all laughter and warmth. The guy had bounced us clear around the lineup to a reserved table in the dining bar.

All the guitars hanging inside the bar seemed to be in one piece. They'd been played in superstar rock bands like The Who, The Doors, Led Zeppelin. We walked by a signed pair of Ringo Starr's drumsticks, David Bowie's purple saxophone, and Elvis Presley's red-hot leather pants.

One wall of the bar looked like a cross between a rock stage and an altar. The message, *Don't blow it—good planets are hard to find*, hung above a bunch of neon symbols from different world religions. In the middle was a big brass Buddha wrapped in a horseshoe of blue light. Three golden words, that seemed to burn into my brain, shone brightly from inside the halo:

Stop Look Listen

"Hey, thanks a lot, amigo," Becca said as the bouncer pulled out a chair for her.

"*De nada*," he said, waving a server toward us. "They call me Snuffer. You got trouble, I snuff it out. Just doin' mah job."

And he hadn't even asked for ID.

As alien as I felt in this frantic new world, I began to think I could actually stomach New Yorkers. That maybe they wouldn't eat us alive on the Carnegie stage.

Gabe loosened up after inhaling a basket of bread sticks. As we waited for our jumbo order of baby back ribs and home fries, I caught myself imagining that, after our gala performance, maybe somebody might want to hang up one of our Inuit drums in this place. I'd even sign it for them, no charge. It would look cool up there beside the Buddha, like a pale moon rising.

DEMOPHOBIA

MACY'S DEPARTMENT STORE
DECEMBER 13TH, 6 PM

Just when I was beginning to think I could survive in New York, when my stomach was full and we could hit the sack, Rosie announced that we just absolutely had to go shopping at Macy's.

"Don't you get it?" she'd said. "We're talking here the biggest god-damned department store in the world. How could we *not* go there? At Christmas? You know, *Miracle on 34th Street* and all that jazz!"

"That old movie where the Macy's shrink locks Santa Claus in a nuthouse?" Becca said.

"And he gets bubblegum all over his beard!" Gabe said.

"The one and only. Same Macy's."

"I'm in," Becca said.

"Me too," Gabe said. "Maybe they've let the old guy out by now."

"Whatever," I said.

So we went.

Becca, who'd made a hobby of phobias, called it demophobia, a deathly fear of crowds. They used to give me a buzz. We'd drummed for packed halls across the Arctic. I couldn't wait to strut on stage in my kamiiks and cape.

But that was before the lightning. It did something to my head. Not just the bald spot over my right ear. It shifted something inside. Now crowds freaked me. That morning I'd almost passed out when we stepped off the plane into LaGuardia airport.

So, on day one in New York, the last place on Earth I should have gone was Macy's department store. But somehow Rosie suckered me into it and we threw ourselves into a blizzard of stressed-out Christmas shoppers.

"Cripes, Rosie," Becca said as they almost carried me, arm in arm, out of Macy's. "Don't you know she can't handle crowds anymore?"

"She's a big girl," Rosie said, like I wasn't even there. She stuck her arm up and pointed to the top of the Empire State Building. "Hey! A trip up there oughta clear her head."

"Since when were you appointed tour guide?" Becca said.

"Got any better ideas?"

"How about sleep?" I said, shaking off Rosie's arm.

"C'mon, you can sleep all winter when we get home," she said.

"Lemme at it," Gabe said. "We can look for King Kong while we're up there."

THRUMMING

The tables turned at the Empire State Building. Rosie went all silent the instant we stepped into the elevator. The higher we got, the whiter she looked. At around the fiftieth floor, she actually reached for my hand.

"I never knew you were afraid of heights," I said.

"It's not the height. It's this flying coffin. Elevators get stuck, you know. Or the cable snaps and they drop like a bomb. Or people get stranded between floors."

"Like the guy who got trapped for, like, almost two days," Gabe said. "Caught it on CNN."

"Thanks for that, Gabe," I said.

"No, really. It happened right here in the Big Apple."

"Forget it, Gabe."

We were sharing the elevator with an old British lady and her freckle-faced granddaughter. The kid was about six years old, a real squirmer.

Becca's an information junkie and had been poring over the Empire State Building brochure without noticing the color of Rosie's face. "Funny you should mention it, Gabe. Listen to this.

"Saturday, July 28, 1945. A B-25 bomber pilot makes a wrong turn in the fog and crashes into the seventy-ninth floor of the Empire State Building, creating a flaming hole eighteen feet wide and twenty feet high. The impact snaps the cables of two elevators, both of which free-fall to the bottom of the shaft."

Rosie went pale and covered her mouth. The little kid clamped both arms around her grandmother's legs. We still had twenty more floors to go. "That's just marvie, Becca," I said, "but, uh, maybe later."

"No, no, it's okay," Becca said without looking up. "Nobody died." She read on.

"*By the time the elevator cars crash into the buffer pit below, a thousand feet of cable has piled up beneath them, serving as a kind of spring. A pillow of air pressure, compressed below the speeding cars, further cushions the impact. By good fortune, only one elevator is occupied. By a miracle, the lone woman on board is severely injured but alive.*"

"I'd rather be dead," Rosie muttered.

The kid started screaming. "Grandma! Get me out of here!"

Gabe plugged his ears and flipped into his rocking routine.

I prayed for the doors to open.

Finally, on the eighty-sixth floor, we're freed. Rosie dashed through the gift shop straight for an outside door. I found her clamped to a railing, gulping the cool night air. I noticed a sign beside her that read: *Warning. Climbing observatory fences is dangerous, unlawful and prohibited.* "Duh," I said to myself.

"What?"

"It says jumping's against the law."

"Fine. Just don't ... don't let me get back on that elevator."

"You mean—"

"I can't do it, Ash."

"You're gonna walk back down all those—"

"Yep."

"You're sick."

"Yep. Must be a name for it."

"*Claut*ophobia," Becca said.

"You mean claustrophobia?" I said.

"No, really, clautophobia," Becca said. "Scared of elevators."

"Scared shee-it-less," Rosie said.

"Just hold your breath on the way down," Becca said. "You'll be okay."

Rosie looked back at the elevator door like it was a charging polar bear. "That's a hell of a long way to hold your breath."

"Works great for hiccups!" Gabe offered. He'd thrust his arms through the railing and his long musician's fingers danced to subtle ripples in the wind.

I realized I'd been holding my breath for much of the time since stepping off the elevator. The view had stolen it from me.

The dizzying height, the glittering lights, the pounding beat of the city echoing through high-rise canyons—it all made my head reel and I lurched sideways for a second.

"What are ya, drunk?" said Becca who was on her tiptoes looking over the edge.

I tightened my grip on the railing. "Not unless you spiked my tomato juice."

"Must've been that Tabasco sauce."

"Uh-huh." I took a deep breath and shook my head. "Not quite Nanurtalik, eh?"

"No kidding."

I thought about the night view of our tiny village. Mom had made it a tradition to haul everyone out of the house and climb Anirniq Hill every winter solstice, the shortest, darkest day of the year. It was kind of a New Age thing for her but everyone got into it once we were out the door. Even at forty below, we'd scramble up there and set off some fireworks to celebrate the planet's swing back into the light. After the last blast of sky candy, we'd all huddle on a couple of sealskin rugs, sip hot cranberry cider from a thermos, and look down at our blip of humanity. Shrouded in a streaming tail of ice fog, the few lights of town glowed like a comet drifting in a dark blue void of frozen tundra and sea ice.

Manhattan Island, on the other hand, was a whole galaxy spinning below us.

I looked straight up through a curved metal grate at the rocket-shaped tower that crowned the most famous building in New York.

Red and green spotlights made it shine like a Christmas tree. I knew there was another observation deck up there on the hundred and second floor, but I didn't want to push my luck with Rosie. She'd begun to unwind and had wandered off somewhere with Gabe.

I looked down at a river of cars nudging white flares ahead of them, trailing a red wake behind. Columns of insect people still marched over the sidewalk, most of them piling in and out of—yuck—Macy's. I felt much saner up here.

At least, until the whispering started.

At first I thought it came from some tourist. But it was a nippy night, for New York at least, and most of them had disappeared after a quick spin around the deck. All but the British grandmother with the kid we'd spooked in the elevator. I must have given her a funny look. She clutched the little girl's hand and made a beeline for the gift shop.

"I better check on Rosie," Becca said as she took a few steps away from me.

I shot my arm out to her. "Shush!"

"What?"

"Do you hear that?"

"Like, traffic?"

"No."

"That whimpering kid?"

"No. She's gone. Listen. Sort of … like a breathing noise."

Becca rolled her eyes. "Must be altitude sickness."

"No, really."

"No, I mean really," Becca said, gesturing to the now empty deck. "There's nobody here. It's all in your head, girl." She grabbed my arm. "We better get out of here before Gabe cracks up, too."

"Wait! Shut up a minute."

What was this urgency I felt?

I heard it again, a breathy, pulsing sound like a warm-up to throat-singing. I stared at Becca. "That."

Becca shrugged.

She was right. It was inside my head. But it had a direction to it, a source, as if something or someone was trying to beam a message straight into my brain. I glanced up at the tower, along the metal railings, at the deck's limestone floor. I looked for birds, cockroaches, bats, any living thing. Since the lightning strike, I'd got used to cueing in on animals whenever I heard that sound.

Nothing.

The whispering got shriller, more urgent. I heard the flap of wings in the darkness above me.

I stuck my nose through the grillwork and peered down. In the green glow of one of the spotlights, some dark shape caught my eye. It lay on a square metal plate at the base of a radio tower. I squinted at the twisted remains of a pigeon. Something had ripped it apart.

Above the whispering, I heard the sound of knife edges slashing the air, like I'd once heard on the tundra, just before a young snow goose exploded into feathers before my eyes.

A falcon? Way up here?

The whispering seemed to streak past me, tugging my attention downward. I pressed my face against the wire mesh. My gaze fell eighty-six stories, locking onto an open pit beside Macy's. Floodlights bathed the site in a raw orange light as a giant power shovel clawed at a pile of shattered concrete. I yanked out the tiny pair of beat-up binoculars I always carry in my backpack.

"What? What?" Becca said.

"I dunno."

The whispering died but soon gave way to a low throbbing hum. Not a machine. It was more like the sound my grandmother made when sewing kamiiks. I closed my eyes and felt it spread into my chest. It was somehow soothing and scary at the same time. I opened my arms and listened with my whole body.

"Cripes, Ash. I don't think you're cut out for city life."

"Shut up."

I opened my eyes and waved a finger toward the streets. "It's coming from there."

"Maybe it's like, the subway again? I think there's one right down—"

"No, no. Not this."

I watched spellbound as the machine dug deeper and deeper through an open wound in the city's concrete skin. Like a brain surgeon's scalpel, it peeled back layers of diseased tissue, exposing naked bedrock and raw soil—healthy flesh of the Earth that had probably been buried for centuries.

I couldn't hear the power shovel above the traffic. But the gentle thrumming sound seemed to leak straight up to me, loud and clear, from the bottom of the pit. Like the falcon had wanted me to hear it.

Impossible!

I lowered my binoculars. My guts swirled with a mix of fear, sadness, and something else. Anger. The anger that boiled my blood whenever I watched a rising ocean eat my Arctic town. The anger that made me burn down a carbon criminal's trailer. The anger that only a wounded Earth could trigger in me.

I blinked away hot tears. Manhattan disappeared.

Cars, streets, skyscrapers vaporized in a soft green mist. Forests sprang out of the glow. They were broken by sprawling marshes, sparkling beaver ponds, and lush meadows dotted with grazing deer. A pair of bald eagles soared above a high rocky ridge that formed the backbone of a living, breathing island.

I blinked again. Manhattan returned. And with it, the crush and clamor of the city.

What the hell was that?

I was suddenly gripped by this sickening feeling that the whole island, once so incredibly beautiful, was now stone dead. Like so much in this world, we'd killed its soul. Drained it, flattened it, smothered it with cement and steel. And there'd never even been a funeral.

As this knowledge sank in, the thrumming from the pit got louder. It climbed up my spine like a snake, a slow pounding hum that finally coiled in my throat. As it reached a crescendo, my mouth fell open. I took a deep breath, not knowing if I was about to sing, scream, or throw up.

I must look ridiculous.

The instant this thought invaded my brain, an ax fell and the thrumming died. I buried my face in my hands.

"Let's get out of here, Ash." Becca said. "You're a basketcase."

LISTENER

CENTRAL PARK, A CLEARING BESIDE THE POND
DECEMBER 13TH, 9:30 PM

A horse wouldn't last long in Nanurtalik. Between roving wolves and marauding polar bears, something would take it out pretty quick. Not to mention our hard-core blizzards. Until New York, I'd seen as many giraffes. Zero, actually. I didn't know how to act around horses. I didn't like the shifty look in their eyes. I kept stepping in their crap. Give me a stampeding herd of caribou any day.

Now a horse clomped past us every five minutes as we sat around a candle in Central Park.

A line of horse-drawn carriages a block long had greeted us as we entered the park off Seventh Avenue. Rosie chatted up one of the drivers wrapped in an orange blanket. He was a Turkish guy about our age whose Spanish boss had given his Tasmanian horse an Italian name: Mario. I was quickly learning that this was what New York was all about—people from everywhere doing anything to make a buck.

Rosie seriously wanted to take Mario for a spin but, luckily, there wasn't room for all of us in the carriage. My legs still ached from our brutal plane ride. My brain had been lost in a fog since the Empire State Building. That was Rosie's idea. Central Park was Becca's. All I wanted to do was sleep, survive the concert, then get the hell home.

Central Park was another world, separated from the city by nothing more than a low stone wall. On one side, the chaos called Manhattan. On the other, a semi-wild chunk of nature where the only vehicles were horse-drawn carriages, the odd cop car, and a few fit-freak parents pushing baby strollers. A cute bellhop at the hotel had told Becca it was okay to walk in Central Park at night as long as we stayed near the edge and didn't party too hard.

Becca insisted on doing some kind of Earth-friendly blessing to give thanks for our safe journey and get psyched for our Carnegie gig. Becca, the neo-hippie. She got on well with my mom.

We found a clear area beside a big pond that had a few teeth of ice around the edge. There was no snow, but the ground was cold and damp.

"Let's get on with it, your royal high priestess," Rosie said, squatting precariously in her new bad-ass boots.

"Chill out, Rosie," Becca said. "You agreed to it."

"We did?" Rosie and I said together.

"Just go with me on this."

Becca had decided that Central Park was a no-brainer choice to get "grounded," as she said, since everything else had been paved over, built on, or plowed under.

"My butt's wet!" Gabe groaned.

"We'll be in the hotel hot tub soon, Gabe," I said, watching Becca jam the candle into the cold ground.

Becca finally got it lit, then gently cleared away all the dead leaves that lay within its shaky circle of light. A couple of big black beetles wobbled off like drunks into the darkness. A worm slowly pulled itself into the rich black soil. We sat staring silently at our private patch of naked Earth.

Gabe started getting restless, rubbing his hands and making faint whiny noises. I opened one of his hands and placed it over the exposed ground. He calmed down instantly.

Becca leaned forward and started talking to the dirt and the bugs and the leaves, like she was in church. "We greet you, Mother Earth …"

Gabe giggled. "Who are you talking to, Bexie?"

I squeezed his hand. "Shhh, Gabe."

"Oh my God, Becca," Rosie said.

Becca gave Rosie the evil eye. "Shut up, would ya?" she said and continued her little chat with Mother Earth. "We give thanks for your living skin that feeds us and protects us and stretches under this crazy city all the way to our Arctic home."

The throb of distant traffic blended with the click of horse hooves. Then, from somewhere above us, that whispering sound.

I tried to act normal.

Becca started singing softly. *"Under the cities, lies a heart made of ground, but the humans will give no love—"*

"Holy crap, Becca," Rosie said.

"No, wait!" shouted Gabe. "That's … that's …"

Becca looked up from the candle. "'Horse With No Name.'"

"Right!"

"Sort of fits, eh?"

"Bang on, Bexie!" Gabe shouted, jumping up and rubbing his hands.

"Oh-oh," I said, watching him bop around with an ear-to-ear smile. Gabe was a mean lyrics machine and once anybody even hummed a few lines of a song, there was no stopping him. Press Gabe's music button and he'd rewind, start all over, and sing every last verse.

"There goes your séance, Becca," Rosie said. She stretched and walked down to the edge of the pond as Gabe's booming voice rang through the trees.

"On the first part of the journey, I was looking at all the life; there were plants and birds and rocks and things …"

A puff of wind off the pond knocked over the candle and killed the flame.

"Shit," Becca said.

I leaned back on my elbows and looked around. A hunk of bedrock beside us rose out of the ground like a breaching whale. The wind was picking up. Bare branches clattered overhead against a sky stained orange by the vomit of city lights. I felt a jab of homesickness.

I shook my head. "God, look at that. Maybe twenty stars."

"Pitiful," Becca said. "More like a million back home."

"The heat was hot and the ground was dry, but the air was full of sound …"

The whispering seemed closer. It came from a huge tree beside the pond.

As the wind rises, the old tree's branches knock together, sending dull thumps down through the trunk and filling the den.

The raccoon stirs. She stretches her long forelegs and opens her glove-like hands. The thumping dies down. She slips back into a dream …

Her nose twitches with the discovery of a dead squirrel in the middle of the road. It has not been dead for long; the blood is still warm. Beside the road on the grass, her two kits are caught up in a fierce game of chase and pounce. The mother raccoon calls them closer with a shrill grunt. With the kits at her side, she loses herself in the squirrel's sweet flesh until she hears a long, low growl behind her. She turns to see a huge black dog baring its teeth. The raccoon sweeps her kits behind her, sits up on her haunches and, with claws held up like a boxer's, screeches and hisses at the intruder …

It's not the thumping branches that wake the raccoon. It's not the dream dog. She opens her eyes to a dark, empty den. For a moment she looks around for her kits, then remembers. They left her long ago when the rosehips first ripened.

There is another presence nearby, closer than the raccoon's own family. A special human presence. Closer than her breath.

A listener has come.

I squinted at the old giant through the darkness. A thick branch hung like an arm down one side of the tree, then bent back toward the trunk like a woman covering her breasts. Where the armpit would be, there was a deep, dark split in the tree. Where the sound came from. The more I focused on it, the louder it got, a persistent, almost frantic whispering. I became aware of a raw, prickly sensation taking hold of my chest, as if something was trying to claw its way in.

The whispering floated down from the tree, surrounded me, entered invisible wounds in my chest, made it ring like a drum. I clutched myself with one arm, unintentionally striking the same pose as the tree.

"*In the desert, you can remember your name, 'cause there ain't no one for to give you no pain …*"

Becca looked up from the dead candle. "What's wrong, Ash? Freaked by all the trees?"

"Trees?"

"You know, dendrophobia? A lot of Eskimos get it when they come south."

"What? Uh … no. No, it's … it's not the trees."

JAMIE BASTEDO

"'Fraid of a few snapping turtles?" Rosie said, rejoining the circle. "I heard Central Park's crawling with them."

"What? Turtles? No ... There's something ... something in that big tree."

Becca stood up and looked at the tree. "*In* the tree? Like, a woodpecker or something?"

"No ... Not a bird. I don't know what it is."

"You see, I've been through the desert on a horse with no name. It felt good to be out of the rain ..."

I kept staring at the tree. "Gabe, shhh."

Of course he kept on singing. *"La laa, laa, la-la, la-laa-la ..."*

I jerked my hands off the ground, suddenly feeling a strange vibration like the one that reached for me from the pit beside Macy's.

A blinding flash painted the tree silver.

Lightning!

I covered the right side of my head—where I got struck last time—and dove for Gabe. We hit the dirt, landing face down on a clump of rose bushes.

"What ya doin', Ash?" Gabe yelled in my ear. "I wasn't finished! Where the hell's the fire?"

I heard Rosie's horsey laugh. "It's a freakin' raccoon!" she shouted.

I jumped up, helped Gabe to his feet, and plucked a rose thorn out of his chin. "Sorry about that," I said. "I thought it was lightning."

"A freakin' raccoon! Check it out!'

Rosie shoved her digital camera at me. "First horses, now raccoons. Never seen one of them."

The image was blurred but I could clearly see the masked face of a raccoon, sticking out of the crack below the big branch. Its eyes, like golden headlights in Rosie's flash, looked straight down at me.

I looked up at the crack but saw only darkness.

Somebody whistled from the quiet street behind us. We turned to see a horse-drawn carriage clomping by. It was full of tourists, boozing it up in the back seat. The driver had an orange blanket over his shoulders and was waving in our direction.

Becca waved back. "There you go, Gabe. A horse *with* a name."

"Is that ol' Mario?" Gabe said.

"The one and only."

"Then I'll sing for *him!*" And Gabe picked up where he'd left off before I'd tackled him, la-laaing his way to the bitter end.

THE END IS NEAR

SOUTH EDGE OF CENTRAL PARK
DECEMBER 13TH, 10:15 PM

On our way out of the park, we heard insane shouting near the Seventh Avenue gate. We weren't about to fool around with any knife artists, so we cut across the grass, hoping to jump the stone wall.

The shouting followed us, echoing off the naked trees. "Prepare to die!"

"Oh my God!" Becca said, as we booted it for the wall.

"*Becca!*" I panted. "I thought that bellhop told you Central Park was safe!"

Rosie started laughing. "Maybe Gabe's singing drew in the freaks."

I looked behind to see a skinny guy, with a wild, foot-long beard, trotting after us. A big sandwich board dangled over his shoulders.

"The clock is ticking!" he shouted. "The holocaust is coming! Prepare for the end!"

JAMIE BASTEDO

After some rude pushing and shoving, we managed to scramble over the wall and land feet first back in the urban jungle. Giggling like school kids, we ran full tilt down the cobblestone sidewalk until we got to Seventh Avenue. We dashed hand in hand across the wide street, through a red light, straight for our hotel. I nearly filled my pants when a red Hummer screeched to a stop a few inches from Gabe's leg.

"What the fuck are you thinking?" yelled the driver who was half out the window. "What are ya', blind?"

"Damn rights I am, Buster!" Gabe yelled back. "Like, *totally*. Have mercy on the handicapped!"

Cars honked at us from all sides. The driver struggled to get out of his Hummer, like he was so pissed off he couldn't find the door handle. We froze in the middle of the intersection like deer in the headlights, wrapped in a steaming cloud of road rage.

The driver finally threw his door open and jumped out. A taxi blasted him from behind. The man shook his fist at us, at the taxi, got back in his Hummer, then squealed past us, missing my toe by a hair.

We played dumb tourists, waving and smiling at the ring of revving cars, then booted it to the curb.

"Holy smokes, Ash!" yelled Gabe. "I thought you were supposed to take care of—"

"Change your ways while you still can! The end is near! Repent! REPENT!"

I spun around to see the bearded whacko pacing back and forth, shouting at passing cars. Somehow he'd beat us back to the Seventh Avenue gate.

"How'd he *do* that?" I said.

"I dunno," Becca said, grabbing my arm. "And I'm not gonna stick around to find out!"

Rosie cupped her hands around her mouth and yelled back at him. "So the world's gonna end! Get over it!"

Under the glare of orange streetlights, the message on his sand-wich board jumped out at me:

Repent! All hell is about to break loose!

SILA QATLUNAATITUT

ISAAC STERN AUDITORIUM, CARNEGIE HALL
DECEMBER 14TH, 9:15 PM

My courage went down as the lights came up. The crowd at Macy's department store had been a demophobiac's nightmare. At least up here on the sprawling Carnegie stage I had a little more elbow room as I squinted at three thousand people staring at me.

You could fit three of my towns into those red velvet seats. But instead of ball caps and blue jeans, most of the audience was dressed like royalty. I spotted one woman wearing a coat trimmed in Arctic fox fur. To ease my stage fright, I decided on the spot to sing to the spirit of the animal draped around her neck, a familiar friend who might have lived wild and free on the tundra near my Arctic home.

As the crowd settled, I looked over at my fellow Dream Drummers. A couple of years back, when our group sprouted wings, Mom sewed Rosie, Becca, and me red and white outfits, designed like traditional women's dance parkas, complete with amauti pouches in the back and long tuxedo-like tails. She sewed Gabe a traditional men's parka, all black with a wolverine-rimmed hood and a Suluk Delta braid around the cuffs and lower hem. Aana made amazing kamiiks for all of us. Dad had hunted the seals within earshot of our house and tanned the skins himself. Using different shades of gray and black seal-skin, Aana had stitched a flock of ravens flying up the sides. To crown our Eskimo duds, as Rosie called them, we'd made sexy headbands with rainbow beads that trickled down the sides of our faces.

Rosie was already swaying back and forth to some inner drumbeat. Becca, a Caucasian blonde born on the prairies, looked more than pumped to play. She was the daughter of a transplanted RCMP officer, and she looked right at home in a fringe Inuit drumming group that had become famous by breaking all the rules. No one loved an audience more than Gabe, who was wearing a huge smile as he clutched his fiddle under his chin and waited for the first strike of my *qilauti.*

In community arenas up north, we usually performed back to back with local garage bands dabbling in Inuktitut rock and country tunes. Tonight was different. Parked beside us, wearing red tuxedos and white basketball shoes, were the Kromatiks, a string quartet known internationally for their off-the-wall music. It was their cello player, Jeffery, who'd been blown away by our tunes on the Web.

During our afternoon rehearsal, Jeffery told me it was my voice that had really grabbed him. "It's so string-like," he'd said, "so multi-layered, like you carry a string quartet in your throat. I told my crew we just *had* to perform with the Jimi Hendrix of Inuit throat singers!"

We'd agreed to start with our smash hit single, "Sila's Revenge." The Kromatiks chose to take a back seat to our lead, so it was up to me to launch the show. I stepped up to the mike, gave it a tap, and cleared my throat. I silently saluted the Arctic fox in the crowd and dove in.

"*Ai.* Hello. We are the Dream Drummers from a little Arctic village called Nanurtalik, the place of the polar bear."

I pulled back a touch from the mike, afraid it would pick up the galloping of my heart.

"Tonight we'll sing about *Nuna,* our land, about the tundra and the sea and the ice and the animals who live there. But our land is changing. It's not like it used to be when my grandmother grew up, or even my dad. You read about climate change in your newspapers. Well, we live it. We feel sometimes like the land is falling apart. My grandmother says it's because Sila, our weather spirit, is angry with people messing up the Earth. She speaks of *Sila qatlunaatitut,* Sila's revenge. She says if you try hard and listen for Sila's voice, you can learn how to help fix the world before it's too late. Maybe you'll hear Sila's warning in our song."

I caught Jeffery's eye. He gave me a cheery nod. Becca and Rosie raised their drums. I took a deep breath, paused to listen to the silence of three thousand souls, then tore into a frantic heartbeat on my drum, the signature riff for "Sila's Revenge."

One strike of my drum and I could feel at home anywhere. That night it told me I would survive the concert—and then some. I imagined performing for all those well-heeled strangers from the top of Anirniq Hill.

The Kromatiks had told us to "simply do your thing," and they'd improvise over top of us. Once our drums took off, Gabe jumped in with a grinding workout on his fiddle. It sounded like sea ice breaking up in a winter gale. The Kromatiks followed suit with explosive rumblings from the cello and the shriek of brain-numbing winds from the violins and viola.

Nothing like a bang to kick off our first gig on the world stage.

I closed my eyes and opened my throat. Out came a high octane mix of grunts and growls, gasps and wails, all layered over a bed of moans and sighs that told a story of rising seas and falling skies. More than any other piece we did, "Sila's Revenge" always shook me to my Uitajuq core. Though we'd performed it maybe a hundred times, when it ended, I always felt, *Like, wow! Where the hell did that come from?*

I opened my eyes and lowered my drum, its echo still bouncing off the pillared walls. I could hear Becca and Rosie panting beside me,

Gabe tapping his fiddle bow against his pants, Jeffery, the cello player, leaning back in his squeaky chair.

But not a peep from the audience.

Did they get it? Did they feel it?

"Are they gonna throw bricks or bouquets?" whispered Becca through a frozen smile.

The answer came from one of the four balconies above us. That's where the clapping started. It spilled over the edge, flooded the ground floor, and crashed onto the stage like a giant wave.

They loved us.

Carnegie's rafters shook to thunderous applause and wild cheers.

I knew then that it was more than the novelty of our music that got them so pumped over us. There was a powerful current in the air and we were the light bulbs that tapped it and made it shine.

But there was more work to do. We had to conjure up a pod of breaching belugas, map the flight path of a thousand migrating snow geese, paint song pictures of northern lights and the midnight sun— all pulled from thin air by our voices and our drums and the playful accompaniment of strings.

Our final shrieks were greeted by the same stunned silence.

I thought maybe this time we'd gone over the top.

But no. They got it, all right. They felt it.

This time, everyone jumped to their feet for the biggest and longest and wildest standing ovation the Dream Drummers could ever dream of.

I think I floated off the Carnegie stage.

MR. MASTERS

BACKSTAGE CORRIDOR, CARNEGIE HALL
DECEMBER 14TH, 11:15 PM

"You guys really kicked ass out there," Rosie said as we packed our drums away.

Jeffery threw back his tuxedo tails and bowed low before us. "Why, thank you. An extreme pleasure. Let's do it again sometime."

Becca bowed. "How about our turf next time? Do drop in when you're within a thousand miles of Nanurtalik. We'd be happy to share the stage with you at Tuktu Hall."

"I'm afraid I haven't heard of ... what did you call it?"

Gabe clapped. "First Carnegie Hall. Next Tuktu Hall! Can you get more famous?"

"Bring your penguin suits," Becca said. "Not a lot of penguins up north, especially red ones."

Jeffery started loosening his bow tie, then suddenly straightened up and fixed his eyes on something behind me. "Well, well," he said under his breath. "Speaking of famous."

I turned to see an old man in a wheelchair approaching us from a dark corner offstage. He rolled straight for me. The guy must have been pushing eighty, but he pumped the wheels of his chair like a gymnast. He bore down on us so fast I had to pull Gabe aside to save his toes from being run over. Rosie held her ground. A tall black dude with a pockmarked face and a white suit kept pace right beside him.

Jeffery extended his hand. "Why, good evening, Mr. Masters. What a pleasant surprise to see you backstage."

Without taking his eyes off me, the old man smiled vaguely and extended his hand sideways to Jeffery. "Good evening, Jeff," he said in a thick Australian accent. "Could you introduce me to your young singing troupe here?"

Becca stepped forward holding out her hand like some pin-up princess.

He gave her a token handshake while still staring at me.

"We're the Dream Drummers at your service, sir. Becca Crawford's the name." She swept her free arm toward Rosie and me. "And here—"

"Masters, Jack Masters. Pleased to meet you." He was a chunky man, wearing a black suit over a crisp blue shirt with white collars. His eyes were green like a cat's. His thin silver mustache wormed sideways when he spoke. His nose was red and puffy, too big for his face.

Masters thrust a diamond-studded hand toward me.

My heart skipped a beat when I saw a polar bear etched on top of one fat ring.

"And you, Miss. Are you the one they call *Uitajuq*, Open Eyes?" He spoke my Inuktitut name like an Elder in an iglu.

"Ah … most people call me Ashley. But how could you—"

"It's in the program."

"Oh."

His smile was total plastic, showing lots of crooked teeth. His gaze was hard, almost predatory. He seemed to be searching for something behind my eyes. I reluctantly took his hand. It was tough and beefy. My hand instantly broke a sweat in his. He made me more nervous than the Carnegie crowd. I yanked my hand away.

"So you liked our music?" Becca asked.

"Your music?" he said, with his eyes still locked on mine. "Bewdy. Spellbinding. Lifted me right out of my wheelchair. But what I liked most was what you said. Before your Sila song. About climate change."

"Uh, yeah. There's a lot going on up there," I said, wiping my hand on my side. "Everything's sort of falling apart. I just scratched the tip of the iceberg."

Gabe lunged from the couch where he'd been zoning out. Before I could get to him, he tripped over Masters's wheelchair, almost falling in his lap. In less than a heartbeat, the dude in the white suit reached for something in his jacket. Masters grabbed the guy's arm and he relaxed.

"That's the trouble, Jack," Gabe exclaimed, still crumpled on the floor. "No icebergs up there now. They're all melting."

"So I've heard. And you would be …"

I pulled Gabe to his feet.

"Gabriel Anowiak, your humble servant, sir." Gabe bowed to the tall dude, who backed off an inch. I steered him back toward Masters.

"Blues harp whiz, fiddle fanatic, radio poisonality, band manager, and conservationalist."

"That's *conversationalist*, Gabe," I said. "Excuse my *tiguaq*. He's a bit of a social animal."

Masters tilted his head back, squinting slightly. "Tiguaq," he said as clear as day. "So, that would make Gabriel your adopted brother, right?"

"Well, yeah. How did you—"

Masters's gaze silenced me. "I've organized a little climate change gathering across town and wondered if you would care to join us."

"Well, thanks but, uh, we came here to perform, not to hear speeches about—"

"No, I want *you* to speak at the conference."

"Me?"

"Yes, you. Maybe say a few words about what's going on in the Arctic. Tell us how your weather's changing, how it impacts your land, your people. You and your friends here live on the front lines of global climate change. What's that really like? Give us an eyewitness account. The world needs to hear your stories." Masters barely raised one finger and his silent companion whipped out a business card and held it under my nose. I could tell that even through his mirror shades, this dude was processing everything around him like some android.

Before I could pull away, Masters rolled right up to me, gave my arm a fatherly pat, then abruptly backed up his wheelchair. "I'll slot you in for tomorrow morning's session. There should be a good crowd from all over the world. Report to my office by eight-thirty sharp. My secretary will give you security passes." He spun his wheelchair and shot down the dark corridor with Mr. Clean on his heels.

"But what can I—"

"I know we can work together!" Masters shouted over his shoulder.

Before I could say anything else, the two of them were swallowed by an elevator.

I stared at his business card. "Holy shit!"

Rosie grabbed it. "Freakin' United Nations! A complete stranger just suckered you into talking at the UN!" She looked up at Jeffery. "Who *was* that?"

Jeffery yanked off his tie. "Handy guy to have around. A *big* arts booster. Even lives upstairs."

"In Carnegie Hall?" Becca asked.

Jeffery nodded. "Rents a whole floor of the studio towers. Must cost a bundle but, well, you saw his rings. They did a big facelift here a few years ago and guess who paid for most of it."

"Masters?" I said.

"Yep. Millions!"

"He made a mint at the UN?" Becca said.

Jeffery chuckled. "Uh, no."

"So where'd he get his dough?" Rosie said.

Jeffery shrugged. "Well, that's really none of my business. But you know, tonight was the first time I've ever seen him backstage. He must have *big* plans for you guys."

"I think he's a Mafia hit man," Gabe said.

"A Russian spy," Becca said.

"A serial killer," Rosie said.

I didn't find this helpful. One minute I was floating off the Carnegie stage, totally pooped but happy. All I wanted was to sleep, pack up, and go home. The next minute, this bossy old guy in a wheelchair rolls in, pats my arm, and takes charge of my last day in New York. "Come and wow the world with a few horror stories about climate change." Sure. As if I needed another overdose of stage fright.

"Did you see the way that dude reached into his coat when Gabe fell over the old guy?" Becca said. "Some kind of animal reflex. Like his bodyguard or something."

"So what if Mr. Clean's an animal?" Rosie said. "I think he's cute."

"Why would an old guy like that need a bodyguard?" I asked, turning back to Jeffery. But all the Kromatiks had escaped to their dressing room.

"Hey," Becca said. "What happened to all the penguins?"

Rosie threw up her hands in mock horror. "What? No party after a show like that?"

"Hey, this is New York, Rosie," Gabe hooted. "It's one non-stop party out there!"

GREEN BEAST

IN A TAXI, BATTLING RUSH HOUR TRAFFIC MANHATTAN-STYLE
DECEMBER 15TH, 8:35 AM

"Come on," said Becca, pounding her knees. "Boot it, Buster. We've got a planet to save!"

JAMIE BASTEDO

"That's a bit over the top, don't you think?" Rosie said, with her eyes glued to the glitz and glitter of Times Square.

"This is important, Rosie." Becca said. "It's not every day someone from Nanurtalik gets to speak at the UN. Like, on the *hottest* topic on Earth. It's a global time bomb out there, baby! Like the old guy said, we're living on the front lines."

"Sure," I said. "But what about *this* war zone?" Our taxi wrestled through a sea of gridlocked traffic. Drivers threw the finger at each other—at us. I turned away, my eyes landing on the taxi's video screen that advertised the latest in poodle sunglasses.

I buried my face in my hands.

"Keep your bra on, Becca," Rosie said "You're freaking out the poor girl."

I sat up and saw a street person vomiting into a garbage can. With long silver hair, a grungy coat, and baggy pants, it might have been a man or woman—I couldn't tell. On a brick wall behind the street person, somebody named Daniel had spray-painted me a message: *You are nobody with nothing to say.*

"So tell me again," I said. "Exactly *who* am I supposedly speaking for? We're not, like, with Greenpeace or anything."

"Oh, that's brilliant, Ash," Rosie said. "They're *real* popular up north, screaming bloody murder about saving seals."

"Just make something up," Becca said. "Like, I don't know … Eskimo Freedom Fighters for a Clean Climate."

Gabe started rocking back and forth in his seat. "Right on! Eskimo Freedom Fighters!"

"Cool it, Gabe," I snapped. "Are you nuts, Becca? That would really go over well back home. *Eskimo?*"

"Okay," Becca said, "so Eskimo's a bit—what would your mom say?—*passé*. How about … Circumpolar Climate Crusaders?"

"Perfect!" Gabe said. "What's circumpolar mean?"

"Bullshit." I said. "I can really speak for every circumpolar nation on Earth."

"What's *circumpolar* mean?" demanded Gabe.

"It means all us iglu-loving seal-eaters, Gabe," Rosie said, craning her neck as we hung a sudden left on Forty-Fifth Street. "Wow, did you see the red-hot boots on that chick?"

"Nice work," Becca yelled to our turbaned taxi driver, who was separated from us by a thick window, probably bullet-proof. "Keep it up. We tip big." She grabbed my arm. "So who's going to check your credentials? There'll be hundreds, maybe thousands of people there from around the world. Like, this is your big chance to get something off your chest." She let go. "Beats setting fire behind enemy lines."

I wanted those ashes to cool fast. The jury was still out on who torched the trailer. "Just leave it, Becca. So I went a little crazy. I'm not planning to—"

Rosie waved her hands in front of us. "No! I've got it! You're speaking for ... for all the noble sons and daughters of the Arctic! You got all the credentials, Ash. Born on an ice floe like the rest of us, seal blood in your veins; you read snow like a book."

"What? A *halfer* like me?"

"No, it's perfect. Politically correct. Kinda poetic. The noble sons and daughters of the Arctic." Rosie let out a grand sigh. "It'll really twang their heartstrings."

Becca wiped away fake tears. "You'll make 'em weep, Ash. Just tell them what's going on back home. You know, starving polar bears, wicked storms, collapsing roads—"

"Tell 'em how our cemetery opened during that Labor Day storm," Rosie said. "And all those bodies popped out."

"They'll love it," Becca said. "Skeletons sliding into the sea, hunters falling through thin ice, houses swallowed by melting permafrost. Wake them up with a few horror stories. They might read about this stuff in the papers over their Italian lattes and twelve-grain toast. But we're breathing it. We live with this screwed-up climate in our faces twenty-four-seven."

A train-sized horn blasted us from behind. Seconds later, a lime-green Lincoln about a block long pulled up beside us and screeched to a stop for a red light. Through the heavily tinted glass I caught a glimpse of a man's diamond-studded hand signaling the driver. Before the light turned green, the limo lunged into the intersection, almost taking out a biker pulling a kiddie trailer. The car grazed his front wheel, toppling both bike and trailer. The guy smacked his helmet against the pavement and skidded to a stop. Over the traffic noise I could hear a little kid screaming in the flipped trailer.

Rosie threw the finger at the retreating limo. "What an asshole!"

"New York is full of assholes, miss," an East Indian voice said through a speaker above us.

"What could these crazies care about climate change?" Becca said. "They're too busy running over each other. But look out, folks. Manhattan's going underwater one of these days."

Rosie shrugged. "So, whatever. Just tell it like it is, Ash. The whole world will be watching." She bolted upright. "Hey! While the media's eating out of your hand, why not drop in a word about the Dream Drummers? Flash our CD around in front of the cameras."

"Sure." I jammed my scribbled notes into my jeans. "I could puke."

Gabe fumbled for the window switch and leaned back in his seat. I ripped opened my backpack, stuffed with my treasured amauti and kamiiks, imagining them covered with barf. "Don't worry, Gabe," I said, clenching my teeth. "I won't puke on you."

"Good news," he said as a cloud of bus fumes gushed through his window. "'Cause I'm choking in all this smog."

Rosie put her arm over my shoulders. "It's only butterflies, Ash. Just wing it."

"Yeah, right," I said. It felt more like a caribou herd tromping through my guts.

She squeezed me tighter. "Hey, nothing wrong with butterflies. The trick is getting them to fly in formation."

KILLING THE CLIMATE

OUTSIDE THE UNITED NATIONS TOWER
DECEMBER 15TH, 9:05 AM

"Thirty bucks for a ten-block taxi ride?" Becca fumbled in her wallet for the exact change. "We could've walked here in half the time."

"Hey, this is New York!" shouted Gabe. "Whadya expect?"

"Three bucks a block," Rosie said. "Well, those nice folks at Empire Oil worked their butts off to pay for our road show. Why miss a chance to spend their dough?"

Becca shoved the money at our driver. He glanced at it, then gave her a pleading shrug.

"Hey, we tip big!" Rosie said in her best Becca voice.

"Oh yeah," she said, handing him an extra dollar.

The driver rolled his eyes, then slouched over the steering wheel while we bailed out.

Rosie whistled. "Hey, real live Greenpeacers!"

Gabe had his nose in the air like a sniffing bear. "There's water nearby," he said. "Big water. I can smell it."

"We're right beside a river, Gabe," I said, grabbing his hand.

We stared at a crowd of granola types gathered in front of the UN under a banner that said: *Save the climate!* They cheered on a little road-roller plastered in Greenpeace stickers. The street echoed with a strange popping noise, like we were under attack by a popgun army.

Gabe's face screwed up like a walnut. "What in God's name is that God-awful noise?"

A megaphoned voice shouted, "What do we want?"

"Carbon taxes!" the mob shouted back.

"When do we want them?"

"Now!"

Becca tugged my arm. "C'mon, Ash. Let the greenies have their fun. There's better ways to save the planet. The whole world's in there waiting for you!"

"Male-icious," Rosie said, eyeing the blonde dude driving the road-roller.

Gabe stormed backward, almost into the path of a double-decker tour bus. "No way! Not yet!"

I lunged for Gabe, almost knocking him flat. "Shit, Gabe!"

"What the hell's that n-n-n-noise? That noise! I g-g-g-gotta know."

Gabe had the ears of a snowy owl. He had perfect pitch and an incredible memory for lyrics. He'd devour new sounds, grind them up, then spit them out in bizarre ways. Like a couple of falls ago, the first time he heard a moose call on the tundra—they're coming north as things warm up. He went around for a week, squeaking a rutting moose out of his fiddle. It was hilarious until Mom went nuts and kicked him outside. Then half the town went nuts. If Gabe heard something he couldn't explain, there was no stopping him, especially when the stutters started.

"Okay, okay," I said. "I'm on it."

A tour guide waved at us from the bus's open upper deck. I gave her a quick thumbs-up and hauled Gabe back onto the sidewalk. The guide's Hollywood voice drifted down to us as the bus moved on. "... Completed in 1950, the thirty-nine-storey UN tower is located in a garden setting along the scenic East River. Believe it or not, the land it stands on is not part of the United States. It is truly international soil, belonging to all of the 192 countries that have joined the United Nations since its birth in 1945. Up ahead you can see …"

A big cheer from the Greenpeacers drowned out the tour guide's voice. We dove into the mob, Rosie leading the pack. They seemed friendly enough, mostly gum-chewing twenty-somethings, a few moms with little kids, and some gray-heads. The driver backed up his machine, triggering another round of popgun thunder.

"Holy crap!" shouted Becca. "The guy's smunching a million light bulbs."

An official-looking guy in a hard hat gestured us to stand back. Drawn on his yellow overalls was a big light bulb hanging from a noose-shaped wire. Underneath, it said: *Ordinary bulbs are killing the climate.*

Gabe waved his arms in the air. "Hey, stop! Do you know what we pay for light bulbs up north?"

I yanked his arms down.

A pint-sized granny jerked down her parka hood and stared up at Gabe with narrowed eyes.

"These are the evil kind, Gabe," Becca said. "Real pigs on energy. That pumps a lot of carbon in the air. Our sea ice melts. Then polar bears come knocking at our doors. Get it?"

"Huh?"

"Later, Gabe," I said.

Something grazed my cheek. An orange sucker landed at my feet. A tall skinny guy dressed like a compact fluorescent bulb was clowning with the kids and tossing suckers in the air. I stared dumbly at the weird circus.

Becca grabbed Gabe and me. "Wakie, wakie, Ash! You got a gig in there."

I stared up at the gleaming blue skyscraper. It looked like a skinny fish tank propped on its side. I sensed a shark lurking inside.

"This way," Becca said, pointing to a long line of tourists. She suddenly turned. "Cripes, Rosie! Where the hell are you?"

I spotted her inching through the crowd toward the cute driver. "Over there, preying on white men."

"Hey, Rosie!" Becca yelled. "He's gonna pancake you. Let's go!"

SOME INTELLIGENCE

OUTSIDE THE UNITED NATIONS TOWER
DECEMBER 15TH, 9:30 AM

We waited in line for, like, half an hour, long after the greenies popped their last evil bulb. I was the walking dead, totally whacked-out from our Carnegie Hall gig. Since the lightning strike, I'd needed a lot more sleep. The night before, I'd had maybe two hours.

Rosie kept thumbing her cell phone, jamming it into her pocket, then whipping it out again. All our phones were useless in New York, but she was addicted.

Becca had chewed her purple nails almost to the bone.

"I thought you were growing big coke nails," I said.

"Gave up cocaine."

"Yeah, right. Just like your cop dad gave up hustling pot."

Becca shrugged, still chewing.

Thank God, Gabe flipped into zombie mode, his usual escape hatch after a lot of excitement.

A clammy gust shot through the canyon of office towers. "Do you believe it?" I muttered, pulling up my collar. "Snow."

Becca stuck her tongue out, then made a sour face. "City snow. Yuck!"

Some Japanese tourists behind us aimed their cameras at the sky, at each other, at the snow-flecked sidewalk.

"Save my place," I said to Becca and walked away from the line. I wanted to be alone with the snow.

I studied the flakes on my denim sleeve. Deranged star crystals and soggy pellets.

I thought of the giant frost crystals we dug out from under our tundra snow. They made the best tea in the world. Dad called it sugar snow. He knew snow inside out, like any good *Inullarik*. He never talked much in town. When he did, it was usually about his station, or money hassles, or who's beating who across the street. But on the land, hunting caribou or musk ox, he used to teach me different words for snow. Like the best kind to chink cracks in drafty iglus—*qikuutitsajaq*. Or clumps of snow that form around polar bear tracks after a blizzard—*qaqiqsurniq*. He taught me different words for snow, depending on the sound it made when you stepped on it—like *qiqiqralijarnatuq*. I loved saying that. *Qiqiqralijarnatuq*. Making tea, building iglus, finding directions, tracking animals, reading the land. Snow glued our culture together.

But Dad couldn't read snow like he used to. The glue was coming unstuck. We all knew why. Our screwed-up climate, the very thing that had brought me to the United Nations front door. Give me thirty-five below and a calm, clear day hunting caribou. Not this shivering in New York City's warm, wet excuse for winter.

With telescopic eyes, a peregrine falcon gazes down from the roof of the United Nations at a flock of pigeons far below. The flock moves as one body, swerving around a long row of flagpoles, dodging treetops in its path. It circles above a line of humans, as if deciding whether to beg for handouts. The pigeons' wings flash white and brown as the flock banks.

The falcon's eyes widen at the sight of three darker birds at the edge of the flock. She watches them intently, her eyes moving as they move, her half-open wings quivering. She selects her target, then launches off the roof with a few shallow flaps of her dagger-like wings. At first her flight is unhurried, almost casual, as she mirrors the motion of the pigeons. Her circle tightens. Her wing-beats quicken for a moment, then stop. She tucks in her wings and dives.

The sound of rushing wind fills her ears. The joy of lightning flight floods her chest. Her unblinking eyes remain fixed on a dark pigeon trailing the flock. In a full stoop, the world's fastest creature closes the gap, from roof to pigeon, in less than three seconds. Just before impact, she thrusts out her wings and extends her razor-sharp talons.

The pigeon dies instantly in an explosion of gray feathers. It hangs limp in the peregrine's talons as it darts to a feeding perch on the highest tree. The falcon rips open the pigeon's belly and enjoys the satisfying tang of fresh blood. She tears off a beakful of meat. It is deliciously sweet and tender. For a peregrine, this is the taste of life.

She rips out the pigeon's still-beating heart, then stops in mid-gulp. Sensing a strange power, like the pull of gravity, the falcon lifts her head and stares through the veil of naked branches. She forgets her pigeon meal for a moment and fixes her black marble eyes on one human, standing alone.

Something caught my eye. Actually, not my eye. My heart. Something clawed at it. I looked up in time to see some dark thing drop like a stone through the swirling snow and, with it, that sound I'd heard on the Empire State Building— knife edges slashing the air. Whatever it was plunged out of sight behind a bunch of trees.

Another falcon?

Something else fell out of the sky, slowly, fitfully, as if batted by a cat. When it finally landed on the sidewalk, I ran over to pick it up. A beautiful feather. A fresh drop of blood hung from its shaft.

In the crazy urban jungle, I found an odd comfort in this tiny slice of wild nature.

Rosie came up and plucked the feather away. She twiddled it between her fingers. "Pigeon, you figure?"

"Probably." I grabbed it back.

"One less rat with wings."

I slowly turned the feather. Its purple tip glittered, even under the flat city sky.

Rosie yawned. "Swell souvenir from a town polluted with pigeons."

"I think a falcon took it out."

"Like the one you imagined on the Empire State Building."

"I believe you were touring the stairwells at the time."

"Hah."

"Over there," I said, pointing to the trees.

I felt a jolt inside, like a door was being flung open.

It came back. That whispering.

"You okay, Ash?" Rosie said.

I realized I'd been clutching my stomach. "Uh, yeah. Fine. Concert hangover, I guess."

"You better get your shit together. Like Becca says, the whole world's waiting for you."

"Right."

Things started to shake loose all around me, vibrating somehow. The bald trees, the steely waters of the East River, even the pigeon feather in my hand— all cracks of untamed nature in a paved-over world. A low, rolling hum leaked from them into me, just like from the Macy's pit and the undressed ground of Central Park.

There it is again! I thought. *First the whispering, then that thrum. Am I going crazy?*

The vibration seeped into my bones, rattling them loose, thumping my skin from the inside out. My whole body became a drum. I had a sudden urge to connect with the drummer.

That goofy song Becca sang by the candle in the park barged into my head. *Under the cities, lies a heart made of ground …*

A heart now crushed in concrete.

I slowly looked around at the grimy skyscrapers, the filthy streets, the stinking traffic. What I would've given, right then, for a monster monkey wrench to pry the scab of Manhattan off the living flesh I knew for certain was down there, that gorgeous green skin I'd seen from eighty-six stories up.

"Come on!" Becca yelled, waving madly.

I shook off my brain fog and ran straight for her, like my life depended on it.

A gust slapped my back. The whispering returned, now almost like a shout. I stopped and looked back at the trees. Some intelligence called me from the highest branches. I stared up through the wet snow.

Listening.

Like I was waiting for a huge email to download. Waiting for some mysterious message from another world.

Rosie caught up and grabbed my hand. "C'mon, space cadet!"

"Cripes, Ash!" Becca yelled. "No time to smell the flowers. We're in!"

PINK BIKINI

INSIDE THE UNITED NATIONS TOWER
DECEMBER 15TH, 9:45 AM

Gabe made a big stink when a UN security guard asked for his harmonica. They were about to kick Gabe out, maybe even arrest him, when he weaseled it back and played a bluesy round of "Arkansas Traveler." The guards softened. The Japanese tourists smiled and bowed. We all squeaked through.

We played tourist for a minute, gawking at the entrance hall. It looked like a sci-fi movie set, with weird stairways built for giants and curvy balconies that rose out of sight.

I ducked into the nearest can to slip on my amauti, kamiiks, and headband. I used to feel like an imposter wearing this outfit in public. But after tons of gigs, it felt like a second skin. I'd never felt more like hiding.

Somewhere between Carnegie Hall and the UN, I'd lost Jack Masters's business card. All we had to go on was his name and our smiles. At first it was like trying to visit the Pope.

"I'm sorry, folks, but Mr. Masters doesn't receive visitors without an appointment," said a gorilla-shaped guard beside the elevator.

"But we do have an appointment, sir," Becca said in ever-so-sweet tones.

The guard shook his head. "Nope. Impossible. He never sees anyone until after lunch."

"Hmm, lunch." Rosie muttered. "There's an idea."

"I'm hungry," Gabe announced.

On top of everything else, Gabe was hypoglycemic. If he didn't eat every half-hour he'd go wrangy. I reached into my pack. "Here, Gabe. A Milky Way. Can't get these up north."

"You're my guardian angel, Ash," he said, tearing into it like a sled dog eating frozen fish.

The guard studied Gabe as caramel goo ran down his chin. "The next tour starts in half an—"

"We're not tourists!" Becca said. "We're invited guests at the climate change thingy."

"The conference," I said. "Mr. Masters invited us ... well ... me, to speak at some climate change conference."

The guard sighed. "Uh-huh. Look, Miss—"

Becca almost jumped on him. "Please, sir. This is a chance of a lifetime!"

"Is there a cafeteria?" Rosie asked.

I scrunched my nose at Rosie, Inuit style. "Look, sir, couldn't you just phone the guy's office? He's expecting us."

"Not in my job description," he said. "Anyway, Masters runs a pretty tight ship up there. Try the tour desk." He aimed a pudgy thumb at a small town's worth of Japanese tourists.

"Good God, not again," Rosie said. "Let's hit up some stores on Fifth Avenue. Buy something cheap and cheerful. You know, a little retail therapy?"

I just wanted to go back to bed.

"Hey, this is New York, Rosie!" Gabe said. "Ya gotta line up to take a pee."

Becca sprinted for the tour desk. "C'mon. We'll jump the line!"

Halfway down the hall, I skidded to a stop in front of a kid-drawn poster of a polar bear standing on a melting iceberg. The sky looked red hot. The sun huge. Water poured off the iceberg into a steaming ocean. The bear was peeling off its fur to reveal a pink bikini underneath. This was how some twelve-year-old Russian girl named Katerina saw my world. Except for the bikini, she wasn't far off.

More artwork stretched down the hallway, the winners of some climate change poster contest. To my artist's eye it looked pretty Mickey Mouse. But where the kids lacked in talent, they more than made up for it in power. Youth from around the world had drawn the Eiffel Tower half under water, a tsunami wiping out New York, a parade of skeletons dancing on a bone-dry field, the Earth being swallowed by tongues of fire. I could've cried.

"Cripes, Ash!" Becca yelled.

I waved her toward me. "Hey, you gotta see this. A polar bear with—"

"Later, baby," she said. "I've got Masters's secretary on the phone.

She needs to talk to you."

"Do you realize, young lady, how awfully important this is?" scolded his secretary. "Get that guard on the phone this instant!"

Whatever she said to him worked. Gorilla man even pressed the "up" button for us. The only trouble now was that one of our band members freaked the second we stepped into the elevator. And I don't mean Gabe.

"I can't do this," Rosie said sticking her high-heeled boot in the elevator door as it closed. "I just can't."

"What?" Becca asked.

"I can't go up there," Rosie said. She sprang back into the hallway so fast she almost knocked over King Kong. The guy actually reached for his pistol.

"But you're our fearless tour guide, Rosie," I said.

Rosie hugged herself like it was fifty below. "Thirty-nine stories, Ash? No way."

"Suck it up, Rosie," Becca said. "He's only on thirty-seven. You survived the Empire State Building. We were up, like, over eighty stories."

"I'm kinda hungry. I'll meet you in the cafeteria after your gig."

"You're outta luck, missie," the guard said. "Closed for repairs."

"Well, then I'll meet you at—"

The elevator started bonging as I leaned against the galloping door. "It's happening in the General Assembly Hall. Just go straight there."

"I don't know, Ash." Rosie looked up at all the numbers above the elevator door. "What floor's it on?"

"It's just downstairs."

"I don't feel so good."

"You gotta be there for me, Rosie. Can't do it without you." I let go of the door. "Oh, and if anybody gets in your way, phone the battle-ax upstairs."

JACK'S JUNGLE

THIRTY-SEVENTH FLOOR, UNITED NATIONS TOWER
DECEMBER 15TH, 10:00 AM

It was like walking through a military parade. Six green guards lined the long narrow hall to Masters's office. No hidden handguns for these guys. Six guards, six machine guns. At least as many security cameras.

"Good morning, gentlemen," Becca said, as if they were underwear salesmen. "We have an appointment to see Mr. Masters."

"You're late," the biggest guard said. "Masters likes things punctual."

"Do you ever sleep in?" Becca asked coyly.

"Still on Eskimo time, I guess," Gabe said.

The guard cracked a faint grin. He sized us up, his narrow eyes coming to rest on my kamiiks. "Those booties wouldn't be made out of baby seals, by any chance?"

"Oil, actually," Becca said. "Hundred percent synthetic."

The guard nodded vaguely and motioned us on. "Last door on the left."

We stopped in front of a wide brass door.

"Man," Becca said. "This thing must be bullet-proof."

Gabe stroked its polished surface with his all-seeing fingers. "Bomb-proof."

Here were the mysterious words I'd seen on Masters's business card.

SETI
Stable Earth Treaty Implementation
— Remote Sensing Center —

I sucked in my breath. Above the words was a brass knocker

shaped like the head of a polar bear. As I reached for it, the vault-like door slid sideways with a faint electric hum. A curtain of heavy plastic strips hung from the inside door frame. A thin, bent woman in her late sixties stuck her head through them and greeted us with a frown.

"It's high time you got here. Did those nasty guards rough you up?"

Without waiting for an answer, she leaned into the hall and clucked at them. "Boys, you take it easy on these folks. They've come an awful long way to speak at Jack's conference."

All the guards jumped to attention like she was a five-star general. "Right, Jean-Anne," barked one of them.

"Is it true you people have polar bears knocking at your doors these days?" she said, herding us into Masters's office.

"By the looks of it, so do you," I said.

Jean-Anne jerked her head like a pigeon. "Jack does have a thing for bears."

"What's with the shower curtain?" Becca asked.

Jean-Anne chuckled. "Keeps in the critters. Jack lets nothing escape his little jungle."

Masters's office could have passed for the lobby of a fancy jungle hotel. Wooden floors, wooden walls reaching three stories up to a diamond-shaped skylight. Even a glassed-in fireplace burning real wood.

And God, the plants! Orchids, bamboo, huge ferns, all kinds of bizarre flowering trees. Tiny bolts of color jumped from plant to plant.

"Who's that chattering?" shouted Gabe.

I detected a fast, high-pitched chirping, like an angry mouse.

"Jack's fond of hummingbirds," Jean-Anne said. "Don't be alarmed if they—"

I felt a puff of wind on my face as a green and red hummingbird slammed on its airbrakes about an inch from my nose.

"See what I mean? It probably thinks your pretty headband is a flower."

The bird and I locked eyeballs until it zoomed away with a peevish chirp. That's when I noticed the butterflies. Blue, green, yellow, orange, flitting from flower to flower.

Becca pressed against my shoulder. "You got snakes in here?"

The old secretary smiled, showing even-edged dentures. "Not that I'm aware of."

Above the fireplace hung a huge painting of a naked woman sprawled on a red couch surrounded by jungle flowers. She seemed to be listening to the lions and monkeys that sat at her feet. I knew this painting well. I'd discovered it in some art book at school. Spent hours sketching it. I loved the woman's thick, braided hair. A real bush woman. Reminded me of Uitajuq.

I pointed to it and looked at Jean-Anne. "That can't be—"

"The original?" She tsked. "I'm afraid so."

"It's … it's called *Dream,* right?"

"Yes. Another of Jack's frivolous purchases. Imagine buying a dream!"

I snapped my finger. "By … what's-his-face … Rousseau?"

"Yes, very good. Henri Rousseau. 1910. The art museum told Jack, 'No way, sir! Not for sale! This is a public treasure!' But you know old Jack. Never takes 'no' for an answer. He basically said, 'Take my offer or I'll shut you down!'" Jean-Anne shuddered. "Oh, heaven help anyone who gets in Jack's way."

I didn't like the sound of that. Jack Masters had asked me—more like ordered me—to speak at his climate thing and I'd said yes. Well, sort of. He took off before I could say anything.

What if I'd said no?

For now, I wasn't going to sweat about Jack's power trips. There was too much to look at.

Hanging through the center of Jack's private jungle was a huge ball made of plastic junk. Bottles, cups, food containers, fish netting, nylon rope, shopping bags, six-pack rings, bath toys, even a Mickey Mouse hat.

Every piece dangled from its own string, carefully arranged by color to make oceans, continents, clouds, ice caps. In the subtle air currents that rippled from the darting birds, Jack's hovering Earth seemed to breathe.

I couldn't take my eyes off it.

Jean-Anne glanced up and shrugged. "Some people call it junk. Jack calls it art. You don't want to know what he paid for it."

"A real live plastic planet," Becca said.

"Like I said, junk. Flotsam and jetsam washed up on beaches. Jack picked it up all over the world when he ran Empire Oil." Jean-Anne shook her head. "Odd kind of beach-combing if you ask me."

My stomach lurched.

Empire Oil?

The energy thugs who wanted to pave the tundra with pipelines and compressor stations. Who starved Nanurtalik out of fuel while pumping it from our backyards. Who sponsored every penny of our tour and now owned us. Who were head-hunting for someone who got a bit careless with some matches and a few gallons of gas. "Did you say Masters *ran* Empire Oil?"

"For sure, sweetie.

Above the tropical flowers and fruits I detected a new smell. Oily, stinky, black money. I'd fallen smack into the lion's den.

I gotta get out of here.

But Jean-Anne put one thin arm around me and flapped the other over her head. "Oil, the UN, diamonds, NASA. Look around this palace. Jack didn't get here by selling peanuts in Times Square."

"Hot nuts! Hot nuts!" hooted Gabe.

She shot him a quizzical look. "Oh, yes. Jack's had his fingers in a lot of pies. Still does."

The Earth ball floated above a weird rock garden carpeted with silvery pebbles that were raked into spiral patterns. The garden was encased in a bubble of thick glass.

Though my feet said "Run!" I had to look in.

"What's with the shiny gravel?" Becca said.

"Aluminum pellets. Actually, aluminum and ... what was it? Oh yes, gallium. One of Jack's little experiments. You don't want to sneeze on his Zen garden or the whole place might blow up."

I pulled back from the glass. "What?"

Jean-Anne brought two fingers to her lips and shook her head. "Pardon me. That's really none of my business. Ask Jack about it. He'll tell you, if he's in the right mood."

A cabinet full of carvings lured me further into his office. "Whoa," I said, under my breath. Soapstone polar bears—hunting, dancing, drumming. The kind of carvings that jump around at night when no one's looking.

Rosie whistled. "Where the hell did Jack find these?"

"Somewhere in your neighborhood, I suspect," Jean-Anne said. "Jack likes to collect beautiful things. Paintings, sculptures, butterflies, plastic junk. Oh yes, and Earth data." She picked up a remote and aimed it at a wall of plasma screens. Above the screens was a flashing digital display.

CTP 0150:46:57

The numbers were getting smaller, like a countdown.

"Look at this mess," Jean-Anne said as the screens blinked on, showing views of the Earth from space. Burning jungles, clear-cut forests, spreading deserts, melting glaciers, smog-choked cities. "Jack's very own spy satellites," she said with some pride. "They collect data on everything from blue whales at the bottom of the sea to carbon levels in the atmosphere."

"His own *satellites*?" Becca said. "Like, how rich is this guy?"

"He's made his quid, as Jack would say. Let's just say he's got enough to support his one and only passion: checking the pulse of his precious planet. That's what we do up here." She watched the hodge-podge of disasters drift across the screens. "And I'm afraid that pulse is weakening by the day."

My eyes suddenly welled up, like I could feel the old guy's love for our sick planet. The same heartache that gnawed at me more each day, especially since the lightning strike.

But a big oil bastard?

I quickly wiped my eyes like I'd got dust in them. "So, who's we?"

Jean-Anne didn't hear me as she fussed with the remote. Below the screens was a glass door framed by banana trees. It, too, was covered with a butterfly screen, but I could make out shapes moving behind it, all wearing white lab coats.

"There we go," Jean-Anne said, and another screen came to life. It showed a close-up of some nerd in a puke-green suit and coke-bottle glasses. The man's tinny voice stabbed the hushed air of Jack's jungle: "… that as a climate change scientist, I put my faith in the facts and only the facts. And I believe that time will prove me correct when I say that we need not jump to conclusions about the dangers of …"

Jean-Anne peered at her tiny silver watch. "Heavens! No time for chitchat. You might be up next, Ashley." She slapped four plastic cards marked *SETI Delegate* into my hand. "Take these to the General Assembly Hall." She tapped her bony chin. "No, wait. There's only three of you. Jack told me—"

"Rosie had a spaz attack in the elevator," Gabe said.

"She's downstairs," I said.

"Then go, my children. Go!" And Jean-Anne herded us toward the door.

As we ran out, I had a strange urge to look up at the big skylight. It was partly covered in snow, but through a gap I spotted the unmistakable silhouette of a peregrine falcon. The bird looked down at me through the glass, its dagger-like wings fluttering madly.

SCUMBAG

GENERAL ASSEMBLY HALL, UNITED NATIONS
DECEMBER 15TH, 10:30 AM

CTP 0150:01:57

We found Rosie talking up a hunky cashier in the UN gift shop.

"C'mon Rosie!" Becca said. "We're, like, over an hour late for Ash's gig!"

With Gabe in tow, we dashed up a winding staircase, flew down a hall, then piled into each other like a train wreck in front of the General Assembly Hall. I handed our passes to a security guard, hoping he'd reject them, but he waved us in like VIPs.

The giant hall made Masters's office look like a closet. The domed roof, ten stories high, looked like a space port for flying saucers. A huge United Nations logo hung on the front wall—a blue Earth hugged by two planet-sized olive branches. The man in the puke-green suit still blabbed at the podium. Over a thousand people were listening to him, sort of.

"So this is Jack's idea of a small gathering." Rosie said.

Becca shoved me from behind. "C'mon, girls."

I spotted four empty seats at a table near the back labeled *Cambodia.* We tried to sneak in, crouching like commandos, except for Gabe, who stood tall and smiling as I tugged on his hand. He was at his best in crowds. I was at my worst.

The second we set foot in the hall, the crowd started groaning. Rosie laughed. "I told you they'd love you, Ash."

"Hey, that's the same geek we saw on the boob tube upstairs," Becca said.

Rosie plunked down in a seat and yanked the binoculars from my backpack. "Oh, how perfect!" she said with a horsey laugh.

"What?" Becca said.

"Blofeld. Norman Blofeld. What a lovable name."

"Sounds like a blowhard to me," I said.

"No, I got it!" shouted Gabe, who was still standing.

I wrenched him into a seat. "Gabe, shh. Let the guy crucify himself."

"No, I got it," he croaked. "Blowhole. It's Blowhole. He's spouting hot air!"

The speaker droned on: "… and so, my friends from around the world, we need not worry too much about climate change. Humans have been down this road before and survived. Quite happily so, in fact. The last time the Earth's climate warmed significantly, ten thousand years ago, it gave rise to civilization …"

Edgy chatter smoldered through the hall.

"Yeah, come north, buddy," Becca said. "We'll show you some happy campers—sinking their snowmobiles through rotten ice!"

"What a turkey," Rosie said.

Butterflies crawled up my throat. As sick as Blofeld was, I'd happily let him talk all day so I could hide. Sitting behind Blofeld at a speakers' table were a small man with white hair and owlish glasses, a female Buddhist monk wrapped in purple robes, and a chunky old guy in a black suit. I caught the flash of diamonds from his folded hands. Jack Masters. There were two empty chairs beside him. I grabbed the binoculars, almost choking Rosie with the neck strap. "Shit!"

Right in front of me, an Indian woman dressed in a red sari turned around with fire in her eyes. I gave her my best saccharin smile and sunk back in my seat.

"What? What?" Becca said.

"They spelled my name wrong."

"Huh?"

"There's a name thing up there, for the chair beside Jack. It says Aisley Anowiak."

"Cripes, Ash!" Becca said. "You better get up there."

Blofeld was on a roll. His squeaky voice filled the hall. "... No one can deny that carbon dioxide levels have risen somewhat over the past century. But let me point out that this rise is tied not so much to the fossil fuels we must burn but to the clearing of forests ..."

Rosie huffed. "He's gotta be some oil company stooge."

"... Since the day when Columbus discovered America in 1492, humanity has cut down nearly ten billion acres of trees ..."

Rosie slammed the arm of her chair. "Wasn't that when *we* discovered Columbus?"

"... and, of course, trees convert heat-trapping carbon dioxide into oxygen, the very stuff we breathe. By cutting down trees, we deplete the Earth's ability to make vital oxygen. Carbon dioxide builds up, the planet warms. So, wherever we live, we should all do our best to grab a shovel, get out there and plant a tree for our children and our ..."

Groans erupted from the crowd.

"Makes me puke," Becca said. "He's trying to sound green without pointing a finger at gas-guzzlers."

"... Furthermore, quite apart from carbon dioxide levels, the sun and stars can explain most if not all of the warming during the last few decades ..."

More groans and guffaws.

"... Let me show you the scientific proof." Blofeld projected some mysterious graphs on a giant screen. "You see, since 1970, the sun's magnetic field has increased, sending significantly more energy toward the Earth ..."

Blofeld's graphs looked like the work of a deranged kindergarten class. Even with binoculars, I couldn't read a word.

"... So, as you can plainly see, we must look beyond our use of precious fossil fuels to explain global warming, a link that is at best unproven and at worst pure fantasy. Furthermore …"

A burst of angry words drowned him out, shouted in a language I'd never heard. He looked up blankly and waited for the shouting to stop.

"… Furthermore, I believe it would be foolish to rush into costly actions on climate change without fully understanding its chief causes and potential impacts, which …"

A long, loud boo filled the ten-story hall.

I turned to Rosie. "You want me to run up in front of these animals?"

"He's the animal, Ash."

"A real warthog!" Gabe said.

"Pure scumbag," Becca said.

Blofeld bowed politely, like he'd just rehearsed his stupid talk in front of a bathroom mirror. That old anger reared its head. My cheeks burned.

Rosie peered at him through the binoculars. "Aha! Just as I thought. Strings!"

"What?" Becca said.

"He's an Empire puppet. Paid to pump out lies."

Becca grabbed the binoculars, pulling Rosie's head into my lap. "I don't see any strings. What are you talking about?"

Rosie looked up at me with a mischievous smile. "Hey, with that beaded headband and sexy kamiiks, you'll get a standing ovation."

"A freak show," I said.

"That monk isn't sweating," Becca said. "Why should you?"

I snatched the binoculars. The monk's eyes were half-closed and she wore a faint smile. I swung my gaze over to Masters. He was looking right at me.

Becca elbowed me in the ribs. "Get up there, Ash! Time to kick butt and save the world!"

Gabe slapped my knee. "I'll get these cheerleaders dancing in the aisles, Ash!"

The Indian woman turned around again, this time glaring at Gabe. He wore a big smile, while doing a silent pantomime of a cheerleader on steroids.

"Go get 'em, Uitajuq," Rosie whispered in my ear.

Without thinking, I stood up and bolted for the stage.

LISTEN!

GENERAL ASSEMBLY HALL, UNITED NATIONS
DECEMBER 15TH, 10:45 AM

CTP 0149:29:41

I could feel Masters's eyes on me as I hurried down the long green aisle. I stood at the foot of the stage, staring up at him as he thanked Dr. Geek. I pressed both hands over my chest to stop my thrashing heart from leaping out.

"You've certainly given us much to ponder, Dr. Blofeld," Masters said, his crusty voice ringing through the great hall.

Blofeld nodded slightly with a tight-lipped grin.

"Your supporters may be inspired to plant more trees on this good Earth. On the other hand, your suggestion that the sun and stars are the main climate change culprits seems to have struck a chord with this audience, albeit a minor one. And so I thank you for throwing some thought-provoking fuel on this debate."

Maybe five people clapped.

"And now, ladies and gentlemen, let me introduce our next speaker from the Great White North ..."

Masters paused, looking directly at me with a big plastic smile.

I felt a thousand people staring at me, strangling me with their eyes, robbing me of air.

On the outside, it must have looked like I'd simply tripped over the stairs to the stage. On the inside, it felt like a second lightning attack.

I don't remember falling. I don't know how long I was out. My next memory was a bunch of beeps and flashes. I fought to open my eyes.

A smiling little girl looked down at me through the wrinkled old face of the Buddhist monk. Her lips moved slightly as she chanted some prayer in a sweet singsong voice. I liked this stranger instantly. She was everybody's grandmother.

It was cameras that beeped, tons of them. My eyes stung with each flash. A dozen reporters formed a mob around us. *What a photo op*, I thought. An ancient Buddhist monk crouched over a young, traditionally dressed Inuk woman sprawled on the United Nations stage.

She leaned close, ignoring the microphones shoved at us. "Welcome back," she said, almost in a whisper. "You bring much hope to our troubled Earth. Listen to her messengers. You will know what to do. *Listen!*"

I had no clue what she meant. But her words, spiced in a thick Asian accent, went in like Cupid's arrow. It was like she was talking directly to my Uitajuq core.

As I struggled to my feet, the hall burst into applause. The monk pulled a white silk scarf out of thin air, placed it around my neck, then bowed to me with pressed palms. I automatically did the same to her. It felt surprisingly natural, important.

More flashes. More applause. This wasn't at all what I'd expected but, hey, I'd found a friend in the lion's den. And Rosie was right. The crowd seemed to love me.

I looked up at Masters, then back at the monk, searching her face for some clue to the riddle of her words. But the magic had passed and a couple of UN aides ushered us onto center stage.

TIPPING OVER

CENTER STAGE, GENERAL ASSEMBLY HALL, UNITED NATIONS
DECEMBER 15TH, 10:55 AM

CTP 0149:19:14

Masters patted the empty chair beside him. He looked at me with a big, satisfied smile, like he'd just collected a rare butterfly. I was creeped out, sitting so close to him. His breathing was short and choppy, like mine is when I'm tumbling into an asthma attack. He gave off an invisible smog that reeked of money and power. He wore a blue United Nations pin on one side of his black lapel. On the other, a green dinosaur, the dreaded logo I'd seen on the trailer I torched: Empire Oil.

I pulled away. *Could I be in deeper shit?*

My shoulder knocked Dr. Geek himself, Norman Blofeld. He sat with his hands clamped so tight that his knuckles were white. But his thumbs twitched constantly, scratching and poking each other like angry cats. His skin was pasty, the color of beeswax, and I detected a faint smell of formaldehyde, like he'd just hopped out of a large specimen jar.

I felt trapped between a laboratory frog and a Tasmanian devil. What I'd give to sit beside my new Buddha buddy. I leaned forward to check her name plate. *Pema Rinpoche, Nepal.*

Masters punched his table mike. "Friends, on second thought, I think we'll let our Arctic guest catch her breath. Instead, I present Dr. James Livingstone of the British Academy of Global Limits and author of the international best-seller, *Bursting the Bubble of Life on Earth*."

Enthusiastic applause.

The man with owlish glasses spun around in his chair and unlocked a metal trunk behind him. As he drew back the lid, he disappeared in a puff of blue mist.

A wave of excited chatter swept through the crowd.

Livingstone bent over his trunk and pulled out an old-fashioned fish tank and a pitcher of water, which he carried to the podium. Without a word, he sloshed water into the tank, switched on a battery-powered propeller attached to the bottom, then carefully poured a vial of oily blue stuff into the water. After a few seconds, a swirling blue doughnut hovered in the middle of the tank. All this was captured by video on the two big screens above us.

The crowd seemed riveted.

Next, he hauled out a bicycle pump and a kid's inflatable palm tree, complete with coconuts. He blew this up and set it on the podium beside the fish tank.

Finally, out came a Styrofoam cooler and orange rubber gloves. He placed these on the cooler lid without opening it. Ribbons of blue mist escaped from around the edges.

With his toys in place, Livingstone spread his hands on the wide marble podium and leaned back. "Ladies and gentlemen of the Earth," he began in a royal British accent.

Applause.

"We hear a lot these days about tipping points, critical thresholds, and runaway warming of the planet. We've all heard the many doomsday news reports about climate change. Let me simplify things for you. Only three great disasters await us. You needn't worry about anything else, since nothing could so effectively bring human civilization to its knees."

Livingstone spoke like a TV evangelist, lifting his arms, pounding the podium, raising his voice, then lowering it almost to a whisper.

In spite of my stage fright and Masters's slimy glances, I was sucked right in.

"For now, these tipping points exist only in computer models. We know they have shaken the Earth in the distant past. Given today's pace of climate change, it seems we're due for another shake-up."

Livingstone waved his magician's hand over the fish tank. He glanced up at the video screens to make sure it was on camera. "The first great disaster: collapse of the Gulf Stream. Imagine the unthinkable. This blue swirl in my fish tank is the healthy Gulf Stream. It circles the Atlantic as a rushing river of warm seawater a hundred miles wide and half a mile deep. It brings warmth and moisture to much of North America and Europe. It makes our winters livable and farmlands productive."

He pulled a little bottle out of his tweed jacket and held it over the fish tank.

"Now, as our climate warms and sea ice melts, frigid Arctic waters pour into the North Atlantic.

"The warm Gulf Stream disintegrates just as this cleaning solvent breaks down the blue oil in my tank. Our climate does a quick about-face, from warming to cooling. The next ice age begins."

Livingstone slowly tipped the bottle. The swirling doughnut frayed at the edges then collapsed. The whole tank turned a washed-out blue. He flipped his palm to the ceiling, like he'd pulled a rabbit out of a hat.

"Once the Gulf Stream collapses, expect a plunge in temperatures within two winters. Parts of Scandinavia become uninhabitable. Farm production across the Northern Hemisphere is cut in half. Fish production drops by twenty percent worldwide. Mass starvation, migrating hordes of environmental refugees, economic collapse, war, pestilence—you name it."

Livingstone set the fish tank aside, like he was removing wilted flowers from a funeral parlor. He pulled the blow-up palm tree toward him.

"The second great disaster: collapse of the world's rainforests. It's no news that we're already losing these natural treasures. The latest count is one hectare or two football fields *every second*. But what slashing and burning won't destroy, climate change may well finish off."

He grabbed the toy tree just below the leaves, as if strangling it.

"As we dump more carbon into the air, rainforest plants start behaving in strange, self-destructive ways. Normally these plants create their own rainfall, so vast is the moisture given off when they open their leaves to inhale carbon dioxide. But as these concentrations rise, they finish their carbon meal quicker. Their breathing holes, called stomata, open for briefer periods. They release less moisture. Which means less rain. Much less. Get the picture?"

Livingstone popped the air valve on the tree. He folded his arms and silently watched it collapse into a heap of crumpled plastic.

"As rainforests fall to drought, the decaying plants and exposed soils discharge massive amounts of carbon, further warming the climate. The remaining plants release even *less* moisture, worsening the drought. Eventually a tipping point is reached where rising carbon and dwindling rain trigger runaway warming."

I stared at the pathetic plastic tree. I'd probably never see a rainforest, but this kooky scientist had somehow breathed life into it for me.

Then killed it.

I looked out over the sea of faces from all over the world. I searched in vain for my friends. Words from a goofy kid's song popped into my head: "Red, yellow, black, or tan. There ain't no difference, a man's a man." I squinted and they turned into a bowl of jujubes.

My head hurt. I'd had enough bad news for one day. I wanted to curl up under the table and sleep. But Livingstone had another disaster up his sleeve.

"And now, the third great disaster." He slipped on the orange gloves and ripped off the cooler lid. A puff of blue mist flew up in his face. He slowly pulled out a steaming hunk of muddy ice. He broke off a piece, set it on the marble podium and held a lighter up to it. "Behold," he exclaimed, "the ice that burns!" And it burst into flames.

A wave of oohs and ahhs.

Livingstone raised a hand to his ear. "And listen."

The crowd fell silent.He held the remaining chunk to the microphone. The great hall filled with a weird hissing, popping sound. "Frozen methane. Massive amounts of this stuff lie trapped in deep ocean floors. The world's biggest stockpile lies below the Arctic Ocean, where intense water pressures and cold temperatures keep methane gas harmlessly locked away in frozen form. But, as temperatures increase, so does the threat of a colossal release of methane. Planetary flatulence."

Nervous laughter.

"But I warn you," he said, knitting his forehead so that his bushy gray eyebrows met. "There is nothing funny about methane. If you thought carbon dioxide was a greenhouse gas villain, methane can warm the atmosphere sixty times faster. It is, without doubt, the arch villain of a safe and stable climate."

He folded his arms and stared at the evil farting ice.

"Many paleontologists believe that the escape of frozen methane caused the biggest biological catastrophe of all time. Instead of humans, it was a massive volcanic eruption 245 million years ago that suddenly boosted global temperatures. At some terrible tipping point, oceans warmed enough for an explosive release of methane. Temperatures climbed higher still. More methane escaped, unleashing an upward spiral of fire that pushed nine out of ten species on Earth to extinction."

"And it could happen again. The release of frozen methane from the sea floor is the third great disaster that would change the face of life as we know it."

Livingstone's little bonfire bravely flickered, then died. The other chunk farted away, releasing methane gas into his face. He leaned over the podium, pivoting on his elbows and clamping his fingers together as if in prayer.

"The most terrifying aspect of these potential disasters is that, once past the tipping point, there's no turning back. The Earth will show us no mercy. Let me explain.

"Many of us treat the Earth like a driverless spaceship drifting aimlessly around the sun. But the Earth is much more than this. Life is not just a passenger on this ship but an active participant, controlling the very conditions that sustain it. Life itself created its atmosphere and it is life that regulates it. The atmosphere, oceans, soils, plants, and animals are like the organs in our bodies. Call it a superorganism. Call it Gaia, after the Greek Earth goddess, or Terra, the Roman equivalent. Call it what you like. By whatever name, the Earth itself is *alive*. It is a planet-sized being that knows how to take care of itself."

I knew exactly what he was talking about. Here was Sila in a lab coat.

"Climate change is a normal part of the Earth's life story. What's unusual about today's crisis is that *we* are the cause of it. Nothing so fast or so severe has hit the Earth since the days of the dinosaur. You could look at climate change as her response to getting rid of an irritating species— us—or at least cutting us back to size. The Earth is changing, according to her own rules, to a state where humans are no longer welcome."

I gave my head a quick shake, dislodging the echo of Aana's warnings about Sila running out of patience and striking back.

"From the thin blue film of our atmosphere to the sea floor of our deepest oceans, we are unplugging the planet's life support systems. Warning lights are flashing all across spaceship Earth as we race blindly toward a massive system failure.

"The good news is that the Earth is a tough bitch. The planet itself will eventually recover from these disasters. The bad news is that what's really at stake is not the planet, but human civilization. The time has come for Mother Nature to lay down the law, fight back, if you like, and bring this burning house down on our heads."

Livingstone sounded like the Dr. Jekyll version of that crazy guy who chased us through Central Park, screaming bloody murder about the end of the world.

"We still have time to put out this fire, to befriend the living Earth before she becomes an enemy. How? All of the countries represented in this hall must slash greenhouse gas emissions deeply and promptly. We must switch to carbon-free energy sources like wind, water, solar, hydrogen, even nuclear. Our governments must punish polluters and reward wise energy users. From riding a bicycle to building a wind farm, we must do whatever it takes to decarbonize our lives, and fast.

"I believe that, as a species, we stand at a crossroads. One path leads to a social, economic, and technological *breakthrough,* where humans find a new harmonious place on the planet. The other path— business as usual—leads us to a *breakdown* of civilization and a full-on climate catastrophe."

As Livingstone wound up for a roaring finish, Masters covered his mouth and let out a huge yawn.

"Never doubt the power of the Earth to kill. Look at recent climate disasters. Hurricanes in the southern States. Firestorms in Australia. Flooding in Bangladesh."

At the mention of Australia, Masters nudged me with his elbow and wiggled his eyebrows. I jerked away, knocking over my glass. One kamiik filled with icewater. Masters righted my glass with a fawning look.

What's with this guy?

"The Earth has merely to shrug to send millions of people to their death," Livingstone continued. "If we don't take care of her, rest assured the Earth will take care of herself. If, in the process, that means eliminating us, so be it.

"Breakthrough or breakdown? I give us ten years, max, to shape our future. The time to choose is now. Any delay could trigger the three great disasters that loom just around the corner." Livingstone swept his arm over the flattened palm tree, the sickly blue fish tank, and the steaming hunk of methane. "Once we've tipped over the edge, I'm afraid all we can do is stand back and watch the planet burn.

"Thank you."

The General Assembly Hall burst into applause. Everyone jumped to their feet. Livingstone politely bobbed his head at the crowd, packed up his toys, and sat down.

Masters shook his hand, then swung around and looked me dead in the eye. He was so close I could smell the rank sweetness of booze on his breath.

"Ya ready, girl?"

The bottom fell out of my stomach. I'd been so wrapped up in Livingstone's magic act I forgot I was up next. That's when I realized his doomsday message had set off a depth charge inside of me. It blew open the song I called "Sila's Revenge." I had to bite my lip to stop it from leaking into the world.

ASH RULES

CENTER STAGE, GENERAL ASSEMBLY HALL, UNITED NATIONS
DECEMBER 15TH, 11:20 AM

CTP 0149:04:59

Masters puffed himself up and tugged on his shirtsleeves, revealing diamond cufflinks big enough to retire on. He could turn the charm on and off like a light switch.

"Ladies and gentlemen. Climate change impacts us all. But all of us are not impacted equally. Those least to blame for the problem are taking the biggest hits. Nowhere is this more true than in the Arctic where shrinking sea ice, melting permafrost, and extreme weather are crumbling the foundation of northern landscapes and cultures. Today we are fortunate to hear a personal testimony from the front lines of global climate change. Ladies and gentlemen of the world, I present to you a young climate change crusader from the Arctic, Aisley Anowiak."

Polite applause.

I was still a wild card to this stuffed-shirt audience. And to myself. Hearing my name botched set me up for another identity crisis. Who was I to be up here, speaking to the world? And what was my message? The graffiti I'd seen downtown came back to me.

You are nobody with nothing to say.

I slowly stood up with ice water in my veins. As I shuffled to the podium, Pema, the monk, reached out and touched my arm. Her face was all sunbeams. I managed a weak smile.

I took a quick look at my notes scribbled in the taxi. I could barely read a word. I turned them face down on the black marble podium. I pulled the pigeon feather from my pocket and set it on my notes. Like

Rosie said, time to wing it.

"*Ai.* Hello. My name is Ashley Anowiak. You can also call me *Uitajuq*, my traditional Inuit name. It means 'open eyes.'"

Something stirred inside. I threw back my shoulders.

"I live in a tiny Arctic village called Nanurtalik, the place of the polar bear. I'm here to speak on behalf of …"

Who?

I lifted my chin. "On behalf of all the noble sons and daughters of the Arctic."

From somewhere near the back of the hall I heard a horsey laugh, one I'd heard a thousand times before. My scattered cloud of butterflies drew together.

Some people clapped. I'd barely opened my mouth and they were applauding.

"We're a group of Inuit and non-Inuit, family and friends, who are trying to do something real about climate change."

I was hitting my stride.

"You may think I'm crazy but I love the cold. I have to laugh when I walk these streets. It's barely cold enough to snow and New Yorkers are bundled up like it's forty below. For us, cold isn't some pain to ruffle our hairdos. It's not something to get over with like the flu. Cold is something we celebrate. It defines our land, our culture, who we are. This may sound funny but we can't live without cold.

"When the cold comes each fall, when the snow comes and the ice starts forming on the sea, we're happy. We know we can soon travel across the ice, hunt seals and caribou, and enjoy the land together.

"But now we can't read the weather like we used to. We can't trust the ice anymore. We can't even find decent snow to make iglus. Animals, too—they're suffering. Like polar bears. When the ice changes and they can't find seals, they come into town, sniffing out garbage or chomping on sled dogs. They usually end up dead, shot in the name of public safety, or they get too close to somebody and *they* end up dead. In the past five years, nine polar bears have been shot at the edge of Nanurtalik alone. A good friend of mine was eaten by one not far from town. Torn up like roadkill."

A sudden movement far back in the audience caught my attention. I lifted a palm over my eyes and squinted. I picked my buddies out of the crowd. Like Olympic judges, they waved three big pieces of paper scribbled with the words: *ASH RULES!* Gabe held the exclamation mark.

My butterflies merged, then disappeared.

"The footprint of my village wouldn't fill one city block in Manhattan. All the people in our village wouldn't fill the elevators in our hotel. There're not many of us up there but we feel like we're at war with the climate. The United Nations was set up to end wars. Well, we come here today to ask you to stop the war on our culture, our land, our livelihoods."

More applause.

"There's no more time to pussyfoot around with carbon targets fifty years from now. Nothing personal, but most of you will be *dead* by that time. We're the ones who'll still be here, shaking our fists at today's decision-makers.

"I've seen my friend's house get bowled over by a freak storm. I've seen my own dog crushed to death in a mudslide triggered by melting permafrost. I've seen my father lose a foot to frostbite after his snowmobile went through some weird ice in the middle of winter. I've seen bullet holes in my living room window from someone shooting at a starving polar bear, driven into our village by shrinking sea ice. I've seen fish meat rotting in the sun before it can properly dry because it's getting too hot in summer. I've seen Elders break down and cry because they can't predict the weather anymore. I've even been struck by lightning, something that was once as common in the Arctic as muskox in Manhattan."

A gasp spread through the great hall.

"I said you could call me *Uitajuq*—Open Eyes. I've seen all these things happening to our land, to our animals, to our people. And I invite *you* to come and see them, too. We'll welcome you. There's lots of room in our house and my mom is a pretty good French cook."

Ripples of laughter.

"But if you never get up there, please believe that everything I've said is true. That climate change is legit and we in the Arctic are feeling it first and worst."

I nodded to Dr. Blofeld and faked a smile.

"It used to be that anyone, even scientists, who warned about climate change were called whackos. Today, it's the ones who say it's not real whose heads should be examined."

Big applause.

"It's real, all right. Take it from me."

Bigger applause. My sails were now as full as they'd get.

"As we flew down to New York, I read on the plane how fifteen percent of Americans think the Apollo moon landing was staged on a movie set. I also read that five percent still believe the Earth is flat." I leaned forward and stood on tiptoes. "Well, I think all the flat-Earth types and climate change deniers must get together on Saturday nights and *party!*"

"Right on, Ashley!" Gabe yelled like he was at a hockey game, "Let's party!"

Explosive laughter.

"*Taima, nakurmik.* Thank you."

Half the hall jumped to their feet. Another standing ovation. I felt like I was back in Carnegie Hall.

Masters was the last to stop clapping. He declared a coffee break, then wheeled over to me. He seemed particularly jolly. Even tried to pat me on the back. I ducked out of the way as civilly as I could.

"I have only one more request," he said, still smiling but looking miffed. "Would you and your friends like to join me tonight for a bit of tucker and tea?"

"Tucker?" I said.

"Dinner. At my flat."

"Flat?"

"Apartment."

"Sorry, my Aussie's a bit rusty."

I glanced at my friends who had joined me at the podium. Becca flashed me a quick thumbs-up. She looked totally game for another Cinderella adventure.

Rosie shrugged.

"Who can say no to a free lunch?" Gabe said, "Even if it's suppertime?"

I felt split in two.

Masters had swept me onto the UN stage. I'd told the world how screwed-up things were back home and got a standing ovation. Overnight, he'd changed a fugitive arsonist into a climate change crusader. The makeover felt good. Really good.

Forget the torched trailer. How could he ever know?

Still, Masters scared me. Behind his toothy smile was a greedy look that made me feel like one of the hummingbirds trapped in his office.

I looked down the speakers' table. Livingstone was dragging his toy trunk off stage. Pema sat with folded hands like she was at her own kitchen table. She gave me another warm, wrinkled smile.

Blofeld beetled off the second I finished.

Thank God.

I decided to bank on safety in numbers. "Yeah, I guess we could come. Don't have any real plans. Do you think Pema could join us for supper? Maybe the professor guy, too?"

"Consider it done," Masters said.

Becca elbowed me and held her arm up as if holding a torch.

"Uh, right," I said. "We sort of planned to climb the Statue of Liberty."

"Fine, then," Masters said, checking his watch. "I'll pick you up at the Liberty Ferry terminal. Look for a green limo. Six PM sharp." With that he spun his wheelchair around and ducked out a side door with Mr. Clean.

Becca gave me a squishy hug.

Rosie added a layer of arms. "You did good, Ash," she said. "But you forgot the bit about skeletons falling into the sea."

"My notes sucked. The only ones I could read were your signs."

"Ash rules!" shouted Gabe and he reached out to join the hug.

I closed my eyes, surprised to find them wet with tears. "Thanks for the cheerleading, guys. Maybe we made a dent in their thick heads."

GOOD INSURANCE

MASTERS'S STRETCH LIMOUSINE
DECEMBER 15TH, 6:15 PM

CTP 0141:15:59

"Sorry we're late," Becca said as we poked our heads into the monster limo to see Masters frowning in his wheelchair. "We got tangled up in the Statue of Liberty's spiky hairdo."

"The clock's ticking, mates."

"What's the rush, Jack?" Gabe said as I steered him through the limo's gaping door. "We're on holidays and you gotta be retired at your age."

"Not quite. Get in, quick."

I felt like we'd stepped into a movie set. We sat down on a plush leather couch that wrapped three sides of the limo. The floor was made of frosted glass with pulsing blue and white lights that made it flow like water. A mirrored ceiling twinkled with tiny lights arranged in familiar constellations. I spotted the Big Dipper. Back home we called those stars *Tukturjuit,* dancing caribou. Orion's belt was *Ullaktut,* three hunters lost on the sea ice. To us, Taurus the Bull was *Qimmiit,* five dogs harassing a polar bear. The rim of Jack's on-board planetarium glowed yellow, green, and pink—just like northern lights.

A row of video screens showed the same kind of messed-up Earth views we'd seen in Jack's office: angry hurricanes, burning forests, collapsing glaciers.

With a glass of whiskey in hand, Jack was parked at the end of a curvy bar that stretched along the opposite side of the limo. The bar was stuffed with crystal glasses, beer mugs, champagne bottles, and what looked like the best booze money could buy. There were fancy pastries and chocolates, bowls of exotic fruit, and a watermelon carved into an angelfish. Within arm's reach of Jack's wheelchair was a mini Zen garden like the one in his office, complete with glass dome and gravel that looked like silver licorice nibs.

At the other end of the bar, a rat-faced dude wearing a shiny green vest and black bow-tie welcomed us with a polite nod. A surround sound system drowned out the city with calls of tropical birds.

The limo was so long it was a few minutes before I noticed Mr. Clean sitting at the far end. I gave him a little wave.

Not a twitch.

We'd visited Madame Tussaud's wax museum the day before in Times Square. He would have fit right in.

Becca was in her social butterfly mode. "You like statues. I'm surprised you haven't tried to collect the big girl herself."

"What?" Jack said.

"The Statue of Liberty. It might even fit in that humongous office of yours."

Masters chuckled. Becca could soften up a stone. "You might be on to something, young lady," he said. "I'll put a man on it." Jack sent the rest of his whiskey down the hatch. "Please have a drink. Anything ya like. You all look legal to me." He turned to Mr. Clean. "Quincy, what's the drinking age in New York these days? Eighteen? Nineteen?"

Masters's bodyguard tightened his lips and gave a quick shrug.

"Twenty-one, sir," offered the bartender, giving us a dubious look.

Masters shrugged him off. "Hell, who cares. The UN bought me this limo so, technically, it belongs to all nations. Surely you're legal *somewhere* on Earth. Help yourself. I insist."

"That's right nice of you, Jack," Gabe said, reaching both arms toward the bar. "I turn twenty-one next month. Steer me to the beer."

I gently pulled his arms down. "Gabe, you know alcohol doesn't mix well with your tranquilizers."

"Always the mother hen," Gabe said.

It's true. I often felt my mother leaking out during long stretches of Gabe-sitting.

"Okay then," he said. "How's about a Muddy Water?"

Becca giggled. "What the heck's a—?"

"Try it, you'll like it," Gabe said.

The bartender set to work, pulling out a frosted mug and pouring in half coke, half orange juice.

"Puke," Rosie said.

"He would if he had a beer right now," I said.

"And you girls?" Masters asked.

Becca ran what was left of her purple fingernail over the cocktail list. "I'll have ... a Boo Boo's Special."

"Any old beer for me," Rosie said as she idly surfed through endless images of a wounded world. "Don't you at least have any, like, Discovery Channel or something? I mean, God, Jack, this is all pretty downer stuff."

"God didn't do this," Masters said. "We did." His speech was slurred like he'd had a long liquid lunch. He swung an arm at the screens. "Lest we forget! You can't be reminded enough how we've royally screwed this planet. Now, Aisley, what can Gino pour you?"

The bartender swept a raised hand over the bar.

"It's Ashley. No thanks, I'm good. Look, uh, Mr. Masters. Do you know you almost ran over a biker this morning?"

Becca straightened. "Now I remember where I saw this thing."

Masters took a final swig of his whiskey and carefully set the empty glass on a neon-rimmed side table. I noticed his hand shaking. "Gaw, that's awful. Must've been another stretch Lincoln. Manhattan's crawling with them."

"A lime-green limo?" Rosie said. "We've been here for, like, two days and the only green machines cruising Manhattan seem to be yours and the one that almost demolished Biker Bob."

Masters wiped his lips with a blood-red napkin. "Not lime. Parrot. A Brazilian parrot. I studied it back in grad school. Got along like chums. Now it's gone. Extinct, like so much bloody else in this world."

"Parrots, toads, whatever. We're talking about endangered bikers."

"No worries, I've got good insurance."

My mind replayed the scene of the crime—the diamond-studded hand waving on the driver, the guy's helmet bouncing off the pavement, the kid screaming. "Sorry sir, but … how can you be so gung-ho to save the planet and not give a shit about some biker dad and his kid?"

Jack froze for a second, then tossed the napkin down like it had bitten him. He slowly turned his head and locked onto me. His eyes widened and I could see the white rim of decay lurking at the edge of his pupils. Then, from behind the darkness, something like tentacles reached for me, wrapped around me, and I felt my chest collapse. My breath came in gasps.

I saw an anger in there I couldn't believe.

I recoiled in my seat, smashing the back of my head against the window.

"Cripes, Ash!" Becca said. "Take a hit."

I fumbled for my backpack and found my puffer. As I sucked back the cold vapors, that satisfied smile I'd seen on the UN stage flickered across Masters's face.

"My job is to help safeguard the Earth's life support systems," he said, calmly folding his hands on his lap. "Once things stabilize, people can bloody well look after themselves."

With her back to Masters, Becca fired me an *Is this guy mental?* look. I nodded.

Becca and I pressed together like spooked bear cubs. Meanwhile Rosie got more chatty. With or without beer, nobody scared her.

"Sounds like a big job, Jack," Rosie said. "Aren't you about ready to retire?" She cast her eyes around the limo. "I mean, it's not like you need more dough."

Masters scoffed. "I'll retire the day my candle goes out. Until then there's plenty of work to be done, spending my hard-earned quid to set things right."

Masters glanced at Gino and pointed to his empty glass. Gino sprang forward with a silver-coated bottle and filled his glass to the brim. Masters took a deep swig and smacked his lips. "Glenfiddich Royal Reserve. Twenty thousand bucks a bottle."

"Not exactly a cheap high," Rosie said.

Masters ignored her, turning his head toward his Zen garden. He seemed lost in a strange rapture.

"What's the shiny stuff?" Rosie asked.

"Aluminum pellets." He raised his whiskey to the garden. "Made from recycled beer cans. And a good pinch of gallium."

"Gallium?"

"It's an odd one, that. Imagine a metal that'll melt in your hand. But mix it with aluminum and you've got a magic brew that can change the world. Fix it right and proper."

"That's your job, right?" Rosie said.

Masters pointed to the glowing floor. "You hear that purring?"

I became aware of a low, breathy rumble.

"That's the sound of the future," he said. "Hydrogen. Fires this limo. Runs on water, basically. Add water to these pellets and boom, a miracle cure for what ails the planet." Master's let his head sink forward. "Or at least ... so I used to think."

"Unless you sneeze on them first " Gabe said. "BOOM"

"Ahh, Jean-Anne's been on ya. Well, she's right. Powerful stuff, hydrogen. Doesn't take much to ignite it. Fuels the sun." Masters spread his hand over the glass dome and stroked it like some kind of pet. "We like to keep it under wraps. A leak could get messy."

Somebody pissed off our driver who leaned on a train-sized horn.

"Gosh," Rosie said after a big gulp of beer. "That horn sounds *awfully* familiar. The biker blaster maybe?"

Masters shot her a black look, then dove back into his tiny perfect garden.

I looked back to see who he almost ran over this time. A grandmother in go-go boots shuffled back to the curb. She clutched a toy poodle while shaking a fist at us. Bathed in the crazy, flashing lights of Times Square, she looked like an angry ghost that had popped out of the pavement.

Seconds later, a police cruiser pulled up beside us with lights flashing and siren wailing.

Gabe started rocking back and forth, rubbing his hands together. "Could be a big owie, Jack! The law's on our tail."

Jack didn't even look up. A couple of feet from my nose, I could see two cops studying our limo for a moment. Then they killed their lights and siren and ducked down a side street. We'd just run a red light, almost flattened an old lady, and the cops couldn't touch him. Or wouldn't dare.

Becca looked at me wide-eyed.

I shrugged.

Then I'm in her lap.

Our driver seemed to lose control. The limo lurched right, headed straight for a brick wall.

"Shit!" I said, instinctively pulling Gabe's head away from the window.

Becca screamed.

"Hey, watch my beer!" Rosie yelled.

I squeezed my eyes shut and braced for impact.

But it never came.

"Welcome back to Carnegie Hall," Jack said, cool as a cucumber.

I opened my eyes to see Quincy flinging open the limo doors while a wall slid shut behind us. We'd driven into a luxury garage with a brass floor and walls paneled in the same fancy wood as Jack's office. The only sounds were the peep of tropical frogs over the limo's sound system and the weird rumble of its motor.

"No worries about fumes, folks," Jack said as Quincy unclamped his wheelchair. "Hydrogen, remember. A few puffs of water vapor won't kill you."

A wheelchair ramp shot out from under the limo.

"Did you say Carnegie Hall?" I said.

"Yep. Had to make a few renos before moving into this joint. I'm not fond of public garages. Give me the willies.

"How come?" I asked.

Masters shuddered slightly and his cheeks went all hollow. I felt a ripple of crazy fear race through my guts. His fear. For a moment,

Masters's armor fell and he was just a tired old man in a wheelchair.

"Some other time," he muttered. Then, with a wave of his diamond-studded hand, he was back in control of his world, shooing Gino out of the way as he burned rubber down the ramp and across the gleaming brass floor.

PARASITES

MASTERS'S APARTMENT, STUDIO TOWERS, CARNEGIE HALL
DECEMBER 15TH, 8:45 PM

CTP 0138:45:59

Rosie had no time to freak before getting on Masters's private elevator. With dirty looks and chin pointing, Quincy had herded us on like corralled reindeer. After filing through another parade of green-clad security guards, we arrived at the door to Masters's penthouse apartment, supposedly for tucker and tea.

An arched doorway slid open. My jaw dropped.

Making his own fantasy worlds was some mad hobby for Masters—his jungly office, the stars and streams in his limo, and now, his home above Carnegie Hall.

It was the light that first blew me away, a clear sizzling light that bounced off a red sandstone floor. Scattered clumps of spiky grass blended perfectly with wall-sized desert murals. I couldn't tell where plants ended and paintings began. I expected a mob of kangaroos in the background to bound away from us any second. A couple of pink parrots—real ones—preened their wings on top of a red rock shaped like a two-ton marble. A flock of painted parrots watched them from the branches of a slender tree with ghost-white bark. A powder-blue sky stretched across the domed ceiling above a ridge of purple hills. It was dotted with popcorn clouds that seemed to move.

I licked my lips. The air was paper dry. A welcome change from Manhattan's clammy winter.

Even my blind *tiguaq* picked up on the otherworldly feel of the place.

"Crikey, Jack!" Gabe said, sniffing the air and reaching his arms out. "What planet have you brought us to now?"

Jack wheeled toward a long glass table set for a king. "Right nice, i'n'it? A little piece of home. Reckon you'd like to see the real thing?" he said, winking at me.

"*OUCH!*" Gabe screamed after stumbling into a clump of stiff grass. "Not me, thanks!"

I yanked a couple of thorns from his leg and clamped a motherly hand on his arm. Like sheep, we followed Masters deeper into his world.

His apartment ended in a round wall of windows. Big plasma screens hung beside them, showing more satellite scenes of a wrecked Earth. Two digital displays flashed above the windows. The one we'd seen in his office counted down the seconds to something that would happen in a few days. The other display, labeled WPC, showed a long string of ten numbers. The tail end moved in a blur.

I wasn't surprised to see another sparkling Zen garden. It was exactly like the other two—shiny gravel, reddish rocks, glass dome—but plunked in the middle, sitting on an easel, was a framed photo, the centerpiece of Masters's altar. It showed a twenty-something guy standing in a jungle, smoking a pipe. He had a big grin on his face and an incredible green parrot on his shoulder. The bird seemed to be whispering in his ear. Its iridescent wings were spread wide, showing every shade of green on the planet. Its red, blue, and yellow tail feathers were unbelievably long, spilling over the man's arm like a liquid rainbow. The guy's mousey mustache and green eyes told me it had to be Masters.

Rosie tapped the glass dome with a fingernail. "Is that your lime-green limo bird?"

"So to speak, yes." Masters wheeled over from the table and stared at the photo for a long time. "*Amazona splendens*," he finally said. "Brazilian emerald parrot. Swore like a devil once we got to know each other. Could recite the dictionary backwards, given half a chance. Probably speak Inuktitut."

I noticed his knuckles going white as he clutched the arms of his wheelchair. I felt a sudden stab of pain in my chest.

"But we missed that chance. Wiped out soon after I left Brazil. Time to put a stop to all this nonsense. Bloody well *all* of it."

"What's all the black out there?" Becca said. She had her nose against the curved window. "Power go out?"

Masters looked up from the photo and blinked hard. A single tear ran down his wrinkled cheek. He sighed deeply as the blood flowed back into his knuckles. "Right, I suppose you're used to that up north. Ravens getting fried on the power lines and all. No, that's Central Park. Black at night. Green by day. Reminds me there's more out there than bricks and pavement."

I thought of the golden-eyed raccoon down there that had called me from the giant tree.

Why had it clawed at my heart?

I heard a clatter of dishes and a ridge of cliffs broke open, revealing an invisible door. A waiter dressed just like our limo bartender pushed a cart piled high with food that smelled of home. Masters snapped his fingers at us, like he did to his servants, and pointed a thumb at the table. "Come. Eat. Tucker's on."

"I thought the professor and that monk were coming," I said.

Masters shrugged. "Got tied up, I guess."

I knew he was lying. He'd never asked them.

But I was starving. Other than snarfing down a blueberry muffin in the taxi, I hadn't eaten anything all day. I loaded Gabe's plate, then my own, with fish, meat, and potatoes. One bite of the fish and I was back in Nanurtalik.

Masters smiled smugly as he watched me chew.

"Arctic char?" I said.

"Uh-huh. Not cheap in New York, I'll tell ya."

"And caribou?" Gabe said with a hunk of meat in his teeth. He was sawing it apart with a steak knife, Inuk style.

"Yep."

"And muskox. *Muskox!*" Becca said.

"You bet."

I looked down at my plate. It was edged in gold. The knives and forks were gold. The serving dishes were gold. We were eating in a museum.

Masters snapped for the waiter and pointed to a cloth-covered basket. The cloth was embroidered with the Suluk Delta braid sewn only by Inuit Elders living just down the coast from us. The waiter lifted the cloth. Deep-fried bannock full of checkerboard holes. Might have come fresh from Mom's wood-fired oven.

"Eskimo doughnuts!" Becca said. "Where the heck did you—?"

"Used to make 'em myself. Got the hang of it after a while up there."

"You lived in the Arctic?"

"That I did. Took some getting used to after Australia."

"What'd you do?"

"Ran away from home when I was fourteen. Somehow ended up on the flip side of the planet working for the Hudson's Bay Company. Apprentice fur trader."

"A real live Bay Boy!" Gabe said, lifting a mug of ginger ale toward Masters.

"That explains the polar bear carvings," Becca said.

"The best money can buy."

"How'd you end up in Brazil?" she said.

"Took a liking to birds up north. All them geese and swans ya get along the coast. Bloody well darkened the skies in springtime. Nested by the hundreds right behind our trading post. Used to sit on the tundra and watch 'em for hours."

Masters snapped for another whiskey. He was getting pretty lubricated. "My father finally tracked me down and hauled me by the ears back to Australia so I could finish school. But I still had birds on the brain. And when a prof at the University of Queensland invited me to the Amazon, well, what the hell could I say?" Masters lifted his glass to the photo of the extinct parrot. "'Come to Brazil,' he'd said, 'to study the most beautiful bird in the world!'" Masters downed his whiskey in one gulp. "That's what killed it," he said, staring into his empty glass. "Too damned beautiful for its own good. Everyone wanted to pluck those goddamned beautiful feathers. Pluck a feather, make a buck. Pluck a feather, make a buck. Pluck. Pluck. Pluck." Masters slammed his glass onto the table so hard that even his waiter jumped. "Plucked it clean out of existence, they did!"

We all stopped chewing. Masters slowly looked us over, one by one, from some faraway place. Then his eyes fell shut and his head thunked to his chest.

Nobody moved, not even Gabe. I became aware of a rustling noise, like wind blowing through stiff grass, and the distant cackling of birds. Something skittered across the sandstone floor. I gasped. Two lizards chased each other under my chair. I watched them through the plate glass table. Their bodies were orange, all covered with thorns, and they danced around each other, with their tails in the air like pygmy dinosaurs entering battle. I held a finger to my lips and pointed down for Becca and Rosie to see. Becca covered her mouth. Rosie stifled a laugh. If those lizards ran up Gabe's leg or over his foot, he would jump up screaming and flip the whole table over on Masters. Quincy would whip out his gun and shoot us all, and I'd never get a chance to finish my Arctic char.

Luckily the lizards took off without a fight. They skittered back toward a rock and vanished. It was like they'd jumped out of the painted desert and back again.

I looked at the waiter. Maybe this was routine for him, Masters passing out every night after tucker and tea. The waiter calmly stroked his nose, looking sideways at Masters as if waiting for the next finger-snap.

The wail of a siren drifted up from the streets far below, reminding me I was actually in New York, not the middle of the Australian outback. It seemed to piss off the pink parrots. They started screeching blue murder and rocketed straight for Masters.

I thought they might rip his face off. Instead, they landed on his shoulder, one on each side, and started nibbling on his neck. After a few nuzzles, the birds had Masters giggling like a schoolboy. He lifted his head, opened his eyes wide, and gave each bird a quick kiss on the beak. It struck me that, with a black eye patch and a fishhook hand, Masters would make a perfect pirate.

"These galahs are anything but extinct," he said, like nothing had happened. "Australia's skies are polluted with pink cockatoos. Noisy buggers." He puckered his lips at the birds. "But good kissers."

He made a little cooing whistle between the gap in his front teeth and they flew back to their rock. With a snap of his fingers, the wheelchair general was back in command of his world, ordering the waiter to fill our plates for a second round.

Gabe leaned back in his chair and rubbed his hands. "Gee, thanks, mate. I'll take more of that marvelous *muktuk*."

I held my hand over my plate. "No, thanks. I'm good." I looked at the spread of northern specialties—Arctic char, muskox, caribou, and muktuk, raw whale blubber. Even igunaq, fermented walrus meat, which my people drool over. It dawned on me that Masters had invited us for supper just a few hours ago. "So, uh, Jack, do you eat country foods like this all the time?"

He popped an olive into his mouth. His jutting jaw moved in circles like a caribou chewing cud. "It's been yonks. Decades, really."

"So how did you rustle up a meal like this so fast?"

"Let's say I had a strong hunch you'd be joining me tonight."

"Yeah, but it must've taken weeks to get all this—"

"Good planning, I guess," he said with a fake smile. "Just enjoy it." His tone basically said: *Shut up and eat.*

Above the char, I smelled something awfully fishy.

"You spoke well today …" Masters groped for a word.

"Ashley," I said.

"Right. Ashley. You brought those eggheads to their feet." He was buttering me up for something.

"They didn't much like your Dr. Blowhard," Rosie said.

"Oh, Blofeld. He's a bit of a boofhead. Keeps the public riled up, though. Helps spread a little chaos. The media love him. Used to work for me."

"Wait a minute," Rosie said with a mouthful of muskox. "He's a big oil plant, right?"

"Empire Oil, actually," Masters said.

Rosie slapped Becca's shoulder with the back of her hand. "What did I tell you, Becca?"

"The puppet man," Becca said.

I stared at the green dinosaur pin on Masters's lapel.

Rosie leaned forward with a lawyer look on her face. I'd lost track of how many beers she'd downed. "So, that makes you an Empire man yourself."

I hadn't told her yet. I didn't want to believe it.

"Vice president, in fact." Masters snapped for another whiskey.

"Hmm," Rosie mused, studying the photo of Masters and his beloved bird. "So, how does an Earth-hugger like you end up working for the dark side?"

This got Becca stirred up. She once confessed to me that before she moved north she used to be a Greenpeacer. "Yeah, like, it's only the world's biggest oil company. Raping the land. Fouling the seas. Filling the air with carbon. You worked for *them*? Like, what's up with that?"

Masters chuckled. "Cheeky Sheilas, aren't ya. Reckon I'm a bit of an Aussie Robin Hood. Ya know, steal from the rich, give to the poor. Pump some of that big oil quid back into the poor old Earth before the shit hits the fan."

"You mean all the disasters that professor guy talked about? Like, Mother Nature taking revenge on us?"

"Exactly what I mean, Miss."

"It's Becca."

"Right."

"So, you're pouring oil money into hydrogen cars, solar panels, stuff like that?" Becca said.

"Building a million nuclear reactors," Rosie said.

"Popping a million light bulbs!" Gabe said.

Masters heaved a deep sigh and shook his head. "I used to believe in all that. But it's too little, too late, I'm afraid. All Band-Aids. Like telling a terminal lung cancer patient to stop smoking. What the hell good is *that?*"

Masters waved a hand at the plasma screen behind him. An ugly brown cloud hung over most of Asia. "Ol' Doc Livingstone's misdiagnosed the patient. Oh, there's no flies on him, of course. First-class scientist. Real showman. Mind you, he's a bit of a panic merchant." He popped a chunk of caribou into his mouth and chewed thoughtfully. "Actually, that's what I like most about the bloke."

"Sounds like you enjoy stirring up shit," Rosie said.

Masters banged his knife and fork on the table like some royal prince. "Most certainly! Chaos is the ultimate weapon against planetary shutdown."

I didn't like the sound of that.

"Trouble with Doc, he's away with the pixies when it comes to numbers. His predictions are rubbish. *Ten years* to get our act together? Hah! Our data shows we're *months,* not years, away from the little disasters he pulled out of his hat." Masters made a big show of leaning sideways in his wheelchair. Quincy jumped up and nudged him back into place. "Can't you feel it?" Masters roared. Our host was coming undone. "The tipping point's just round the bend. We're passengers on a cruise boat, drifting merrily above Niagara Falls, for God's sake, and the motor's about to go tits-up!"

"So, forget the light bulbs?" Becca said.

"Bless the hearts of my Greenpeace friends, but you can forget the goddamned light bulbs! Besides, green is the color of mold and corruption."

"And hydrogen cars?" I said. "Your *green* limo?"

"Hah! Forget hydrogen cars. Still twenty years to mass production."

"But I thought your little silver thingies—"

"Nobody believes they'll work. They all think I'm a kook."

Becca looked at me and rolled her eyes.

"And nuclear reactors?" Rosie said. "Could be handy up north. Kiss goodbye all our power failures."

"Yeah," Gabe said. "And when they break down, all's you gotta do is invite a glowing raven into your house for extra light!"

"Takes ten years to approve 'em," Masters said, "and at least another five to build 'em. Forget the goddamned reactors. Don't have that kind of time."

He took a long swig of whiskey, glancing up over the rim of his glass at the flashing displays.

I pointed to them. "What's ticking away up there?"

A dreamy look came over Masters's face. "Your future."

"The big one, WPC, what's that?"

"That would be us. The plague of the planet. The deadly virus causing this fever of runaway warming. Behold, my Arctic friends, the UN's official World Population Clock."

I stared, amazed at the whizzing numbers, bumping up about three times a second. Each flash a new human life.

"It's damned well time to stop the clock before the Earth tips over the edge. She'll be right once we pull out a few weeds, shake up the soil a bit, give the Earth time to heal before handing it back to us parasites."

"Parasites?" Gabe said, scratching himself. "You mean, like, fleas?"

"I mean like seven billion brain worms. Screwing their way into the Earth's central nervous system. Driving her mad." Masters banged the table with a wrinkled fist. "Time to yank those bloody numbers down any way we can!"

"*Any* way?" Becca said.

"'Fraid so, sweetie."

I grabbed her hand under the table.

"And, uh, the other clock?" I said, bracing myself, like I was about to get punched. "CTP?"

Masters gestured for the waiter to leave. The cliffs opened and, like the lizards, the waiter melted into the desert. Masters looked toward the door where we came in. It, too, had vanished into a painted sea of red sand. No doorknob. Nothing.

A ripple of panic washed through me. The hot dry air seemed ready to ignite. I saw myself clawing the walls to escape.

Masters nodded to Quincy as if wrapping up a security check.

Quincy nodded back.

"Remember those tipping points that Doc Livingstone preached about?"

Vivid images of an exploding blue doughnut, a collapsing palm tree, and farting ice came to mind. "Like, the Gulf Stream and rain-forests pack it in? That methane stuff gases off?"

"Yep. All time bombs set to blow global warming through the roof. All *uncontrolled* collapses. I can't let that happen. We've bloody well messed around long enough with spaceship Earth. Royally screwed up every one of her life support systems. We're chock-a-block with people. Crossed the line. Something's gotta give and I'll be god-damned if it's the Earth!" Masters was weaving in his chair.

Quincy stepped closer.

"Like the professor said, the Earth's a tough bitch. And her rule is that when any species gets too big for its britches, she fights back. So I say, hell, why not give the old girl a little help? That's where my CTP comes in. Time for a *controlled* tipping point!" He blinked at the flashing display. "Well, almost time."

Even Rosie seemed a little spooked by Masters's tone. "So, uh, which time bomb are you going to set off?"

Masters ignored her. "We're shaping the Earth's destiny here, Aisley."

"Ashley."

"Whatever." Masters drove his index finger down hard on the table. "That destiny lies in the hands of a few very powerful people. You and I are among them."

"What? Me?"

"You and your little music troupe here can help ..." Masters turned to Rosie. "How did you so eloquently put it?"

"Stir up shit?" Rosie said.

"Exactly. Last night, you had the Carnegie audience spellbound. Felt it meself. And again today at the UN. Your eyewitness stories and songs from the Arctic war zone make climate change real for people. Help spread a little shock and awe, fear and trembling. I like that."

"Actually, the idea wasn't to freak people out," I said, "but to get them to do something positive like—"

"Don't you see?" Masters shouted. "The more convinced people are that this is a huge goddamned problem—as big as the planet itself—the more powerless they feel to do anything. That's where my controlled tipping point comes in. Paralyze the public with scary news. Knock 'em down. Then hit 'em hard. Boom!" Masters snapped backwards over his wheelchair, almost flipping it over. He shook his head as if waking up, then pressed both palms on the table to steady himself.

I squirmed inside as he gave me a long bleary-eyed look.

"Besides," he said, oozing phony charm, "I really like your singing. Makes me homesick for the Arctic."

"I'm feeling a little homesick myself," Becca said in a trembly voice.

"I can make you world famous, Aisley. Uh … I mean, Ashley. Imagine, the biggest aboriginal music festival the world has ever seen." Masters chuckled to himself. "And the last, too, I suppose. It's big bloody business these days, ya know. Throwing on the war paint, beatin' the drum for Mother Earth. I call it the Scorched Earth Concert. A big climate change powwow. Native musicians from the Andes to the Arctic, Melbourne to Mongolia, all cryin' the blues about a dying planet. The whole thing'll be wired for TV, radio, the Internet. Those broadcasts'll suck in an audience of … oh, I'd say about three billion bleedin' hearts. My boys are trucking in outhouses for a live audience of half a million."

"Outhouses?" Gabe said. "Won't they freeze their butts?"

"Not a chance, mate. The party kicks off on the twenty-first."

"The winter solstice?" Becca said.

"*Your* winter solstice. Our summer solstice. It's happening right on my farm. Bit of a farewell party, you might say."

"Farewell party?" I said.

"Dead right. A last blast. I reckon the best way to honor Mother Earth is for us to step aside for awhile. So I say, why not go down singing?" Masters fumbled for his fingertips then pressed them together. "My job is to ward off one global collapse by triggering another," he said very slowly. "And you can help me."

I sprang to my feet, spilling Rosie's beer.

"Shee-it," Rosie said.

I started lifting Gabe out of his chair. "Uh, I think maybe it's time we headed back to the hotel. Would you mind calling us a—"

"No need," Masters said in an oddly drawn out way. "Hang on. Relax. We still have a few days."

"*Days?*" I said. "But we fly home tomorr—"

"Actually, I was hoping I could tempt you with a little fame and fortune."

Rosie was already on the plane, flying straight for Australia. "Half a million people, Ash? Like, that's one hell of a gig."

I shot her my best *Are you crazy?* face. "On second thought, Jack, we can call a cab downstairs." I scanned the painted desert for a door-knob. "Uh, if you could just show us the way out."

Becca grabbed Gabe's other arm. Three blind people looking for a door. Quincy grinned at us in a way I didn't like.

"I'd really like you to come to the concert," Masters said gruffly. It didn't sound at all like an invitation. "Besides, you might want to let a certain little fire die down before you go home and face the music."

Becca turned to me with big eyes that shrieked two words: *He knows!*

HOODWINKED

CTP 0137.55.59

There was no escape. Not tonight, at least. In less than twenty-four hours, Mr. Jack Masters, a rich old fanatic in a wheelchair, had roped us into some harebrained plan to save the world from humans. We were pawns in a high-stakes game with the instructions missing. All I knew was that he'd given us no choice but to play along. Masters had laid his cards on the table, offering fame and fortune with one hand and blackmail with the other.

"How the hell could Jack know you burned down that trailer?" Becca asked. She was flopped on one of the king-sized beds in Masters's guestroom, staring at the clouds on the ceiling. The room was painted like his dining area, complete with kangaroos and cockatoos. We'd found all our bags and instruments from the hotel stacked neatly in a corner. Everything in order except for a crack in the wooden rim of my drum. Masters had dumped us here after inviting us "to consider his proposal" overnight. We were trapped in an Australian desert floating high above Carnegie Hall.

"Beats me," I said. "Good connections, I guess."

"There's a reason they call it *Empire* Oil," Rosie said. "Like, they're everywhere. Probably had security cameras on you the whole time you were slopping gas all over the place."

"No way," I said. "The place was pitch—"

Then I remembered. A blinking Webcam above the last computer I doused.

Rosie read the alarm on my face. "What can he do to you? So you got caught red-handed burning down a dumpy trailer."

"It was brand new, Rosie. Lots of fancy gizmos in there. Stuffed with computers. Giant video screens." That anger stirred again. "Maps of our land covered in their roads and pipelines."

"A base camp to spread the evil Empire," Becca said. "Good you took it out."

"I just ... I just went friggin' crazy."

Rosie shrugged. "Okay, so plead insanity."

"They catch kids burning down stuff all the time back home," Becca said. "Like what's-his-face, that Tungilik runt?"

"Leon?" I said. "He's just a dumb kid. I'm eighteen, Becca. They could lock me up. Goodbye, art school."

"It doesn't mean you have to kiss the old guy's ass for the rest of your life," Rosie said.

"You mean *his* life," Becca said. "He said himself his candle's going out."

Rosie shook her head. "No, I mean humor him. Feed him some of your awesome throat-singing. Tell him Arctic horror stories about our screwed up climate. He'll soften up. Anyways, what's the harm in a little Christmas shopping in sunny Australia?" Rosie shoved her face toward mine. "With a nice *global* gig on the side? Hard to pass up, huh?"

"I call it kidnapping."

Becca jerked her head off the bed. "He's probably listening to us right now," she said in a low voice.

"*Aamittara,*" I said.

"What?"

I held a finger to my lips. "Careful."

Gabe let out a ripping fart. "That'll teach you to eavesdrop, Jack!"

"Remember what that Jean-Anne lady told us," I whispered. "How Jack likes to collect beautiful things. You get the feeling he's trying to collect *us?*"

"He's already collected our stuff without asking," Gabe said, who had amazing ears. "*Stole* it, I mean! Right out of our hotel room. What's up with that, Jack? I know you can hear me, Jack, you big crook! What's up with that?"

"Cool it, Gabe," I said. He was putting a leather rocking chair through its paces, rubbing his hands like mad.

Becca pointed to her open mouth.

"Uh, right. Gabe, did you take your tranquilizers at supper?"

No answer.

"Your pills, Gabe. Did you take them?"

"No, Ma'am."

I rummaged through his suitcase, amazed at how tidily it was packed. When we raced out this morning, our room looked like it had been carpet-bombed. One of Jack's henchmen had broken in and burglarized all our stuff. Yet he'd also put fresh soap and toothpaste in Gabe's toiletry kit. "Here, Gabe," I said. "Take two. Could be a long night."

"Shouldn't we call somebody?" Becca said.

"Like the cops?" Gabe said. "Your dad's a cop, Becca. Sic him on Jack!"

"Like my mom," Becca said, "who's going to shit her pants if she calls the hotel and finds we've checked out."

"My folks don't even know I've left town," Rosie said. "Hell, half the time I don't know where *they* are."

"We'll phone in the morning once we get out of here," I said. "Nobody's going to call. They'll figure we're just out partying on our last night in the Big Apple."

"Instead of being locked up by a madman," Becca muttered, "who wants to save the Earth by dissing humans." Her cheeks were all flushed and swollen like just before one of her weeping fits.

I wanted to hug her but just sat there, frozen on the bed, too chicken to show how trapped I felt.

Gabe threw his hands in the air like he was under gunpoint.

"Uh ... what are you doing, Gabe?" I asked as calmly as I could.

"We've b-b-been hoodwinked and hijacked, p-p-partners! Ambushed and k-k-kidnapped!"

Becca grabbed a fat pillow and squeezed it tight. The dam broke on her tears. "I just remembered something else old Jean-Anne said."

"What, Bexie?" shouted Gabe. "*What?*"

"Heaven help anyone who gets in Jack's way!"

RAINBOW JEWELS

GUEST BEDROOM OF MASTERS'S APARTMENT,
STUDIO TOWERS, CARNEGIE HALL
DECEMBER 15TH, 11:15 PM

CTP 0136:35:17

As I lay my head on a fat feather pillow, I felt like a rare zoo animal. Pampered. Imprisoned. Carefully packed clothes—somebody had actually cleaned and pressed everything right down to my panties. Fresh towels and bubble bath at the end of a king-sized bed. A mouth-watering meal of traditional Arctic foods. A spotlight on the UN stage. And now, an offer to perform at some mega concert in Australia.

On Masters's terms, of course.

I'd had enough fame for one trip and was more than ready to go home.

My head spun like a top as soon as I closed my eyes. I finally fell asleep to classical piano music wafting up the air vents from the Carnegie stage.

I'm late for a plane. I can't find the airport. I look at my watch. Red numbers flash by too fast to read. I'm lost in an urban jungle, running barefoot through streets packed with honking, stinking traffic. A police siren chases me. I desperately try to flag down a taxi. There's no one at the wheel. There's no one on the sidewalk. Just cars, cars, cars.

I see a patch of green up ahead. I find new strength and almost fly over the pavement. The green opens up, takes me in. Grass, flowers, sunshine, safety.

I'm in Central Park!

Some playful impulse tugs at my chest. A raccoon catches my eye, then dives into the woods. I leap after it. I hear cracking sounds. Bark splits and pops off the trees. They're growing. Fatter, taller. Blocking the sun.

I'm in a rainforest!

Thunder crashes above me. Rain comes down in buckets. Water pours off giant leaves, down trunks, around my bare toes. Then ... silence. Dead branches crash to the ground. Trees collapse all around me and crumble to dust. Red dust.

I'm in the Australian desert!

I follow lizard tracks squiggled in the sand, past sea-green bushes, silver trees, bald hills shaped like purple bread loaves. A black eagle with gold-tipped wings drops from the sky, punching a hole in the desert, opening the Earth. Sand pours in. I run from the hole. It spins like a whirlpool, sucking me down. My feet break through to ... nothing.

I fall into a warm, welcoming darkness dotted with jewels of rainbow light.

ARCTIC STAR

CTP 0124:36:17

My nose woke long before my eyes. Cinnamon rolls.

Yum!

Mom always baked a bunch for Christmas holidays. I imagined her downstairs, crooning as she pulled a fresh batch out of our wood-fired oven and piling them into a homemade willow basket. I lay still, debating whether to give in to hunger or sleep. After a minute or two, sleep won—until I awoke with a start to the sound of Gabe snoring.

Gabe? Sleeping in my room?

I opened my eyes. A strange creature with a rabbit-like face and the ears of a deer stared at me expectantly. A painted kangaroo. A dozen more grazed on dry grass behind it. A distant police siren rose above Gabe's snoring. I groaned and pulled a fat pillow over my head.

"How's about a little brekkie, folks?" It was Masters's crusty voice blaring over a ceiling speaker.

How did he know I just woke up?

My eyes darted around the room looking for a security camera.

Gabe screwed up his face and covered his ears. "Good God! It's the voice of Big Brother!"

"It's well past a sparrow's fart," boomed Masters. "Plane to catch, ya know."

I threw off my pillow to see Becca next to me, wiping tears from her eyes with a corner of the sheet.

"Thank God!" she said. "The old bugger's changed his tune."

"Been crying again?"

"Well, duh! Like, I totally planned to be held hostage for the holidays!"

"Sounds like he's sobered up a bit." I looked at my watch. Almost ten. "We've got lots of time. Our plane's not till five."

"Great, but what about Ashley, the arsonist? If you don't sing and dance for him down under he's gonna stick you with a police record you'll never shake off."

My stomach cringed like I'd swallowed something awful. "I'd forgotten that little detail."

A pillow landed on my head.

"Yeah, and what about Ashley, the Arctic diva?" Rosie said, lining up for another shot. "What about that mother of all gigs?"

I dodged the second pillow, which knocked over a lamp.

"Are you seriously going to pass up the chance of a lifetime?" Rosie threw a pillow at Gabe, still sprawled on a giant leather couch. "Correction. Four lifetimes. We're all in this together."

"Just 'cause you've got no home life to go back to!"

I instantly regretted opening my mouth.

This time Rosie drilled me with one of her high-heeled boots. "You got us into this mess!" she snapped.

Nobody could twist my insides like Rosie. We'd crashed and burned together many times. Pulled each other out of the deepest ditches. Drummed ourselves to the moon. Laughed our guts onto the floor. And, like sisters, we could scratch and claw to the bone. This was so not the time to start a brawl. I needed her strength.

"Hey, like, I'm sorry," I said, rubbing my booted arm. "What the hell should we do?"

"Call your mom," Becca said.

Rosie laughed. "Yeah, right. And try to explain all the shit you're in? She'll blow a gasket."

"What's stopping us from just getting on that plane?" Becca said.

"Like, no door, for one thing," I said. "And an Empire Oil firing squad."

"What's stopping us from partying in Australia?" Rosie said. "It's not like the old fart's chained us up on a bread and water diet." She swept an arm around our luxury guest room. "Let's live a little."

"So, okay, we go down there," Becca said. "Do the gig. You think we could be home by Christmas?" I could tell she was slipping off the fence.

"Piece a' cake," Rosie said. "It's on the twenty-first, remember."

"Right. The solstice," Becca said. "That would give us plenty of time."

"We zip down there," Rosie said. "Beat the drum for Jack. He forgets about Ashley's pyromania. We get world famous. Bring some boomerangs home for Christmas. What the hell can we lose?"

Becca and Rosie stared at me. Gabe sat up on the couch with an ear cocked in my direction.

Waiting.

"He creeps me out," I said after a long pause. "And that tipping point stuff? He's got something big up his sleeve."

"Goodbye, parasites!" Gabe yelled. "Boom!"

"His weird clock says he'll pull the pin sometime around the concert," Becca said.

"We'll be at the other end of the planet by the time he tries anything," Rosie said.

"What about that Quincy guy?" I said. "You trust him?"

"He's a puppy with a pistol," Rosie said.

Without a knock, our door slid open and Masters's waiter wheeled in a silver breakfast dolly. Masters and Quincy pushed their way past him.

"Speak of the devil," Becca whispered as she gathered the sheet around her shoulders.

I grabbed a sweater and pressed back against the headboard.

Masters tossed a thick newspaper on the foot of our bed. "Didn't I say I could make you famous? You made page three of the *New York Times*. We'll get you on the front page next time."

Rosie scooped up the paper and flipped it open. Her eyes went wide. "Let's see, let's see!" Becca said, reaching for it.

Rosie held it away. "No, listen to this. *Arctic star of Carnegie Hall wows UN climate change forum.* Shee-it, Ashley! Can I have your autograph?"

"Go on!" Becca said.

> *If you thought climate change was only a problem for people living in grass huts by the sea or maybe your great-great-grandchildren, think again. At this week's climate change forum at the United Nations, Ashley Anowiak, a groundbreaking Inuk throat singer fresh from the Carnegie stage, stirred the international delegation with shocking first-hand testimonies of life on the front lines of climate change.*

Masters beamed at me. "Shocking! I like that."

Rosie read on:

> *Anowiak, a native of the tiny coastal village of Nanurtalik, Canada, described an Arctic world that is undergoing a hurricane of change, rocked by the relentless stresses and storms of an angry climate.*

Masters raised a fist. "Oooh, angry climate! That's perfect."

Rosie shot him a funny look over the newspaper, then continued:

> *The eighteen-year-old climate change crusader told passionately of how her dog was crushed to death in a mudslide triggered by melting permafrost. How her father lost a foot to frostbite after crashing through abnormally thin ice. How her living room bears the scars of bullets aimed at a starving polar bear driven into her village by shrinking sea ice. And, most terrifying, how she was struck down by lightning, which, before climate change hammered the Arctic, was once, in her words, 'as common as muskox in Manhattan.'*

"Terrifying!" Masters said. "That's bewdy."

Just before stepping on the UN stage, Anowiak collapsed as if overcome by stage fright. She quickly revived with the kind assistance of a visiting Buddhist speaker from Nepal, Pema Rinpoche. The UN chair and retired oil tycoon, Jack Masters, later called her to the podium where she wowed delegates with her real-life stories of climate change in the flesh.

No stranger to the spotlight, Anowiak and her traditional Inuit drumming group performed at Carnegie Hall the night before as part of their world tour. She earned a standing ovation from both audiences.

Rosie whistled. "One for the scrapbook."

"World tour?" Becca exclaimed. "Who fed them that crap?"

Masters shrugged, studying his fingernails.

"Give me that," I said, grabbing the paper from Rosie.

There we were, me, decked out in full Eskimo duds, and Pema, in her purple robes, bowing to each other with pressed palms.

I barely recognized myself.

"Good on ya, girl," Masters said. "We'll do better next time."

"Yeah, nice," Rosie said, "but next time you're fainting in front of all those cameras maybe you could flash a copy of our CD on the way down."

The waiter whisked away silver lids, revealing a pile of steaming cinnamon buns, eggs, bacon, and hash browns.

Gabe shot up and stumbled toward the dolly with open hands. "Awfully nice of you, Jack, putting us up like this. How's about laying one of those baked goodies in my mitts?"

Nothing calmed Gabe down more than food. It seemed he'd instantly forgiven Jack all his sins.

I stepped way around Masters and loaded a couple of rolls on a plate for Gabe.

Jack rolled up beside him like they were old buddies. His charm button was switched on. "Coffee, Gabriel?"

"Why sure, Jack. And some juice would be nice."

Masters snapped to the waiter.

"Say, Jack, you're a bird man. What's a sparrow's fart sound like?"

"What? Oh, a sparrow's fart." Masters laughed so hard he almost choked on his bacon. "It means dawn in Australian, for God's sake. You'll get an ear for the language. I had to learn a whack of Inuktitut in your neck of the woods."

"No trees near our home, Jack," Gabe said.

While Gabe chit-chatted with the enemy, I wanted to run for my life.

"Speaking of home," I said, "didn't you announce something about a plane to catch?"

"Bloody right I did. My plane. My home."

I sat, stunned, looking out the window toward Central Park. The sun shone on treetops dusted with fresh snow. I could see kids running from tree to tree, dodging snowballs. Farther away, couples skated hand in hand on an outdoor rink. I felt like a prisoner looking out at the free world through cell bars.

I spotted something black drifting above the park straight toward us. A helicopter. Moments later it swooped so close I could see the pilot through his bubble window. He wore a shiny green vest like all of Jack's staff. Painted in gold on the side of the helicopter were the letters S-E-T-I. My head tilted back as the helicopter slowed, then disappeared directly overhead. The thwack of its rotors got louder and louder until I thought I saw the painted clouds shaking above me.

"Sounds like our airport taxi's arrived," Jack shouted above the racket. "Right on schedule."

"Whose schedule?" I yelled, still staring at the ceiling.

"Mine of course."

PART 3

SIMPSON DESERT, AUSTRALIA

To truly listen,
You have to be able to let go.
Listening is the best thing we can do as human beings.
– Shine Edgar, Australian didjeridu master

There is something quiet coming out of the Silence, quieter than a whisper—
A heartbeat, a breath, a rhythm, a sensing of bright colors,
Or a transparency of nature.
– Harold Heritage, Quaker Elder

Underneath the silence rolled the deep, comforting thrum.
– Karsten Heuer, *Being Caribou*

VANUATU

CTP 0055:54:27

"You heard right. I don't have a clue where we are."

The pilot looked at me over her shoulder and wiggled a finger.

"Wait a minute, Mom."

She pulled a map off her lap and pointed to our position. I nodded.

"Yeah, well it looks like we're flying over ... the Coral Sea."

"Where in God's name is that?" Mom said, her voice filling the sleek cockpit of Masters's private jet.

Kind of weird having complete strangers eavesdrop on a heated exchange between my mother and me. Masters had insisted that we tour the cockpit, and when I heard the co-pilot wishing his kid a happy birthday, it hit me.

Shit! I haven't phoned home yet!

Masters agreed but asked the pilot to put us on speaker phone, so, as usual, he could stay in full control. I'd meant to call when we'd stopped in Hawaii, but Masters had showed us such a good time there—a submarine tour, whale-watching, cutting loose on the beach to watch hunk surfers—I'd completely forgotten we'd been kidnapped.

"It's somewhere down in the south Pacific."

The pilot tapped her finger on the map over a cluster of tiny islands. We seemed to be flying awfully low.

"Yeah, we're just coming up to a place called ... uh ... Van-u-a-tu. Vanuatu."

"South Pacific? Vana-what? Did you step on the wrong plane in

New York?"

"Actually, we didn't really have much choice but to go with this rich guy who—"

Masters cleared his throat behind me like he'd swallowed a lemon. When I turned around he pulled a lighter out of his jacket, flicked it, and casually lifted the flame to within a foot of my nose.

"I mean, well, maybe you should talk to him."

"Put the man on."

"Good morning, Mrs. Anowiak," Masters said as he tucked away his lighter. "I'm already on. Jack Masters here."

"It's Le Beau. And it's evening here. How dare you steal my children and their friends away from us at Christmas! Have you any idea how upset the whole community has been since they didn't get off the plane yesterday? And what are you doing listening to our conver—"

"Please, please, Ms. Le Beau," Masters said in a voice that would soothe a baby in wet diapers. "Let me explain. Everyone's fine and happy here." He raised his eyebrows like he wanted me to nod in agreement.

I scowled at him.

"I'm afraid it's entirely my fault no one called. I was so impressed by your daughter's performance at Carnegie Hall that I invited her to speak at a United Nations climate change conference the next day."

"United Nations?"

"Yes. She brought the house down. Her second standing ovation in twelve hours."

"Standing ovation? My Ashley?"

"Yes, indeed. I arranged for a copy of yesterday's *New York Times* to be couriered to your door. You'll see what a smash hit she was. We've had a very busy schedule ever since and—"

"Where are you taking her?"

"I can understand your concern, Ms. Le Beau. I'll give you my wife's cell number near Alice Springs so you can—"

"Where the hell are you taking her?"

Masters smirked at the speaker.

"It was a tough decision for all of us but—"

Rosie let out a horsey laugh. Jack glared at her.

"Is that Rosie?"

"Yeah. Hi, Carole," Rosie said, pushing past Masters into the cockpit. "Jack's taking us to a big music powwow on climate change in the middle of the Aussie desert. Supposed to be millions of people plugged in all over the world. Once it's over, you and Moise can retire on our CD sales."

"Who is this Mr. Masters?" Mom said.

"A solid Earth-hugger, Carole. You'd love him." Rosie winked at Masters who ignored her. "He, uh, found more Empire dough for us."

"He works for Empire Oil?"

Rosie glanced at Masters, who nodded sternly. "Uh, yeah. Things went so well in New York they decided to sponsor a little detour to Australia for this concert and—"

"Mon Dieu! Detour? To Australia?"

"Well, yeah. He wants us to, you know, beat the drum about climate change. Stir up some—"

Masters barged in. "I assure you, Ms. Le Beau, that their performance will pay substantial dividends, both in terms of fighting climate change and enhancing your family's financial security."

"And what about Christmas?"

"We'll fly them home well before that."

Static filled the cockpit.

I could almost hear the wheels turning in Mom's head.

"This is an Empire sponsored event, right?" she said.

"A hundred percent," Masters said. "You can check out our Web site at Scorched-Earth-Concert.com." He even spelled it out for her twice. "You'll find it's all quite legitimate."

"They'll be paid for their performance?"

"Handsomely. Plus a large per diem until the day they fly home."

"Before Christmas, right?"

"On an Empire jet."

"Really? I see."

I shook my head in disbelief. Masters had reeled my hard-headed mother into his pocket. I wondered how the hell he knew we were barely scraping by. Mom had lost her stewardess job with Arctic Air months ago. Things were tight at Dad's radio station even before he lost his foot to frostbite and fell into a deep depression. Ever since we moved into Nanurtalik's biggest house, he'd had a mortgage monkey jumping on him twenty-four-seven. If Masters spilled the beans about my arson trick, that just might break my father's back.

Masters twiddled with his polar bear ring. "Again, I apologize for any inconvenience, Ms. Le Beau. I will personally see to everyone's needs."

"Including Gabe's, I hope? Ashley, can you hear me?"

"Yes, Mom."

"Are you taking good care of Gabe?"

"Yes, Mom."

"Hi, Carole!" Gabe shouted from the rear. "All's hunky-dory down here."

"Like Jack said, everyone's fine and happy," Rosie said. "I guess you could pass that on to my folks. That is, if you can find them."

"Mine too," Becca piped in, sounding panicky.

Masters tapped the pilot on the shoulder and spun a finger in the air. The pilot throttled back and steered us into a steep dive toward a high volcanic island dead ahead.

"Will do, girls. When's the concert again, Ash?"

The island drew my eyes like a magnet. Its black cone towered above a soft green skirt of unbroken forest. It shone like a jewel in a smooth turquoise sea.

"Uh, the twenty-first."

"The winter solstice!"

We dropped suddenly, aiming for a steep diamondback ridge that leapt up one side of the volcano. A bank of cotton-batting clouds trailed off the other side like hair on a grandmother's head. The forest rushed past below us, pulsing with mysterious life forms I would never know. And yet, something familiar called me from the green.

"The solstice, yeah. I mean, it all depends."

The pilot made a tight left-hand turn, tipping the wing to give us a better view of the mountain. The hem of trees ended abruptly at an apron of jagged lava rock.

"Depends on what?"

Above the engine noise, phone static, and Masters's heavy breathing, I thought I heard a whispering.

What's happening to me?

"Uh, depends on where you ... I mean, down here it's ... it's, like, summer solstice."

"Oh, that's nice, but what day do you fly home?"

I was trying to concentrate. My brain unplugged. My chest was bursting. "What? uh ... I don't know exactly ... for sure in time for Christmas—"

I shot out both arms and clutched the back of the pilot's chair. It lasted only a second or two, my glimpse down the cavernous mouth of the volcano. It was blacker than black. Bottomless. Like the whirlpool in my desert dream. Something down there wanted to suck me head-first into the Earth.

"Ash! Are you still there? Ashley!"

The island raced away behind us. A flock of white birds fanned out over the sea. Still clutching the pilot's chair, I looked over at Masters. He'd been watching me closely, like he knew what had just roared through me.

"No worries, Ms. Le Beau," he said without taking his eyes off me.

JAMIE BASTEDO

"Just doing a little flight-seeing. I think your daughter's a bit knackered with all the fun."

The copilot offered me a barf bag.

I waved it away. "No. No, thanks."

Masters fired Mom a phone number. "Ring up Rita any old time. My wife'll have a fix on us."

"Fine, fine. But do tell Ashley to call often ... Ash? Can you hear me?"

"Yes, Mom."

"Good luck, sweetheart."

"You, too, Mom."

"*Taima,* then," Masters said, showing off his Inuktitut. "*Assunai.*"

"What? Oh yes, goodbye to you, too, sir. And, uh, thank you ..."

"Do you believe it?" Rosie said, once we'd settled back into our cushioned corner of the jet. "I thought your mom would have at least one tit in a wringer. But nope. Good ol' Jack. Softened her up pretty quick."

"Total schmoozer," I said. "Even suckered you."

"*What?* Come on, Ash. I know a good gig when I smell it."

Becca stared down at the red carpet floor. She'd been crying again and looked wrecked. "What was that shit with the lighter?" She stole a glance at Jack at the other end of the plush cabin. He was slumped in his wheelchair, snoring like a bear. A limp hand was draped over yet another of his weird silver gardens. "Sugar daddy, my ass. The guy's friggin' nuts!"

"I'll protect you, girls!" yelled Gabe, bobbing his fists at a vase of daffodils.

I had to laugh in spite of a trickle of tears that sprang from a creeping feeling that we were falling off the edge of the world.

RITA

CTP 0050:54:31

"Welcome to the land of Oz."

I knew instantly that this woman was aboriginal, at least, partly. Maybe a halfer like me. I sensed minestrone blood in her veins from a mixed bag of Australian immigrants. But the native blood was there. I could see it in her face, a blood that bubbled from the red desert sand as surely as mine did from the Arctic ice.

This woman. Rita. Jack's wife.

"You must be right knackered," she said, swinging open the thick wooden door.

"Knackered out, tuckered out, liquored up," said Gabe, who hadn't had a sip of booze since we left Nanurtalik. "Nice place you got here, Mrs. Masters." He paused at the marble threshold, probing the unusual circular doorway with his all-seeing fingers. "Would make a nice hobbit house."

Rita smiled, showing remarkably white teeth for a woman in her eighties. They were big and bold like a kangaroo's. She had a graceful poise about her that reminded me of Pema, the Nepali monk who'd picked me up off the floor of the UN. They could have been sisters.

"You like it? Jack stirred all kinds of styles into this place— Russian, Japanese, Mexican. He wanted our home to be a microcosm of the whole world. He was reading *Lord of the Rings* when he built it, so, yeah, I reckon there's a bit of The Shire in here, too."

Deep wrinkles meandered across Rita's face like dried-up riverbeds.

A thousand smile lines flowed out from the dark pools of her eyes. She wore a loose yellow sarong and had a flowery scent about her, like incense. I got the feeling the desert breeze could pass right through her body.

Jack was all bark and bluster. Rita, softness and light. I was floored by their differences.

What could she ever see in him?

Rita clicked the door shut behind us. I realized that, for the first time since Jack had picked us up by the Statue of Liberty ferry, he'd left us alone. He was pretty hungover after the flight and had dumped us in front of Rita's house without a word. We stood, jet-lagged aliens, watching his hydrogen-powered Land Rover disappear in a swirl of red dust. I didn't know where he was going or what evil plans he had for us. All that mattered was he was gone. No more fatherly pats. No more booze breath in my face. No more mad rants about filthy humans.

We were out of Jack's meaty clutches. This nice lady would keep us safe. We could escape. We could go home.

"How d'ya like the heat?" Rita asked, leading us toward a wide cushioned sill beneath an arched window that Jack might have stolen from King Arthur's castle. "Would you like some lemonade?"

"That'd be swell," Gabe said, rubbing his hands in utter delight.

Sometimes I envied Gabe—in spite of his blindness, autism, and fetal alcohol issues. The guy was easy to please. At home everywhere. A friend to all the world.

"Is this it?" Becca asked, wiping sweat off her neck. "Like, does it get *hotter*?"

Rita pressed a button on a wall intercom. "Darri, dear, a pitcher of lemonade for five, please."

"Yep," said a husky voice over the speaker.

"I'd take a cold beer," Rosie said.

"Yep."

"Lucky you," Rita said. "You've hit the peak of our summer. A nice break from freezing in the dark, huh?"

"We kind of like the cold," I said. "What's left of it, anyway."

"Jack told me about your speech at the UN."

"He did?"

"How you had everyone rapt over your climate change stories from … what did you call it?"

"I dunno. A war zone. Ground zero. Whatever."

"Things really melting up there?"

"Really."

"Sea ice? Permafrost?"

"Uh-huh. It's all true, that stuff you read." But part of me doubted my own words. A bad case of brain fog and Jack's Cinderella world of money and power made all the climate crap back home seem so far away. It was scary how fast it could fade off the radar. And I *lived* it. No wonder so many people could care less about climate change.

The slap of sandals and clinking ice announced the arrival of our drinks. Thank God. A large dark woman shuffled toward us with a tray of lemonade and cold beer. She wore a simple white blouse and a printed cotton skirt with big fat ants and snakes crawling over it. She'd wrapped her forehead in loose strands of red and orange yarn topped with a string of bright red seeds. Something about her woke me up. My hand itched to draw her chiseled leathery face.

"Thanks, Darri," Rita said.

Darri set the tray down before us on a wicker table and folded her thick arms. "The Arctic, huh?"

"Yep," Becca said, lunging for the lemonade.

"Polar bears?"

"Yep."

Darri pursed her lips and shook her head. "No, thanks. Gimme snakes or crocs any day." She watched as we guzzled our drinks, then shuffled back to the kitchen.

"I hear it's even tough to build iglus up there," Rita said. "Your snow's gone all funny, has it?"

"Funny?" I said. "Yeah, I guess."

"And your people, how are they holding up under all that strange weather?"

Visions of Dad's stumpy leg came to mind. Jacques disappearing under a mudslide. The high school flag at half-mast with yet another suicide. "Uh, not so good."

"It's heartbreaking, really, that those least to blame for climate change are the worst hit."

"It sucks."

Rita sighed heavily. "Isn't it amazing? We live in a world where we don't need to see what we do, whether it's bombing another country or simple things like using a plastic bag at the store for three minutes, then pitching it in the dump for two thousand years. People don't see the consequences."

"But they're coming," I said with a firmness that surprised me.

Rita looked at me funny. "Beg yours?"

"Consequences," I said.

"You mean, like all Jack's talk about the planet fighting back?"

"Yep."

"He told me you have a song about that," Rita went on.

"Uh-huh."

"What do you call it?"

I bit my lip and looked at my friends. Rosie was lost in her beer. Becca gave a little shrug.

"'Sila's Revenge,'" I said, almost in a whisper.

"Sila?"

"Uh-huh."

"What's that?"

"You mean, *who's* that," Becca said.

"All right. Who's that?"

"Kind of like duct tape," Gabe said.

"I'm sorry?" Rita said.

I had to laugh. "An old Inuit spirit."

"Sila!" Gabe hooted. "You know, found everywhere, holds everything together! Just like duct tape!"

Rita's eyes brightened. "I see."

"That would be Sila," I said. "Especially weather stuff. Wind, rain, storms, and—"

"Lightning," Becca said.

"That, too." I rubbed the bald spot over my right ear. I felt a tingle at the base of my spine.

"And the air we breathe," Becca added. "All life, actually."

"The Breathmaker," Rita said quietly.

The tingle crawled up my back. "Yeah, something like that. That's the way our Elders talk, anyway."

"Us, too," Rita said. "Here we call her Yhi. They say if we mess around too much with her body—"

"Her body?" Becca said.

"The Earth, of course."

Rita declared this with such conviction that my elbow slipped off my chair and I spilled lemonade all over the place.

"Yes," Rita continued, while I tried to mop up. "If we cross the line, well, Yhi just might steal our breath away."

The tingle rose to my throat. I could feel Sila's song erupting. I covered my mouth with a lemonade-soaked napkin.

"Jack actually buys that spiritual stuff?" Becca said.

Rita slowly shook her head. "Not a word. Sure, he'll work with the local fellas. Hires lots of them. Loves the desert as much as they do. But he's got no time for their stories. To Jack, no problem's too big to fix with a hammer. If our climate's going to hell—"

"Is it?" I interrupted.

"Oh, yes. Hotter and drier than ever. Australia's been locked in a drought for seven years. Rivers drying up. Massive crop failures. Bushfires everywhere. I forget what rain looks like."

"What do you mean, a hammer?" Becca said.

"Jack's tools. Money, machines, manipulating people. That's how he fixes things."

"Like, you don't mean Australia's climate?" I said.

Rita laughed softly. "I mean the *planet's*. Remember, Jack thinks big."

Rosie shook the last drops from her beer bottle. "S'cuse me, but I don't think Jack flew us down here to talk politics or religion. Like, where's the party happening?"

"Ah, yes, the concert," Rita said.

"Like, yeah! The Scorched Earth Concert." Rosie said these words slowly, like she was savoring good chocolate.

Rita pointed her chin to the window. "Right here. Hot Rock Farm."

Rosie screwed up her face. "Half a million people. *Here?*"

"Maybe more. Jack owns a big chunk of desert. His private kingdom, full of cockatoos and lizards."

I stared out the window at a landscape as familiar to me as Mars. Burnt red sand. Shriveled clumps of spiky grass. Spindly trees that reached like dead fingers to a powder blue sky. A distant lump of purple hills that floated above the ground, suspended by heat waves.

Here in bone-dry flesh was the fantasy world painted on the walls of Jack's Manhattan apartment.

"You call this a *farm?*" I said.

"I reckon," Rita said. "Fed the bunch of us for forty-odd years. Now we grow energy."

"Energy?"

"You'll see."

I remembered the concrete guardhouse, security cameras, and

ten-foot-high razor-wire fence that greeted us miles back on Jack's private road. When Rosie had asked him what was up with that, all he said was, "Keeps out the rabbits."

"Are we talking nuclear reactors here?" I said. "With that huge fence and everything?"

Rita laughed. "Not likely. We've got nothing to hide. Jack likes his peace and quiet, that's all. Built a little safe haven for himself."

"What's he afraid of?" I said.

Rita looked at me funny. "Another time."

"Jack's gonna let a bunch of New Age hippies crawl all over this place?" Rosie said.

"Jack'll throw the east gate open for the concert," Rita said, collecting herself. "He's hired a small army of security staff to keep the peace."

"What did you call this place?" Rosie said.

"Hot Rock Farm. Named after the TAG below our feet."

"Tag?" Rosie said.

"Sorry. T-A-G. Stands for thermally anomalous granite. Kind of a household word around here. There's a big old rock down there that's bloody hot. A real gold mine of geothermal energy."

"Is that why he moved here?"

"Oh, no. Discovered the TAG years later. Jack was on a back-to-the-land kick in the early sixties and dreamed of greening the Australian desert with the new miracle crops coming out in those days. He uprooted from his seaside home in Queensland to start his own little kingdom here in the Red Center."

"How did you meet?" Becca asked. She has a nose for this kind of stuff.

"I was principal of an aboriginal school just down the track and Jack used to drop in to borrow my jeep whenever his broke down, which seemed an awful lot, really. One day he took a look at my vegetable garden and I reckon he decided I was the girl for him. The first thing we planted was forage crops for camels."

"Camels," I said.

"Yep. Camels don't really belong in our desert. Helped build our railroads years back. But they've kind of moved in since and gone wild. Jack has a thing for camels. Lassoed a few, then started breeding them. He'd ride them all over the map."

"Jack on a camel," Rosie said. "Now that I'd like to see."

Rita smiled, deepening the lines around her eyes. "He claims they're way smarter than horses. Good to go in the hottest weather. And Jack made a lovely cheese from their milk."

"*Camel* cheese?" Becca said.

"Oh, yes. A big hit in the Alice market." Rita tapped a whitewashed wall with her knuckles. "And we had enough straw left over from those first camel crops to build this house."

"Uh-huh," Gabe said thoughtfully. "A straw house … like the three little pigs!"

Rita smiled and gently picked up his hand, guiding it to the wall. "More or less. There's hundreds of straw bales behind this plaster."

"*This is the straw that lay in the house that Jack built,*" Gabe crooned while tapping the wall like a drum. "Cool."

"Stays cool no matter what the outside temperature. Super eco-friendly. Jack built all the buildings around the farm with straw. One of his many kicks. People thought he was crazy until they stepped inside."

I looked around at the ceiling's sexy curves, the owl-like windows, and an airy hallway that could have been carved by the wind. "It's nice."

"Jack's always way ahead of his time. But his so-called miracle crops failed miserably, so we added camel meat to our veggie diet. And rabbits. *Lots* of rabbits."

"And now you grow *energy?*" I said.

"Working for Empire Oil, Jack could clearly read the writing on the wall. By the early seventies, he knew the end of dirt-cheap fossil fuels was just around the corner. That's when he switched from planting

Indian dates and cactus apples to farming sunshine."

"A real tree-hugger," Rosie said.

Rita laughed. "More like a one-man army. They used to call him Sol Man. He pumped millions of oil dollars into building a massive solar farm. Stormed ahead with construction even without buyers for his power."

"How come?" Becca said.

"'Too far away,' they said. 'Not dependable.' Told him the same about his wind farm." Rita gazed at the sun-scorched landscape. "Back in the seventies, the world just wasn't ready for Jack's kind of thinking."

"So, where do the hot rocks come in?" Becca asked.

"Jack took to caving, as an escape, when the weight of the world got too much for him. Our property's loaded with them. He'd disappear for hours, sometimes days. Underground. All by himself."

"Solo spelunking?" Becca said.

"Solo. Imagine what *that* did to my nerves!"

"What was he looking for?" I said.

"Oh, sussing out bats, blind lizards, opals, fossils, peace of mind. I don't know. But he always took climbing gear, sleeping roll, billies, and tucker. Without warning, he'd slip out the back door and leave a note saying, 'Off to church.'" Rita paused. "He'd always come home a little calmer. Except the day he found the TAG. He barged in the house, bruised and blistered, waffling on about how he'd dropped into a frightfully deep cave and almost got poached alive. How he'd got so excited he smashed his headlamp, then had to scratch his way out."

"Squirming through pitch-black caves?" Becca said.

"He had to swim up scalding sulfur streams. Wade through stinkin' bat guano. Squeeze through tunnels so narrow they would've had to break his collar bones if he got stuck." Rita shuddered. "All in hellish darkness."

"And all alone?" Becca said.

"Too right."

"No, thanks."

"But Jack's a driven man."

"We kind of noticed," Becca said.

"He knew he'd discovered something big. Real big. And he had to live to tell the world. Turns out that one rock alone throws enough geothermal heat to supply all of Australia's power needs for yonks, maybe a hundred years. Without emitting an ounce of CO_2."

Becca said. "Australia's energy and carbon issues solved in one swoop."

"So he thought."

"Another dud dream?" Rosie said.

"I'm afraid so. It almost broke his heart. Spent years trying to tap this awesome power source and the world ignored him."

"How come?" Becca said.

"Geothermal energy was going nowhere back then. Still isn't. Government didn't understand it. Power companies didn't trust it. His Empire Oil mates blocked it. And really, the technology to tap the power here is still decades away."

"What about hydrogen?" I asked. "Jack seems pretty hepped up on that."

"Same story. He threw himself into promoting it, developing new uses, new fuel systems."

"Like those silver thingies he swoons over," Becca said.

"His invention. He holds the patent. Made millions on it. But still, the world couldn't move fast enough for him. The technology's still so young. So he gave up on that, too."

"He seems freaked that we're running out of time," I said.

"Certainly *his* time is running out. He's fought emphysema for years. And lately he's suffered from peculiar fainting spells."

Images of Livingstone's magic act on the UN stage popped into my head. Flattened palm trees, collapsing doughnuts, farting ice. "He talks crazy stuff about these, uh, tipping points."

Rita nodded with tight lips. "His latest obsession. Defusing the time bomb of global warming. Humans armed the bomb, he says, but soon the planet will pull the pin."

"Then, *BOOM!*" shouted Gabe, which startled us all. He'd been snoring in a wicker chair moments earlier.

"That's the revenge part, right?" I said.

"Right," Rita said. "Jack will do *anything* to stop this from happening."

"A one-man army against the world," Rosie said.

"That's kind of how he sees it."

"What's this *controlled* tipping point thing?" Becca said.
Rita shook her head. "I really don't have a clue. Something to do with his UN work."

"That stable Earth stuff," Becca said.

"*SETI*. Yes, I think so."

"What goes on up in that weird office of his?" I asked. "I mean, besides birds and butterflies."

"I believe it has to do with satellites."

"Yeah, his personal spy satellites," Becca said. "Beaming down horror movies of a dying planet."

Rita tsked. "He does seem stuck on that. Not healthy, really. There's so much good news out there. People waking up, greening their lifestyles, making a difference."

I thought of how I'd tried to fix things. To tackle climate change head-on. By burning down a trailer. *Hah!* Once the ice road was in, Empire trucked in a new one that was twice as big. "But it's too late," I said. "I mean, like, what can anybody do about such huge problems?"

"Never think that way," Rita said, almost scolding. "Societies change one person at a time. Your songs and stories are part of all that."

"Sometimes I think they just scare people."

"Never lose hope, Ashley. This concert's all about hope."

"Is it?"

"Of course."

"Jack called it a farewell party."

Rita shrank a little. "He did?"

"A last blast," Rosie said.

Rita paused, looking out at the desert. A pair of pink cockatoos preened themselves on top of a rusty water tank. "That's Jack's problem, I'm afraid. He's lost all hope."

"In people, for sure," I said.

Rita stood up suddenly. "Oh, it's probably just whiskey talk. He's not well, you know. The ravings of an old man, projecting his own looming death on the whole world."

Becca was chewing the paint off her nails again. "Like he wants to take out everybody else along with him."

"To save the planet, of course," Rosie said.

Becca looked up at Rita with a pleading look. "He calls us parasites!"

Rita slipped an arm over her shoulder. "Oh, Jack's mostly all bark. Just enjoy the concert and then you can—"

"There's something fishy going on up there," I interrupted.

Rita arched an eyebrow. "Where?"

"At the UN. Behind Jack's jungle. People slinking around in white lab coats."

"All cloak-and-dagger stuff, it seems." Rita sighed heavily. "We don't talk a lot these days. Knowing him, it's something Earth-shaking." She rubbed her hands as if flicking off dirt. "Anyway, you must be starving. Why don't you—"

A bird-like, trilling sound broke the still air of the house. "Excuse me," Rita said as she pulled a cell phone out of a fold in her sarong. She checked the call display and frowned. Her whole body stiffened.

I had no doubt who was on the other end.

"Yeah ... sure, but ... yeah, I realize that, but ... no, they haven't even had lunch ... okay, give us an hour, at least ... all right, half an hour ... Gotcha. Thanks, honey."

Becca knitted her forehead. "Speak of the devil," she muttered.

"Guess who," Rita said, forcing a smile. "Uncle Jack's got plans for you."

JACK'S BACK

RITA'S HOUSE, HOT ROCK FARM, AUSTRALIA
DECEMBER 19TH, 3:00 PM

CTP 0049:46:23

My stomach clenched when, just twenty minutes later, I heard the blast of Jack's horn through the thick straw walls. Darri had brought us an amazing spread of local tucker. Kangaroo fillets, bush tomatoes, lemon myrtle linguine tossed with yabbies. These were like little lobsters, only much sweeter, according to Rita, who took pains to explain each dish in detail. We'd barely had two mouthfuls before Jack pulled up.

Rita leapt from her chair. "I'm sorry, but my husband has a bad habit of believing the whole world revolves around him."

"Oh?" Rosie said.

Rita went to the window and gave a hurried wave. "You really don't want to get in Jack's way."

I'd heard that line somewhere before.

"Jack's way or the highway!" Gabe yelled through a mouthful of kangaroo. "Well, that's just fine for you guys but I'm not going!" He stabbed his fork around the table probing for another fillet.

"Just a little farm tour," Rita said.

I seized Gabe's roaming arm and helped him spear another slab of meat. "There you go, Gabe. So, like, you're definitely not coming with us?"

"I'm a musician, not a tourist. A *hungry* musician. Just point me to the stage and we'll rock the place."

Gabe's voice was beginning to squeak, a sure sign that a meltdown was just round the corner.

"Then we go home, right, Ash?" he yelled. "Then we go home!"

Gabe had somehow held it together on a trip two days and ten thousand miles longer than planned. Like I promised Mom, I hadn't left his side since we left Nanurtalik. But he needed a break and, honestly, so did I.

Two more long blasts.

"I'm in," Rosie said, opening another beer for the road.

Becca shrugged. "I guess it'll kill time."

I pulled a vial of pink tranquilizers out of my backpack and pressed a couple into Gabe's hand. "Okay, Gabe. But I'm not leaving until you take these."

Gabe downed the pills in one gulp and waved a steak knife in the air, almost slicing off my nose. "Go on, then!" he squeaked. "You don't want to keep your kidnapper waiting."

Rita stared at Gabe. "What? *Kidnapper?* But surely you planned to—".

"Uh, he's ... he's just kidding," I said. It was too early to spill our whole story to Rita. Besides, as gracious as she seemed, I didn't know who to trust anymore. "It's just that everything's happened so fast."

"I see," Rita said. "No worries, then. He'll be right. Darri's good with guests. Has a blind son herself. She'll take care of 'im." Rita punched the intercom with her thumb. "We're off, Darri. Leaving Gabe behind. Keep an eye on 'im, would ya? Maybe hook 'im up with Willard."

"Yep."

Rita grabbed a few buns and bananas off the table and dropped them into a canvas bag. "Let's scoot. You don't want Jack's blood pressure rising."

FENCED IN

SETI VAN TOUR, HOT ROCK FARM
DECEMBER 19TH, 3:15 PM

CTP 0049:31:12

"'Bout time. Get in," Jack said, sticking his pudgy nose through the front passenger window of a black van. As I climbed in I noticed gold letters painted on the side: *SETI*.

Rita gave Masters a quick peck on the cheek before scrambling in the back with us. He flashed her a syrupy smile, then brushed his face like a fly had landed on it. In spite of his crisp Aussie bush clothes and outback hat, he looked wrecked. His face was drained of color, except for his swollen nose and the purple bags under his eyes. I noticed his hands shaking and a new twitch to his lips. Parachuting into this heat after a twenty-hour plane ride would cause most men his age to keel over.

But not Jack. Not yet, at least.

JAMIE BASTEDO

Rita had also read the signs. "What is the rush, love, working yourself to the bone like this?"

Jack grunted. "My dear, the roving hordes who muck around with this planet aren't taking a day off. How can I?"

Rita frowned.

Quincy, still in white suit and shades, greeted us with his usual stone face and slammed the van door behind us. Sweat poured off his brow in spite of the air-conditioning.

Rosie rolled her fingers at him. "Hot enough for ya, Quincy?"

He huffed. "*You're* the ones in the hot seat."

Our driver was a dark guy about my age, well muscled, with a frizzy pony tail. He wore faded blue jeans, sockless tennis shoes, and a dingy T-shirt that read THOUGHT CRIMINAL. Hardly the uniform of Jack's other employees.

Leaning up against the driver's seat was a thin yellow dog. By the big pointy ears and the wild look in its eyes, I figured it must be a dingo. It sat on its haunches, watching us with a faint snarl on its lips. When I leaned forward to get a better look, the dingo drew back its ears and showed me a healthy set of razor-sharp teeth.

"It's okay," I said. "Nice pup."

The driver subdued the dingo with a glance, and the animal obediently curled up on the van floor.

Jack snapped a finger and the driver floored it, spilling Rosie from her seat.

"Awesome power, man," she shouted, still clutching her beer. "But, like, could you ease up on the hydrogen?"

I caught the driver staring at me in the rearview mirror, a searching look that probed too deep for my liking. I had to turn away, fixing my gaze on the Martian landscape blurring past

The road slashed a ragged wound through a thin skin of sun-baked grass and scrawny shrubs. It wove around the odd stand of ghost-white trees and piles of red rock that looked like dinosaur turds. Whoever put this road in barely disturbed a rock or stick when choosing a route.

I was too zonked to care where Jack was taking us. Becca sat in the back of the van, arms folded, eyes closed, with her head almost plopped on Quincy's shoulder. He sat like a block of wood, still sweating and staring straight ahead in his android way.

We never lost sight of the chain-link fence. I couldn't believe how high it was. And how long. On one close pass by the fence, Jack sprang forward in his seat and shook a fist at it.

"Just look at the *crap* that blows in here!" he bellowed.

That's when I noticed countless blobs of plastic spattered along the fence. Cast-off shopping bags hung in shreds from the razor wire. They flapped in the wind like crucified crows.

"That's some kinda weird art, Jack." Rosie said.

Jack huffed. "Bah! The consumer society hard at work."

"But ... there's nobody out here," I said. "Where's it all come from?"

"Oh, maybe Alice Springs, Barrow Creek, Ti Tree. Hell, this crap could've blown in from Brisbane. Not much to get in the way out here. First law of ecology."

"Huh?" I said.

"Everything leaks. Everything ends up somewhere."

"Feels like *nowhere* to me," Becca grumbled from the back seat. Rita passed around frosted bottles of lemonade from an onboard fridge. "It'll grow on you."

"This fence goes around your whole property?" I said.

"You bet," Jack said. "All fifteen hundred square miles of it. About the size of Rhode Island."

"Like, you mean the *state* of Rhode Island?"

"No less. A man's gotta have *some* land to call his own. Fence keeps out the riff-raff. Not one ratbag species on the property."

"Except humans," Rosie said.

Masters laughed. "I mean exotics like foxes and cats, pigs and rabbits. They'll tear up the desert if I let them in."

"Real pests, eh?" Rosie said.

"It's the human bastards who shipped them from God knows where in the first place. They're the *real* pests!"

Rosie whistled. "Must be big rabbits."

My eye caught some animal bounding through the bushes on the far side of the fence. It seemed to be shadowing us, struggling to keep up. "Like *that* one?" I said.

The guy at the wheel snorted and shook his head.

Rita lightly tapped my knee. "Red kangaroo."

"Right." I felt pretty stupid, but then this wasn't exactly Arctic tundra.

She glanced at it again. "My, that *is* a big one."

I turned back to the window so fast I almost goose-egged my head. My heart raced. I was dying to catch another glimpse of the kangaroo.

Why?

Now, I was always game to learn about new animals and plants. Mom says I've been that way since before I could walk. And this was, after all, Australia, land of some of the weirdest creatures on earth, like the platypus, koala, and wombat. But this urge to connect with the kangaroo had nothing to do with curiosity. It grabbed my guts and seemed to burn them from the inside out.

Just as the road veered away from the fence, I heard that whispering again. Urgent. Frightened. Somehow, this time, I knew exactly where it came from. The kangaroo that just disappeared behind a wall of thick shrubs closing behind us.

I stared at the dusty van floor, feeling betrayed, like a precious gift had been stolen from me before I could open it.

"What about camels?" Rosie said. "I hear you've got a thing for camels." She seemed more talkative than usual. Probably the beer.

"None on the property," Jack said. "They'd trample everything.

Trouble is, roos can't get in either. I miss seeing 'em hop about."

"What about hippies?" Rosie said.

"What about them?" Jack said.

"The concert. You're going to let thousands of hippies take over your farm?"

"We'll only open the east gate. Built an extra fence to keep them penned in. Wouldn't want 'em crawling all over the place now, would ya?"

"Why not? I mean, what are you hiding?"

Jack spun around and glared at Rosie. "Enough interrogation! You're here as performers. Got it?"

"Jack, please," Rita pleaded.

He ignored her. His face went beet red. "You're fresh-faced performers from the great white north. Not FBI agents! *Got it?*"

Rosie recoiled in her seat and shook her hands like she'd touched a hot stove. "Whoah! Yesss-sir."

HIDDEN POWER

PERIMETER OF NORTH FENCE, HOT ROCK FARM
DECEMBER 19TH, 3:45 PM

CTP 0048:58:11

The huge fence clatters and groans in the wind. A male kangaroo, almost six feet tall, bounds along beside it. His gait is fast, steady, direct. He leaps with almost reckless determination over every boulder, bush, and creek bed in his path. His short forelegs paddle the air with each bound as if to boost his speed.

The kangaroo stops abruptly in a clear patch of sand and stares intently through the fence. He raises his battle-scarred muzzle to the sky. Seeing nothing unusual, catching no new scent, he resumes his anxious flight along the fence.

From a familiar rocky outcrop that straddles the fence, he spots a shiny black thing moving just ahead of him on the other side. He stops again, panting heavily in the late afternoon heat. His ears spring to full alert, twitching backward and forward, straining to locate the source of this new vibration in his former territory.

Not since his first memories, when the fence had grown out of the sand and divided the land, has he so longed to be on the other side. Following rain clouds, hoping for the flush of green grass, his mob roams widely over the desert. But their beaten trails always circle back to the sweet grazing lands at the foot of the red mountain. Where the first kangaroo mother sat against the stone and, with her wet tongue, smoothed the furry path to her pouch. The most important path of all, which every newborn kangaroo must follow.

Something in the wind tells the kangaroo that this path is now threatened, that a widespread sickness could stop all rains and whither all grass. He has rushed to the red mountain far ahead of the mob, lured by an urgent quivering in his heart.

A strange power swept him here, as if he were caught in a fast-flowing river engorged with rain. A hidden power that waits, that listens, that can heal. Somehow he knows he must connect with it, to communicate his fears of a broken world and beg for healing.

The kangaroo thrusts his long muzzle through the fence. He confirms the source. This power radiates from the shiny black thing, now moving quickly away from him.

He knows there are humans inside.

One of them carries the power.

He splays his foreclaws and rakes at the unyielding wire. He walks stiffly on all fours with his back arched. He tears up hunks of grass and pounces on a shrub as if goading it to wrestle with him. He lets out a harsh cough while eyeing the fence like a rival male in springtime. With one final snort, the huge kangaroo coils back on his tail and, with all his might, pummels the fence with his powerful hind legs.

WARMALA

SETI VAN TOUR, HOT ROCK FARM
DECEMBER 19TH, 3:50 PM

CTP 0048:53:19

A heavy silence fell over us after Jack's little tantrum. Rita sat with her hands folded on her lap and eyes closed. Given who she married, I figured she must be praying.

I pressed my nose against the window, feeling like I always did when Jack was around: trapped.

My eyes fried in the brutal desert light. I squinted into a world of shimmering heat waves. Bizarre mirages danced across the horizon. Trees floated over it. Clouds quivered below it. Rocky hills stretched like rubber bands into the sky.

A giant black skull hovered above the road. It morphed into a honeycomb. Then a spiral of dominoes. Finally, a sea of sparkling solar panels that stretched to the purple hills.

"Well?" Jack said, "Aren't you going to ask me about this?" He sounded almost hurt, like a little boy whose favorite toy had been ignored.

"You just said no more questions," Becca said.

"Ah, but this. *This!* The biggest solar array on Earth."

Rita snapped out of her spell, looking remarkably calm. "Oh, we're here already."

We whizzed past row after endless row of panels.

"That was once upon a time, love," Rita said. "Portugal and Germany beat you out long ago."

Masters ignored her. "Over a hundred acres of panels, fifty *thousand* of them, cranking twelve megawatts straight from the sun. Enough clean energy to power the whole town of Alice Springs, and then some."

"I was proud of you, love," Rita said. "It was an amazing solar farm."

"What do you mean *was?*" said Becca, who had caught her second wind. "Seems pretty amazing to me."

"Look carefully at the panels," Rita said, then tapped the driver on the shoulder. "Ease up, Jirra."

The blur of navy blue panels cleared. I could see that the glass in many of them was badly cracked and their metal frames partly melted. Behind them, wires dangled freely in the wind, trailing ugly lumps of burnt plastic and fused copper. Here and there, blackened cement foundations had crumbled, leaving panels lying face down in the red dirt.

"What happened?" I said.

Rita tsked. "Another dream up in smoke. About a month after we cut the ribbon and turned on the juice, a wicked grass fire took out thousands of panels. Some said it was a lightning strike."

"This must have cost a *bundle!*" Becca said.

"You're damned right!" Jack shouted. "Early technology. It took me years to find enough sponsors. Spent a pile of me own quid."

"Lightning, eh?" I said, absently stroking my bald spot.

"Damned funny lightning, I say. Not a storm cloud in sight."

Rita leaned toward me. "Some said it was the hills."

"The *hills?*" I said.

"Rubbish!" Masters scoffed, going redder than ever.

Rita pointed her chin at the bald hills quickly rising ahead of us, like purple bread loaves.

"Kulini Ngura," Rita said. "The listening place."

Jack started rocking his head as if on a swaying ship. Suddenly, he slumped over like he'd passed out. One arm fell over the dingo's back who sniffed it with a low growl. The driver barely lifted a finger from the steering wheel and the dingo backed off.

Rita watched him for a while, her lips tightening. "One of his spells, I'm afraid. Doctors say it's the emphysema. He gets so worked up these days he just runs out of steam."

Good riddance, I thought.

Rita turned to us and spoke quietly. "Jack's heart was in the right place. But his solar farm wasn't. The local fellas saw it as a scar on the Earth. For them, Kulini Ngura is a signpost left by the Ancestors when the world was new. Back in Dreamtime." Rita paused, looking up at the hills with narrowed eyes. "Oh yeah, very sacred. The fellas warned Jack about *warmala.*"

"Warma-who?" Becca said.

"*Warmala.* About the land taking revenge if he changed it too much." Rita gave me a probing look." You know, like your song?"

I felt caught off guard, like Rita had barged into a room inside that I'd barely explored myself. "Uh, yeah."

"But Jack was too wrapped up in his dreams to listen to theirs. The old fellas told Jack, 'Watch out. It won't last. Too close to the hills.'"

Rita glanced at the driver. He'd slowed down almost to a crawl. The look on his face in the mirror told me he'd been listening intently to every word. When our eyes met, he sat up straight and hit the gas.

Rita turned back to the panels, her dark eyes flitting back and forth as they raced by. "However it happened," she said, "the whole project backfired in Jack's face. Almost killed him."

I stared at the hills. As we got closer, they changed shape—stuff did that out here on the desert. They'd morphed from bread loaves into breasts. Great heaving breasts that poked out of the desert floor, complete with low-cut cleavage and house-sized nipples. Their color changed, too, from hazy purple to a stark brick red. Layers of sandstone curled across the rock face like fossil tidal waves. I began to make out other details. Deep frowning caves, black streaks that covered some hills like a woman's hair, and some kind of white fuzz floating above the highest domes.

Rita followed my gaze to the top of the hills. "Can you spot them?"

A forest of white bristles brushed the sky. Something was gyrating up there. Giant propellers.

"Wind turbines," she said. "From solar farm to wind farm."

Becca leaned across Quincy to look up at the towers. Quincy pressed back into his seat like she had the plague. "Crazy," she muttered.

"So right," Rita said. "Jack *was* crazy about 'em. He loved to boast how these turbines work like fans in reverse. Instead of making wind with electricity, he'd make electricity with wind. Enough to light the streets of Brisbane and twenty thousand homes. And not one ounce of carbon to make it."

"But …" Becca said, "he built them smack on top of their sacred site."

Rita nodded slowly. "Uh-huh."

"I bet that went over well with the locals," Rosie said.

"Nope."

I became aware of a rising hum in my chest. It got stronger as we closed in on the hills. I got the feeling there was some power here that Jack could never tap.

A sad smile stole across Rita's face. "Jack saw himself as God's gift to clean energy. That fire took a big piece out of him. But Jack's no quitter. After soaking his wounds in booze for a few months, he bounced back with a new plan to save the world. Wind. And he knew the perfect place to harness it." She bent forward, pointing to the hilltops. "Up there."

The road veered sharply and now we cruised right beside the base of the hills. They rose straight out of a carpet of red sand and bomb-shaped boulders. "Jack tried to change the fellas' minds. Offered them good quid. But they wouldn't take his money. Wouldn't listen to his plan. They'd scatter every time he tried to talk about it. In the end, Jack had to bring in migrant workers all the way from Indonesia to build these towers."

I craned my neck to look up at them. They looked like monstrous storks marching across the ridgeline.

"The local fellas kept telling him, 'Don't climb those hills. Don't put nothin' up there.'"

"Or else," Becca said.

"Uh-huh. My brother Mani actually led the resistance."

That's when I noticed that none of the giant pinwheels were spinning. The blades on some towers were bent backwards as if toyed with by Godzilla. On others there were no blades at all, just a gleaming white tower, dead from the neck up. Like Jack's solar panels, these towers of power had taken a hit from something big.

"Another dud?" I said.

Rita nodded slowly. "Ironically, it was wind that took them out."

"*Wind?*" said Rosie, Becca, and I all at once.

Rita chuckled. "Some said it was faulty parts, maybe sloppy labor. But the local fellas knew what did this."

"*Warmala?*" I murmured.

"Right. The signs were everywhere. This was much more than a run of bad luck. Two people died in a helicopter crash, airlifting a tower to the highest dome." Rita leaned forward. "This dome, in fact. Mount Wara, the tall one."

The mountain rose above a ring of lower hills that seemed to bow down to it. A string of caves reached up the side, making a perfect ladder for a giant. The mountain wore a sandstone crown of deep, bulging folds, like fissures in a human brain.

"The day after they finally installed a tower up there, a worker fell off and plunged to his death."

"Was the guy blown off?" I said.

"No. The big wind came after. A week later, another worker was beheaded by a spinning blade."

"Ouch," Rosie said.

"But, of course, Jack had good insurance. Good lawyers, too. He just paid 'em off and plowed ahead."

Jack was still doubled over and beginning to snore.

"The big wind came about a week after they hooked up the last tower. In the middle of the night. Hundred-mile-an-hour winds out of the north. Gusts to almost twice that. Hit like a hammer. It only took a couple hours to knock the stuffing out of Jack's wind farm. Died as quick as it rose." Rita snapped her fingers. "Poof. Just like that. No one, I mean, *no one,* had ever seen such winds out here. Over in Alice there was hardly enough to ruffle a flag. Very strange."

"But, like, isn't that the whole idea?" Becca said. "More wind, more power?"

"Right, up to a point. These things, they have a cut-out wind speed. Above that you're only making trouble, not power. That's when you hit the brakes. Furl the blades. Slow 'em down before they fly off. It's supposed to be automatic, but something knocked out all the brakes that night."

"Every single tower?" Becca said.

"Uh-huh. All fifty of 'em. Every generator, fried. The blades spun out of control and buggered the whole works."

"Bye-bye, wind farm," Rosie said.

"Uh-huh. What's left of it's been flapping in the breeze ever since."

"*Warmala*," I said again.

"I reckon."

"Is that some of the junk that fell off the mountain?" Becca said.

I followed her gaze to a thick grove of mop-topped trees, hugging the base of a cliff. Bright metal structures rose above them, flashing orange in the late afternoon sun.

"That's Jack's latest project," Rita said. "Grain silos."

Besides a few flowers in front of Rita's house, I hadn't seen anything planted by human hands on Jack's so-called farm. For sure, nothing you could call grain. No farm animals, either. "I thought you said all those miracle crops were a bust."

"Uh-huh."

"So what's he put in those silos?"

"Tells me it's camel feed."

"What? I thought the big fence kept them—"

Rita shrugged. "That's right. He says it's some sort of biofuel experiment. Corral a few camels, scoop their poop, convert it to gas. Potent stuff."

As we raced past the grove of trees, I glimpsed six big silos. I whipped out my binoculars. They stood in a circle around a glittering cone-shaped pile of something I couldn't identify. A spider web of conveyor belts radiated out from the pile to the top of each silo. Behind the ring of silos was a long, low building, all white with a red-tiled roof, like Jack's straw-bale house, but with just one tiny window. Perched on top of the building was a satellite dish so big it would have made my father drool.

I spotted some movement beside the building. Two guards were having a smoke in the shade. They were dressed in green battle fatigues and they toted rifles that would bring down an elephant. In a clearing behind them sat a camouflaged military helicopter. The whole compound was surrounded by two rows of extra razor-wire fence.

I whistled. "What's with the hard-core security?"

"Keeps out the dingos," Rita said.

Becca huffed like she does when stuck on a math problem. "So they don't bother the camels, right?"

Rita nodded dubiously.

"Which are nowhere in sight," Becca said.

Rita shrugged and flipped an upturned hand to Jack whose head now tapped the dashboard. "That's the way he tells it, anyway."

Just before the trees closed in on my view, I focused on the shiny pile. It was shrink-wrapped in clear plastic from top to bottom. I slowly lowered my binoculars. Here was a mini mountain of those silver pellets that Jack swooned over in his weird Zen gardens.

I turned to Rita. "What the hell does Jack need camel poop for when he's got so much power locked up in those pellets?"

"Ah, he explained those, did he?" Rita said. "The hydrogen bit. How you just add water—"

"And *BOOM!*" Rosie shouted, sounding exactly like Gabe.

Rita had fixed her eyes on a white speck hugging the horizon. Her outback home. Her armor of calm had cracked since telling us all about Jack's disasters. I detected something lost and lonely leaking out. Like she, too, felt trapped. "To be honest, girls," she said, "I haven't the foggiest what Jack's up to this time."

I squinted at the dashboard GPS for a clue. A flashing red dot marking the silo site dropped toward the bottom of the screen. Just before it disappeared, I managed to read the letters beside it: CTP-LP. As I opened my mouth to pass this by Rita, I detected another message, equally mystifying, beamed straight for my third ear, Uitajuq's ear.

That whispering.

FULL STOP

KULINI NGURA RING ROAD WEST OF MOUNT WARA
DECEMBER 19TH, 4:10 PM

CTP 0047:33:37

This time, the whispering was steady and strong and closing fast.

I stared, dumbstruck, through the windshield. All around us, spears of oven-baked grass leaned away from the wind as if trying to escape. Shrubs like giant porcupines seemed to shudder in terror.

Something unseen lay dead ahead. Something precious, calling to me like the raccoon, the falcon, and, just back there, the kangaroo. Something larger than life that we dared not hit.

I have to know!

I ripped off my seatbelt and grabbed the driver's arm. "Stop!" I yelled. "You gotta stop! NOW!"

I guess I used a little too much force.

The driver slammed on the brakes, sending lemonade and beer all over his dingo—who sprang into his lap. I flew forward as the van almost keeled over on two wheels, then lurched to a stop.

I let out a tentative breath, lying face down on the floor where the dingo had been seconds before. A hydrogen motor growled beneath my bruised forehead. Wind-driven sand clawed at the van, trying to get in. I slowly rolled onto my back. The dingo stared me down with a nasty look that said: *You got us into this mess*—which, of course, I had.

The driver sat frozen with eyes closed, still clutching the steering wheel.

My hip and elbow felt like hamburger. I rubbed my forehead, feeling a goose egg rise under my fingers.

I dragged myself to my knees and rested my chin on the dashboard. We'd spun ninety degrees and now faced the sacred hills. The van teetered over a deep, dry creek bed that disappeared under the road through a giant culvert.

I strained my Uitajuq ear, testing the desert wind for a whisper. Nothing.

The guy at the wheel suddenly lifted his head. He peered down the road, looked at me, then back at the road. It was empty. By the looks of it, there was nothing between us and the Indian Ocean half a continent away. He slowly spun in his seat, eyes wide with astonishment.

"Crikey! You *heard* it. Well, I'll be stuffed."

A huge hand clamped down on my shoulder, squeezing so hard that all my other bumps and bruises drowned in a purple haze of pain.

GRANDFATHER LIZARD

KULINI NGURA RING ROAD WEST OF MOUNT WARA DECEMBER 19TH, 4:15 PM

CTP 0047:28:16

With perfect slowness, Grandfather Lizard steps out onto the hard-packed road. Like a tiny clockwork toy, he staggers forward on bowed legs, freezes, then rocks up and down. His push-up dance is jerkier than it should be and he almost tips over. A sickness in the wind throws him off balance. It has been that way for many lives. Getting worse.

He tilts one shrewd eye to the sky and watches for winged shadows. He basks in the road's extra heat, warming his wide belly. He knows the sun will leave soon. He must reach the big drop before the sun sleeps. He knows he will find shelter there from the cool night winds. He will be safe beneath his clump of grass or broken tree or drift of sand. He will be safe as long as everything does not fall apart.

From that sickness.

A few more unsteady steps. He pauses, rocks again, steps, pauses. One side of his forked tongue picks up the scent of his favorite food. He turns left. Step. Step. He cocks one eye, then the other, toward a column of red ants snaking across the road. He lunges for the closest ant, clamping down on it with toothless jaws. The rest of the ants scatter. The captured ant's legs tickle the roof of his mouth on the way down.

Grandfather Lizard plods forward, pausing this time to study the squashed remains of a distant relative. Its rear legs and tail are flattened. Ragged strings of bloody flesh and a few half-digested ants trail from its mouth. One lifeless eye stares at the sun. He knows the dead lizard's breath has returned to the wind, carried back to the red mountain where the first of his kind hatched.

Where giant lizard began his journey with the dance.

He lifts a front leg, about to take another step, when he feels a strange tremor come up through the four long toes of each of his hind feet. Something shakes the ground, coming fast like a dust storm. Above this, Grandfather Lizard senses a looming presence streaking toward him. Before he can even duck, it arrives invisibly, piercing his tough, scaly skin.

The lizard squeezes his eyes shut as a strange, shielding power wraps around him. It is like the yolk he once floated in as he grew inside an egg. An invisible pathway opens above the roadbed, connecting the lizard with the source of this power.

He knows where it comes from. Generations of his kind have waited for this day. Longed for it. The power comes from a special human who can hear the land's healing song.

As the lizard feels when the rains finally come, when the bright plants open and the land is full of insects, so he feels now. A river of sound, as sweet as a honey ant, floods his body. Something beyond his skin and senses swells, until he feels his barbed head about to brush the clouds.

Grandfather Lizard opens his huge mouth and gulps a valley's worth of healthy wind. He releases it in a voiceless call for help, for healing. He rears up on giant legs and rocks. He rolls.

He dances, sure and steady, as in the early days.

Until he sees the black thing rushing at him.

NGIYARI

KULINI NGURA RING ROAD WEST OF MOUNT WARA
DECEMBER 19TH, 4:20 PM

CTP 0047:23:41

"Mr. Masters ain't about to put his head through no windshield if'n he can help it."

It was the longest sentence I'd heard the guy string together. "*Ouch!* I gotcha, Quincy! Like, I really meant to crash us. Can I have my shoulder back?"

After a final wicked squeeze, the vice opened and my bones moved back into place, more or less.

I twisted around, ready to snarl. Quincy's mirror shades had flown off. I gasped.

One of his eyes was deep brown, like a grizzly bear's. The other was totally clouded over, like he had no pupil at all. His pockmarked face was drenched in sweat.

He reached for where his shades should be, then quickly pulled away. "For God's sake, Jirra, what kinda plonk ya been drinkin'?" Jack was back in fine form. He sat up, rubbing both temples and glaring at the world.

The driver, still looking at me funny, shook red dust from his head. "Sorry, boss. Cheeky back-seat driver."

"Cripes, Ash," yelled Becca from the back. "Are you mental?"

"Ditto," Rosie said.

"I dunno," I said. "Must be heat stroke or something."

Rita watched me, while stroking Jack's back. His body seemed to melt under her hand. Everyone relaxed.

Except our driver, Jirra. He whipped open his door and jumped out like a skydiver. The dingo leapt out on his heels. The van tipped forward. The horizon tilted. I braced myself for a nosedive into the creek bed. Then, as quickly, the van thumped back onto its rear wheels.

Barely breathing, I watched Jirra bound in front of the van, then climb out of the creek bed. He slowed down, almost tip-toeing, and held out his arms above the road. It reminded me of Dad doing what he called a "dummy check" whenever we'd leave a campsite—looking for stray knives or forks, a gas can lid, maybe one of Gabe's harmonicas, or bits of trash.

"What the hell?" Rosie said over my shoulder.

"Beats me," I said. But part of me knew that whatever Jirra was doing had something to do with the whispering.

Jirra took a few more slow-motion steps, then turned suddenly and fell to his knees. He stared at something in the middle of the road.

"What in God's name?" Jack grumbled.

Becca slowly opened the van door. We carefully stepped out. Just as Rita's foot touched the red gravel, the rear wheels rose about two feet off the ground, leaving the van, with Jack and Quincy still inside, teetering over the culvert.

The stream of blue murder that poured from Jack's lips would have melted a glacier. With his wheelchair clamped to the floor, he wasn't going anywhere. And if Quincy moved to help him, he might upset the whole applecart, sending Jack over the edge.

Let them work it out, I thought. They were both out of our hair for a while.

After the air-conditioned van, I felt like we'd hopped out of a space-ship onto the plains of Venus. I shielded my eyes from the blinding light, the blistering heat. The red desert sprawled away in front of us, ducking over the horizon in a tangled mess of squirming mirages. As I took a few feeble steps toward Jirra, I got the feeling I was walking over the hide of some great sleeping beast. Faraway dips and ridges poked through its mangy skin like so many ribs. I looked over my shoulder at the sandstone hills that towered above us. Flooded by a harsh west light, the breast-shaped rocks seemed obscenely exposed, as if daring me to look at them.

What the hell was Jirra staring at?

Becca sidled up beside him, took one look, then locked her hands on her hips and turned to me. "You almost killed us to save *this?*"

"Whoa," Rosie said. "Bad case of road rash."

"Wasn't us," Jirra said, watching his dingo trot down the road with his nose to the ground.

"Huh?" Becca said.

"Dead too long," Jirra said.

Spread out on the road in front of Jirra's knees was a road-killed lizard, its back end flattened like a pancake. It might have been an old shoe or tossed orange peel for all I cared. One glance told me this was not what I was looking for.

"What's the big deal?" Rosie said. "Like, is this some endangered species, or what?"

"*Ngiyari,*" Jirra said, his eyes still fixed on the dingo. "Thorny devil. There's a few about."

I took another look at it. No rose bush ever had more spines than this creature. It was striped like a tiger with a crown of yellow and brown thorns. A pygmy dinosaur.

"Cute," I said, unable to grasp what I was seeing.

"Bloody cute," said Jirra, standing up so fast he almost knocked me over. He sprinted after the dingo.

I could hear Jack yelling in the van. Rita had stayed behind, trying to calm him down. Quincy, still trapped in the back seat, was waving a hand around while talking on his cell phone.

I felt a strange tug in my chest. Without thinking, I bolted after Jirra. His dingo was toying with something at the side of the road, picking it up and tossing it in the air the way an Arctic fox plays with a lemming before downing it.

"Puli!" shouted Jirra. "Wiya. *Wiya!*"

The dingo instantly dropped the thing and stood aside with its tail between its legs. Jirra carefully cupped the creature into his big hands.

Another thorny lizard. This was bigger than the squished one, meaner looking, and very much alive. Its tail was shorter and bleeding like it had just lost the tip. Probably stuck to one of our tires.

As the lizard thrashed about in Jirra's hands, it stopped randomly, did a couple of funny little push-ups, then tilted its spiny head, peering directly at me. I couldn't take my eyes off it.

I realized with a start that Jirra was also looking at me. His piercing eyes cut through me as if he were tracking a far-off animal through binoculars.

He thrust the lizard toward me. "Here. Get to know each other."

"What?" I said, recoiling. "*That?* What's there to know?"

"Lots," he said matter-of-factly.

It was like he'd sliced me in half with one word. Part of me bled panic, wanting to run madly into the killing desert, away from Jack and Quincy and this crazy farm, away from Jirra's taunting grin and the bizarre creature he held up to my face.

Another part of me watched the whole scene through steady, searching eyes, as if this creature had much to teach me.

Everything slowed until the whole world stopped turning, caught in this single hovering moment. Fingers of windswept sand loosened their grip on my ankles. Becca and Rosie stood very still by my side, waiting to see what I would do.

Jirra had turned to stone.

I blurted a weak laugh as I felt my arms rising, my hands opening, reaching out for the lizard. Invisible strings took control of my body, my thoughts, my heart. At that moment, I wanted nothing more than to cuddle this tiny wounded soul, to protect it, to enter its territory beneath the sacred mountain.

Jirra let the thorny devil crawl into my hands. I flinched, almost dropping it, but the devil hung on by the claws of one foot. Jirra prodded it back onto my palm. It thrashed once, twice, then lay still.

No one breathed.

I thought maybe it had died of shock, until the whispering returned.

The lizard twitched, then sprang up on four bowed legs. It rocked sideways, up and down, then sideways again. For such a clunky-looking beast, it moved with amazing class. It repeated this routine over and over until some steady inner beat switched off and it again lay still in my hand, as light as a sparrow.

The whispering died.

A crazy, simple dance, yet it reset the world's axis, now turning on the lizard's broken tail.

I felt something volcanic moving inside of me. It rumbled up from my pelvis, shook my belly, and startled my heart. It erupted from my lips as a gigantic, bone-rattling, bubble-bursting laugh.

Soon Becca and Rosie were splitting their sides over the lizard's fancy footwork. Even Jirra joined in the laughter.

The hills themselves seemed ready to uproot and dance.

Until a low, pounding, insect noise shattered the sky.

EAR OF THE WORLD

HELICOPTER OVER KULINI NGURA
DECEMBER 19TH, 4:40 PM

CTP 0047:03:46

"I shoulda bloody well thought of this in the first place." Jack's crusty voice blasted into my headset. "Let the van rot. Give those soldier boys something to do."

I ripped off the headset. The ear-popping roar of the helicopter was unbearable. I flipped it back on, choosing the lesser of evils.

"I would've punched a road through these hills if they weren't so damned stubborn."

I looked at Rita for some explanation. Even strapped into a monster helicopter with a headset clamped to her head and shaking all over, she seemed right at home. "Stubborn?" I shouted.

Rita smiled and shrugged, pointing to the microphone on my headset. I swung it around in front of my lips. "How can hills be stubborn?"

"Jack wanted to build a road directly into the theater," she said. "But every time he—"

"Theater?"

"That's what he calls it. More like an amphitheater."

"What happened?" I asked.

"Somebody put a moz on it," Jack grumbled. "I just wanted to open up one little canyon that led straight inside. Instead of driving way around Hell's half acre. But, damnedest thing. Our dynamite wouldn't fire." Jack chuckled grimly. "Least, hardly ever."

Jirra sat beside me, his bare leg occasionally knocking against mine. I stole a glance at him. He was staring at the back of Jack's head. I saw his lips moving but his mike was off.

Rita pursed her lips. "Blew up in one worker's face. Lost an eye and most of his hearing. Another lost an arm. That put an end to Jack's road."

I stuck my head in a bubble window off the chopper's side. From this far up, the sandstone hills had shape-shifted yet again. I looked down at rolling folds on the stomach of a very large, very chubby woman.

"This is it?" I said. "The theater?"

"Yeah," Rita said. "The local fellas say it's an ear. Called it that for thousands of years."

An ear. Of course. Not bread loaves. Not giant breasts. Not Mother Earth's tummy. But an ear. I could see it right away. Along the east side, a series of high ridges formed a C-shaped curve around a wide central bowl. The west side, where we'd ditched the van, was dominated by Mount Wara, which cast a deep shadow into the heart of the bowl. The bowl itself was veined with faint ribbons of green that spilled over its barren red skin. From the air, these puzzle pieces fit together to make a picture-perfect ear.

"That's one honkin' ear," Becca said, her voice crackling in my headset.

I pulled back from the view as a bigger puzzle hit me. "How could anyone see this thousands of years ago? From the ground, I mean."

"Good question," Rita said. "On foot, the ear is invisible. Like those strange lines on the deserts of Peru."

"Oh, yeah," Becca said. "Saw 'em on TV once. The Nazca lines."

"Right," Rita said. "They make no sense on the ground. But fly over them and you'll see giant spiders, monkeys, birds. So, we've got an ear. A bloody big one. Kulini Ngura. They say it's the ear of the world."

"Imagine that," Jack blared. "On *my* farm!"

"Listening to what?" Becca said.

Rita raised her eyebrows. "Can't say, really. But it seems it's a good place for a little music."

"You mean, like, their music?" I said.

"I mean their music, *your* music. Same roots. Welcome to the concert site."

"It's the first goddamned project of mine the local fellas supported," Jack roared. "Been doing it for ten years now. Bigger each year. Tried different themes—Green Man, Water Music, Power For Life. And now, *now,* Scorched Earth! This'll be the first one on climate change. And you can be damned sure it'll be the last." Jack's brittle laugh crackled over my headset. "The apocalyptic holy grail!"

The pilot banked the helicopter away from the setting sun. I got my first clear look at the spot hidden by the shadow of Mount Wara. If the eastern hills formed an ear, this had to be the ear canal.

As my eyes adjusted to the shaded ground, I made out a strange C-shaped pattern that perfectly matched the arc of the surrounding hills. We plunged deeper into the shadows. I suddenly got it. Spread out over the crazy ripples and folds of the desert was a perfectly symmetrical street plan. The empty streets, marked with long red, yellow, and black flags, radiated out from a huge central stage. A bunch of trucks, tents, and camper vans were packed in behind the stage. Workers moved like ants across the sand and climbed over a bank of scaffold towers that rimmed the platform.

Jirra flashed me an odd smile and tapped his knees like he was beating a drum.

Jack waved a thumb in front of the pilot's nose, and moments later we were powering down in the center of the Scorched Earth stage.

VIPS

SCORCHED EARTH STAGE
DECEMBER 19TH, 7:00 PM

CTP 0046:04:17

"Just two more days and every Earth-hugging bastard and his dog'll be pouring in here," Jack said, after rolling out of the helicopter onto the plywood stage. He flicked an arm toward a wall of sun-drenched hills on the far side of the bowl. In the low-angled light, they looked positively molten. "The east gate's just behind those hills. Once we swing it open … well, I say, bring it on! Let the farewell party begin!"

At this, Rita looked sideways at Jack. It dawned on me that there was a lot she didn't know about this man. But the love was still there. I could sense it. Flowing out of sight, like a warm, deep river below a waterless land.

How could she love this creep?

She turned to face the black silhouette of Mount Wara, then walked toward it across the massive plywood stage. Her body swayed as if prompted by some inner song. Jirra slipped by her side and they both tilted their heads up at the mountain. They seemed pretty buddy-buddy, those two, like they were tuning into the same wavelength.

The towers lining the back of the stage held rows of stadium speakers and TV cameras. Huge video screens lined the flag-draped streets that spread out from the front of the stage like spokes on a wheel. We stood at the hub, the dead center of the bowl, the gateway to the Earth's inner ear.

From this angle, due east of the setting sun, the dome of Mount Wara drew a perfect pyramid on the sand. Even weirder, this shadow pierced the dead center of the stage. I didn't need my New Age mother around to tell me this was some kind of power spot. The stage wasn't placed here by accident. Somebody knew exactly what they were doing when they told Jack where to put it.

"God, I've never seen so many outhouses," Becca said.

Besides the stage, the workers' tents and trailers, and the rows of wooden flagpoles, the only other structures on site were bright blue outhouses lining the outer streets. There must have been a hundred of them.

"Impressive, i'n'it?" Jack boasted. "The whole operation will be zero impact. Local fellas insisted on it. Everybody brings all they need. Food, water, shelter. Buy nothing. Sell nothing. All litterers will be shot, jailed, and pissed on, in that order."

"So, like, how many spectators was it again, Jack?" Rosie said.

Jack stormed to the front of the stage, almost rolling over the edge. "There'll be no spectators at my party. Sure, lots of hippies, punks, greenies, eco-freaks, rebels, seekers. But no spectators. Everybody's part of the show."

Rosie cleared her throat. "Okay, so that was—"

"Mobs and mobs," Jack exclaimed, raising his arms in a great V. "A half-million, give or take. Advertised all over the bloody planet. Crackerjack Web site, TV ads, major newspapers around the world. Shit, cost me an arm and a leg." Jack frowned. "Can't believe you missed the hype."

"Uh, we didn't exactly have Australia on our radar for Christmas," I said.

"Right," Jack said. "Well, it's good you finally came to your senses."

"Actually, this was *your* idea," Becca said. "You didn't give us a lot of choice."

Jack rubbed his chin like this was news to him. "Hmm, right again."

"So we took the scenic route home," Rosie said. "What can we lose?"

"Now that's the spirit," Jack said.

"Girls, our fans are lining up at the gates," Rosie said. "*Panting* for us. Think of the publicity. The CD sales! We'll never, ever top a concert like this. Not in a thousand years."

Jack chuckled to himself. "Yep. That's about how long it'll be until the next one."

Becca leaned over Jack's wheelchair, trying to catch his eye. "Just what's that supposed to mean?"

The sound of piano music cut the air, a haunting classical riff you might hear at Carnegie Hall. Jack waved Becca off like she was a pesky mosquito and reached into a shirt pocket. It was the ringer on his cell phone.

"Yeah, what," he said.

Becca and I backed away as we watched furrows carve deeper into Jack's forehead.

"What the fuck do you mean you can't get it through the gate?" he shouted.

Rita and Jirra ignored him as they talked to one of the workers over the edge of the stage. I motioned to Rosie to come over, quick.

"Who's the piking bastard in charge down there?" yelled Jack.

In spite of the fast-cooling air, he'd started to sweat buckets, as if it was high noon. He was puffing like a steam engine. His free hand gripped the arm of his wheelchair so tightly I expected to see bones pop out of his old blotched skin. "Can you believe it, Ash?" Rosie said. "Like, this is performer heaven."

"Yeah, perfect," I said. "Except for our self-appointed manager.

Just look at him."

Jack's complexion had turned from beet red to purple. He clawed at his shirt collar like it was a tightening noose. "Damn it, whining won't fix it," he sputtered between gasps. "Now you listen to me ..."

"He's a whacko megalomaniac," Becca said.

"A powder keg," I said.

"Come on, girls," Rosie said. "He's our sugar daddy, 'member? Just kinda fell head over heels for our music, that's all."

"And, like, threatened me with blackmail if we didn't dance to *his* music."

"Oh, yeah," Rosie said. "The arson bit. Forget it. Jack's a bit obsessive, maybe. But see how *bad* he wants us."

"Yeah," Becca said. "But for *what?*"

Rosie stomped one of her high-heeled boots. "To perform on this very stage."

"That's all, eh?" I said. "Do you really believe that?"

"Well, yeah," Rosie said. "And maybe stir up some shit."

"The chaos bit," Becca said.

"He seems to get off on that kind of stuff," Rosie said. "Rock the world with a few tunes. Shake it up with a couple of Arctic horror stories. Jack forgets about the torched trailer. We fly home to stardom."

"That simple," I said.

Rosie shrugged. "What am I missing here?"

"Okay, we fly home," Becca said. "But *when*, exactly? Like, has anybody seen a plane ticket?"

"Well ... no," Rosie said. "But hell, Jack could fly us door to door in one of his fancy toys. Like real VIPs."

I looked up at Mount Wara. Its shadow had completely enveloped the stage and speared its way to the base of the eastern hills. A warped ocher moon, almost full, sprang out from behind a sandstone ridge. I imagined it rising, calm and cool, above the blue-green sea ice of home.

A dull knife raked my stomach. "I know we're not bound and gagged or anything," I said, "but don't you feel just a little bit like hostages?"

"Yeah, VIPs, all right," Becca said. "Very important *prisoners*."

"Screw the darkness!" yelled Jack. "We don't have any more time to piss away. We'll have to airlift the sucker over the fence ... you got it ... so how many extra men do you need? ... Right. Round up every jackaroo who can walk straight, and I mean fast ... *What?* ... I know it's a goddamned Sunday!" Jack glanced at his diamond-crusted watch. "Gate opens in forty hours, mate. You can forget about sleep until then. Now get your shit together. We're on our way."

DEVIL DANCE

FIREPIT AT EMOH RUO SETTLEMENT
DECEMBER 19TH, 8:30 PM

CTP 0044:26:32

Skipping all niceties, as usual, Jack had dumped us behind a cluster of aborigine homes near the east gate, grabbed some extra workers, then taken off into the night to "kick some drongo arses," as he'd said. Rita told us we'd be in good hands and stayed in the chopper, hoping to check up on Gabe before we got there. As he took off, Jack stuck his head out the chopper window and yelled that he would send a vehicle for us "eventually"—whenever that was.

Compared to back home, night here fell like a guillotine. From what I could see in the pale moonlight, all the homes were made out of straw bales like Rita's place, only they seemed more run-down, with rusted tin roofs instead of clay tiles. There were about ten of them, spread out in a circle around a large central firepit draped by a ring of gnarly gum trees. That's what Jirra called them, anyway.

Far to the east I could hear the faint thump of a helicopter.

"Why's Jack so nuts on abo music?" Rosie asked Jirra, after we'd all had a taste of kangaroo steak and cold beer.

Jirra seemed to have two faces. Cold and quiet for Jack. Warm and funny when he was out from under his fat thumb. I caught myself watching him closely.

"Ya probably noticed Uncle Jack's kind of fanatic about—"

Becca waved a hand. "No, wait a sec. *Uncle* Jack?"

"Uh-huh. Great Uncle, actually."

"God," Becca said. "Poor you. So, what's the connection?"

Jirra pointed across the firepit at the silhouette of an old guy moseying toward us across the compound. "Him." The man held a long pipe close to his chest, the same way my dad would carry a rifle.

"Who's him?" Becca said.

"Mani. Rita's brother. My *amari.*"

"Huh?"

"Oh, right. My grandfather." Jirra paused, watching him shuffle toward us. "Shit-hot didj player."

"Didj?"

"Didjeridu." Jirra pointed to the pipe. "He's playin' at the concert."

"So who else is on stage?" Rosie said.

"Who *isn't?* Reckon something like fifty acts. From all over. Amazon, Africa, Siberia. Grass huts to iglus." Jirra took his eyes off the fire to look us over. "You guys really live in iglus?"

"For sure," Rosie said. "Twenty-four-seven."

"Yeah? Uncle used to talk about your iglus. Said he built one once.

And your … what's-it? … midnight sun? They say it stir-fried his brains. The guy thinks he can save the world."

"From humans," I said.

"Yeah, pretty much. Messy ones, at least. Thought solar panels would do it. Then it was windmills."

"Then hydrogen," I said.

"Uh-huh."

"Then hot rocks."

"Yep. You name it. Tried all sorts of power trips. Flavor of the month. Then it was us."

"Who's *us*?" Becca said.

Jirra studied Becca for a moment, taking in her blonde hair and fair skin. "Well, most of us. You know, aborigines, *maruku,* redskins, first people, jungle bunnies. Whatever. Jack calls us … Inheritors."

"What's that supposed to mean?" Becca said.

Mani staggered up to the fire and stood behind Jirra. He looked as old as my Uncle Jonah in his last days, easily pushing ninety. He wore khaki shorts and a ripped yellow T-shirt. His kinky snow-white hair poked out from under a red and orange headband just like the one Darri wore. His body was lean and wiry. Soft wrinkles filled his milk-chocolate face. He had the shortest, widest nose I'd ever seen.

Mani halted at the edge of the firelight. His eyes were closed but I felt he was peering at me. He seemed sleepy or drunk, I couldn't tell. His mouth was open and, above the crackling fire, I could hear his heavy breathing, like he was snoring on his feet.

"We're survivors," Jirra said after a long pause. He chucked a log into the flames, sending up a volcano of sparks. "Think about all the shit that's gone down. They steal our homelands. Smash our tradition-al life. Make slaves out of us. Infect us with their diseases. Throw booze at us. Dump us in schools where they whip our language out of us." Jirra horked deep in his throat and spat in the fire. "Oh yeah, and they put a bounty on our heads and shoot us down like rabbits. And guess what. *We're still here.* We keep bouncing back."

"Must be doing something right," Rosie said.

Jirra laughed, flashing Rita's kangaroo teeth. "Uncle Jack reckons it has something to do with our special connection to the land. To the Earth. No one's been able to beat that out of us."

Mani seemed to wake up. He carefully leaned his long pipe against a tree and sat down on a rock. He scooped up an armful of sticks and hurled them on the fire. "Not yet, anyways," he said in a low, even voice.

Jirra nodded thoughtfully. "So Uncle reckons that if the shit hits the fan and the world falls apart, we'll be the only ones left to pick up the pieces."

"Or maybe stop it from happening?" I said.

"You wish," said Jirra as he leaned forward to examine a half-burned log. Something green was oozing out of the log's unburned end. Ants. A horde of fat green ants, most of them clutching egg cases. They spilled out across the sand, drew crazy circles in the dust, then dove back into their burning home. A few skittered madly over the bark within inches of the flames. In spite of the roaring fire, I felt cold and dizzy watching this pathetic show.

I glanced at Mani. He sat like a wooden statue, fixed on the flames. I realized something in me had cracked the moment he sat down.

I looked back at the crazy ants. The smoking log became our baking planet. We were the ants. I wanted to break down and bawl.

The sound of Becca's voice pulled me back from the brink. "So, like, if your people are so-called Inheritors …"

Jirra tilted his chin at Rosie and me. "Them, too."

"Okay," Becca said cautiously. "Then what's that make people like me?"

"*Piranpa.*"

"Ah, right. Is that good?"

Jirra shrugged. "Dunno. White people. Non jungle bunnies. In

Jack's books you're Intruders. You don't belong here. At least, not the messy ones."

"Like, just *where is here?*" Becca said.

Jirra gingerly pulled the ant log out of the fire and tossed it onto the cool sand. "On this planet, basically."

"But … but your Uncle Jack's as white as I am."

"Not for long," Jirra said, whacking the fire with a stick. "On his last legs, old Jack. Then he's dust. White dust."

Becca shuddered. Rosie and I flung an arm around her shoulders.

Mani laughed. "Crikey, Jirra. You're scarin' the shit out of the sheilas. Let's call up some good ghosts." He reached for his long pipe. It was dark red, about five feet long, with a slight flare at one end. Orange and white snakes slithered over its shiny surface around a central spiral of bright green dots. In the center of the spiral was a brilliant gemstone that flashed every color of the rainbow.

So that's a didjeridu, I thought.

Mani looked up at me, an odd twinkle in his old eyes. He nodded slightly, like he'd read my mind.

He started tapping his didjeridu with a straight peeled stick. The sharp clicking sound blended with the crackling fire and bounced off the sheltering trees. His feet beat the sand as if the desert floor were a giant drum. I noticed his feet were cracked and dry like some sort of animal hooves.

Closing his eyes, he placed the narrow, waxy end of the instrument over his lips. At first the low buzzing sound that came out seemed ridiculous to me. A five-year-old with an empty paper towel roll could do this. I watched Mani closely, waiting for him to take a breath. But he never did.

That's when I knew there was some magic afoot.

It started with the fire. The flames danced as they had before Mani started playing. But something had changed. They brightened. They slowed. They gained form and substance. They took on the shapes of animals. As Mani tore into his didjeridu, I swear I saw a falcon, a raccoon, a kangaroo, a thorny devil, all peering out at me as they danced in that fire.

The buzzing opened up—or had my ears? It parted and split like sunlight through a prism, like a flash flood rushing down a dry creek bed, like wind singing through the desert grasses. I heard the sound of laughing parrots, skittering lizards, thumping kangaroos.

Mani was painting the whole desert with his droning palette of sounds.

He squeezed the didjeridu between his knees and waved his free arm in the air like a helicopter blade. For some reason, my eyes were drawn to the spiral of green dots. They, too, seemed to spin, echoing the movement of the panic-stricken ants.

With a strange grin on his face, Jirra suddenly vaulted backwards over his rock and crumpled in the sand. He lay there perfectly still like he'd been speared. Mani's music faded to a whisper.

A whisper!

That same haunting sound that had chased me from one end of the Earth to the other.

A wave of goosebumps swept over me. I felt my skin loosening as if Mani was prying it off with his didj, peeling me like an onion down to my raw Uitajuq core.

Time stopped as all of my awareness zoomed in on Jirra's crumpled form.

Mani sped up the tapping on the side of his didj, faster and faster. The drone rose to a fever pitch. His music seemed to call Jirra back from the dead. Jirra twitched. He lifted his head and cocked one eye toward the smoking log. A ring of green ants marched around it. He sprang to all fours and staggered forward on bowed arms and legs. He stopped above the log, his body obscured by smoke. I got a strong sense he was protecting it, saving it from disaster. He jerked up and down, almost burning his chest in the tongues of fire that still flickered on the bark.

Through the smoke I thought I saw another face with a leering grin, wide-set eyes, and a crown of thorns. Then it struck me. I had seen this show before. The push-up dance of the thorny devil. Jirra perfectly mirrored its bizarre jig, performed on the palm of my hand. He pitched awkwardly from side to side. He lunged forward and back, almost doing a face plant in the sand.

After a long pause, when the moon seemed to hold its breath and the stars stop twinkling, Jirra's dance exploded. He jumped into a handstand, flinging his legs into the air. He twirled them sideways like a propeller, then stopped abruptly, balancing on one hand. He sprang into a barrage of pretzel hops, butt spins, and back flips. His writhing body became a blur in the campfire light.

Dropping into a low handstand, he froze with his face just inches from the smoking log. He watched the circling ants with such intensity I thought he might lap them up with a forked tongue.

The devil dance ended as fast as it began. All that remained of Mani's music was a faint, droning whisper. With one final boomerang flip, Jirra leapt away to the edge of the firelight. He did a classic stop, drop, and roll routine in the sand, as if his clothes had caught fire. But I saw no smoke, either from him or—and this rattled me—from the ant log. It looked stone cold, as if Jirra had danced away the flames.

I watched, stunned, as all the ants climbed safely back inside their log home.

After a few timeless moments, Jirra rolled onto his back and propped his hands behind his head like he was settling in for some casual star-gazing.

From a faraway place, I heard Becca's voice. "What the hell was *that*?"

"Shee-it!" Rosie exclaimed "That was insane! Lizard man break-dancing his ass off."

I couldn't speak. Most of me was still tuned in to the hum of Mani's didjeridu. But when I turned to look at him my jaw dropped. He was staring into the fire, sitting cross-legged with both hands on his knees. The didjeridu lay silent across his lap.

The hum trickled from somewhere else, from inside of me, a thrumming in my chest. I felt a warmth rising in me that had nothing to do with the campfire. Whatever Mani had jump-started with his didj now seemed to leak out of me, rippling into the desert, setting it in motion—the fragrant curtain of gum leaves, the stark profile of Kulini Ngura silhouetted against a sea of stars, the moon itself, all pulsing in time to this soft, soothing voice.

Is this a bad case of jet lag?

With that thought, the thrumming faded. The whole scene became a mirage: the trees, the fire, even my friends. I tried to focus on the hills but everything blurred.

I closed my eyes and held my chin in both hands.

"Hey, Ash, you okay?" It was Becca's voice.

I managed a weak nod. The howl of distant dingoes invaded the silence. The only other sounds were the crackling fire and the soft rush of air entering and leaving my lungs.

I suddenly got this weird feeling that I was holding a skull, a living skull, which I was able to ponder as if from outside. It dawned on me that there was enough room inside it to contain the whole world. The boundary between my body and the cool night air dissolved. I couldn't tell where *I* ended and the rest of the planet began.

For a split second, this distinction seemed hilarious to me and I burst out laughing.

Mani's music and Jirra's dance had cracked me open. I was all mush inside. But happy mush.

"What, *what?*" Becca said.

I opened my eyes, surprised to find a moonlit desert misted over by tears of joy.

I reached for her hand and squeezed it. "I'm okay, Becca. Really, I'm okay."

INTO KULINI NGURA

FIREPIT BEHIND JIRRA'S HOUSE
DECEMBER 20TH, 9:00 AM

CTP 0031:44:37

I'm walking barefoot over hot red sand. I choose each step carefully. The ground is scarred with grass stubble that pokes through circles of smoldering ash.

A small group of naked aborigines marches ahead of me. The men carry wooden spears. Most of the women carry babies. A little girl just in front of me clutches a large orange-bellied lizard by the throat. In the other hand, a brown snake hangs limp from a stick. They are walking toward a high ridge of purple hills.

I sharpen my dream eyes. I know these hills. Kulini Ngura. The listening place.

There is a rhythmic hum to the desert that reverberates in my chest. Not like an engine hum. I mean a voice. A low, soothing voice like an old woman singing to herself. I try to run up beside a gray-haired lady trailing behind the group, to see if she is making this sound. But she shuffles ahead with amazing speed, not letting me catch up. I notice that the wrinkled skin on her back is marked by a swirling pattern of raised bumps, like lizard tracks in the sand.

I can't talk to these people but feel oddly at home with them. I know that as long as they are near, I will be safe in this hellishly hot landscape.

As we get closer to the hills, bright green shoots emerge from the charred ground. The shrubs get thicker, taller. The trail leads through a clearing and ends abruptly below a steep wall at the foot of the hills.

The group stops in the clearing. The ground looks beaten down by generations of dancing feet. An old woman shouts. Everyone scatters into the bushes and melts into the green.

The hum is much louder here, almost shaking the ground. It seems to swell from the hill itself. It leaves me dizzy, confused. I peer into the silver-leaved bushes.

I know I am being watched.

A big hollow log sits in the middle of the clearing. Two worn sticks lie on top of it. I reach for them and tap the log once, twice. A deep ringing thump echoes off the rock wall.

I hear a child giggle.

The thrumming gets stronger, faster, like the wound-up beat of an aching heart. I try to follow it, feeling klutzy at first, but eventually finding the groove. As my drumbeat and the land's heartbeat merge, a golden warmth pours from my chest into every cell of my body.

I look down at my hands, surprised to see Uitajuq's small fingers gripping the drumsticks.

At that moment my aborigine guides burst out of the bushes, jumping and laughing. They dance around me with arms spread wide above their heads, then dash for the hill. In a flash they disappear again, this time swallowed, one by one, by the solid rock wall.

SUCKER

CTP 0031:34:51

Something cold and wet grazed my cheek. I slowly rolled onto my back and met the cold yellow eyes of a dingo. I scooched away from him, accidently bopping his muzzle with my knee. The dingo let out a low growl and trotted over to the houses.

I heard a familiar chuckle behind me. Jirra sat on a stone by the dead campfire, whittling a hunk of wood with a foot-long knife. "G'day," he said without looking up from his work.

My brain felt like cold molasses. My chest still rang with the echo of drumbeats. I flopped back in the sand and stared at the gum trees gently swaying above me. The desert sky was dotted with high popcorn clouds. Over the clicking of Jirra's knife I detected the faraway sound of cars honking, people shouting. And there, quite distinct, the beating of drums. I sat up and looked at Jirra. "What's with the drums?"

"Huh?"

Am I still dreaming?

"Can't you hear it?" I said.

Jirra looked up from his carving and squinted at the sky. "Oh … that. Guess the savages have arrived."

"What?"

"Mobbing the east gate."

I felt a stab of stage fright. "You mean the concert's started?"

"Don't chuck a wobbly on me. S'tomorrow. They're just killin' time. Uncle won't let a bloody ant get through that gate 'til he gives the word. His G.I. Joe goons'll hold them back."

I looked at the ring of empty stones around him. Something popped between my ears. "Hey, what'd you do with Rosie and Becca?"

"Yer mates?"

"Like, *yeah.*"

Jirra raised a chin to one of the houses. "Sleepin' it off."

"What about Jack? He was supposed to send a—"

Jirra shrugged. "Probably forgot about ya. Lots going on today, ya know. Better off without 'im."

As my brain woke up, I realized I'd shirked my number one job.

"Yeah, but what about Gabe?"

"Who's Gabe?"

"My blind *tiguaq.*"

"Your what?"

"Oh, sorry. My adopted brother. He needs his pills and—"

"No worries. Rita'll look after 'im. Won't need no pills."

"Yeah, but—"

"You was hummin' funny."

"*What?*"

"In your sleep."

I studied the sand around me. It was all kicked up like I'd been in a wrestling match. There were strange etchings I couldn't begin to identify. Imprints of tails, claws, and hooves. Smaller slitherings in the sand. While I'd slept and dreamed, a swarm of mysterious creatures had crept within inches of my body. "You let me sleep *here* all night?"

"None of my business where you sleep. Ya kinda passed out. A mob of wallabies give you a sniff. Maybe a couple scorpions. Puli chewed on a typey for ya."

"A what?"

"Taipan. Nastiest snake in Australia. One chomp and you're done in half an hour."

"Oh, that's nice." Jirra's dingo lay sprawled in the shade of a tree with one sleepy eye still trained on me. "I don't think he likes me."

"It's snakes he likes." Jirra blew shavings off his carving and stared at it for a long time. Then he shot me that same piercing look I'd seen when he shoved the wounded lizard in my face. A mix of doubt and wonder. "So then, what was ya hummin'?"

My mind drifted back to the weird drum dance at the foot of Kulini Ngura. How my naked guides had run full tilt into solid rock. "Just a dream."

Jirra pulled on his thick lower lip. "Around here, dreams count."

I scooped up a handful of red sand and let it trickle through my fingers. I must have done this ten times or more. Something about this jackaroo made me want to open up, something I didn't trust.

He coaxed me on with a long grin.

"Well … there was this hum out there."

"Where?"

I tossed some sand toward the sacred hills. In the morning sun they were the color of cornmeal.

Jirra's eyes widened for a second, then he rolled off his stone toward me. The way he moved, like a well-oiled gymnast, I thought he was about to fly into another break-dance routine. Maybe a kangaroo knee-dropping into a belly swim. Instead he lay sidewise in the sand, casually propping himself on one elbow and folding his hands. He was so close I could smell the campfire smoke on his shirt. "Okay, lemmee get this right. You dreamed of *those* hills?" he said, pointing a finger over my shoulder. "Kulini Ngura?"

"I guess so."

"That's where it came from?"

"The hum?"

"Yeah, yeah."

"Seemed like it. There was, like, this pulse or a—"

"Heartbeat?"

I pulled back. "You've heard it?"

Jirra looked down at the sand and stabbed it a few times with his knife. "Dunno. Not exactly." He idly drew a circle in the sand. "You alone out there?"

I'd already told him too much. My dream was too fresh, too hot to be blabbing about it to anyone, let alone this muscle-bound desert rat lying close beside me.

I stood up and brushed sand off my legs. "It's all kinda fuzzy." I scanned the ring of houses for signs of life. A wisp of smoke from one chimney, a flock of scrawny chickens, Jirra's dozing dingo with one eye still on me. That was it. These houses had certainly seen better days. "So, which one are they in? We need to go rehearse and—"

"I know a good place to warm up," Jirra said, sounding almost playful.

"Uh, I just *have* to get back to Gabe."

"It's not far."

"You know, I could sure use a bathroom."

"You'd like the place."

"I, uh, I really should call my folks. You got a phone out here?"

Jirra's eyes narrowed and he was looking through me again, tracking something I couldn't see. Then the sparkle returned and he came on strong. "Ya know, ya really oughta stretch yer lungs in the open desert. Get used to our air."

I tried to wipe the sleep from my eyes. "Look, I don't have a clue about this stupid concert. And we haven't touched our drums since, like, Carnegie—"

"Let 'em sleep. It's you Jack wants on stage."

"What?"

"Before you got here, word got out he'd found this … this *Wonder Girl* from way up north. From the land of ice and snow." He crinkled his nose. "It's … Ashby, right?"

"Good God, just like your great-uncle. It's *Ashley*."

Jirra tightened his lips and made a smacking sound. "Yep. Thought so. You're the one. Didn't hear nothing about yer mates."

"We perform together or not at all," I said matter-of-factly.

"Uh-huh. Did ya happen to sign a contract?"

I huffed. "We were basically kidnapped."

Jirra chuckled. "See how *bad* he wants ya."

"So why me?"

Jirra slashed a bunch of lines with his knife. A circle of pin-headed dancers emerged from the red sand. He added a big X in the center. "Called you his secret weapon."

My head started to spin off. "Uh … look, thanks for keeping the snakes off me and everything, but we really have to—"

"Yer friends need their beauty sleep. How's about a little walkabout before brekkie?" Jirra stood up, shoved his knife in a hip sheath, and stretched his arms wide. For a moment he looked like one of the dancers in my dream, only with clothes on. He started walking toward a battered pickup truck caked in dry mud. The letters S-E-T-I were barely readable on the side. "There's a dunny behind the house and I got some sossies in me ute. Come on, be a sport, then." He whistled to his dingo. "Let's go, Puli," he shouted, like everything had been decided.

The ruckus at the east gate seemed to rise with the breeze. I couldn't hear any more drumming.

Am I hallucinating?

I stood by the cold firepit with my hands jammed deep in my pockets. My head and bladder were ready to burst. I felt strangely paralyzed. My mouth, my legs, my brain—nothing seemed to work. I felt like the sand was rising around my ankles, reaching for my body, pulling me into the desert heartland.

Jirra suddenly turned around and grinned at me. "Yer pals'll be right. Me mum'll cook up something for 'em. Let's go. It'll take yer mind off the concert."

A gust of dry wind slapped my face and I recovered my legs. I found the outhouse, then ran back to his truck like I was late for a plane. When I swung open the passenger door I almost fell back on my butt.

Mani sat up, yawning like a lion. "'S 'bout time."

Puli jumped in the back of the truck, Jirra cranked it into gear, and we took off to God knows where.

As we bounced off the only road leading out of his village, it occurred to me that kidnapping might run in the family.

What kind of sucker am I?

LIZARD TRACKS

CROSSING DESERT IN JIRRA'S TRUCK
DECEMBER 20TH, 9:30 AM

CTP 0031:14:47

Jirra was an awesome off-road driver. He put the truck into a kind of dance through humps of sand and dead grass. He knew exactly when to swerve around a bush or to flatten it. Dry seed heads showered the windshield like ocean spray off the bow of a boat.

After a couple of star-spangled head bashes against the cab's roof, I reached for something, anything, to hold on to. My hand landed on a chunk of wood crammed between Mani's thigh and mine. I yanked it out and held it up to the harsh sunlight streaming through the open window. Jirra's carving. As it bobbed madly in front of my face, I could make out the torso and head of an old aborigine woman, naked except for a headband drawn tightly around her long, coiled hair. Her lips and cheeks were drawn back, as if she were humming, and she seemed to be concentrating on something far away, or deep inside. Tucked under both arms were the faces of wide-eyed children, looking out on the world with expressions of wonder and belonging.

Jirra sideswiped a monster mogul of sand and his carving jumped from my hands like a flustered frog. Mani's hairy arm shot in front of my nose and he plucked it out of the air before it flew out of the truck. As he cradled it face down in his lap, a chill ran up my spine. I recognized a strange pattern on the old woman's back and shoulders—a swirl of raised bumps like lizard tracks in the sand.

WALKABOUT
DESERT EAST OF KULINI NGURA
DECEMBER 20TH, 10:30 AM

CTP 0030:14:47

Jirra slammed on the brakes in the middle of nowhere. A wall of red dust fell on us from behind. Before I could see much past the windshield, some animal sprang over the truck's cab, thumped on the hood and bounded off into the dust. Then another flew over the truck.

"What the—" I said.

Mani looked at me with an amused pout. "Crikey, they're after you."

"Who?"

"Wallabies."

A third animal followed on the heels of the last. Puli.

We sat in silence as the dust cleared. I could see no landmarks—no distinctive trees, boulders, trails. Nothing. Just red sand, ankle-biting grass, a few mangy shrubs, and the hunchback hills of Kulini Ngura, the listening place. My mental map from the chopper ride put us somewhere near the ear lobe.

My eyes locked on to the sacred hills, already quivering in the mid-morning heat. A parade of wind towers marched across the rolling sky-line. The blades on most of them were bent backward or had fallen off completely. Any remaining rotors swung lamely back and forth like broken pendulums—vandalized by a vengeful spirit wind.

"Right, then," Jirra said as he threw on a grungy cowboy hat. "'S not far."

"What's not far?" I said.

"Little surprise for ya. You'll like it. Only for *special* guests."

Jack's image of drifting passively above Niagara Falls popped into my head. I'd been swept into a storm surge of crazy events, tossed between waves of joy and currents of sheer panic. Some fathomless force carried me farther, faster, deeper into the unknown. And my guts told me I'd soon go over the edge.

I'd forgotten what it was like to get up in the morning, eat Cheerios, read a book, call a friend.

Had I ever lived that way?

"Whatever," I said.

Jirra reached for a cucumber-shaped thing on the windshield and shoved it in my face. It smelled of garlic and roadkill and was plastered with thick dust.

"Ya hungry?"

I recoiled in my seat. "What the hell is that?"

Jirra blew the dust from one end and gnawed off a piece with his kangaroo teeth. "Roo snags. Me mum made it 'erself."

"Shot it, too, she did," Mani said as he tore into the foul-smelling meat.

I jumped out of the truck, ready to puke.

The heat instantly took my mind off my stomach. It was like stepping onto a fresh field of lava. Sand poured into my sandals and singed my toes. "Ow, ow, ow, ow!" I started hopping around in front of the truck until I heard Jirra's hyena laugh from inside.

I scowled at Jirra and Mani as they passed the evil sausage back and forth. Then they piled out, slammed the truck doors, and started hoofing it toward the hills.

"Hey!" I yelled. "Where *are* you going?"

"Like I says, it's a surprise," Jirra yelled back.

"Why don't we drive?"

"Wouldn't want to get stuck out 'ere in one of these dunes now, would ya?"

I squinted around me. The land had changed. Here the sand was sculpted into grass-lined waves that seemed to ride up to meet Kulini Ngura. As if it had just risen out of the Earth like some desert-prowling submarine. Our ride to this point had been the most ass-numbing, head-splitting experience of my life. It made snowmobiling over broken sea ice seem like a carpet ride.

To drive farther would be suicide.

Sweat poured off my forehead, blurring my vision, stinging my eyes. My tongue greedily lapped up whatever moisture fell near my lips. It was a struggle to swallow. I felt my throat closing. Each breath fried my lungs.

I looked to where I'd last seen Jirra and Mani. They weren't exactly waiting for me. And I'd get broiled alive if I stayed in the truck. I had no choice but to follow my captors.

After stumbling along behind them for a few minutes, I glanced up to see Mani standing on a high dune, looking back the way we'd come. He held his arms above his head like he was having a big stretch. The way he swayed them around told me it was more than that. I could see his mouth moving but the only sounds were the slow, mournful song of some unseen bird and the scratch of wind-tossed grass.

When I turned around to see what he was looking at, a gust of wind came out of nowhere, almost knocking me over. Another gust came up right after it from the opposite direction. They joined in a dancing funnel of sand. I'd seen something like this up north, where a small spinning wind picks up loose snow and shapes it into bottles, bowling pins, or flower vases. Dad calls them snow devils. We used to chase them as kids, falling over each other with squeals of laughter. But I felt something sinister here. Like a giant eraser, this mini tornado obliterated my footprints from the desert sand. The slate of my existence had been wiped clean. Not to mention that finding the truck would now be impossible.

When I turned back, Mani was gone. I trudged ahead, cursing Jirra under my breath.

The shrubs and grass got thicker as we approached the hills. A triangular clump of distant trees looked like a thatch of green pubic hair on the mother rock. The plants seemed to open before us, then slam shut behind, choking off escape. But Jirra always found a way, whistling down an invisible trail like he was strolling on a city sidewalk.

I felt an odd temptation to reach out to a tuft of grass. I bent down slowly and put a hand on a clump, only to find my palm stuck with tiny spines an inch or so before I'd thought I'd make contact.

"Oops," Jirra said as he gently picked them out. "You don't want to do that."

"Thanks for the warning."

"*Everything's* spiny in Australia."

"You too, eh?"

"Hah."

Mani, maybe five times my age, had trotted way ahead of us. I'd forgotten about him until he shouted, "Snake!"

I hopped closer to Jirra, brushing against his broad shoulders. He stepped aside like it was his fault.

"Are they all poisonous?" I said.

"Naw. Must be over a hundred kinds in Australia. Only 'bout twenty-five'll kill ya." He cupped his hands over his mouth. "Where, amari?"

Mani swept his arm up and down the trail in our direction.

Jirra picked up a long stick and, without glancing at the ground, kept walking.

I hadn't had a thing to drink since I got up. The sun seemed to boil moisture from the back of my throat. My tongue got so stiff it felt like a dry sponge between my teeth. "You got any water?"

"Naw. Plenty a' water up ahead."

Out of the blue, Jirra started making cat-like hissing sounds through his teeth. Puli, who I hadn't seen since the truck, blasted out of the bushes with bloodlust in his eyes. He ran up to Jirra and jumped to his waist, begging for some command.

"Puli, *liru!*" Jirra said as he thrust his arm at the ground ahead of us.

I jumped to Jirra's side almost knocking him over. "What?"

He grinned. "Like Mani said, snake."

I felt as angry as afraid. "Nice little walkabout through a snake pit. Like, just *where* are you taking me?"

"You'll like it. Puli'll clear out any snakes."

I dug in both heels and looked back the way we'd come. No sign of a trail or truck. Just scorched sand and saber-toothed grass.

"Wouldn't try that if I was you," Jirra said as he continued ahead.

I folded my arms and pretended to hang tough, waiting for Jirra to turn around.

He kept walking.

"Shit," I said, as his rumpled cowboy hat disappeared behind a dune. I took one more look over my shoulder, kicked up a wall of sand, then tore after him as fast as my wasted body would let me.

What really pissed me off was that he knew that I knew my life was totally in his hands.

"No snakes where you live?" he said as I tripped up beside him.

I had to think about that for a minute. My brain was shutting down. "Nope. Not one. No snakes, no scorpions, no crocodiles."

"Just bears. Big bloody bears." He turned to me with a look of true amazement. "How can you *live* with 'em?"

I laughed in spite of my cardboard mouth, aching head, and simmering anger. "Just like you, I guess. Sic me dog on 'em," I said in my first attempt at Aussie talk.

He laughed.

I calmed down.

Then I remembered. Jacques was dead.

I remembered how he died, buried by a hillside of melted muck. I remembered how the hell I'd ended up down here after spilling my guts at a UN climate change conference, how some wacko had lured us onto his private jet with rich food, promises of fame, and threats of blackmail. Now it all seemed like some dreamy play, its script written on water, being vaporized by the desert sun.

We walked on in silence. Time seemed to turn in on itself, like the melted clocks in Salvador Dali's weird paintings. The sun beat down my thirst, my fear, my anger, until they seemed to drip off me like candle wax. Somewhere inside, beyond my muddled brain and weakened body, a wick caught fire, burning with a fierce desire to *listen*.

To what, I didn't know.

The words of Pema Rinpoche, my Buddha buddy in New York, barged into my head. *You will know what to do. Listen!*

I stared up at the red rock, speechless.

A narrow path eventually opened in front of us, revealing a dry creek bed. It was lined with willowy trees covered in shaggy gray bark. Tiny red flowers fell from the flimsy canopy and sprinkled on the bare ground like drops of clotted blood.

The creek bed widened into a round clearing.

I stopped in my tracks. I peered into the bushes, expecting to hear a giggling child. I looked for the footprints of dancers in the sand.

We were alone.

No sign of Mani except for a few widely spaced dents in the sand that led to—guess where—the foot of Kulini Ngura. Its base was pretty much where I expected it, a stone's throw away from the clearing, just like in my dream.

The feeling of déjà vu shook me. I felt like I was watching the rerun of a movie in which I'd played the star role.

My brain clicked back on in the half-shade of the trees. I watched everything around me with cat-like concentration—the bushes, the sand, the rock wall, Jirra's slightest expression.

Though I promised myself I would never tell him, somehow I knew this was exactly where I should be. I felt a strange sense of belonging, as if my whole life had been programmed for this moment.

Above the sharp scent of gum trees, a faint new ribbon in the air made my nostrils flare. I impulsively grabbed Jirra's arm. "Water? *Here?*"

"I reckon," he said, smiling like I'd passed some sort of test.

For the first time that morning, I struck down the path ahead of Jirra. I followed Mani's prints until they disappeared in a thick clump of bushes. I looked back at Jirra, who just shrugged and gave me a dopey grin. I darted along the edge of the bushes, inspecting the ground for some way through.

The rock wall was so close I could see individual pebbles poking out of the sandstone. Some were shiny and threw a strange rainbow light. Wisps of some distant memory, some forgotten dream, floated into my head. The sparking jewels seemed to pull me forward.

"The hell with it," I said to myself and stepped back to take a running leap into the bushes, trail or no trail. Just as I was about to fling myself forward, I heard a low growl, then some scuffling directly in front of me. The bushes bobbed and shook, then out burst Puli with a big brown snake dangling from his mouth. He bounded over to Jirra and dropped it at his feet, tail wagging.

"Good on ya, Puli," Jirra said, scratching behind the dingo's ears.

Jirra picked up the dead snake by the neck. It was close to six feet long.

"Is that one of those typey things?" I said, backing away.

"Taipan? Naw. Only a king brownie." Jirra whipped out his foot-long knife from a hip sheath and, with one flick, cut off the snake's head.

Puli downed the head in one gulp before it hit the ground.

"They won't bother ya unless ya step on 'em," Jirra said, watching blood gush over his hand. "Then it's curtains, I'm afraid." He hung the beheaded snake on the branch of a tree with bark so smooth it looked almost human. "This'll make good tucker for lunch."

"What happened to Mani?"

"Ahh, snakes won't mess with 'im."

"No, I mean, where did he go?"

"Give up?"

"Just *tell* me!"

Jirra stroked his chin. "Jeez. Wouldn't it rot yer socks if we came all this bloody way and lost the trail!"

I could have slugged him.

"Right, then," he said with raised eyebrows.

Jirra walked up to the spot where Puli had appeared and parted the bushes. "You were pretty much on it."

I bent low to study a hard-packed dip in the ground, probably worn down by generations of Jirra's people. The bushes arched over it like a tunnel.

"How could I miss this?" I said.

"'S not for everyone to see, I reckon."

"Like our tracks back at the truck?"

"Yep. Mani's willi-willi swept 'em up good, di'n'it."

"You mean that little tornado thing back there?"

"Yep. Uncle Jack doesn't even know about this place. Couldn't spot it even with all his spy satellites and soldier boys."

"What's so special about it?"

Jirra gestured for me to lead. "Go on, check it out."

"Uh, no thanks. You first."

"Right." Brandishing his knife, Jirra dropped to his knees and started crawling like a commando through the snake-infested bushes.

MALA

KULINI NGURA
DECEMBER 20TH, 12:30 PM

CTP 0028:14:47

Jirra's beat-up desert boots disappeared ahead of me in a spray of red sand. I stood there, dumbly watching the bushes shake and roll as he scrabbled through them. The commotion got my head spinning. My face felt like the crust on week-old bread, my mouth like beef jerky. I'd sweated my last drop of water somewhere, way back, on the disappearing trail.

I would've happily passed out on the spot until I felt a jolt in my chest, as if Uitajuq had elbowed me in the ribs from the inside out.

I fell to all fours and dove in after Jirra.

The bushes closed in around me. They seemed amazingly lush for desert plants, all loaded with feathery leaves. Perfect cover for a pissed-off snake to coil, aim, and strike as I blindly squirmed past. Hours seemed to pass as I scraped my elbows through the coarse sand, dodged branches bristling with spines, ate Jirra's dust, and imagined snake fangs clamping onto my neck. With Puli's hot breath on my heels, I was boxed in from all sides. This iced the cake for pretty much all of my phobias—snakes, crowded spaces, losing control.

I popped out of the green tunnel as if from a birth canal. What I saw melted all my pain. There was Jirra, wiping blood from his knife as he crouched beside a still pond of emerald green water.

"It's okay to drink?" I said, wiping sand off my scratched-up arms.

He turned my way and his face broke into a coy grin. He was staring at my chest. I looked down to discover that my left boob was hanging out through a fresh rip in my tank top and bra.

"Ah, yeah. No worries. Drink yer fill."

I tucked myself together as best I could and knelt beside him. I scooped up handful after handful of water and greedily drank it down. It was delightfully cool, with a faint sulfury taste.

"That'll make ya real strong, all right," he said.

I nodded quickly, now sucking back directly from the pond surface just like Puli.

"The snake blood, I mean."

I stopped in mid-gulp and sprayed what was left in my mouth in Jirra's face.

"Ta for that. Reckon I needed a shower."

I moved as far away from Jirra as I could and was about to dunk my whole head in the water when I noticed another set of fresh boot tracks in the sand. They led one way, right to the edge of the pond.

"What the—?"

"Find another snake? Scorpion, maybe?"

I'd forgotten about scorpions. "Weird. Mani's footprints."

Jirra strolled over and glanced down at the sand. "Uh-huh. What's weird about 'em?"

"They just end."

"Yep. Guess Mani felt like a swim."

"Sure but—" I looked into the cool, clear water. The bottom dipped steeply toward the base of an overhanging ledge of rock. It cast a black shadow over the deepest part of the pond. All I could see was a thin trail of silver bubbles rushing up out of the darkness. I suddenly drew back at the sight of my own sweat-stained face and tousled hair reflected against the naked wall of Kulini Ngura.

I turned to Jirra, who shrugged, kicked off his boots, and dove headfirst into the water.

An impossible number of minutes passed. My throat tightened. I thought I might choke. I gaped into the dark water. A gust of wind set a bush beside the pond swaying, as if daring me to dive in. I jumped to my feet, surprised by my concern for Jirra and a strange longing to be with him—this mysterious kangaroo cowboy who'd dragged me into his scorched alien world.

In my whole life I'd never felt so alone.

After enough time had passed to drown a whale, I caught some movement deep underwater. The whites of two eyes against a dark chocolate face.

"Jirra!" I shouted.

His arms hovered limp at his side as he slowly rose to the surface like a bloated corpse. An explosion of bubbles erupted from his lips just before breaking the surface.

The bugger was laughing.

"What's the frickin' idea?" I blurted.

"Come on in," he said. "The water's grouse."

"Gross?"

"Naw, it's *grouse*. Ya know, excellent."

"Where'd you go?"

"Secret."

"Just *tell* me!"

Jirra sculled toward me. "Tell ya what, I'll *show* ya."

He shot his arm at me with a huge spray.

The shock of water on my face made me want to weep. Or giggle hysterically. I was basically a basketcase.

I let my hand fall into his and he gently pulled me into the pond. We treaded water face to face. I felt suddenly tingly and light, enveloped by a healing presence that lifted my spirits and rewired my brain.

"Right. Now do what I say and ya won't cark it."

"What?"

"Die. You won't *die*."

"Oh, thanks. Just do me a favor and speak English."

"Right. So it's like this. We go down for a bit, then right for a bit. Go left and you're—"

"Carked."

Jirra chuckled. "Totally. It's a maze down there. They'll never find ya. Well ... maybe when this pond finally dries up, some critter'll dig ya out. Chew on yer bones."

"It's shrinking?"

"Like yer ice, I reckon. Pond's been here forever. Twice as big when Mani and Rita were tykes. But, ya know. All that climate shit."

"Here, too?"

"Oh, yeah. Nobody's safe anymore."

We treaded water in silence for a moment. Jirra looked up at the towering flank of Kulini Ngura and his mouth popped open. I followed his gaze to a deep dimple in the rock wall not far above our heads. Staring down at us from the edge of the shadows was a small animal, about the size of an Arctic hare. It stood on its hind legs just like a kangaroo and its tiny humanlike forepaws were clasped together as if in prayer.

"What the hell's that?" I said.

At the sound of my voice the animal started swinging its forepaws from side to side, then threw back its head and spun around three times, like in some kind of crazy trance.

Jirra looked at me with a flicker of amazement, then back at the animal. "Mala wallaby. Seen maybe three in my life. S'posed to be extinct. Mani says this rock wouldn't be here without 'em."

A thrill floods the small round body of the mala wallaby. It spins once for the wind in his blood, once for the red hills he protects, and once to welcome the human presence who hears the land's healing song, who carries it inside her and keeps it safe.

I felt my chest open as something sacred circled our floating bodies. Something alive in the water, in the spiral dance of the wallaby, in the swirl of distant clouds.

I realized that Jirra was still holding my hands.

He fixed his charcoal eyes on me—so much like Rita's—like he'd felt the same thing. "So, yeah, anyways, once you're out of the maze, it's level for a bit, then up for a bit, then you're in."

"In what?"

"You'll like it."

"You keep saying that."

"'S'truth. By the way, you'll need heaps of air."

It dawned on me how constricted my throat had been just minutes ago. "Uh, I'm kinda prone to asthma attacks. Specially if I'm stressed out."

"You'll be right. Just relax. Enjoy the ride." Jirra squeezed my hand. Hard. "Oh yeah, and whatever you do, don't let go. Got it?"

I grabbed his other hand and squeezed back.

He pulled me closer.

Locked in a tight circle, we gulped several lungfuls of air until our breathing came together as one.

"One hand's plenty," he said, prying his fingers out of mine.

He brought his face close, locking onto my eyes, leading our breaths. We took one last gulp of air then plunged, the dark water closing over us.

SILENT SCREAM

UNDERWATER TUNNEL, KULINI NGURA
DECEMBER 20TH, 12:50 PM

CTP 0027:54:31

The last thing I saw on the way down was a rough circle, crudely chiseled into a submerged rock face. As I brushed past it, two gouged-out eyes looked back at me above a mouth locked open in a silent scream.

After that, everything went black.

Between Jirra's broad shoulders and my wide hips, there was barely room for the two of us to squeeze through the underwater tunnel. Of course, I forgot all of Jirra's careful instructions the moment we ducked our heads under. Except for one: *Don't let go.* I could barely tell which was up or down, right or left. All I needed to do was hang on and this desert rat would save my life.

So, guess how I felt when he let go?

It happened at a sharp turn in the tunnel. Still in total darkness, I'd smashed my skull against the wall and, stunned by the impact, accidentally released half of my air. The water swept away my tears. My stomach started rocking in and out like it does when you've hung out too long on the bottom of a swimming pool.

Jirra chose this moment to shoot forward and my hand slipped from his.

His foot bopped my nose.

Two, maybe three precious seconds passed—the longest of my life. I thrashed alone in a watery tomb. Then, like a thunderclap, I remembered the joyful dance of the wallaby. Somehow it gave me the strength to make one desperate lunge for Jirra. My hand connected with his ankle and I clamped on.

The tunnel narrowed even more, squeezing in on me from all sides. But I would not let go. My one cheerful thought was: *If I drown, you drown!*

I was just sane enough to notice a slight upward tilt to our path. The tunnel widened and Jirra shifted back beside me, this time snugging his arm around my heaving waist.

Then, light.

It was a smile-shaped sliver of dappled light, flashing red and white like the gums and teeth of a mother welcoming her children.

We rocketed to the surface, a couple of spent seals shooting for a breathing hole.

I floated on my back, gulping air with my eyes closed. For the moment, I didn't know or care where I was. I knew only that I was alive. I could breathe. For now, at least, no critter would be picking my bones.

BAT SHIT

CATHEDRAL CAVE, KULINI NGURA
DECEMBER 20TH, 1:00 PM

CTP 0027:44:18

"You right?" Jirra's voice seemed to ricochet at me from all directions.

I cracked one eye open. After the total gloom of the tunnel, the sunlight now flooding my face was brutal.

"Ya seem to like the spotlight, don'tcha. Really pours in 'ere this time a year."

I rolled onto my belly and slowly breast-stroked out of the blinding light. My eyes gradually adjusted. I stared up at the head of a giant walrus with six-foot-long tusks, dangling over my crotch.

I yelped, kicking myself backwards and smashing my head against a rock.

"Shit!"

"Gaw, take it easy on yer noggin."

I spun around to see Jirra sitting cross-legged on a hump of rock about three feet above me. I looked back at the walrus, a bizarre sculpture of fused stalactites hanging over the water. Other weird forms, all gray and drooling, seemed to sprout from cracks in the red walls and ceiling. A chandelier of bird claws, a stack of butter-drenched pancakes fit for a giant, vulva-shaped folds as big as a bus.

In the dancing light reflected off the water, I noticed, here and there, the same rainbow sparkles I'd seen outside. Droopy vines reached all the way down from the skylight and disappeared underwater. I was floating on the liquid floor of a natural cathedral twenty stories high. We were hidden, worlds away from anything, in the heart of Kulini Ngura.

JAMIE BASTEDO

You'd think I might have drowned in the aching beauty of this secret, sacred place. One look and I knew it had to be a mega power spot for Jirra's people.

Instead, I felt overcome with a deep feeling of … nothing much. I was exhausted. And hungry. I could have eaten half a caribou. The ridiculous roller-coaster ride in Jirra's truck, the searing march across the sand, the snakes, the tunnel. All for this? Real nice, but there was no rapture here for me. I felt like a tourist who'd busted into a locked church. Something in me died back in that tunnel and I mostly just wanted to go home.

I gazed numbly into the dark edges of the pool, wondering, *Why did Jirra bring me here?* And, more puzzling, *Why did I let him?*

"Room for one more up here," he called.

I tried to claw my way up through a shower of loose pebbles that fell on my head.

"Need a lift?"

"No, thanks … Ouch!"

Jirra politely watched me suffer for a while, then reached down and offered a hand. I grabbed it and he hauled me up with amazing ease.

"Ya done good, Ashley. Hung on like I told ya."

At least he got my name right. "Yeah … until you took off on me."

"Right. A bit tight back there. Couldn't nip through together. Might get dangerous."

"*Might?*"

"'S always a little spooky the first time. Not far, really. You can go first on the way out, if ya like."

It never occurred to me that we'd have to go back through that terrifying tunnel. "There's, like, no other way out?"

Jirra pointed to the crescent-shaped hole in the cave's ceiling. "Not unless ya got a rocket pack."

I pointed to a vine hanging near Jirra. "What about those?"

He reached out and gave it a quick tug. There was an echoing crack high above us and a coil of tangled vine landed in a cloud of dust beside him. "Wouldn't hold two fleas."

I stared up at the gash of light. "Anybody ever climb down, I mean, with ropes and stuff?"

"Must be a million holes in these hills, most of 'em dead ends. Take 'em forever to find it." Jirra inspected a toenail. "Wouldn't make it anyway. Something would happen."

"Something?"

"Can't let just any hippie with a helmet come swingin' in here uninvited."

"Guess I made the grade."

"Not dead yet, are ya?"

"Feel like it."

"See them bones down there?"

I leaned forward to look into the water. All sunlight and shadow. "Uh, no."

"Back there. Where you go in. Not everybody makes it."

"Now you tell me."

"Thought I did."

"What's with the face?"

Jirra twisted his lips into a Jack-o'-lantern smile. "What's wrong with it?"

"On the rock."

"Oh, him. S'posed to keep out the riff-raff."

I glanced up at the leering walrus. The palace walls were closing in on me.

"So … this is it, what you wanted to show me?"

Jirra threw a stone in the pool. The ripples set off another volley of rainbow sparks across the rock. "Not quite."

"So?"

"There's more."

I recalled Rita's story about Jack discovering "miles and miles of caves" in these hills. "Why the hell did you drag me here?" I shouted. Crazy echoes made a mockery of my anger.

Jirra feigned surprise. "Hell, who's the one who jumped in me ute? Who followed me down the trail? Who dove in the pond?" He tugged on his scruffy T-shirt with both hands. "Ya don't see any whips or chains on me, do ya?"

I had to laugh.

"No handcuffs, either. Not my style."

I looked squarely at him for a few seconds. Baffling. Maddening. A genuine horse's ass. But I saw no demons behind his eyes. Not like his great-uncle Jack. "You got any food?"

"Right. Thought you'd never ask." He reached deep into his jeans and yanked out the kangaroo sausage that had me almost puking back at the truck.

I grabbed it from his open hand and took a big chomp out of it. "Hmm. Not bad. A tad salty."

"'S blood."

I took another chomp. "No probs. We drink seal blood all the time."

"I mean, from yer noggin." Jirra leaned close, ran a thumb down my cheek, and held it in front of my nose.

I jerked back, nearly choking on the sausage. I cautiously touched the top of my bashed head. Two goose eggs and an open wound that stung like hell. "Oh, God. What a mess."

"She'll be right. Little souvenir, that's all." Jirra stood up, stretched casually, and walked over to a dark corner of the cave. There was a brief fluttering sound and I thought I saw a shadow streak across the circle of sunlit water. I heard Jirra scratching around in the dirt. He returned with a mass of brown powder in his hand.

"What's that?"

"Magic potion." Jirra studied my head for a moment. "What happened there?"

"Where?" I felt oddly exposed.

He gently touched the bald spot over my right ear. You could only see it when my hair was wet. I'd made sure of that since the lightning strike with a couple of bobby pins.

"Oh, that. I, uh … got in the way of a lightning bolt."

Jirra let out a long, slow whistle. The sound ricocheted off the cave walls and ceiling. "Well, fuck-a-duck," he whispered. "It's true, then."

"What's true?"

"Nuthin'. Hold still."

He spit on the powder a few times and stirred it with a finger. Without a word he reached up and started dabbing it on my fresh wound.

I cringed but didn't pull away. His touch alone was somehow healing. What worried me wasn't the pain but a sickly sweet smell that rose from his hand. "What reeks?"

"'S just bat shit."

I stood up so fast one foot slid over the edge and I fell ass-over-tea-kettle into the water.

Jirra looked down at me, deadpan. "Good idea. Clean ya up a bit."

I sucked in a huge mouthful of water and sprayed it at him. But he was too high and the water fell back in my face.

He leaned out of sight and the cave filled with boyish laughter.

As the last echo faded, a new sound took its place. A sharp, rhythmic clicking that made me stop treading water and sink to my nose. My eyes darted from wall to wall, trying to find the source. I noticed one side of the roof dipped sharply toward the water, ending in another dark tunnel. The sound seemed to come from there.

I heard the plunk of pebbles, followed a second later by Jirra doing a cannonball inches from my face.

"You trying to kill me?" I yelled when he finally popped up on the dark side of the pool. I glimpsed only the glint off his wet curly hair and a pearly glow from his teeth.

"Up for another little swim?"

"Actually, no. Not again," I muttered, blowing bubbles in the water.

I watched the darkness swallow him. "*Not again!*" I shouted, my words mocking me from all sides.

"Come on, you'll like it," came his disembodied voice.

I lifted an arm and slapped a huge angel-wing of spray after him. The only damage inflicted was a wicked sting on my arm. I gulped down my pride and porpoised after Jirra into the dark.

SOMETHING BRIGHT

SWIMMING BETWEEN CAVES, KULINI NGURA
DECEMBER 20TH, 1:20 PM

CTP 0027:24:36

"No worries. Keep yer head up and you'll be right."

If Jirra was really that interested in me, I could think of better ways to get us holding hands. But there we were again, clamped together, swimming in a pitch-black tunnel to God knows where.

At least this time we could stay on the surface. In the pitch-black, I couldn't tell where the ceiling or walls were, so I covered my head with my free hand and held onto Jirra with the other. He basically towed me through the water like a dead weight.

The clicking sound got louder, faster, filling the tunnel, boring its way into my brain. There was something hypnotizing about it, vaguely familiar. Then a new sound, at the edge of hearing, teased my ears. A low, oscillating vibration like the rumble of drawn-out thunder.

I kicked myself forward beside Jirra. I could smell kangaroo on his breath. "Mani?"

"Yep. Reckon he's warmin' up for the concert."

"In *here*?"

"Sure, why not? 'S good a place as any."

The rumble got louder and I recognized the low droning sound of Mani's didj. There was a playfulness in his music that I'd not heard the night before, as if he were trying to catch all the echoes and weave them into one pure sound.

Something bright jumped inside of me. In spite of the darkness, the blood, and the bones, I suddenly felt very safe.

My mind flipped to Gabe, dear Gabe, always living in darkness like this, always listening. He could spend hours listening to the ocean surf crash on the Spit or pulling subtle harmonics out of his fiddle that no one but our dog Jacques could catch. Whatever he heard, lost in his sightless world, it always seemed to put a big smile on his face. My mother called it deep listening. As Mani's music flooded the black tunnel, I caught an inkling of what that must feel like. I almost envied Gabe and his blindness.

A shiver of disappointment cut through me when I saw a crack of light ahead. I actually closed my eyes, clinging to the delicious sound of Mani's didj.

Until it died.

Jirra shot us forward with quick, powerful strokes. The tunnel opened to a pool like the last one, rimmed on all sides by high crumbly walls. Before I could retrieve my hand, Jirra lifted it high. Something like a crocodile paw grabbed it and yanked me out of the water.

MAMA PASH

JEWEL CAVE, KULINI NGURA
DECEMBER 20TH, 1:30 PM

CTP 0027:14:44

"Right nice, i'n'it."

Mani sat cross-legged on a rocky platform above the pool. Like Jirra, Mani had the muscles of a body builder, in spite of his snow-white hair and wrinkled face. He'd pulled me out of the water like a well-hooked char. A black didjeridu crawling with golden snakes sat across his lap. He casually cast his eyes around a cave drenched in a miracle light.

Rings of sedimentary rock wrapped around us in an almost perfect sphere. The bright red and orange layers—the exact colors of Mani and Darri's headbands—broke at the ceiling into a tiny round skylight. A shaft of raw sunshine poured through, bounced off the water surface, and filled the cave with shimmering light. Poking out of the rock layers were the same sparkling pebbles I'd seen by the other ponds. These ones were polished and deliberately set in a tight spiral pattern that swirled up to the skylight. There were thousands of them, scattering thick rainbow beams in every direction. I felt encased inside a diamond.

"It's … it's awesome," I mumbled.

"Opal," Jirra said as he scrambled out of the water. "Opal to die for. Wouldn't a mob a' miners like to get their mitts on this place."

Mani chuckled. "Yeah. When hell freezes over."

I gawked.

"Welcome to Jewel Cave," Jirra said. "Told ya you'd like it."

"Can't let just any bloke wander in here," Mani said.

"Yeah, but … why me?"

Jirra glanced at Mani as if for approval. Mani tipped his chin at a wall across from us. Part of it had been smoothed into a square rock canvas plastered in paintings. Like some kind of prehistoric video screen.

Jirra sprang up like he'd been waiting for this moment for some time and dove into the water. He climbed out just below the paintings. I felt strangely light-headed, almost drunk. I managed to find my legs and tiptoed over to him along a narrow rock ledge above the pool. I passed paintings of big-mouthed stick-people, big-breasted women who seemed to be jumping on trampolines, big-bellied ants dancing in a circle around a coiled snake. Twirling wallabies, soaring eagles, human hands that seemed to glow. Boomerangs, dingo paws, lizard tracks scrawled in the desert floor.

Some of the images looked like doodlings. Others clearly told a story. All seemed as old as the red rock itself.

Jirra watched me closely as he stood beside one of the bigger rock paintings. There was a story here, for sure. As soon as I laid eyes on it, I got all fidgety inside, like Uitajuq was jabbing me in the ribs again.

A big-boobed lady stood in the center, flailing on a pumpkin-shaped drum. A jagged flash of lightning sizzled directly over her head. Above that floated a semicircle of kangaroos, lizards, and other weird animals I couldn't identify. Wiggly arrows sprang out to her from the mouth of each animal. More arrows flew out from her drum to a lower semi-circle of other drummers—lots of them. A thin blue line wrapped all the figures together in a circle, broken at the top and bottom by a roaring campfire.

Something about the lower fire caught my eye. I leaned closer. The flames were moving upside down.

"What gives?" I said.

Jirra tapped a finger on the hot drummer in the center. "You remind Mani of this sheila."

Another jab in the ribs. "What?" I looked back across the pool at

Mani. He sat with his eyes closed, slowly rocking back and forth, the didj still in his lap. He cradled a grapefruit-sized rock in his hands, close to his lips, like he was whispering to it.

"Who is she?" I asked Jirra.

"Pretty spunky, I reckon. Decent boobage. We call her Mama Pash. Bit of a lightning rod, ya might say."

I felt a tickle under my scalp, like the top of my head was about to float off. I heard a loud splash behind me.

Mani's rock.

The ripples set off a kaleidoscope of dazzling light. I scrunched my eyes shut.

Mani chose this moment to let her rip on his didj.

He started with the playful riffs I'd heard in the tunnel, toying with echoes, flying high out of earshot, opening the drone into ten thousand threads. The effect was intoxicating and my body started to sway.

At one point, I felt the steadying touch of Jirra's hand on my shoulder, but something kept my eyes closed.

Mani spun a web of living sound around me that filled the cave, seeped into its walls, then burst out of Kulini Ngura to spread across the desert like the shadow of a welcome cloud.

The music lifted me out of my skin and carried me over the barren red sand. I watched a tide of life spread out before me—desert flowers exploding with red and yellow blooms, tiny chicks breaking out of their eggs, young kangaroos riding high in their mothers' pouches.

Mani soared, lifting me so high I could see forests and mountains rise before me. I watched oceans roll to every horizon, breaking on other lands and—there!—the sea ice of home.

I flew higher and higher on the wings of the didj until the land, water and ice fell into shadow and all I could see was a thin blue line draping the Earth, just like the halo surrounding Mama Pash and all her drummers.

That's where Mani ditched me.

HEALING SONG

JEWEL CAVE, KULINI NGURA
DECEMBER 20TH, 1:50 PM

CTP 0026:56:41

Mani's music cut out as if someone had pulled a plug. I started to fall, slowly at first, almost imperceptibly, then faster and faster like a duck sprayed with buckshot.

I plunged into a black hole of deathly silence.

A tsunami of panic swept through me. I was about to scream when I felt Mani's crocodile hand clap over my mouth.

"No! Listen," he commanded.

I struggled to open my eyes.

His other hand covered them. "*Listen!*"

Mani's rumbling voice came to me as if through a thick door.

I fought against him but he held me with a gentle strength. The second I gave up, his hands dropped away.

A kernel of trust told me to let go and do as he said. I kept my eyes shut and listened. For what, I didn't know. But the more I concentrated, the slower I fell, until I was soon free-floating in a limbo world with my Uitajuq ears on full alert.

It began like a breath. A deep, shuddering breath like the sound of a million surfacing whales. At first it was short and labored, as if fighting some great sickness. There was a raw tightness about it that cut me like a knife. Then, a new sound. My own breaths, rising and falling exactly in time with what had to be, must be, the breath of the Earth, now thrumming with mine.

Sila's breath.

In spite of a creeping pain, I listened with all my might. The sound swelled. It broke up. It filled my floating body with a planet-sized chorus of whispered screams. Screams for help.

Sila's children.

I felt something break inside me as if a hammer had struck and shattered solid rock. What rushed through the cracks was a great gush of love for a wounded Earth.

I opened my mouth. This time no hand clapped over it. I let fly a throat-singing number I'd never heard or sung before. It started off low and slow, like undercurrents in the deepest ocean. Soothing harmonic layers wove their way into the song, creating tones that seemed to wrap the whole world in a healing embrace. It was a tapestry that had a distinct rounded shape like the planet itself.

The second time through I was startled to hear another voice join mine. It seamlessly picked up the thread of my song, like we'd rehearsed it a hundred times before. I carried on, eyes still closed, bathing in the song's healing power. The other voice merged with mine, humming in my flesh, a twin to my own.

It was the drum that opened my eyes.

I saw Mani perched on the rock ledge, leaning back on his hands and swinging his legs above the water. Jirra stood in a shadowed corner of the cave, beating a pumpkin-shaped drum in time with my healing song. He watched me with an intensity I now understood as he sang along in perfect unison.

TEN THOUSAND DRUMS

JEWEL CAVE, KULINI NGURA
DECEMBER 20TH, 2:05 PM

CTP 0026:41:37

As Jirra and I began the third cycle of our song, Mani jumped up, grabbed the drum from Jirra and placed it at my feet. "Your turn."

Our voices trailed off.

I felt unsteady, like a bird settling on a broken tree branch. "Your didj … Incredible … I heard this amazing—"

"Your turn," he repeated.

I stared at the drum. It was made from a huge, barrel-shaped gourd with some kind of animal skin stretched over it. "What do I know about this kind of—"

"Drum's a drum," Mani grunted.

I gave it a tentative swat with my palm. A hollow boom bounced back to me from all directions.

Mani nodded approval.

I looked again at the rock painting, now seeing it with fresh eyes.

I ran a finger along a wiggly arrow that shot from the mouth of a kangaroo to Mama Pash.

"Lotsa talk out there," Mani said. "Lotsa trouble."

It was my turn to nod. My special link to animals now felt as natural as my nose. The Uitajuq in me seemed to stand up and applaud.

I studied the lightning bolt over Mama Pash's head, rubbing the bald spot above my right ear. It was like looking in a mirror.

But the dancing drummers below her still made no sense to me.

Jirra walked over, like he'd sensed my confusion, and followed my finger across the painting. I felt a new power in his presence, like a bridge had been built, suspended by our song.

"Got 'er figgered?" he said, like nothing had happened between us.

"Yeah, I guess." I tapped the drummers. "But who are these guys?"

"Like Mani said, we got trouble in paradise, right? Reckon you do, too."

"Well, yeah. Like, major."

"Don't need a bunch a' scientists to tell us that, right?"

"I'm hearing stuff out there," I blurted.

Jirra tightened his lips, like he knew exactly what I was talking about. "Hell, a million kangaroos can't be wrong."

Mani chuckled.

"Up north, too," I said, feeling a dam crack inside. "There was this crane. Then raccoons in New York. Kangaroos down here. That wallaby thing. I think I even heard plants, once. This little island we flew over, with a volcano on it. It was, like … weird."

"Hmm. Good ears."

"You've heard it?"

Jirra blinked hard.

"That horny devil on the road?"

Jirra laughed. "*Thorny* devil."

"Strange vibes. Like … like something's broken."

"Kinda the same message, i'n'it." He pointed to the ball of fire at the top of the pictograph. "It's all comin' to a boil out there."

"*Pikatjara*," Mani shouted, his voice spiraling up the cave walls and escaping through the skylight.

I looked at Jirra.

"Sick. Mani's sayin' the land's sick. Don't know what's coming but the shit's gonna hit the fan real quick."

"*Warmala?*" I said.

Jirra looked surprised. "Dead right. Big time. Comin' like a freight train."

Mani chucked a pebble into the pool. "Forgettin' the songs. That's what's broke."

Jirra touched the upside down flames. "That's where we gotta go. Where *you* come in."

"What?"

"Backwards fire. Makes things healthy. Sucks out the bad stuff. Buries it in the ground."

Mani reached over and whacked the drum. "Your turn," he said again. "Rehearsal's not over."

"Rehearsal?" I said.

"Right," Jirra said. "So it's like this. Ya sing that song a'yers with, let's say, ten thousand drums backing you up."

"Ten *thousand* drums?"

"Yep. Reckon there'll easily be twice that at the concert."

I pointed to all the drummers at the bottom of the pictograph. "That's these guys?"

"Bewdy. Finally yer gettin' it. So, ya get all them drums rolling with yer song and—"

"*Nganana. Wiru, kunpu,*" shouted Mani.

"Huh?" I said.

Jirra stared at Mani for a moment. "He's sayin' … he's sayin' we'll all be strong and healthy."

"Who's *we?*"

"The works. Animal. Mineral. Vegetable." Jirra folded his arms and looked at the pictograph, then back at me. "See, Ashley, the whole idea is you gotta kick-start this thing. The healing, I mean."

"Me."

"Yep."

"Kick-start the *healing?*"

"Yep. Ya know, wake people up a bit. Turn 'em round so they don't muck things up worse. 'Fore it's too late."

Mani tapped the lightning bolt aimed at Mama Pash's head.

Jirra gently parted the hair over my right ear.

I jerked away.

"Mani says ya got all the right credentials."

I turned to face the old man. "How would *you* know?"

"Clock's tickin'," Mani said, picking his teeth with a baby finger.

His words catapulted my mind back to that crazy guy in Central Park, screaming about all hell breaking loose, to Jack's babbling about tipping points and eco-disasters, and to Rita's quiet prophecy about Yhi, a Sila look-alike, who would take our breath away if we didn't clean up our act.

What the hell could I do about all that?

"Is that why you brought me to this crazy cave?"

Mani turned his attention to a fat opal on the wall and started polishing it with his thumb.

"My grandfather spotted you a mile away," Jirra said.

Performing in front of half a million people was one thing. Saving the world was another. "But I live, like, how many miles away? In iglus, remember?"

"Don't have to be a dinky-die Aussie," Jirra said. "Job's a job. Fits ya like a glove."

"Don't matter where yer from," Mani said. "Same song."

Something inside me shrank. I could almost hear a door slam shut. A magical song that minutes ago seemed to save my life, that thrilled me when Jirra's voice joined mine, now terrorized me.

I impulsively grabbed Jirra's hand. "Yeah, but you could do the song," I pleaded. "You seemed to pick it up pretty quick."

"*You* gotta start it," Mani said flatly. He flicked his chin at the pictograph. "Says so right here."

I glared at it, wanting to claw it off the cave wall with my fingernails.

Jirra shrugged. "Wouldn' a' believed it meself. The lightning. How the animals talk to ya. That song. But Mani smelled ya a mile away. He's saying you're it, sugar."

Mani tapped the drum between Mama Pash's legs. "Your turn."

I frowned at my latest captors. First Jack. Now this pair of outback clowns. "So what about your deranged great uncle? Is that why he dragged me all the way to Australia? To stand in for *her?*"

Jirra shook his head. "Uh-uh. No way. Jack wouldn't know Mama Pash from Madonna." He studied me for a moment, scratching the stubble on his chin. "Maybe ya make 'im homesick for his younger days in the Arctic. I dunno. Seems to like ya, anyway. Treats ya almost like family."

I snorted. "Which isn't saying much."

Jirra chuckled. "Ya got that right. Truth is … we don't have the foggiest as to what Jack-o's cookin' up this time."

"Our luck, I guess," Mani said, pushing the drum against my shins. "Now play."

LISTENING TO EVERYTHING

DESERT EAST OF KULINI NGURA
DECEMBER 20TH, 3:05 PM

CTP 0025:41:37

In the end, I killed the rehearsal.

"You gotta sing yer way outta here," Mani had threatened.

But I refused. I would not sing. I would not drum. To be honest, I couldn't. I'd buried my healing song too deep to dredge it out. Smothered it with fear.

The journey out of the underwater tunnel was only half as terrifying as the one in. I now knew enough to take a gigantic breath in Cathedral Cave and I collected no more souvenirs on my skull. As for Jirra, I locked onto one of his ankles from the start, which worked way better for steering and my basic sanity.

Still, my lungs were frantic by the time we exploded through the surface of the outside pool. I lay panting at the water's edge for several minutes with my forehead on my hands.

Mani popped up beside me breathing calmly, like he'd just dunked his head in a bathtub.

As I was about to lift my head, something wet and snakelike slithered across my bare neck. I jerked upright and found myself nose to nose with Puli. His tail wagged as he licked the water off my face.

"Reckon you passed the test in Puli's books," Jirra said as he flipped on his grungy leather hat.

Mani hissed.

Puli backed away.

The old man climbed out and stood above me with his hands on his hips. I suddenly felt very small.

Maybe I should have sung for him.

Behind the usual mischief in Mani's eyes I detected a gold vein of power. "Just *think* a' telling anyone about this place and—" He made a gurgly sound with his mouth while slashing a thumb across his throat.

"Right," Jirra said, scratching Puli behind the ears. "Could get messy."

"Are you threatening me?" I cried.

"Nuthin' to do with us, ya know," Jirra said, squinting up at the sacred hills.

"*Mulupa!*" grunted Mani.

"Huh?"

Jirra flicked a pebble into the pool. It glanced off the screaming face, then sank out of sight. "He says we're not shittin' ya."

Once I'd calmed down after Mani's warning and we'd started walking back to the truck, I was surprised to notice how the desert had changed. Or was it me? Though everything around me was still strange and unknown—bushes, trees, birds, bugs, all nameless to me—I felt less uptight in this world down under. Like the landscape had put on a new dress, its colors brighter, the air clearer, and the contrast between stone, sand, and sky much sharper. Even the brutal heat had less of a bite.

The birds seemed to be singing their heads off and we were followed by a continuous fluttering of wings. The slow whistled notes of the bird that had haunted me on the way out now sounded almost jolly.

"Butcherbird," Jirra said, noticing my interest.

"What a sick name for such a nice bird."

"Skewer ya right through the heart if you let 'im."

A black-hooded bird with a bright blue beak darted out from a tuft of dry grass, hovered in front of me, then disappeared behind a dune.

"That's if you're a bug," Jirra added.

Though I couldn't see them, I now felt the presence of small creatures moving with us through the grass, even under the sand.

At one point I laughed out loud when I caught myself watching a clump of bushes for signs of naked dancers.

It wasn't just the physical world that had changed. The land seemed charged with a new power. It vibrated beneath me as though the ground itself was a living instrument. Neither loud nor subtle, it was an urgent beckoning that teased the outer limits of my awareness. It was a thrumming I had heard many times since the lightning strike. But now, for the first time, it was steady. It was safe.

I trudged through the sand with my head down and eyes half-closed, straining to hear the baseline melody humming through the land. I got so wrapped up in it that I stumbled into Mani as I crested a steep dune. I tripped over my own feet and landed on my ass.

I got the sense he'd been standing there for a while.

"*Kulini kulini, kulini kulini,*" he chanted with a faint smile on his lips.

"Huh?"

"The real thing," he said slowly, "is *listening* to everything."

"Uh … yeah," I said. I closed my eyes for a second and smiled.

It was still there.

Mani actually offered me his hand.

I refused it but tried to look half-polite as I straightened up and marched on ahead of him.

I couldn't see Jirra but I stuck to his tracks like a locomotive to rails. I walked faster. The thrumming kept up. It spread out in front of me, washing over the land, spilling to the horizon and beyond. I broke into a run, ignoring the heat, forgetting my thirst, wanting only to share this discovery with Jirra.

I finally spotted him standing on top of a tall, curling dune. I could see his truck not far ahead. His back was to me but I knew something was wrong. I could *feel* it.

I ran up beside him, puffing like a race horse.

He didn't say a word, just pointed to a huge plume of dust rising in the east.

"What is it?" I said.

"Looks like he opened the gates. Party's on."

Above the gentle thrumming I heard a faint rumble of vehicles, shouting voices, and the random beating of drums. I felt a familiar stab of stage fright.

Jirra suddenly spun around in the sand and peered into the southern sky. "Shit. He found us."

My heart sank as the thrumming fled from the slash of chopper blades. I never got a chance to ask Jirra if he'd heard it.

CRASH

CTP 0024:41:52

Everything seemed to fall apart. Long before Jack's helicopter landed in front of Jirra's truck, the symphony of birdsong caved in like a house of cards. The sky faded to a paler shade of blue. The colors of the desert seemed bleached. The sun took on a savage brilliance and every pore of my skin now stung in the heat. The sacred hills of Kulini Ngura retreated into a haze.

What had been a rich landscape humming with life had suddenly turned harsh and sterile. In a matter of seconds, the land and sky fell out of alignment.

"Tell 'im we was out bird-watchin'," Jirra shouted above the shriek of the chopper.

"Better nick off," Mani said to Jirra.

Mani shot me a spooky wink, then the two of them bolted down the dune for Jirra's truck.

"No worries," Jirra yelled over his shoulder. "He'll treat ya right."

"Wait!" I started after them but tripped on a clump of ankle-biting grass. By the time I found my feet, Jirra had already whipped the truck into reverse, spraying the nose of the chopper with sand. He pulled a wild backwards U-ee, then took off into the desert like a bucking bronco. The scene reminded me of one of those kooky old black and white war movies set in the Sahara. I would've laughed if I wasn't half-dead from heat exhaustion.

As I watched Jirra's truck dissolve into a rising fist of dust, a wave of dizziness almost knocked me over. Though I couldn't see Jack, the scent of money and worldly power oozing from the cockpit told me he was on board. Jirra and Mani had escaped like a couple of thieves, carrying off another kind of power, rooted in the land. Two worlds had collided, crumpling me in the middle like a bumper in a head-on car crash.

One of Jack's guards jumped out of the chopper, looking like he'd had a very bad day. He unslung his rifle and fired a burst of bullets high into the air.

I dove behind the dune and tumbled down the other side. I rolled to a stop beside a twisted dead tree that offered as much cover as a parking meter. In the heat of the moment, this seemed like as good a place as any to shrivel up and die like a road-killed lizard.

ALINGA

GUEST ROOM, RITA'S HOUSE
DECEMBER 20TH, 6:35 PM

CTP 0022:11:48

"Cripes, Ash, you coulda fried out there!"

Becca's voice came to me as if from a dream. It took me forever to open my ten-pound eyelids. Instead of Becca, all I saw was a blood-red blur. I blinked. It didn't go away. "My eyes," I mumbled. "I can't—"

I felt a gentle hand on my cheek, then everything flashed white. I slammed my eyes shut.

"No rush, Ashley. You'll be right."

The sound of Rita's voice was like a cool drink and I fell back asleep, still feeling totally wasted but safe.

I dreamed of lemonade and strawberry ice cream, swimming off the Spit, and nude sun-bathing on a slab of spring sea ice.

This time I woke to the playful refrain of "Turkey in the Straw" hammered out on a harmonica. My eyes filled with tears and I blindly reached out both arms. "Gabe!"

I felt his big warm hands fumble for mine. "Got ya covered, Ash!"

"You know I hate that song," I said as we hugged.

"Worked, didn't it?"

I forced my eyes open. I was surrounded by the brilliant white walls of Rita's guest room. She stood smiling at the end of my bed with a red washcloth draped over her folded arms.

Becca leapt to her feet and pried Gabe off me. "Time's up, buddy," Becca said, squeezing me until my bruised ribs protested. "You buggered off without telling anybody anything."

"Sorry, Mom."

"What was that shit in your hair?" Rosie said from her bedside chair.

I gave her a blank stare for a minute, then remembered Jirra's hand on my head. "Bat."

"*What?*"

"Bat shit."

Rosie huffed, then took a turn in my arms. "These Earth Mother binges are gonna kill you."

"Just a little walkabout."

Rita laughed. "Now that's the spirit."

"But there's tons of snakes out there," Becca said.

"Only saw one. Jirra took it home for lunch."

"Right tasty," Rita said.

"You trust that guy?" Becca said.

I looked back at Rita. "You trust his great aunt?"

"Oh yeah, sorry," Becca said. "He just seems, I don't know, *odd*."

"Fair enough," Rita said with that same mischievous twinkle I saw in her brother Mani's eyes.

"Your neck," Rosie said. "It was caked in blood. What the hell was that about?"

The image of Mani slashing his throat came back to me. "Uh … bumped my head, I guess. Swimming."

"*Swimming?* In the desert."

"Well, yeah. Just a puddle." I wondered if I'd already spilled too many beans. "In some trees." I reached up to check my goose eggs. Both had vanished. I was amazed to discover that the wound beside them had completely healed over.

"Whatever," Rosie said. "But how's about no more sexcapades with lizard man 'til *after* the concert. We need you alive and kickin' on that stage tomorrow."

Tomorrow. A thousand butterflies did loop-de-loops in my stomach. Dodging deadly snakes seemed less threatening. And what if Mani shows up at the concert, taunting me to perform some Earth-shaking song I'd long forgotten?

"We don't really have to play," I said. "Like, we never signed a contract or anything."

"Well, no," Becca said. "If you're not up for it, we could maybe just watch the concert, then—"

Rosie whipped a lighter out of her jeans and held it up to her face. "Forget something, girls?" she said with a Jack-like sneer.

Rita's forehead went all crinkly for a second.

I couldn't read her. Did she know I was a fugitive arsonist? Did she know about Jack's threat to rat on me if I didn't perform? All I said was, "Oh, *that*."

Rosie tucked the lighter away. "Anyways, who wouldn't *pay* to perform in front of the whole world? Jack's gonna beam this concert to every damned TV and computer screen on the planet."

"Sounds good to me!" shouted Gabe, who was sprawled over a white wicker chair. "Better keep my chops up," he said and tore into a kick-ass version of "Whiskey Before Breakfast" on his fiddle.

"First Carnegie Hall, then the world!" Rosie said. "What can we lose?"

Good question, I thought. At that moment the stakes felt big. Very big.

"So who's the cutie?" said Becca, who'd wandered over to a curved wall plastered with photos.

"Alinga," Rita said, moving to her side. "Our little sunshine."

"Your kid?" Becca said.

"Born in the Hot Rock heydays. Jack was on top of the world, just finishing his solar farm. Named her for the sun."

"Who's the hippie?" Rosie said, pointing to another photo.

Rita slipped on a pair of reading glasses that hung around her neck. "Now, that would be the man I married."

My curiosity got the better of my brain fog and I threw off the sheet and spun my feet onto the cool sandstone floor. I wanted to know more about my kidnapper.

My head reeled to one side as soon as I stood up. I could feel the planet beneath me turning in space.

The next thing I remember is standing over a bathroom sink as Rita splashed water on my face. "You really should rest, Ashley. There's no plane to catch, you know."

I nodded slowly. "Yeah. Thanks for reminding me." I stared numbly at the mirror, studying a face I barely knew. In spite of a wicked headache, my dust-caked hair and sautéed skin, I detected a subtle strength in that face, a faint glow behind my eyes that reflected a new flicker in my heart.

Something had caught fire in that cave.

With her arm tucked under mine, Rita tried to steer me back to bed, but I wriggled free and shuffled over to the photo wall.

Rosie stood in front of a gold-framed picture of a thirty-something guy smoking a pipe. I'd seen that face before, back in Jack's Manhattan apartment, only here he wore a long, blond ponytail. He stood, smiling, beside a wheelbarrow full of tomatoes.

"*That's* Jack?" I said.

Rita sighed. "Ah, yes. My Jack. He was the very picture of hope and happiness back then. Quite an eco-holic."

"A what?" Rosie said.

"A back-to-the-lander, if ya like. Jack threw himself into building a sustainable eco-community in a world that seemed addicted to carbon-rich energy and environmental plunder. He called it an epicenter of hope."

"But I thought he worked for Empire Oil," Becca said.

"Right. Still keeps his hand in. In those days he worked swing-shift. A full-on month with Empire, then a month here, pumping oil dollars into the farm. He led a kind of double life."

"Sounds schizo," Rosie said.

"Worked for him. Jack was everybody's friend." Rita pointed to a framed newspaper clipping from the business section of the *Brisbane Times*. One picture showed a black-suited Jack, posing for the camera as he cut the ribbon on a huge offshore oil rig. The other showed Jack dressed like Crocodile Dundee, shaking hands with an aboriginal chief at the opening of a new national park. The headline read: *What to make of Jack?*

"Even after he became a VP of Empire Oil, Jack carried on as chairman of the Australian Parks and Wilderness Society."

"Looks like a poser to me," Becca said. "That would drive me nuts. I mean, wearing such different hats?"

"Jack took pride in building bridges, not walls." Rita moved to a picture of a laughing Jack running after a brown-skinned little girl on a bike with training wheels. In the background was Rita's house, still under construction. "But the first cracks started when Alinga was born."

"A tough kid?" I said.

"Hardly. An angel. Jack adored her. But the state of the world came back to haunt him. Soon after she was born, an amazing bird he'd studied—"

"Went extinct," I said.

"He told you about that?"

"Uh-huh."

Gabe jumped out of his chair and stood behind us, playing a soothing version of "A Cuckoo's Nest" on his fiddle.

I remembered seeing a tear run down Jack's wrinkled cheek after his rant about this lost bird. In Manhattan, his story left me empty and cold. Now, it was as if my own cheek stung. "He was pretty pissed," I said. "Shouted something about … I dunno … putting a stop to all this nonsense."

"Bloody well *all* of it," added Becca with an Aussie twang.

Rita chuckled. "Sounds like our Jack."

Rosie tapped another photo. "Same bird. Insane colors. What'd he call it?"

"Brazilian emerald parrot. That really took a piece out of Jack. His specialty became bad news."

"Uh, we noticed," Becca said.

"Burning rainforests, spreading deserts, dying reefs, starving polar bears, soaring cancer rates. Jack couldn't get enough of it. He got so consumed with worry over the planet that sometimes his stomach ached too much to eat. The more he learned about looming catastrophes, the more pessimistic he got about Alinga's future. He obsessed on the real chance that his little sunshine would face a global ecological breakdown."

Rita moseyed past a string of photos mapping out her daughter's life. "The good news is that, as Alinga grew older, she turned out to be the best medicine Jack could ask for."

There was young Alinga, proudly holding a frill-necked lizard under her father's nose. Alinga and a screaming friend, jumping hand in hand off the top of a monster sand dune. Alinga showing off a bucket full of orange and purple berries.

"She restored her daddy's hope. He worked harder than ever to fix the world for her."

"Pretty musical kid?" asked Becca who'd moved ahead of us.

"Alinga had many gifts. Sang long before she could talk. Lovely tunes that she pulled out of thin air."

Becca had stopped by a photo showing Alinga on an outdoor stage with a guitar in one hand and a bouquet of orange roses in the other.

"She won the Alice Springs talent show five years running."

Another showed her playing the didj beside a campfire with perhaps a hundred people circled around her.

"A real crowd pleaser, she was. The workers would drop everything to listen to her sing or play the didj. Like iron filings to a magnet. When nobody was around, she'd wander out into the desert and sing to the birds and lizards."

Gabe broke off from his fiddle. "Hey, I know about that! Played for a polar bear once. Got him up dancing!"

Rita turned and smiled at him. "Good on ya, Gabe."

"Is that Mani?" I said, pointing to a big man seated near Alinga at the edge of the firelight.

"Right. Uncle Mani. Took a liking to each other from day one. Her didj teacher. Language, too. She was fluent in Pitjantjatjara."

I looked at Rita. "And you?"

She gave a quick shrug. "Oh, I get by. Too much school, I guess."

I leaned closer to the photo. A black didjeridu crawling with golden snakes lay across Mani's lap. The same one he played for me in Jewel Cave.

A series of newspaper articles announced the opening of Jack's solar farm—then its freak trashing. Same for the wind farm. He was a media star.

A bunch more photos of Alinga, now as a teenager—feeding

camels, cupping an injured bird in her hands, hugging a koala. One close-up showed her lowering a pair of binoculars like she was trying to hear some far-off sound. I could see a hint of Mani's mischief in her eyes and her father's jutting jaw. Her skin was smooth, like polished sandstone, her face somehow wise beyond her years. I recognized the hypnotic profile of Kulini Ngura in the background.

I wanted to meet this person, now a woman, I assumed. "So, where does she hang out now?"

Rita closed her eyes for a few long seconds.

"Oh, I'm sorry."

"What?" Becca said.

Rita waved a hand at the last photo on the wall. It showed Alinga in some urban flower garden, cooing with a pink cockatoo on her shoulder—the way her dad did in his Manhattan apartment. Her skin was blotched and pale. Her arms hung like broomsticks out of a faded green hospital gown.

"Sometimes I think she was too sharp for this world."

"What do you mean?" I said, fighting back tears.

"She had the eyes of an eagle. She'd spot snakes or birds long before we'd see anything. It's like she felt them more than saw them. Or *heard* them."

"Like they were calling her?" I blurted.

Rita gave me a surprised look. "Why, yes. Even in the house she seemed to be constantly connected with life on the desert. When she was little, she'd suddenly jump up from a meal, run to the window, then come back to the table humming a new tune. That's where all her songs came from. Sometimes it got too much for her, like she couldn't turn it off, and she'd disappear into her room for days."

"So, what did her dad think of all this?" Becca said.

"After one scary bout of withdrawal, he took her to see a psychiatrist in Brisbane."

"A *shrink?*" Rosie said.

"Jack thought she might be manic-depressive or something. After lots of fruitless visits, the doctor finally came up with a label for her. Empath."

"What's that?" Becca said.

"Basically it's someone who can tune into the feelings of others. I mean, actually *experience* them."

"Like, both the good and bad stuff?" Becca said.

"That's right. The doctor warned us about empaths being tortured by the pain of others."

"Do you really think she was one?" I said.

"It's a bit clinical sounding, but Jack seemed satisfied. The local fellas have other names for it. They say it wasn't so unusual years back."

My grandmother Aana would be the first to agree. I didn't know the Inuktitut word for it, but Alinga's powers sounded awfully familiar. When I was a kid, Aana loved to tell me stories about how her mother, Uitajuq, the ancestor I'm named after, would get sick whenever the sled dogs got sick, how she'd stand on the shore singing to beluga whales, or how she'd hear the caribou coming long before anyone else. Empath. I hated labels. But this one seemed to stick—to Alinga and to that part of me where Uitajuq still lived. "We're talking people *and* animals here?"

"In some cases, yes. Alinga seemed especially in cahoots with camels and roos, that is, until Jack fenced them out. When she was younger, she'd speak of songs leaking out of the sand and the rocks. In time, she clammed up about all that. Her school chums would rib her. Called her a boofhead. But I got the sense that the playing field got much bigger for her, like she sponged up the pain of the whole world."

The whole world. The pain of the whole world. What I felt in Jewel Cave.

My knees turned to mush. I shot both hands out, knocking a photo off the wall.

"Are you all right?" Rita said, clutching my arm. "You really should rest."

"Yeah, it's just … nothing." I straightened up and faked a smile. "I'm okay."

Becca grabbed my other arm. "So, this empath thing, is it lethal?"

Rita's face softened. "I don't think so. Alinga died of leukemia. Jack was positive something nasty in the environment killed her. In our water, our food, in the air. God knows. Any hope Jack held for turning things around died with Alinga. He basically gave up on people. Any hope he had turned to anger."

"How old was she?" I said.

"She would have been …" Rita studied my face for a moment. "What are you?"

"Eighteen. Why?"

Her eyes widened, just for a second, then she abruptly turned back to the photos. "Oh, nothing. Same age, that's all."

Gabe stopped "The Cuckoo's Nest" in mid-flight. "Just like you, Ash!" he yelled. "Watch out! Jack's looking for a replacement!"

"*What?*" I said.

Rita spun around and stared at Gabe. "Replacement? What do you—"

"No kidding, Ash. He's got you m-mixed up with Alinga!"

"How would *you* know?"

"D-Darri told me. Had a few good ch-ch-chats with her while you were out on your little whatsit, your s-s-sexcapade."

I felt a cork pop in my head. I looked at Rita, who had suddenly clutched her neck. "Is that true?" I demanded. "Jack's using me as a stand-in for your *daughter*? I'm some … some pretty bug he's collected. To pin on the wall?"

Rita put a hand on my arm.

I brushed it off.

"You certainly charmed him, but—"

JAMIE BASTEDO

"But what? What the hell's he up to?" I shouted.

"I honestly don't know. He goes on and on about … about giving the planet a rest. Whatever he's planning, the safest thing would be to do as he says, at least 'til after the—"

"We're not some windup toys he can just plop on a stage for his crazy concert."

"Of course not. But, like Rosie said, what can you lose?"

Rosie put her arm around me.

I brushed that off, too.

"Right on, Rita!" she said.

"Once it's all over, I'm sure he'll arrange a flight home for you," Rita said.

"How do you know? He might—"

A crusty voice blared over the intercom. "Rita!"

"Speak of the devil," Becca whispered.

"Would you just stop saying that?" I said. "Like I need reminders?"

WE'RE GOING DOWN

SITTING ROOM, RITA'S HOUSE
DECEMBER 20TH, 7:45 PM

CTP 0021:01:53

"Just thought I'd check on my star performer," Jack bellowed as he snatched a glass of whiskey off Darri's tray. Sitting on a futon couch beside Jack's wheelchair was a small man with white hair and owlish glasses. It took me a minute to place the guy until Becca marched up and shook his hand. She seemed relieved to see him.

"Dr. Livingstone, I presume?" she said.

He stood up in true British form. "Indeed. James Livingstone. Should I know you?"

"Becca Crawford. We caught your magic act at the UN."

"Ah, yes. Just five days ago. Seems a tad hypocritical, jet-setting around like this, burning up heaps of carbon, in the name of climate change."

"Hey, if Al Gore can get away with it," Becca said, "why not you?"

"You're doing your thing on stage tomorrow?" I asked.

"Just a few words. Jack's idea."

"Stir up some shit," Jack muttered into his empty glass. He was breathing like he'd just run a marathon.

Livingstone glanced at him over his glasses. "I couldn't resist the invitation. What with the eclipse and all."

"Eclipse?" I said.

"Why, yes. Same day as the winter solstice. Remarkable convergence, really."

"You mean summer *solstice,* Doc," grunted Jack. "You're on my turf now, remember?"

"Of course. *And* a window of totality lasting a whopping six minutes, thirty-nine seconds, swinging right above Alice Springs."

"A benediction on my plan!" Jack shouted to the ceiling.

Livingstone ignored him, extending his hand toward me. "Now I remember you. The Arctic climate change crusader."

I gave it a limp shake.

"That's *my* Ashley!" Jack said in syrupy tones that made me retch.

"I'm not your daughter!" I snapped.

Jack lowered his glass and slowly looked up at me. His eyes narrowed to slits like he was hiding some huge pain behind them.

I felt a sudden gash in my guts—no, in *his* guts. The hair rose on my neck as some tender thing leaked out of that gash. No amount of booze or bluster could mask it. A bittersweet love for his long lost daughter. I had a crazy impulse to reach for his wrinkly old wrist and apologize. Until it dawned on me that he was trying to foist that love on me.

I flung my hands behind my back and turned to Livingstone. "Crusader?" I said. "Ah … that's kind of pushing it."

"You're here to perform, of course," he said.

I cringed at the thought. "Actually, no, I don't think—"

"Damn rights we are," Rosie said.

"I'll second that," Jack said with his happy mask back on. He raised his empty glass toward Darri. She stood across the room holding a tray with a bottle of whiskey on it.

"I think you've had enough, Jack," Rita said as she politely waved Darri out of the room.

Jack belched. "My dear, I may have given you this house but I still pay the staff. Darri! I'm dying of thirst!"

All eyes fell on the arched hallway where Darri had escaped.

"Darri!" he shouted again. "Another shot for the road!"

An orange gecko shot out from under Jack's wheelchair, squeaked at him, then took off after Darri.

Jack slapped Livingstone on the back. "Do you smell a mutiny, old boy?"

Livingstone grimaced. "Might do you some good, Jack," he said, pulling out a handkerchief and wiping sweat from his neck. "I understand alcohol can actually increase one's thirst in heat like this."

"Sounds like a porkie to me," Jack roared. His breaths came in short, labored puffs. He yanked a mickey flask from his khaki shorts and filled his glass to overflowing. "How about you, Ashley? Hot enough for you and yer chums? Must feel pretty grouse after fifty below."

I refused to look at him. I could feel his predator eyes all over me.

"Good God!" He exclaimed in mock horror. "What did those savages do to ya?"

I'd forgotten I still wore the grime from my walkabout. "Savages? Must run in the family."

Jack chuckled into his glass. "Only difference is I got more money."

It was my turn to stare at him. "For this Earth-shaking *plan* of yours."

"Hmmm. Earth-shaking. I like the sound of that."

"I thought you loved the Earth."

Jack gazed out the window.

It was what Jirra called the orange hour. That magic time I'd witnessed the day before, standing on the empty concert stage, when the sun throws a peach-skin blanket over the desert.

Jack's breathing slowed for a moment. "I reckon. More than anything."

"More than people?"

"Now, there's the rub," he said, flushing red as a beet. "I have seen the enemy, and he is *us!*"

Becca stood over Jack. I could see her knees twitching. "Yeah but, like, if we caused the problem, we gotta fix it, right?"

Jack stared into his glass, slowly shaking his head. "I used to believe that. I thought renewable energy could save us. Even nuclear. But now I know it's all a crock. Sure, swap your SUV for a hybrid car and you can drive more efficiently, all right. *Straight into hell!* All Band-Aids. Too little, too late."

Becca turned to Livingstone. "But there's still time, isn't there? Didn't you say we've got another few years before … what did you call them?"

"The three great disasters," he said solemnly.

"Yeah, like, when things start falling apart. Ocean currents and rainforests and stuff."

"And frozen methane."

"Yeah, that too. There's still time, right?"

Livingstone nodded. "But not for dilly-dallying."

Jack clapped his hands like a football coach. "Sorry, folks. Time's up. We're going down." He leaned forward and cupped a hand to one ear. "Can't you hear it? The roar of the waterfalls? There's nearly seven billion of us parasites out there. Eighty million more every goddamned year. Not to mention a billion belching cows and farting dogs. Just by breathing, humans pump out a quarter of the world's carbon dioxide. That's four times all the airplanes on Earth. Just by bloody *breathing!*"

"I got it, Jack!" Gabe yelled. "Alls we gotta do is take turns holding our breath!"

Jack exploded into laughter, spilling half his whiskey. "That's a right *fine* plan, Gabe. A tad cheaper than mine. And while we're at it, maybe we could all sprout gills and jump in the ocean for a few hundred years. Give the land a break. Or maybe grow green skin, eh? Soak up all that extra carbon dioxide, just like bloody gum trees!"

Jack folded his hands in his lap and tilted his head way back. His barrel chest heaved up and down like a bobbing whale. "No, my friends, I've done my homework and I'm afraid the bubble's about to pop. It's now or never. I can't leave it up to the unwashed masses to fix things. In these matters, I'm a big believer in the power of one."

"And just how are you going to fix everything?" I said.

Jack sucked back the last drops from his glass. "Come on now, sweetheart. What's a surprise party without a surprise?"

ZERO SUM GAME

SETI LAND CRUISER, EN ROUTE TO CONCERT SITE
DECEMBER 21ST, 2:00 PM

CTP 0002:46:33

"He's nuts, right? Totally friggin' nuts?"

Becca had a knack for sussing out friend or foe. Her tone told me she'd given Livingstone the thumbs up, even though he and Jack seemed to be buddies.

The professor gazed out the van window at the south side of Mount Wara, baking in the noon sun. It seemed taller today, hovering on a cushion of sand kicked up by a growling north wind.

Jack had sent Jirra and one of his soldier boys in a stretch Land Cruiser to pick us up at Rita's.

"I'll watch you on TV," she'd said as we piled in. "Best seat in the house."

Jirra had his work face back on and was hunched over the steering wheel, staring down the road like he was expecting an earthquake. I bobbed my head around, trying to catch his eye in the rearview mirror. Even though he'd almost killed me yesterday in the underwater tunnel, smeared my head with bat shit, and dumped me when Jack's chopper landed, I felt a surprising comfort in his presence. He had refused to look, but I knew we'd connected when a faint grin leaked from his stony face, like the one I'd seen after we'd sung together in Jewel Cave.

"Eyes on the road, kid," grunted the guard.

I noticed the guy's rifle dangling close to Jirra's foot. It dawned on me that maybe Jack knew we'd tapped into something big on our walkabout and the guard had orders to keep us from getting too chummy. No more sexcapades, at least.

At Becca's question, the guard leaned way back in his seat and cocked an ear toward us.

"Nuts?" Livingstone said. "Quite possibly. Jack's heart is in the right place. It's his head I'm worried about."

"But you work for him," Becca said.

"*Used* to. On the Stable Earth project. Now he just rings me up for the odd circus act."

"What is that anyway?" I said.

"SETI?"

"Yeah."

"It stands for Stable Earth Treaty Implementation. Jack was the mastermind behind it. A kind of global Ten Commandments. Supposed to put the brakes on a species skidding out of control."

"That would be us?" Becca said.

"Correct. The whole idea was to stabilize the Earth's climate support systems before they irreversibly collapse."

"*Was?*" I said.

Livingstone sighed. "Many countries got cold feet and pulled out before the ink dried on the treaty. Most of the biggest carbon emitters like the U.S. and China never even signed it. So Jack took matters into his own hands."

"The power of one," I murmured.

"Indeed, if money is power. Jack was a multi-millionaire at age five, when his father died and left him everything."

"Oil money?" I said.

Livingstone shook his head. "Built railways across Australia."

"Ol' Jack's a bit of a steam engine himself!" Gabe said.

Livingstone laughed. "He poured a fortune into keeping the treaty alive. Lobbied the UN for his own staff and research lab. Launched cutting-edge satellites to monitor the state of the Earth. Traveled the world spreading the Stable Earth gospel. And for all his efforts, Jack received a bullet in the back."

"*What?*" Rosie, Becca, and I said together.

"Gunned down in a Paris parking garage."

"Who?" Becca said.

Livingstone shrugged. "Jack has his enemies. Disgruntled oil thugs who think he's too green. Eco-terrorists who think he's sold out to the mega-machine. Whoever it was only knocked out his legs. He rolled out of the hospital feeling he'd been saved for some higher purpose."

"To save the Earth, no doubt," Rosie said.

"Indeed, to stabilize the Earth before it's too late. But, of course, on Jack's terms. He feels we're in a zero sum crap game with Mother Nature and somebody's got to take the hit." Livingstone's eyes narrowed. "And guess who that would be?"

"We have seen the enemy," bellowed Gabe in his best Jack voice. "And he is *us!*"

Livingstone lightly tapped Gabe's arm. "Precisely, my young man. And Jack's not content to wait for nature's backlash to keep us in check."

The hair on the back of my neck stood up. This sounded a lot like Sila's revenge. Like Yhi stealing our breath away. Like worldwide *warmala*. Whatever. Labels suddenly didn't matter.

I jerked my head, like somebody'd smacked me from behind. It hit me that Jack and I were basically fighting for the same thing. To stop the shit from hitting the world's climate fan.

Becca asked, "So, what do you mean, backlash?"

"I mean, widespread misery. Mass starvation. Natural catastrophes. Basically, a breakdown of civilization as we know it."

"Oh, that," Rosie said. "So, are we almost there yet?"

"Very close," Livingstone said. "Though I believe not as close as Jack thinks."

"No, no. I meant the concert."

"No worries," Jirra said. "Lotsa time." He still wouldn't look at me but I could tell he'd been listening intently.

"After a few too many drinks," Livingstone continued, "Jack once told me that the planet's last hope is to bring fat-cat nations to their knees—as soon as possible, for as long as possible."

"That's totally insane," Becca said. "How's *one* guy supposed to do that?"

"Jack has a long history of instigating projects designed to shake the world. And he does have quite a flair for the theatrical."

"Like you and your smoking trunk," Becca said.

"A little hocus pocus does help to grab people's attention. Jack knows that as well as I do."

"Whadya think Uncle Jack's gonna pull out of his hat this time?" Rosie asked.

"All I can decipher from his latest rants is that he's planning some kind of eco-sabotage on a very grand scale."

"Can't somebody stop the guy?" Becca asked. "They should lock him up and throw away the key!"

"Like any good magician, Jack keeps his rabbits well hidden. He'll pull them out of his hat how and when he pleases."

"Couldn't you, like, tip off some hotshot reporter to dig out the facts?" Becca said. "Expose him for what he really is? An evil eco-loony."

"That's just it. The media doesn't know what to make of Jack. Greedy industrialist or bighearted conservationist? Jack has cunningly woven a chameleon cloak that he slips on and off as he chooses."

"When do you think he'll hatch his little Earth-shaking plan?" I asked.

Livingstone smiled at the security guard who had turned to us with a devilish grin. "We may soon find out."

NO ESCAPE

CTP 0002:16:51

The wind had picked up by the time we entered the concert site. Clouds of whirling red dust shrouded the massive stage and the thousands of people now gathered around it.

"Oh, well, 'A' for effort," I said. "I can see the headlines now. Global powwow nixed by sandstorm."

"Oh, I doubt that very much," Livingstone said. "Jack's not going to let a little bluster spoil his party."

Becca put her hand on my knee. "You're trembling, Ash."

"Just a chill. Guess I'm not used to air conditioners."

"Yeah, sure. Like, your whole body?"

I could have slept for another week after our walkabout. It wasn't so much the heat and the thirst that left me knackered, as Rita would say. Not even the tunnel. It was what happened in Jewel Cave. Hearing Sila's breath. Feeling her pain. Finding that healing song. Sharing it with Jirra—then losing it. And later, walking back to the truck, being welcomed by the desert, electrified by its thrumming beat—then losing that, too!

I felt like one of those little sealskin toys, hanging by a thread, that we high-kick in our iglu games. That was my heart. Kicked around so many times the rawhide thread was about to snap.

"Come on, Ash, get your shit together," Rosie said. "This might be as close as we'll ever get to a religious experience." She hung half-out of the Land Cruiser window, drinking in the bizarre view.

A man wearing an eagle feather headdress and smoking a cigar peered in at us as we drove by. Four shirtless old guys, with discs of wood in their lower lips and fans of yellow feathers in their hair, beat skin drums as they jammed with a Rasta man playing reggae guitar. Three hunks in grass skirts, their faces plastered with tiger-stripe tattoos, danced in a circle, waving spears and chanting warlike cries. A ring of women in red robes, wearing turbans the size of watermelons, sat in the sand, slapping their knees to some Arabian beat and making weird cooing sounds with their tongues. A gypsy-looking woman draped in an orange sarong rocked a sand-caked baby at her breast.

In the day and a half since I'd stood on the Scorched Earth stage, a throbbing city of tribal musicians and their fans had sprouted from the sand.

"What a zoo!" Becca said, rolling up her window.

"Hey, save a cage for us!" shouted Gabe, who was madly rocking in the back seat. "We'll fit right in!"

This I could not handle. "Speak for yourself."

Rosie hauled herself back through the window and felt my forehead like I had a fever. "Don't you get it, Ash? We're talking the holy mother of all gigs here! Imagine going home now, after all this, and not doing a couple of little numbers for our *millions* of new fans."

"Yeah," I said. "Imagine. Going home."

"You've got to hand it to old Jack," Livingstone said, as he waved to three topless women walking arm and arm, their braided hair dripping with red and white beads. "He knows how to throw a good party. Fifty different acts. A select bunch of indigenous performers from all over the world. These ladies here, Xingu Indians from the Amazon. And look, the ones with the colorful capes: Quechua from the Andes. Those tattooed fellows, Maori from New Zealand. And there, Ainu from Japan, Tuareg nomads from Timbuktu. Marvelous!"

"No shit," Rosie said. "There's really such a place?"

"Timbuktu? Of course. In the Sahara desert."

"Well, *they* must feel pretty at home here," I said glumly.

"What about you?" he said. "Feeling a bit like a fish out of water?"

"Like, majorly."

I looked beyond the chaos and colors closing in on me, beyond the trailers and tents, the flags and the fences. I lifted my eyes to Kulini Ngura. A string of black clouds lurked behind its eastern face. A wide slope of sand leaning into the hills was covered with windswept dunes shaped just like snowdrifts back home.

I squinted.

The desert dust and campfire smoke became a ground-hugging blizzard over bald-ass tundra.

I blinked.

The desert mutated into what my grandmother Aana calls "Nuna"— Our Land. For a flash, I knew that deep below the surface, whether covered in sand and snakes, or snow and caribou, it was all the same land.

All one.

My body stopped shaking.

I thought I could hear the land thrumming again.

Until the guard barked at Jirra. "That one, mate," he said, pointing his lizard chin at a green and black trailer. It was exactly like the one I'd torched in Nanurtalik.

My throat tightened. As we pulled up, I spotted Empire Oil's dinosaur logo painted on the door above the words: *Proud Sponsor of the Scorched Earth Concert.*

Mani sat on the grated metal steps, chewing a piece of dead grass.

Rosie hopped out of the Land Cruiser and started pulling our drums out of the back. "Let's go, gals. Time to warm up in the green room."

"Fully air-conditioned," Livingstone said. "Jack wants you to be comfortable while you wait."

I felt anything but.

"When are we on?" Becca said as we stepped into the blazing sun.

Livingstone reached into his tweed jacket and handed her a concert program. "Four-fifteen, I believe. Right after me, just like New York. Then Mani and Jirra."

Becca took one look at the program, then laid her wide eyes on me. "Hey-hey! Cover girl!"

I grabbed the program. "God! That bastard! How could he?" There I was, on page one, a full-color close-up of me in my finest Eskimo duds, throat-singing my heart out on the Carnegie stage.

"Aha," Becca said thoughtfully. "Sneaky bugger."

"What?" I said.

"Don't you remember? Jack promised he'd get you *on the front page*."

"Look at that," Livingstone said. "It is you. I must say, I hadn't made the connection. You look … different somehow. Quite smashing, really."

Jirra peered over my shoulder and whistled. "I'll be gobsmacked. Can ya spare an autograph?"

I glared back at him.

Even the guard came over for a look. "Hmm," he grunted.

Rosie put her arm around me, beaming. "There's no escape now, Ash. They'll be screamin' for you."

WAAHI TAPU

EMPIRE OIL TRAILER, CONCERT SITE
DECEMBER 21ST, 3:00 PM

CTP 0001:46:33

I might as well have been back in Nanurtalik dumping gas on the floor.

The Empire Oil trailer was laid out exactly like the one I'd torched. Part of me felt like doing it all over again.

But another part of me had already kicked the monkey-wrenching habit. Like the gash on my head from our little tunnel tour, that cave seemed to heal something deeper in me. Raging against the megamachine that was screwing our climate had lost its zing for me. The flames of my anger had begun to fizzle. Maybe I could find something better to do than pull up stakes and burn down trailers.

Still, the irony was no less disgusting. Here was the world's largest fossil fuel predator sponsoring a concert to help fight climate change. *Hah!*

It could have gone either way.

I just might have lit another match if it weren't for half a million witnesses. Besides, jail looked better to me now than going on that stage.

"What the devil is that?" Livingstone said.

Instead of rehearsing, we'd all crashed in front of a widescreen TV, showing live coverage of the concert that was going on just a stone's throw away. After zooming in on a bunch of acts, including the tiger-striped guys from New Zealand and the half-naked women that waved at us, the camera angle had changed to a wide view of the whole stage and the sea of fans in front. Livingstone pointed the remote at a gigantic round object that hovered over the stage.

"How could we have missed *that?*" Becca said.

"It's just, like, floating there," Rosie said.

Livingstone hopped from the couch and ran out the front door. Everyone but Jirra and Mani leapt after him.

Livingstone took a look at the stage and gave one good clap. "Bravo, Jack!"

What looked like a hot air balloon wearing a dress was suspended over the stage by a spider's web of thin wires. It was draped in a light blue fabric that perfectly matched the desert sky. In the mid-afternoon sunlight, the whole thing was virtually invisible.

"Like I say, Jack has a flair for theater," Livingstone said. "A real master of illusion."

Rosie let out one of her horsey laughs. "That must be the thing he was cursing at the other night."

"What do you mean?" Livingstone said.

"He was screaming something about … airlifting the sucker over the fence. Wouldn't fit through the gate."

Livingstone played with his lower lip. "I see. It's certainly a big sucker. I wonder what he's cooking up."

As we piled back in the trailer, I noticed our guard standing at the bottom of the stairs. We must have spooked him, the way we burst outside, and his finger twitched near the trigger of his rifle. What irked me was that I didn't know if Jack had assigned him to protect us—from what? No other acts had security guards—or to keep us from escaping.

Livingstone plopped back in front of the TV and turned to Jirra and Mani, who were sprawled on the couch. "So, what do you fellas make of that?"

"Reckon just another a' Jack's toys," Mani said. "Kept mum with us."

"Well, he's got an awful lot of people guessing," Livingstone said. "Everything we see here is being streamed live around the world to thousands of TV networks, radio stations, and Internet servers. Jack's aiming for an audience of three billion, give or take."

"That's, like, half of the people on Earth," Becca said.

"Almost," Livingstone said. "Quite a daunting audience."

"Better not pick your nose while we're up there, Ash!" Gabe said.

I just shook my head and gawked at the screen.

A trio of Mongolian sheep yodelers were packing up their twenty-foot-long horns as the MC invited a new act on stage. He had proud dark eyes, a long gray beard, and hair that fluttered in the wind. He was dressed in a blue and gold robe and wore a reed crown with a carved black bear's head sticking out of it.

"Who's his royal dudeness?" Rosie said.

"Handsome devil, isn't he?" Livingstone said. "An Ainu Elder, probably from the mountain country of northern Japan. I did some ocean studies there years back. *Intensely* spiritual people. I once saw an Ainu woman bow to a cricket, like she was at some holy altar."

"Of all the world's indigenous people," the Elder said in remarkably crisp English, "our next guests are among the hardest hit by climate change. Their native home is literally washing away as global warming melts ice caps and causes sea levels to rise. Would you please give a warm welcome—but not *too* warm …"

Laughter from the crowd.

"… to the Kaitiaki singers from the Marshall Islands Republic."

Huge applause.

A well-built guy in his forties stepped up to the mike, a red sarong around his waist and rings of long grass around his knees. He wore his jet-black hair in a tight bun, and a corkscrew shell hung from a fine gold chain around his neck.

I ran a hand through my hair as if readying it for a close-up shot like his. I realized that if I had a piece of popcorn in my teeth or something rude dangling from a nose hair, it would be caught on camera for all the world to see.

Four gorgeous women stood beside him, wearing grass skirts and the strangest brassieres I'd ever seen.

"What are those chicks wearing?" Rosie said.

"Ah, those would be polished coconut shells," Livingstone said.

"Did a study of those, too, eh, Doc?" Gabe said.

Livingstone chuckled. "I'll never tell."

Each woman wore a lip-cracking smile that would melt an iceberg. They gently swayed back and forth as if on a ship.

The man hailed the crowd with a slow wave of both arms. The

camera cut wide. Everyone saluted him with the same gesture. He'd turned the crowd into a gently rolling sea.

"We need a gimmick like that!" Becca said.

"Shut up," I said.

"We come from a liquid continent," the guy began. "You call it the Pacific Ocean. We Polynesians call it *Moana.* Ninety percent of us ocean people are indigenous and we try our best to live according to her laws. *Moana* gives us rain for our crops. She gives us fish for our tables. She gives us our stories and our songs. *Moana* gives us life."

The camera zoomed in on his bronzed face as he paused, sweeping his eyes over the crowd and the desert landscape behind them. He held half a million people in his palm.

He opened his wide, smiling mouth and continued. "So, you must think we feel a bit lost in the middle of the Australian desert."

Boy, could I relate!

"Not so, my friends. For sure, you have made us feel right at home. But there's something else going on here. The land's the land, no matter where you live. Sand here. Water there."

"And don't forget *snow,* buddy!" shouted Gabe.

"Shhhh, Gabe," I said.

"It's all part of the living, breathing skin of Mother Earth. At the level of spirit, it's all the same. We all know that or we wouldn't be here today. Can't you feel it?"

The crowd cheered.

This guy is talking my language. Here was pure Nuna. Sila's skin.

"At the level of spirit, the land itself has welcomed us here."

More cheers.

"You'll hear us sing about *waahi tapu,* the sacred place. We're singing about our island in the middle of the sea. But we're singing about your home, too, wherever you live. *Waahi tapu*—all land is sacred. We know, at the spirit level, that your home and ours are only one percent different and ninety-nine percent the same. *Waahi tapu.* We can't touch this spirit. We can't see it. But something is there. We feel a presence in the land, between each other. *Waahi tapu.* It's all one!"

Applause.

"Please say it with me, *Waahi tapu!*"

"*Waahi tapu!*"

"One land!"

Cheers.

"One people!"

More cheers.

"One voice!"

Wild cheers, whistling, applause.

"The guy's a freakin' evangelist!" Rosie said.

"Right you are," Livingstone said. "An *environmental* evangelist. And a damned good one."

"We first nations of the world have *first* knowledge about climate change. Why? Because we live closest to the land. Closest to our mother. And she's feeling a bit under the weather these days, if you know what I mean."

Waves of laughter.

"Do you know what I mean?" he shouted.

"Yeah!" roared the crowd.

"We indigenous peoples of the world contribute *least* to greenhouse gases. We have the *smallest* ecological footprints on Earth. Yet we suffer the *worst* impacts of global climate change. In our small island nation, coastlines are falling into the sea. Our land and drinking supplies are being flooded with seawater. Traditional travel routes are no longer safe because we can't predict the weather any more. Traditional species that we depend on for food have changed their migration patterns—we can't find them! New species we've never seen before are invading our region. The list goes on."

"Check, check, check," Becca said. "Sounds like home, eh, Ash?"

"Sort of."

"Just add polar bears!" Gabe shouted.

"My friends, we are close to the edge. We are reaching the limit of our mother's patience. The Earth is telling us loud and clear that humans can't break her laws. We can only break ourselves against them."

Huge cheer.

"Climate change has wounded the Earth from top to bottom. In my home. In your home." He raised his arms again. "Can you feel her pain?"

A much louder "Yeah!"

"Her pain is *our* pain."

Applause.

"Are we going to let this go on?"

"No!"

"I CAN'T HEAR YOU!"

"NO!"

"Are we going to heal our mother?"

"YEAH!"

I thought I felt the trailer walls shake.

The guy slowly lowered his arms and poised his big hands over a beautifully carved conga drum. Hammerhead sharks chased stingrays below a wreath of coconut palms. The base of the drum was a spiral of ocean waves curling over the back of a sea turtle. The camera pulled back, showing two other guys dressed just like him, one holding a ukulele, the other a simple bamboo flute.

"We call ourselves *Kaitiaki*, which means guardians. May we all guard the piece of the planet we call home. And may this song give strength to each one of you to carry out this task."

The loudest cheers yet.

This time I *knew* the trailer shook. Like thunder.

Becca stood up and pointed at the screen. "Can you believe it? The guy's got 'em eating out of his hand and he hasn't even played *one note!*"

I pushed her out of the way with my foot.

The drummer kicked off with a lightning beat. The women pulled sticks of split bamboo from behind their backs and started whacking them together in time with the drum. The other guys tore into a high-powered song about swaying palms and breaching whales.

"Check those flying hips!" Rosie said.

The dancers went into high gear, spinning like tops, setting their grass skirts on fire.

"This could be a hard act to follow," Becca said.

I ran to the fridge and pulled out a gooey lemon Danish. I wolfed it down, pacing the trailer floor like a caged polar bear.

"Oh my God, Ash, loosen your shorts," Rosie said. "You're making even *me* nervous!"

"Shut up, will you!"

In my mind I was weighing the odds of dodging destiny. They didn't look good. Unless I got shot by a twitchy guard, arrested for arson, or struck down by another bolt of lightning, I knew that, in less than an hour, it would be my face glued up on that screen.

I stood over the couch, staring at Jirra as I wiped lemon goo off my lips.

He looked up from the screen, cracked a kangaroo smile, and poked his right cheek. "Ya missed some."

I wiped off the last goo and plunked down on the couch right beside him. I wanted to feel his strength, hoping just a little might rub off on me.

THE LID'S OFF

CTP 0000:31:49

"That galah gives me the shits," Jirra said as he looked over his shoulder at our guard, retreating into the empty trailer. "I thought he'd never nick off."

We were walking up a long plywood ramp behind the stage. For me it was a long last walk to the gallows.

"Looks bad on TV," Mani said. "Don't want no goons on stage."

"What do we need *him* for?" Becca said. "Like we're terrorists?"

"Ask the boss," Jirra said. "First time we've been under the gun."

"Could it be the way you sprayed his chopper with sand yesterday?" I said.

"Had a heavy lunch date," Jirra said. "Couldn't keep me mum waitin'."

"Where the hell *is* Jack, anyway?" Becca said. "You'd think he'd want to come to his own party."

"Pulling strings somewhere. Real control freak, Jack."

"Oh?" I said. "Hadn't noticed."

"Wake up, little Susie. He's got plans for ya."

Part of me did wake up and I suddenly realized I was clutching Jirra's hand. For how long, I didn't know. Even though he'd still played aloof, especially when Jack or his goons were around, some wall between us had crumbled in the cave. Now I couldn't get close enough to him.

My face must have told him so and he gave my hand a quick squeeze. "Don't sweat it," he said. "We're your back-up band, Mani and me." He eyed the long hem of my amauti. "We'll be hangin' on yer coattails."

He seemed more like his wicked old self, even though we were about to step in front of a live audience which, according to Livingstone, was about half as big as Kansas City.

"Why don't you guys go first?" I said. "Break the ice for us tourists."

Jirra craned his neck, looking up at the strange shape dangling over the stage. "Can't do that, sugar. It's Jack's way or the highway."

"The highway looks pretty good to me right now."

A puff of blue mist from the front of the stage told me the professor was up to his tricks, wowing the world with his toy eco-disasters. I glimpsed the back of his balding head framed by the shoulders of Mount Wara. Its knife-like shadow crept across the crowd and would soon skewer the stage. The huge draped thing hanging over us rocked in its wire cradle, batted by gusts of wind thrown off by the sacred mountain.

I could tell from the squeak in Livingstone's voice that he was winding up for a big finish and we'd soon be filling his spot on center stage.

"Ladies and gentlemen of the Earth, the upshot of my simple experiments is this: Our world is about to catch on fire."

The Japanese MC, still dressed in his royal robes, greeted us backstage with his palms pressed reverently together. "You must be the Eskimos."

"Yeah," I said. "Well, actually, no. See, nobody calls us that any—"

"Please, please, come with me." He grabbed my hand.

For a second, I was being pulled apart by two gorgeous guys. Jirra, still holding on, caught my eye, then pushed his face close to mine. "Mani's got plans for ya, too. Best do what he says this time."

Jirra let go as he and Mani stepped aside.

The MC steered me through a sea of cables, scaffolding, instruments, and microphone stands. I reached back for Becca's hand, who in turn grabbed Rosie, who grabbed Gabe. I felt about six years old.

I looked back at Mani, who made a quick drumming motion with his hands, then flashed me a thumbs-up. I shrugged, pretending I didn't get his message.

The Ainu man towed our little parade to a cramped waiting area behind a wall of speakers, then disappeared in a swirl of blue and gold cloth.

"How you feeling, Ash?" Becca said in a loud whisper, still holding my hand.

"That's the trouble. I don't feel anything. I keep wondering when I'm gonna totally have a cow."

"Shit, Ash!" Rosie said, sounding nervous as hell. "Can't you just for once keep it together?"

I gave her a blank stare.

"Just keep thinking," Becca said, "*Carnegie Hall. We did friggin' Carnegie Hall. How good is that?*"

Livingstone's voice filled the ear of the world. It got louder and boomier, as if someone was fiddling with the volume controls. "As dire as it sounds, we can't lose hope. We can't let ourselves be paralyzed by fear like the proverbial deer caught in the headlights of a speeding car ..."

He'd really stirred the pot this time. Below his voice I could hear a new murmur in the crowd. Like the sound of the sea that's just out of sight. A storm was brewing out there, a storm of anguish for the Earth. People were actually screaming. But not like for the Polynesian guy. This sounded more like panic.

Becca heard it, too. "It's starting, just like Jack wanted."

"What?" I said, playing dumb.

"The chaos."

"Come on, girls. They're screaming for *us!*" Rosie said, sounding way more confident than she looked. Her pure Inuk skin had gone pale.

Something else was starting above our heads. The clouds I'd seen lurking in the east now rolled toward the concert site. They folded in on themselves, forming ribs of light and shadow that would soon smother the stage. Meanwhile, from the west, the sword-like shadow of Mount Wara still crept over the crowd, like it was announcing the end of the world.

Something electric hovered in the air.

"Never doubt the power of the Earth to kill," Livingstone said.

I'd heard that line before. While I'd sweated bullets on the UN stage.

"This is it, Ash," Becca said.

"... Look at the natural disasters that are spreading across the world. Most are linked to our messing about with the climate ..."

"It's the real deal, Ash," Gabe said.

A gust of wind shook the tower of speakers beside us.

"... The Earth has merely to shrug to send millions of people to their death. If we don't respect and take care of her, we can be sure the Earth will take care of herself ..."

"We're on, Ash," Rosie said.

"... If, in the process, that means eliminating *us,* so be it."

"Time! Time!" declared the Japanese MC as he skittered past us, tapping his watch.

"... The time for action is now, people. Any delay could tip us over the edge. If we let that happen, I'm afraid all we can do is stand back and watch the planet burn."

A willi-willi, like the one that erased our tracks from Jirra's truck, hopped on the stage and paused beside Livingstone. This one was decorated with plastic bags and coffee cups. He lowered his spectacles and stared at it with a wry smile—until it blew apart his toy disasters. His plastic palm tree flew into the crowd. His chunk of frozen methane shattered into a million steaming pieces. His fish tank fell off a stool and crashed on the stage, spilling blue water all over his leather Oxford shoes.

Of course, all this was captured on the giant video screens and no doubt broadcast around the world.

I could almost hear Jack's gleeful laughter, wherever he was.

Looking shaken, Livingstone scooped up his notes and gave a sheepish wave to the crowd. "Thank you and good luck, everyone."

"Yeah! Good luck, Doc!" yelled Gabe.

I'll never know what caused it. The power of Livingstone's speech? The puckish willi-willi? That buzz in the air? Whatever it was tilted the Earth just enough to rip the lid off the crowd, releasing a gut-wrenching geyser of despair.

The video crew had a field day. As stage hands mopped up Livingstone's mess and set up microphones for the next act—us!—their cameras sampled the crowd.

"What can I do?" pleaded a Native American woman in a doeskin vest and flowered headband.

"*Qué pasará ahora?*" cried a Mexican woman with a hundred silver rings strung on each ear. "What happens now?"

An African woman, dripping in colored beads, held her startled baby up to the camera. "What about my children? And *their* children? What kinda world we leavin' em, for God's sakes?"

"We're up shit creek now, man!" shouted a beery-eyed desert rat in a camo T-shirt.

"The end is near!" declared a burned-out hippie wearing a top hat.

The big screens caught them all.

Livingstone squeezed past us like we were store manikins. "What have I done?" he muttered to himself. "What have I done?"

As I watched his tweed jacket disappear backstage, my drum slipped from my trembling hand. It made a nasty thunk that would have been heard out front if it weren't for all the yelling. The crack in the wooden rim that I'd spotted in New York slowly opened before my eyes. I picked up my drum as if it were a dying bird and tried to close the crack with my thumb. The rim snapped inward, then collapsed. I tapped the floppy drumhead with my willow stick. It had all the ring and power of a laundry basket.

"Shee-it!" Rosie said. "*Now* what?"

"Just drum louder," Becca said.

The MC lifted his arms in a crucifixion pose, his great robe sailing in the wind. "Please, please, people. I ask you to stay calm."

A swirl of red dust smacked him in the face and he had to stop to wipe grit from his eyes.

"Please, please," he continued. "We all know the Earth's climate is in peril."

A pained roar from the crowd.

"That's why we have all gathered here. To give each other strength in these troubled times."

Shouts and general pandemonium.

"The good news, as the professor said, is that we still have time. Together, we can stop climate change from reaching catastrophic levels."

"It's too late!" screamed a shrill voice from the far fringes of the mob. "Too late!"

Livingstone's doomsday message had taken root in fertile soil. The chant spread like wildfire through the crowd. "Too late! Too late! Too late!"

The big screens showed people shouting, sobbing, raising their arms in desperation, hugging each other as if facing a firing squad.

"And now," said the MC, almost shouting into the mike, "it is my great pleasure to introduce our next act, fresh from a climate change benefit concert on the Carnegie stage …"

"Too late! Too late!"

I looked up, wanting to fly the hell out of there. The ribbed clouds moving in from the east now arched over the stage like the closing of a coffin. The sun hung directly over Mount Wara, turning a fast-shrinking patch of sky into the mouth of a blazing woodstove. The orange hour had returned. But today it had a hostile look, turning everything to rust.

"… a group of talented young musicians from the land of iglus and polar bears."

"Too late! Too late!"

My chest burned. I had a sudden impulse to look for Jirra, like he was trying to connect. I peered through the tangle of stage equipment but saw no one.

"Would you please welcome to the Scorched Earth stage ..."

"Too late! Too late! TOO LATE!"

"... from Nanurtalik, Canada—the Dream Drummers!" Forcing a smile, the MC beckoned us on stage with an urgent wave.

Becca flashed the crumpled program cover in my face. "Just find that zone, Ash! Like Carnegie. Remember? The *zone!*"

With Gabe clutching the long tail of my amauti, I stumbled out to center stage, drumless and naked before a crazy crowd of fellow Earth-huggers.

LOSING IT

FRONT AND CENTER, SCORCHED EARTH STAGE
DECEMBER 21ST, 4:30 PM

CTP 0000:16:38

Seconds after we appeared on stage, the chant cut out like the falling of an ax. In the sudden silence I could hear the scaffolding behind me rattling in the wind, sand skipping across the stage, the howl of a distant dingo.

And something more. A whisper, trickling from the sky.

"I *told* you they'd love us," Rosie said out of the corner of her mouth. "They're freakin' dumbstruck."

Becca put a hand over her microphone as she pointed at one of the giant video screens. "Nice try, Rosie, but do you think it might just have something to do with …" She whipped her head around and looked up and over her shoulder. "… *that?*"

Hanging high above the stage was the most exquisite work of art Jack Masters would ever lay his fat hands on. The sky-blue cloth had been lifted like a skirt, revealing a gynormous Earth ball. The continents were perfect in every detail. The oceans shone like polished marble. Cloud pinwheels floated above the surface. The whole thing spun slowly, revealing a dark side dotted with city lights. It seemed to pulsate with life.

People exploded into hysterical cheers. A doomsday funeral for the planet had suddenly morphed into an Earthnik love-in. Somewhere behind the scenes, Jack was pulling strings, working the crowd, steering an emotional roller coaster that carried half a million passengers—not to mention the billions wired in from around the world.

"That's one kickass, amazing planet," Becca said breathlessly.

"Why now?" I said.

"Simple," Rosie said. "You're Jack's little superstar."

"Yeah, sure, but—"

"The eclipse," Gabe said in an unusually soft voice. "It's coming. Can't you *feel* it?"

I wheeled around and faced his hollow eye sockets. "How could you—"

The patch of open sky behind him had changed from orange to a muddy gray.

Rosie tapped the rim of her drum. "Time to get it on, kids. This isn't an astronomy camp. These people paid good money to hear our stuff."

I nodded slowly, ignoring the rising clamor of whispers in my head and pressure in my chest. I tried to keep my performer's face together. The words I'd seen scrawled on a brick wall down a New York side street came back to me: *You are nobody with nothing to say.*

I shot Becca a tentative glance. Thumbs-up. I drew Gabe closer to my microphone. He wore a huge grin, like he always does when he's got a fiddle locked under his chin.

I took a deep breath and dove in. "*Ai.* Hello. My name is Ashley Anowiak. We live at the top of a wounded world ..."

Big applause.

Rosie looked at me with raised eyebrows, mouthing, "See?"

"We are a group of Inuit and non-Inuit, family and friends, who are trying to do something real about climate change."

I was just rehashing lines from my UN spiel. All head stuff. No heart. But what the hell. In spite of a peeling nose, my face looked pretty good up there on those giant screens.

So much for being a nobody.

I flashed a cover-girl smile at the cameras, then, after what felt like a dramatic pause, tried to look grim.

"We are fighting for our future. Coming here today, we have no hidden agenda. Like most of you, our agenda is simple: survival!"

Big cheers.

I felt like an imposter doing a takeoff of myself while in the zone. I looked up at the giant Earth ball but found no heart stuff there. Just another of Jack's toys—a fantastic, tear-jerking, windup toy. My eyes were drawn to the restless sky above it. A big black eagle with gold-tipped wings soared on an invisible thermal staircase.

I ignored it.

The whispering got louder.

I ignored that, too.

Please, not now, I thought. *I'm busy being famous.*

I continued the charade, even raising my arms and stomping a foot on the plywood stage.

"How do we fight for our future? With our songs!"

Bigger cheers.

"With our stories!"

They loved what I was dishing out and the praise went straight to my head. I was playing the crowd, just like Jack.

"Who's our enemy?" I shouted, surprising myself. "Ignorance, fear, denial, the feeling that we're powerless to do anything!"

The pressure in my chest became almost unbearable. The whispers clamored for my attention. Uitajuq thrashed to bust out.

I brushed all this aside and barged ahead.

"You scream that it's too late! Okay, so we just pack up, go home, and wait for the sky to fall?"

"No!" they shouted.

"You say there's no hope! Is that what I'm supposed to tell my little brother?"

"No!"

"My unborn children?"

"No!"

"If we do nothing, the sky *will* fall! All hope *will* die!"

It was a total sham. I didn't believe a word. I'd become a climate change prostitute, tossing out tricks for a few strokes to my half-Inuit ego. It felt wonderful and disgusting at the same time. I'd do anything to bury my stage fright. So I carried on, drunk with my new power to change the world with a few punchy words, rainbow beads in my hair, and a fancy parka.

"Together, we can get through this! We are survivors!"

Why not swipe a few lines from Jirra?

"Think about what we indigenous people have been through. Our homelands are stolen. Our languages banned. Diseases almost wipe us out. But hey, we're still here! We keep bouncing back!"

Cheers.

"And we'll always be close to the land! Close to Mother Earth!"

Now I was parroting the iron-man with grass leotards.

"No one's been able to beat that sacred connection out of us! If anyone can stop this madness, we can!"

I shot both arms in the air, checking a screen out of the corner of my eye to make sure the camera caught my bogus smile full on.

My blind tiguaq saw right through me. "For Pete's sake, Ash," he yelled, his amplified voice echoing off the sandstone hills. "Enough babbling already! When do we get to *play?*"

Laughter.

Who didn't instantly love Gabe?

My arms fell like dead weights. I looked out at my new fans, now a sea of strangers. My eyes fixed on the eagle circling above the crowd. It hit me that this was the source of the whispers now filling my head. For several moments I forgot the whole world was watching and just stared up at it. The camera followed my gaze and soon a million eyes were fixed on that one bird.

A gust of wind knocked me off balance. The Earth ball banged against the metal scaffolding, sending a shock wave across the stage.

Gabe pulled the cry of an Arctic loon out of his strings. "Come on, Ashley! Are you *there*, Ash?"

Becca and Rosie raised their drums and, with a shared nod of the head, tore into a frantic heartbeat, the signature riff for "Sila's Revenge."

I couldn't take my eyes off the eagle.

From the sea of bobbing humans a thousand feet below, Walawuru, the wedge-tailed eagle, searches for the source of healing power that drew him here. He stretches his eight-foot wing span to the limit, then tips over on one wing to study the crowd. He fixes his yellow eyes on a figure standing on a flat wooden hill in front of the huge flock of humans.

That one.

A warm glow fills the eagle's hollow bones. He opens the circle of his flight, barely able to contain his joy.

I felt warm breath on my ear. "The *zone*, Ash!" Becca said. "Find it or we're epic losers."

I heard someone tap a mike.

The eagle's circles got wider and wider, like it was about to head for the hills.

I stepped in front of my mike to keep it in view.

Becca grabbed my arm. "Cripes, Ash," she hissed. "You wanna nosedive off the stage?"

"Hi. I'm Rosie."

Rosie never introduced our numbers.

"We're gonna start with a little throat-singing thing called 'Sila qatlunaatitut.' 'Sila's revenge.' Sila ... uh, that's an Inuit spirit who, like, calls the shots in our weather and ... lots of other stuff."

Rosie's voice was breaking up. She sounded like a twelve-year-old. But she was building a good head of steam.

"I heard Sila's got another name down here ... I forget ... something to do with the Earth's breath. She must get around."

Applause.

The Earth ball thumped and writhed above me as if in pain.

"Start messing with Sila and she fights back. I guess that's why we're all here today. To try and stop that. Hope you like it."

Applause.

Rosie let loose on her drum, like she was trying to wake me up, then lunged back toward the mike. "Oh yeah, if you like our tunes you can find our CD at dreamdrummers.com."

Becca rolled her eyes at Rosie and cranked up her drum, too.

Gabe magically drew the sound of ocean surf from his fiddle, completing the stage for my voice to dance on.

I panicked.

It was gone. A song that once sprang from my throat as easily as my breath had suffocated under a sticky mass of make-believe and Hollywood schlock.

I opened my mouth to see what might come out.

Nothing.

I tried to fake it.

Strangled squeaks and grunts.

I pulled back from the mike and frowned at Rosie like it was all her fault.

She scrunched her face at me and gave her drum one offbeat wallop as if to hammer me on the head.

I turned to Becca. She was sweating bullets, struggling to keep a steady beat. Even Gabe was losing the groove, his fiddle now sounding more like a tortured cat than a storm-tossed sea.

The Dream Drummers were coming undone.

Our little melodrama was being captured, larger than life, on the big screens. I actually heard someone boo.

"Look!" someone else shouted. "It's started!"

A thousand arms pointed to the sky. Heads turned westward to the sun as it plunged toward Mount Wara. Instead of a deeper orange, the land was turning a ghostly gray.

The drums and fiddle fell silent.

The big screens switched from my shell-shocked face to a full-frame image of the sun. The moon had taken a big bite out of its disc and was quickly snuffing out all daylight at a galloping pace. When only a sliver of sun remained, a weird blanket of thin wavy lines washed over the crowd, the stage at our feet, the skin of my broken drum. For a few seconds, the desert ran like a river as alternating bands of light and shadow danced over everything.

Then it happened. Totality.

The sky went black. The wind died. The air chilled. The stars and planets blinked on.

Hovering above Mount Wara was a black sun wearing a pearly white crown of light.

For the second time that day, not a tongue moved.

In the pregnant silence that followed, I was startled to hear the click of claws connecting with the arm of my microphone stand.

I stood eyeball to eyeball with one of Sila's messengers.

A JOB TO DO

TOTAL ECLIPSE, SCORCHED EARTH STAGE
DECEMBER 21ST, 4:37 PM

CTP 0000:09:43

In the eerie daytime darkness, I could just make out the silhouette of a magnificent bird. It was hunched over, its huge flesh-ripping beak thrust toward my face. Here was the eagle that had spellbound the world.

I pulled back so fast, I almost knocked Gabe over.

"Jeepers, Ash!" he said. "It don't mean you no harm."

"But ... but you can't even—"

"Just listen, Ash! *LISTEN!*"

My blind brother's command ricocheted through the audience and across the planet via satellite.

The words of Pema, that nice old monk in New York, popped into my head. *You bring much hope to our troubled Earth. Listen to her messengers. You will know what to do. Listen!*

Instantly, everything shifted. My stage fright, and the need to hide it behind a hero's mask, vanished. A dry and brittle crust split open, revealing a new ache in my chest—to know why this eagle had come. As we stared at each other, unflinching, the memory of a dream came flooding back to me in a tidal wave of joy. A falling star, an Arctic beach, a sandhill crane, Uitajuq's smile. And a rhythmic whisper, almost like throat-singing, that connected me to the stars.

This time I got it. I *really* got it—not in a dream, not in some magical cave, but on that crowded Scorched Earth stage, pouring from the eagle who'd stolen my mike. Passed heart to heart, its wordless message was the same.

Listen.
It's all alive. It's all connected. It's all intelligent.
And we are all family.

I moved closer to the eagle, to within easy striking distance of its huge glinting claws. There was something else. Something urgent.

Help us.

I closed my eyes to the eagle, to the video screens, to the hushed crowd and the snuffed-out sun. I sank far below my stage fright and the need to *be* somebody.

I withdrew to the room where Uitajuq lives—and listened.

There, closer than my breath, I found the thrumming.

If, up until now, I'd been a fish out of water, this was the sound of the sea. It throbbed all around me, in the eagle, in the throng of people below me, in the sand, in the sun and moon now locked in a cosmic embrace. It rose in goose bumps that crawled over my skin. The Earth's baseline melody returned to me like a long lost lullaby. It led me straight back to Jewel Cave and the healing song I'd sung with Jirra.

And it wanted out.

"Cripes, Ash!" Becca whispered in one ear. "What the hell are you—"

I reached for her arm. "Shh-shh. It's okay, really."

"That bird's gonna rip your face off," Rosie whispered in the other.

"Believe her, gals!" bellowed Gabe. "It's O-KAY!"

I felt a hefty hand on my shoulder. "'Ere ya go, Ash. Give it a burl."

I opened my eyes to see Jirra, holding a big gourd drum like the one I'd refused to play in Jewel Cave. He set it at my feet.

I impulsively threw my arms around him. "You're early!"

He pecked me on my lightning scar, then pried me off. "Reckoned you needed some backup."

Mani stood behind him with his black didj in hand, the one he played in the heart of Kulini Ngura.

I didn't remember him carrying that thing out of the hills, but there it was, its golden snakes glowing, even in the unearthly darkness. "Your turn," he said with a piercing stare. "You know what to do."

It was like Pema was speaking through him.

Mani was right. I knew what to do. However I'd got here—standing on the world stage with an Aussie drum at my feet and a healing song in my heart—whether kidnapped by a human-dissing Earth-hugger or drawn by some mystic power as old as those sacred hills, I knew I had a job to do. And it was now or never.

The eagle hopped to the edge of the stage and faced the sun, still shrouded in totality.

Jirra moved up to my mike and started clapping in exact time with the steady thrumming in my chest. My jaw dropped but he wouldn't look at me.

"Just keep that going," he shouted to the audience.

The crowd, already primed with eclipse fever, instantly joined in, a million hands slapping in time.

I gave a few timid taps on the weird drum.

Mani chose this moment to lay down a low, surging drone on his didj, like the rush of an underground river.

Becca and Rosie tentatively raised their drums. Gabe poised a bow over his fiddle strings.

I felt a whale's energy uncoiling inside me. My flesh and blood fell away and I was all energy.

Ashley died for a moment. All that remained was pure Uitajuq.

"This is it, Dream Drummers," I said. "Just go with me on this. A new ditty I discovered on my walkabout!"

I fell headlong into the new rhythm that was shaking my heart. The drum came alive under my flying fingers. A stagehand appeared out of nowhere and positioned another mike on my drum so that soon, the clapping, the drumming, the cheering filled the shadowed sky. Rolling underneath it all was the thrumming.

"Just keep that going," Jirra shouted again into my mike.

While still beating the drum, I moved my lips beside his. "Okay, people!" I shouted, rising on a fountain of primal power. "I can't see you very well, but I can *sure* hear you!"

Huge cheers.

"Isn't this absolutely incredible? A total eclipse on the solstice! Makes you think we're here for a reason!"

More cheers.

"I want to share a little secret with you."

I glanced at Mani who waved his didj at me like a snake charmer.

"A secret this weird and wonderful land taught me. We can start healing this tired old planet right now! Right here! All we have to do is drum up a hurricane of love for Mother Earth!"

The clapping got louder, faster. Gabe added an overlay of joyful loon calls on his fiddle.

"Okay, you've got the rhythm. Now, I want you to grab yourself a drum and beat your heart out!"

An eruption of drums soon drowned out the clapping.

"Great stuff! But I'm talking *ten thousand* drums! That's what we need, to tell the Earth we're really serious about this. To tell her we really mean business about turning things around!"

Becca and Rosie lifted their drums and caught up with my lead, both smiling from ear to ear.

"If you don't have a drum, grab a garbage can lid, a hubcap, a beer cooler! *Anything* to beat on!"

The stage remained unlit. I glanced at the screens. The cameras were still fixed on the eclipse. "Same goes for you people listening or watching at home! Don't just sit there. Join in! Let's shake things up a bit! Together, we're gonna blow the lid off global climate change! Let the healing begin!"

Thunderous cheers.

I closed my eyes and opened my throat, letting the song's multi-layered harmonies pour out. The soothing effect I'd felt in Jewel Cave was multiplied a hundredfold by the beat of so many drums. The intense burning pressure I had felt in my chest evaporated without a trace, as if the Earth herself had accepted the burden of my love.

For a moment, the song choked in my throat when a second voice joined mine in perfect unison. Again, it was Jirra.

The sound of drums became almost deafening, carried higher and higher into the sky by our song, yet solidly grounded by the thrumming. I became aware of a rising chorus of drums from backstage and knew that my fellow performers from the world over had joined in. All around me, above me, below me, inside me was the healing pulse of ten thousand drums.

There was a loud crack over our heads and a blast of orange light. The crowd went nuts.

I opened my eyes just in time to see the eagle take off like a bat out of hell.

I looked up at Jack's toy Earth. My televised scream circled the real Earth at the speed of light.

Antarctica was on fire.

SCORCHED EARTH

FRONT AND CENTER, SCORCHED EARTH STAGE
DECEMBER 21ST, 4:42 PM

CTP 0000:04:57

Argentina was next to go. By the time the flames reached Brazil, my cheeks were burning. Was it the flaming Earth above me or my disgust with Jack and his little games? My terror broke when I realized he was, as usual, just toying with us, fanning the flames of chaos, trying to extinguish all hope by scorching the Earth.

Soon the entire globe was ablaze, throwing a terrible brilliance into the crowd. People were running from the stage, trampling each other, sending up a colossal scream that shook the world.

I felt locked in a power struggle between hope and chaos.

Incredibly, I could still hear the thrumming, louder than ever.

"Drum, girls, drum!" I shouted.

My hands fumbled on the drum. It teetered over and rolled off the stage. Without thinking, I leapt after it, landing on my back ten feet below in a narrow patch of sand. The fall knocked the wind out of me and for a moment I lay stunned, gawking at Jack's inferno. But just touching the Earth seemed to boost my strength. I jumped to my feet, frantically looking for the drum in the dim light. I heard a shout in some strange language and turned around to see the group of old guys with discs of wood in their lower lips. One of them was pressed against a security fence holding the drum out to me.

"Nakurmik," I said to him as I seized the drum. He and his buddies bobbed their feather headdresses at me and clapped.

"Gaw!" yelled Jirra, who was hanging over the edge of the stage with his arm out to me. "Hell of a time to chicken out. Over here!"

I tucked the drum under one arm and, with the other, clawed my way up through a rat's nest of cables. Jirra grabbed my hand and hoisted me back on stage, just like he'd done in Jewel Cave.

This guy's rescued me in more ways than one, I thought as we ran back to the microphones.

Jirra knelt down beside the drum and held it tight for me. "Give 'er!" he shouted.

My hands clicked right back into the groove set by the thrumming. My throat opened and the song flew out as if on eagles' wings. Rosie and Becca joined in reluctantly, staring agape at the flames. Gabe picked up the beat on his fiddle and the Dream Drummers quickly fell back in stride, filling the ear of the world with our healing song.

As if shrinking from our music, the flames suddenly died down, revealing a blackened Earth enveloped by a thick pall of smoke. The screaming subsided. A few drums started up again. The daytime darkness was ending.

"Listen!" boomed a crusty voice that I knew too well.

The rising smoke flickered blue, then a face appeared, five stories high, on the charred world. Its features were warped and wiggling. But the big ruddy nose and wormy mustache left no doubt who it was.

"It's the freakin' Wizard of Oz!" blurted Rosie.

"Keep drumming!" I shouted. "Don't stop!"

"Native sons and daughters of the Earth," the voice blared. "Inheritors of a pained planet. Oh yes, and the rest of you buggers who've been screwing this world for too long. Listen to me!"

Jack sounded really angry. And really drunk.

A gush of flames wrapped the Earth once more, creating a blinding flash that reached far into the crowd.

Shrieks and general pandemonium.

"Just in case you hadn't got our attention, eh, Jack?" shouted Becca.

"Just keep drumming!" I shouted.

"I've been waiting for this moment for a long time," Jack roared.

"Hey, Jack," yelled Gabe "you busted into our best song!"

"Shut up and play!" I shouted

"Sorry to interrupt the festivities, folks," Jack bellowed, "but we've got a problem here. Like Doctor Doom said, our world's about to catch fire. The good news is that I for one am *NOT* going to let this happen!"

Another blast of flames engulfed Jack's face.

More anguished cries from the crowd.

I felt a drop of rain on my flying hands.

"We're going to turn this ship around right now before we go over the edge!" Jack roared.

The moon's shadow passed. A bright speck of light flashed into view on the western edge of the sun. Totality had ended.

A few more drums kicked in, rising above the screams.

"The bad news is that this will be the last satellite broadcast the world will ever see for a very long time." Jack started laughing so hard, the smoke his face was projected on went pink. "I reckon probably a *thousand* years!"

He let out a ripping belch. "The last banking, too. From now on, the buck stops with Jack!" More crazed laughter. "Phone calls, radio, TV—all a thing of the past, I'm afraid! Ya like surfing the Web? Checking your goddamned email? Buying cheap plastic crap on eBay? Forget it. Hopping airplanes all over the bloody place? I wouldn't try that if I were you! All navigation systems: *Kaput!*"

I felt farther from home than ever. But closer to Uitajuq than I thought possible. It was her hands on that drum. I beat the crap out of it. I shoved my mouth closer to the mike, hoping to drown out the voice of my enemy with my song. I clung to the thrumming with all my life.

"Yes, my friends, it's time to kiss goodbye the central nervous system of a civilization that's got a little too big for its britches!"

The shadow of Mount Wara reappeared, about to pierce the stage. Black clouds from the opposite side of the sky reached out to meet it.

"Time to *stick it* to the soft underbelly of a civilization that's got too greedy for its own good!" Jack's voice grew hoarse with yelling. "For the *planet's* good!"

The shadows met over the stage, over the ear canal of the world, and the rain started falling in earnest.

"Once the shit hits the fan, when the gluttonous jaws of global commerce grind to a halt, it's back to the land, baby! Some will figure it out. Some will survive. I'll place my bets on native people like you. To those who don't, to the Earth's *Intruders,* I say, good riddance! You'll be doing the planet a *big* favor!"

Another huge blast of flames. Jack's head swung in and out of view as he laughed uncontrollably.

I stopped throat-singing and yelled up at the hideous face. "*YOU CAN'T DO THIS!*"

Jack's monstrous eyes tipped down toward the stage and opened wide. "You just watch me, girl!"

I turned back to the crowd. "Don't give up people! Drum! Dru—"

Somebody killed all our mikes. But the crowd didn't need us anymore. They were on autopilot, drumming up a storm.

We played on, one drum, one voice, even as the clouds burst open and drenched us all.

The last words we heard from Jack were, "Hit it, Quincy!"

A great silent flash of yellow light filled the sky behind Mount Wara followed, seconds later, by a fireball that seemed to shoot from its bald dome.

Jack's smoky screen flushed crimson as if splashed with blood, then cut out.

A series of tremendous explosions echoed off the sacred hills, drowning out all sounds for several minutes, except for the steady thrumming in my chest.

PARTY

FRONT AND CENTER, SCORCHED EARTH STAGE
DECEMBER 21ST, 4:50 PM

CTP 0000:00:00

It was like the audience had been struck dumb, shell-shocked by Jack's horror show and the crazy booms that ended it. Some nervous laughter, a few whimpers, a handful of babies crying—that was it. And then a new hissing sound high above me. I looked up at Jack's toy Earth, cooling in the rain.

It was like a sign for me, like the healing had begun. We'd let it out of the bag and it was already circling the Earth.

I felt Gabe grope for my shoulder.

I took his hand. It was shaking.

"That was insane thunder, Ash," he said. "It *was* thunder, right?"

I looked at the bald profile of Mount Wara, now blacker than black against the last sliver of orange sky. "I don't know … maybe. Whatever it was, I don't think it was part of Jack's plan."

Jirra turned his face and palms to the sky. "Crikey! Rain!"

Mani walked over to me, his snowy hair hanging in wet ringlets over his eyes. Even in the rain, I caught the smell of gum-tree wood smoke from him. "*Wiru, wiru,*" he said as he shook my hand in his crocodile paw. "Time for *inma.*"

I looked at Jirra. "Huh?"

"Uh … he says you're beautiful. Now we party."

Gabe rubbed his hands with glee. "Now that's my kinda talk, lizard man. Sounds like it's already started."

I cocked an ear to the crowd.

Drumming.

It began with a whoop from way back. It sounded like a garbage can lid but it was drumming, all right. The same driving beat we'd fed them from the stage. It flew like a wind through the crowd. It grew and grew until I could feel the plywood throbbing beneath my sealskin kamiiks.

"Way to crash Jack's party!" Becca said as she threw her arms around me.

Mani spread his legs and started hopping sideways from one foot to the other in time with the beat. He opened his arms wide and flashed a huge smile to the masses below. His boyish moves were irresistible and we all jumped in beside him, Becca and Rosie on one side, Gabe, Jirra, and me on the other. And someone else, hopping about inside of me. Uitajuq.

"Do you believe it?" Rosie yelled. "A frickin' rain dance!"

"I believe it!" I yelled back.

Even though the lights were off and all the screens were dead, the crowd somehow picked up Mani's invitation. Tens of thousands of rain-soaked drummers joined Mani's victory dance, their feet stomping in time to a healing rhythm that now shook the world.

POOR OLD JACK

"So, tell me again exactly what happened to Jack," I said.

"Better yet," Livingstone said as he reached under the plane seat in front of him, "I'll *show* you." He pulled out his laptop and set it on the tray table in front of me.

Rosie and Becca leaned toward me while Gabe fiddled with the music channels on his armchair controls. Though the crew had killed most of the lights and there were snores all around us, we were all still pretty wired from the concert.

Especially Gabe. "Hey!" he shouted. "They're playing our song!"

I squeezed his arm. "Gabe, shh. It's nap time."

But there was no stopping him. *"Well, I've been through the desert on a horse with no name, it felt good to be out of the—"*

"At least *whisper* it," I said.

"Okay," he said with a huge grin. He carried on a few decibels lower. *"The heat was hot and the ground was dry, but the air was full of sound ..."*

I had to smile. *How perfect,* I thought. *Full of sound.*

Livingstone took off his owlish glasses and wiped them with a paper napkin. "You know, Jack might have pulled it off," he mused as his laptop booted up.

"You mean, Jack's evil plan," Becca said.

"I do. Imagine, taking out most of the world's communications satellites with only six dime-store rockets."

"And he told us those silos were for camel feed," I said.

Livingstone burst into a proper British laugh. "Preposterous. He fenced out all the wild camels twenty years ago. Gave away his farm stock to the local fellas."

"Camel burgers," Rosie said.

"Yes, all of them. Not one camel left on Jack's land."

"What do you mean, dime-store?" Becca asked.

"Falcon rockets made in Uzbekistan. Functional but hardly state of the art. Maybe six million bucks each, tops. And Jack provided his own fuel."

"That shiny stuff?" I said.

"That's right."

"Like in his weird little gardens?" Becca said.

"Gallium mixed with aluminum. Extremely explosive. Just add water and—"

"BOOM!" Gabe shouted, waking up half the plane.

I slumped down in my seat and reached across the aisle to squeeze Gabe's arm. "Thanks for that, bro ... but, uh ... maybe later? Like, when you're telling the story over Dad's radio waves."

"It'll need a *really* scary soundtrack," he said.

"We'll help you, Gabe ... won't we, girls?"

Rosie winked at me. "Deal me in."

"Me, too," Becca said.

"You were saying, Doc."

"Yes, Jack's people were on the cutting edge of rocket propellants. But the real genius here is that his fuel and his weapons were the same."

"Huh?" Becca said.

"No pricey nuclear warheads or heat-seeking missiles in Jack's payload. No fancy anti-ballistic guidance systems. Just a nose cone stuffed with bright, shiny pellets."

"He'd fire pellets at satellites?" I asked.

"More of a scatter-gun approach. Just open the payload doors once you're at the right altitude and spew them all over the place."

"Sounds messy," Becca said.

"Precisely. Gravel would've done the job but it's impossibly heavy. Jack solved this problem with his ultra-light pellets. He planned to use them to trigger a catastrophic disruption of satellite traffic by wrapping the Earth in a kind of cosmic junkyard."

"That's crazy," I said. "How?"

"It doesn't take much to knock out a satellite. A bolt that slips from the glove of an astronaut tinkering with the space station. A piece of cable that falls off a solar panel. Not to mention plenty of defunct satellites."

"Space junk," Rosie said.

"Yes, and the real kicker is that, up there, junk begets junk. Things bombard each other, creating more junk, which in turn smashes into something else in a positive feedback of destruction. Jack's pellet clouds would have tipped this process over the edge, sparking a disastrous chain reaction that would render satellite technology obsolete for at least a thousand years."

"He was *serious!*" I said. "A thousand years!"

"Oh yes, likely more. It would take an awfully long time for the debris orbits to decay and all that junk to burn up. Until then, all of today's heavily used satellite trajectories would be useless."

"No more Internet," Rosie said. "No phones, no TV."

Livingstone shook his head. "Kaput, as Jack said so eloquently. Satellite technology is indeed the central nervous system of all our communications systems, banking transactions, global food distribution, ground and air navigation systems, military surveillance. Jack's so-called *controlled* tipping point, his CTP, would have been a massive blow to human civilization, at least in developed countries."

"The worst environmental criminals," I said.

"So Jack believed. Less developed regions and many indigenous cultures …" he bowed his head toward us "… like yours, they would have fared better since people generally live closer to the land."

I nodded slowly. "The Inheritors."

"That's what Jack called you."

"How sweet of him," Rosie said.

"Jack wanted to engineer a collapse of the world's economy *before* its life support systems collapsed."

"You mean, tipped over," Becca said. "Like your plastic trees and stuff."

Livingstone chuckled. "I believe I should rethink my little show after the reaction I got at the concert."

"Sort of backfired, didn't it?" Rosie said.

"They certainly got worked up."

"Dr. Doom," I said. "That's what Jack called you. Maybe focus on the good stuff from now on. The hopeful stuff."

"I'll try, I promise. But Jack was far beyond that. He'd lost all hope when his daughter died of cancer."

"Alinga," I said under my breath.

"Jack's little sunshine, killed by a polluted world—in his mind, at least."

"You and her could have been two peas in a pod," Becca said.

I shrugged. "I don't know."

"I *do* know. And so did Jack. The way he looked at you. He probably had forged adoption papers up his sleeve ready to sign."

"Like, as if one dad's not enough?"

"Yeah, but how often would you see him? Or *anybody* back home?"

"What do you mean?"

"I mean, if Jack had pulled the plug the way he'd planned—what did he say on stage? No more hopping planes all over the bloody place. Well, we'd all be trapped down under. He'd have you right where he wanted, living out his last days on Hot Rock Farm with Alinga Number Two in his pocket."

"Come on, Becca," I said.

"No, think about it. Half-native, just like you, gifted singer, this special woo-woo thing with animals, feels stuff, hears stuff that nobody else does."

"You're crazy," I said, though I knew she was right.

"Actually," Livingstone said, "it's Jack who was crazy, God bless him. Alinga's death was the last straw. Pushed him over the edge. After that, he'd stop at nothing to heal and stabilize his beloved Earth."

"SETI," Becca said.

"Yes, the Stable Earth Treaty. This undoubtedly was his original inspiration, though, I must say, it mutated into something monstrous. It turned an environmental hero into a villain."

Livingstone's computer gave a friendly beep. His desktop picture showed a black sun crowned with a brilliant white halo. "Marvelous, wasn't it?" he said, beaming. "Worth all the bumps. I took the shot myself while Jack was up to his shenanigans."

He powered up the DVD program and double-clicked a file called *Stageview*. "Now, here's what we saw."

There it was again. The eerie sky. The scorched Earth. Jack's deranged face. The downpour. The yellow flash behind Mount Wara. The volley of explosions. And, through it all, our drumming.

"Quite a show, wasn't it?" Livingstone said.

"Was that broadcast?" I said.

"It was. Made a big splash around the world."

I wondered how many people, watching us on TV, plugged into the Web, or listening on the radio, had grabbed something to bang on and joined in. Lots, I hoped. Maybe millions. I knew, with all the cells in my body, that every drumbeat was good for the Earth.

Livingstone paused his cursor over another file, labeled *Jackview CTP-LP*.

"What are the letters?" Becca said.

Livingstone sat back in his seat. "Can you guess?"

"I got it," she said. "Controlled tipping point ... LP, LP ... uh ... lip protector … life preserver … LP … launch pad!"

"Very good. The spearhead of Jack's diabolical dream. He had security cameras everywhere. Rita authorized the release of this particular clip but asked that I not hand it over to any global media until *after* you get home tomorrow. She was concerned it might spook your families."

"Good old Rita," Rosie said.

"And so, here's what Jack saw."

There, lit up by brilliant floodlights, was the grove of mop-topped trees on the back side of Mount Wara.

"This is taken from the top of Jack's command-and-control center. Quite sophisticated, I understand."

"That little white house with the tiny window?" Becca said.

"Correct. Rather thinly disguised with all the razor-wire and such. Like the house, this camera was hardened for the launch blast. It survived the explosion. I'm afraid Jack's house didn't."

All six silos had been peeled back like flower petals. Standing in each was a gleaming silver rocket with a red camel painted on the side.

Rosie laughed. "Shee-it! There's Jack's camels."

Livingstone pointed to the center of the ring. The mountain of shiny pellets we'd seen that first day had shrunk, but a good pile remained. "And there's his Achilles heel."

"Pellets," I said.

"Yes. That's what killed him. After loading the rockets, he'd left a pile of surplus pellets unprotected."

A little digital window at the bottom of the screen showed the CTP numbers rushing toward zero. At the sixty-second mark, the words *Initiate launch sequence* flashed on the screen.

"Now he's cooked," Livingstone muttered.

The rockets came alive. Fingers of fire danced out from under them.

"Isn't that a little crazy?" Becca asked. "I mean, with all those explosive pellets so close."

"Not at all. The pellets are completely inert until … well, just watch."

The flames stiffened, changing from orange to blue. With only thirty seconds to go, the whole scene was suddenly drenched in buckets of rain.

Livingstone thrust his finger at the screen. "Here!"

A great rush of steam rose from the exposed pellets.

"Here comes the hydrogen gas," he said. "A huge, uncontrolled release, triggered by the rain."

Seconds later, flames engulfed the rockets and they toppled over each other like bowling pins. Then everything disappeared in a giant mushroom cloud of fire.

"There you have it. Destroyed by his own invention."

"Like Dr. Frankenstein," Becca said.

"Quite right. That extra flood of hydrogen in the blast zone caught Jack totally off guard. But rain was something he simply had not accounted for. And for good reason. I checked the region's weather records. They go back over a century and there's not one record of rainfall in December."

"Not to mention a seven-year drought," Becca said.

"Astonishing, isn't it?" Livingstone put away his laptop, stretched from head to toe, then folded his hands on his lap. "Poor old Jack."

"Bad luck, I guess." Becca said.

"Bad karma," Rosie said.

"*Warmala*," I whispered as I closed my eyes and tuned in to the soothing thrum of the Pacific thirty-five thousand feet below the plane.

RITA'S GIFT

LOS ANGELES AIRPORT
DECEMBER 23RD, 3:15 PM

Before we parted in Los Angeles airport, Livingstone pulled me aside and slipped me an unmarked DVD envelope. "Rita gave me this for you. A little movie thriller she thought you might enjoy. It's a one-of-a-kind, you might say. You have the only existing copy in your hands. Rita assured me that all the original security footage has been destroyed."

"What's it about?"

"Oh, I don't want to spoil it for you. It's not very long. All I can say is she recommended you watch it in the comfort of your own home." Livingstone leaned toward me with a mad professor look. "Alone."

"*Why?*"

He glanced at his watch. "Sorry, Ashley, but I must scoot. Jolly fun trip it was."

"Uh ... yeah, jolly fun."

He hurriedly shook my hand and took off down the airport corridor, lugging an oversized wheeled suitcase behind him.

"Uh ... good luck, professor," I shouted after him. "Saving the world, I mean."

"You, too," he said with a laugh and a wave.

I thought I saw blue mist leaking from his suitcase.

I stood in the middle of the corridor, staring at the envelope in my hand as people streamed around me. Somebody bumped my arm, knocking the envelope to the floor. A couple of people stepped on it before I managed to grab it back. I stuffed it in my jeans and ran over to the waiting area where the rest of the Dream Drummers were sprawled over half a dozen seats.

"Do you mind watching my stuff a bit longer?" I said. "I really gotta pee."

"Boot it, baby," Becca said. "We board for Edmonton in, like, eight minutes."

"Thanks."

I took a left down the corridor and broke into a sprint.

"The can's the other way!" shouted Becca.

I waved back at her and kept running. What I really needed was a computer, and I'd seen an Internet café down here earlier. I'd decided I couldn't wait to open Rita's gift.

I ran up to the last empty terminal just as a big guy with a viking beard was about to sit down in front of it.

"Uh … do you mind?" I said. "I have a plane to catch."

The guy rolled his eyes but stepped aside. "Don't we all, sweetheart."

I plunked down in the chair, swiped my credit card, then ripped open the envelope. I pulled out a DVD with the numbers 25/8/09 written on it and a little yellow stickie with the words: *You've come a long way, Ashley. Love, Rita.*

It took a couple of precious minutes to get the right computer port to open. When it finally did, I slammed in the disc and hunched over the screen so no one else could see.

Good thing, too.

It only lasted about a minute. But it was long enough to shake me to the core.

It was a fixed Webcam view, really dark, but I could make out a half-opened cardboard box. I adusted the computer screen to maximum brightness. The box was full of Empire Oil brochures, the kind they like to dish out at community meetings in Nanurtalik.

"Holy shit," I whispered as I hunched closer to the screen.

I turned up the volume to hear a sloshing sound. Getting louder.

Something bumped the Webcam and its new angle showed a face all twisted in a crazy kind of anger—just like the look on Jack's face when he'd rage against all the evil planet killers, or the look in his monstrous eyes when he was about to launch his rockets and save the world from us parasites.

Only this wasn't Jack's face.

It was mine.

Another sloshing sound, real close this time, and the view went all blurry. There was a great whooshing sound, some glass shattering, an orange flash, then the screen went blank.

I held my face in my hands, learning how to breathe again, until I felt a tap on my shoulder.

"Are you, like, done yet?" asked the big guy.

"What? Yeah, sure. It's all yours."

I signed off and yanked out the DVD.

As I ran down the crowded airport corridor, half laughing, half crying, I snapped the DVD into about a hundred pieces. I dumped them in three separate garbage cans to make sure no one could ever glue that part of me back together again.

EPILOGUE

NANURTALIK

There are times in life
When a person has to rush off
In pursuit of hopefulness.

– Jean Giono, *The Man Who Planted Trees*

TUULLIK PINGO

Thanks to Rita, there was no more talk about building monster compressor stations in Nanurtalik. Soon after Jack died, she was given honorary membership on Empire Oil's board of directors. Like Jack, she tried her best to green the company from the inside out. Unlike Jack, she believed in people power to turn things around.

Jack's style was to think globally, act globally. If the Earth had a problem, it was bloody well up to him to fix the whole friggin' thing. Rita's style was different. Think globally, act *locally*. Convince everybody to do that, she figured, and we'll be in a lot better shape real soon.

It floored me when she decided to start with my home.

It's as good a place as any to start, she'd written in an email soon after we returned from Australia. *Your village will be a beacon of hope at the top of the world, just like Hot Rock Farm was always meant to be. By the way, we managed to find a big investor to start tapping the heaps of geothermal energy below us. I reckon we'll soon be powering half of Australia! Just like Jack hoped in the early days.*

Hope.

Not a word that stuck on the Jack I knew. God, no. The way Rita told it, his passion to help the Earth followed a dead-end road from hope to anger. I guess for me it was the opposite. These days, hope was as much a part of me as Uitajuq's smile.

From the summit of Tuullik Pingo we had a grand view of two of Rita's pet projects.

About a mile behind Anirniq Hill, a pump-jack slowly rocked up and down, feeding local natural gas directly to our homes. I got permission to paint a green dinosaur face on the pump-jack's head to honor the company that paid for it.

The other project was what Mom called the twelve apostles. A dozen gleaming white wind turbines circled the town like birthday candles, all constructed and paid for with Empire Oil money. Everyone, including Mayor Jacobs, agreed it was a perfect way to harness some of the crazy winds we'd been getting lately. Besides, it was good for business. Tourists, engineers, energy specialists, and yes, indigenous people from around the world had come to see how our tiny Arctic village harnessed local energy to keep warm and cozy in the land of the midnight sun.

It might have had something to do with all the press we'd got at the Scorched Earth concert. Now, no visitors left town without asking us to perform. Our CD was flying off shelves around the world.

The empire even sponsored this summer's Northern Lights Music Festival, an annual party that I lived for. As usual, performers and fans flew in from across the north, and, this year, from somewhat farther away.

"Right nice a' ya to invite me up here for yer concert. As long as I don't cark it on stage."

"Hey, no worries, mate," I said in my best Aussie accent. "I know it's a hard act to follow, but you'll be right. We'll keep the polar bears off stage while yer up there with your didj."

We sat together on the fragrant moss and lichens as a laughing red-throated loon flew straight for us out of nowhere. It circled over us once, twice, three times, then dissolved into the glassy Arctic sky. Jirra tried to call it back by imitating its laugh. That only got me laughing, and soon we were rolling over the edge of the pingo, smothering each other with kisses.

GLOSSARY

AS = Australia, slang
AP = Australia, Pitjantjatjara aborigine
AR = Australia, Roper area aborigine
FR = French
IN = Inuktitut
PO = Polynesian
SA = Sanskrit

Aamittara –	(IN) be careful
Aana –	(IN) paternal grandmother
Amari –	(AR) grandfather
Ai –	(IN) hello
Alinga –	(AP) name shared by several aboriginal groups, meaning sun
Amauti –	(IN) Traditional woman's parka with a deep hood at the back in which babies and children are placed
Anaana –	(IN) mother
Anirniq –	(IN) angel, spirit
Assunai –	(IN) goodbye
Away with the pixies –	(AS) in another world, daydreaming
Brekkie –	(AS) breakfast
Bien sur –	(FR) of course
Boobage –	(AS) Boobs, breasts
Burl –	(AS) attempt, try, as in, "Give it a burl"
Cark –	(AS) die; also, "cark it;" often used of a machine that breaks down, e.g., "The car's finally carked it"

Déjà vu –	(FR) literally, "already seen;" an impression or vaguely familiar feeling that one has seen or experienced something before; also called paramnesia, from the Greek para, "near" and mneme, "memory"
Didjeridu –	(AP) along, wooden, cylindrical wind instrument of Australian aborigine people, traditionally from northern Australia; played with continuously vibrating lips to produce a buzzing drone, while using a special breathing technique called circular breathing; also spelled Didgeridoo
Dinky die –	(AS) true, genuine, the real thing
Drongo –	(AS) someone who is not very bright
Emoh Ruo –	(AS) "Our Home" spelled backward, a common Australian name for one's house
Fuck-a-duck –	(AS) a statement of disbelief, e.g., "No way!"
Galah –	(AS) silly, foolish person, dolt; also a pink and grey species of cockatoo native to Australia
Gobsmacked –	(AS) taken by surprise; "I'll be gobsmacked" = Incredible! Is that so?
Grouse –	(AS) excellent, fine, outstanding
Igunaq –	(IN) rotten meat; often referring to fermented walrus meat, a popular traditional food across the Arctic
Inniturliq –	(IN) old camping site used for a long time; fictional name of closest major town to Nanurtalik
Inullarik –	(IN) a true Inuk; a capable and talented man

Inukshuk –	(IN) stone figure constructed by Inuit across North America and Greenland; used for navigation, hunting marker, food cache, herding caribou into a harvest area, or sacred landmark; also inuksuk; plural inuksuit
Ittuq –	(IN) grandfather
Jackaroo –	(AS) hired hand on a large farm or sheep station
Jirra –	(AP) kangaroo
Kaitiaki –	(PO) guardian or steward; also to have guardianship or stewardship over something
Kamiik –	(IN) traditional Inuit footwear often made from seal or caribou skin
Kulini –	(AP) to listen
Kulini kulini –	(AP) Are you listening?
Kulini Ngura –	(AP) listening place; name of the sacred dome-shaped hills featured on Jack Masters's Hot Rock Farm
Kunpu –	(AP) strong, tough
Liru –	(AP) poisonous snake
Maiksuk! –	(IN) bad thing
Moana –	(PO) sea or ocean
Moz –	(AS) to jinx, e.g., "Put a moz on him"
Muktuk –	(IN) whale blubber
Mulupa –	(AP) True!
Ngiyari –	(AP) thorny devil lizard
Nganana –	(AP) all of us
Ngura –	(AP) home, camp, place
Nakurmik –	(IN) thanks
Nanurtalik –	(IN) fictional name of Ashley's Arctic hamlet, meaning "place with polar bears"
Nick off –	(AS) leave

No flies on –	(AS) smart or intelligent, e.g., There's no flies on that girl = You can't fool her
Panic merchant –	(AS) one who panics easily or spreads fear
Pash –	(AS) to kiss passionately
Pikatjara –	(AP) sick
Piker –	(AS) one who doesn't keep his / her word or breaks promises; doesn't pull her weight
Pingo –	(IN) a conical mound of earth-covered ice found in in the Arctic, subarctic, and Antarctica that can reach up to seventy meters in height and up to two kilometers in diameter; literally means "small hill"
Piranpa –	(AP) white, white person, non-aboriginal
Plonk –	(AS) cheap wine
Porkie –	(AS) a lie
Puli –	(AP) rock, the name of Jirra's dingo
Qilauti –	(IN) traditional Inuit drum made from a narrow rim of driftwood and stretched caribou skin; held in one hand by a short handle, the drum is rotated back and forth and struck on the edge with a wooden mallet, which is often wrapped in the skin of walrus or seal
Qimmiit –	(IN) sled dogs; Inuit name for the constellation of Taurus the Bull
Rage –	(AS) a really good time, a big party
Rinpoche –	(SA) Last name of Buddhist monk Ashley meets on UN stage; a title of honor literally meaning "precious one"
Roo –	(AS) kangaroo
Sheila –	(AS) woman

Sila –	(IN) weather, climate, environment, all that surrounds us; a very strong spiritual power contained in people and the land
Sila qatlunaatitut –	(IN) Sila's revenge
Siksik –	(IN) Arctic ground squirrel (the sound it makes when alarmed)
Sossi –	(AS) sausage
Sparrow's fart –	(AS) dawn
Spunk –	(AS) good looking
Suluk –	(IN) feather
Suss out –	(AS) to find out or investigate
Ta –	(AS) thank you
Taima –	(IN) That's it. That's all.
Thrumming –	sound with a monotonous hum; rhythmic, droning vibration of a stringed instrument
Tiguaq –	(IN) adopted brother
Too right! –	(AS) Absolutely!
Tuurngaq –	(IN) ghost, spirit
Tuktu –	(IN) caribou
Tukturjuit –	(IN) caribou (pl); Inuit name for the Ursa Minor constellation of which the Big Dipper is a part
Ullaktut –	(IN) fast runners; Inuit name for Orion constellation
Uitajuq –	(IN) "His / her eyes are open and stay open." Inuktitut name for Ashley and her great-grand-mother, mother of Aana; pronounced "U-tah-yuk"
Ute –	(AS) utility truck or pickup
Waahi tapu –	(PO) sacred place
Waffle on –	(AS) to talk incessantly without making sense

Walawuru –	(AP) wedge-tailed eagle; this large black eagle uses thermals of hot desert air created to rise to great heights where its keen eyes scan for food; it can kill animals as large as small kangaroos by gliding down and striking them about the head with its massive talons
Warmala –	(AP) traditional revenge party
Willi-willi –	(AS) dust devil; a small vortex of disturbed air made visible by a spinning cloud of dust or debris; forms in response to surface heating during fair, hot weather; most frequent in arid or semi-arid regions
Wiru –	(AP) great, lovely, fine, beautiful
Wiya –	(AP) no; pronounced wee-ya
Wobbly –	(AS) excitable behavior; e.g., "I complained about the food and the waiter threw a wobbly"
Wouldn't it rot your socks! –	(AS) expression of disappointment
Yonks –	(AS) ages, a long time

ACKNOWLEDGMENTS

I am indebted to the many nameless people of New York's Manhattan Island and Australia's Simpson desert who opened their very different worlds for me and helped me discover some common ground.

Many thanks to you, Steve Woods, and your awesome drumming band, Northern Cree. Little did you know it, but that night in Saskatoon where you got nine hundred of us up and dancing, you unearthed the turning point of this story which vibrates to the sound of ten thousand drums.

And to you, Maurice Strong, of the United Nations Environment Program, for uttering the words (off the record of course) that helped Jack Masters spring, fully formed, onto these pages.

Thank you, Glen MacKay, at Yellowknife's Prince of Wales Northern Heritage Centre, for sharing with me an anthropologist's radical opening to the "animate universe," to avant-garde throat-singer, Tanya Tagaq, who blazed Ashley's trail from the Arctic to the Carnegie stage, and to you, Karsten Heuer, for revealing a thrumming land in *Being Caribou*.

Thank you, Gordon Hans, my real live Aussie brother in Melbourne, for your screening of my Australian slang.

For editorial advice, I thank my ruthless teenage assistants Jaya Bastedo and Amber O'Reilly, plus fellow writers David Malcolm and Mindy Willet. I offer a heartfelt thanks to all the supportive staff at Red Deer Press and Fitzhenry & Whiteside, especially editor Peter Carver for, as usual, finding the fire behind the smoke of my early drafts, and to managing editor Richard Dionne, for believing in this project from the word "go."

And finally, thank you, Brenda, for once again supporting my writing habit in so many countless ways.

INTERVIEW WITH JAMIE BASTEDO

WITH TEN EASY STEPS TO HELP FIGHT GLOBAL WARMING

Where did the idea for this book come from?

Most bookstores these days have shelves groaning with the latest best-selling non-fiction books on the perils of global climate change and the urgency of taking action. I wrote *On Thin Ice* to give fiction readers an in-your-face picture of this issue from the front lines of climate change, the Arctic. *Sila's Revenge* moves beyond the hard-core effects of climate change to the question many of us ask ourselves: "Okay, so what can I do?" In this adventure, Ashley is gradually shaped into an heroic climate change crusader who, I hope, will inspire readers to harness their own "power of one" and help tackle this issue head-on.

A number of scientific theories are explored in this story, some of them quite radical. Tell us about the ideas that are most important to you.

Like *On Thin Ice*, this sequel is a work of pure fiction. I made the whole thing up and had a lot of fun doing it. But all the climate science sprinkled through these pages is based on accurate, real-world research. Much of this is revealed through James Livingstone's captivating show at the UN climate change conference where he speaks of the "Three Great Disasters," or global tipping points, induced by runaway warming: a collapse of the Gulf Stream, the death of Amazonian rainforests, and the explosive release of methane from the sea floor. All of these potential scenarios are well documented in both scientific and popular literature (for instance, see *The Weather Makers* by Australian palaeontologist and environmental activist Tim Flannery). Other scientific curiosities in the story that are also factually based include: the hydrogen potential of aluminum-gallium alloy, the geothermal potential of Australia's giant TAG—the thermally anomalous granite lying deep beneath the Simpson Desert—and the fantastic play of light and shadow created by a solar eclipse.

In some ways, what Livingstone describes in his description of the "Three Great Disasters" is frightening, almost to the point of making readers think: well, what's the point? What could I possibly do to offset the tipping points to come? In fact, there are climate doomsayers today— above all, James Lovelock, the originator of the Gaia theory—who are saying, with Jack, that the planet will soon turn its back on civilization to save itself. What is there in your story that can encourage us to think that Doomsday is not just around the corner?

In his recent best-seller, *The Revenge of Gaia* (which inspired the title for this novel), James Lovelock declares that humans are "disabling the planet like a disease." He is confident that Gaia—the mysterious forces that regulate the Earth—will survive but he feels that now may be "much too late" to save ourselves. There's a little bit of Lovelock in Livingstone, but the professor I created is a tad more optimistic about our future.

When I read books like Lovelock's—and there is a fast-growing pile of them—I sometimes suffer fits of despair about our planet's health and wonder if it's too late for *anybody* to do *anything*. Why not just give up, turn off the news, and "drift merrily above Niagara Falls," as Jack says, until we tip over the edge? I suspect anyone who doesn't have similar feelings now and then is out of touch with reality.

Sparked by an onslaught of climate change impacts, Ashley's journey follows an arc from anger to hope—from torching the local headquarters of a "global carbon criminal," to releasing a worldwide flood of healing energy from the Scorched Earth stage. Jack Masters travels in the opposite direction, from hope to anger and ... well ... he ends up dead.

Ashley's victory in the fight against climate change is not merely symbolic. Nor is it restricted only to artistically gifted youth with a shamanic flair. In today's tightly interconnected world, the power of one passionate individual to make a difference is greater than ever before. When such individuals join hands through bold, collective action, they sow the seeds of planetary transformation, while inspiring others to swim against the current of despair. In this sense, Ashley's victory belongs to all who believe in this power.

Ashley Anowiak is a very convincing heroine. Some readers will be intrigued that a male author could get into the head of a strong female character. Where did this character spring from?

Is this not the central fun of fiction? You can be anyone, anywhere, at any time. An Inuit girl or a thorny lizard. All sentient beings are fair game! To get into Ashley's head, I had to become a "literary crossdresser"—a 54-year-old Caucasian male living in the subarctic, writing through the eyes and heart of an eighteen-year-old Inuit girl living in the Arctic. I have two teenage daughters of my own and have absorbed much of today's teen world through them. My oldest, Jaya, was the same age as Ashley when I wrote this story and she served as my most ruthless editor, combing an early manuscript of the book for any sins I may have committed on how Ashley might speak, act, think, or dress. My many visits to schools and outdoor camps dominated by Aboriginal kids, and thirty years working and living in northern Canada have given me a good feel for the kinds of challenges Ashley might face and how she would react to them.

Who is Ashley? She is a composite of many of those kids, particularly those caught "between worlds" through a mix of race, culture, or environment. She also personifies a new breed of sensitive youth that is bombarded with news of a wounded planet and is passionately seeking meaningful ways to help heal it.

The climactic drumming scene on the Scorched Earth stage is Ashley's finest moment. Where did you get the idea of her triggering this amazing event?

The idea came to me as a gift while I was still struggling with the conclusion of this story. I was at a Literacy for Life banquet in Saskatoon that featured a Native drumming group, Northern Cree, led by Steve Woods. After getting all nine hundred of us up and dancing, he spoke passionately of the sacred power of the drum and how traditional cultures around the world—from Mexico to Mozambique—beat the drum in unison every solstice and equinox to promote the healing of Mother Earth. It's officially called the "8,000 Sacred Drums Ceremony" (you can Google it) and has been happening consistently for many years. I boosted the threshold number to 10,000 (hey, remember I'm a fiction writer!) but remained true to the power and intent of this sacred event.

Jack is a great villain. He's brilliant, powerful, rich, and makes plans to destroy civilization as we know it. Tell us about your enjoyment in creating this character—and do you think the final act he attempts is really possible to carry out—or is it in the realm of science fiction?

When I was a little kid, I actually knew a man named Jack Masters. I used to walk a mile to school and he lived along my route. Jack was a big mysterious man and a fierce walker. Whenever I saw him storming down the road, I would always dash to the other side to avoid being trampled underfoot. There's a bit of that Jack in my Jack. More than anything, I loved the name.

From the moment I first conceived of this story, I was on the lookout for a dark character who could help draw out Ashley's light. In our undeclared war on the Earth, sometimes I feel like giving up on humans and cheering for the Earth to beat us down to size. Jack takes this feeling to extremes by hatching his plan to knock out all satellite communication—"the central nervous system of a civilization that's got a little too big for its britches!"

Could he have done it? Most certainly. I like to write what I call science-based fiction, not science fiction. We're talking rocket science here, but nothing too fancy. While laser-guided missiles and nuclear warheads capture the "Star Wars" headlines, there is a solid body of research suggesting that the most effective anti-satellite technology might well be a few buckets of bolts shot into space. As Dr. Livingstone explains near the end of the story, "It doesn't take much to knock out a satellite." A few thousand of Jack's shiny pellets, injected into high-altitude satellite trajectories, could indeed spark a catastrophic chain reaction that would knock out the Achilles heel of our digitally dependent world.

You have had a significant career as a writer of non-fiction. How difficult has it been for you to shift to the role of storyteller?

Over the past twenty years, I have made a deliberate shift away from highly technical, scientific publications in ecology to more popular works that promote wider appreciation of nature and our place in it. It's generally true that the more technical the writing, the fewer people read it. I wanted to reach a wider audience and found that it was the stories in my early non-fiction books that readers seemed to enjoy most. My leap into fiction came with a push from my then young daughters who declared, "No more books, Daddy, until you write a kids' book!" I took up the challenge with my grizzly book, *Tracking Triple Seven,* and found a fun new way to stir natural science into rip-snorting adventure stories. As suggested by one reviewer of *On Thin Ice,* "Sometimes good fiction gives the reader a more intense experience of the real world than non-fiction."

What advice do you have for readers—and writers—who want to do something about the climate change issue, who want to influence how the planet evolves?

As author Betty Reese writes, "If you think you are too small to be effective, you have never been in bed with a mosquito." The buzz on personal actions we can take to combat climate change is everywhere on the web, in bookstores, in schools, and on the streets. Here's an excellent list adapted from the *Global Warming Survival Handbook* by David de Rothschild. In addition to typical actions like these, don't forget to draw upon your unique strengths, skills, and talents such as music, drama, art, writing, public speaking, organizing, and fund-raising to find your own way to, as Mahatma Gandhi said, "Shake the world gently."

HERE'S TEN EASY STEPS TO HELP FIGHT GLOBAL WARMING:

1. *Adjust Your Climate by Two Degrees*
   Turning your heat down by two degrees in the winter and your air-conditioner up by two degrees in the summer can save our planet from more than one-third of a ton of CO_2 emissions per year.

2. *Change a Light Bulb*
   If every household in the country used just one energy-saving light bulb, it would be enough to shut down a major power station.

3. *Stop Appliances from Standing-By*
   Those little red lights on your TV, stereo, and computer? They're on standby, waiting for your remote click, and still sapping energy. Turn them off for real by unplugging them and cut your home energy-related emissions by ten percent or more.

4. *Say No to Plastic Bags*
   The story of the five hundred billion to one trillion plastic bags used each year doesn't have a happy ending. Most end up in landfills, blowing through the streets, or hurting animals on land or in the sea.

5. *Shop Locally*
   On average, each item in your local supermarket has traveled at least a thousand miles to get to you. Buying locally produced food reduces the amount of energy used for transportation.

6. *Bring Your Own Mug*

   Bring your own travel mug. Most disposable cups go directly into landfills where they not only take up space but, as they break down, release large amounts of methane and carbon dioxide, two major contributors to global warming.

7. *Go Public*

   One bus can carry the same number of people as fifty cars. Subways and trains hold even more. All forms of public transport can slash the amount of fossil fuel used per passenger and hence, the amount of greenhouse gases released.

8. *Bike or Walk*

   Bike or walk to work, to school, to the store—doing so will give the planet a much-needed break from the CO_2 emissions of your car.

9. *Say Yes to Short Showers*

   Global warming promises to worsen water shortages around the world. A quick shower uses one-third the water of a bath. Cutting your shower time by one minute can save more than five hundred gallons of water each year.

10. *Plant Something*

    Plants take in CO_2 and pump out oxygen. A single tree provides enough oxygen for two people for their entire lives. Plants and trees provide homes and food for birds and other wildlife.

ABOUT *ON THIN ICE*

The tiny hamlet of Nanurtalik—a place known for polar bears—is thrown into chaos as the community fears that starving polar bears, driven to new habitats by the drastically changing climate, have returned. A teenager, found mangled on a nearby ice road, seems to confirm their fears.

Sixteen-year-old Ashley Anowiak, who has a special bond with the polar bears, is led on a mysterious journey to find Nanurluk—a giant legendary bear that has been haunting her people for thousands of years. Ashley is led from the frozen catacombs beneath her town, through the dangerous ice fields capping the Arctic Ocean. As her inner and outer worlds are torn apart, Ashley is desperate to find solid ground to stand on. This is a story of a gifted young woman struggling to find her true home and purpose in a fast-changing Arctic where climate, culture and the environment seem to be falling apart all around her.

On Thin Ice is both an exciting mystery and a touching lesson in the relationship between humans and the environment ... [Bastedo's] message is sure to resonate with young readers.

–*Canadian Geographic*

While readers will be intrigued by the mystical elements of the story as they are woven into the realistic daily life of a modern Arctic teen, there are also many undisguised messages about global warming, chaos theory, and man's effect on the weather patterns. Human encroachment into the animal habitat is illustrated by a few chapters told from the polar bear's viewpoint, as hunter and hunted.

–*School Library Journal*

OTHER BOOKS BY JAMIE BASTEDO

On Thin Ice (*Sila's Revenge* is the sequel to this novel.)

Free as the Wind: Saving the Horses of Sable Island

Falling for Snow: A Naturalist's Journey into the World of Winter

Tracking Triple Seven

Shield Country: The Life and Times of the Oldest Piece of the Planet

Reaching North: A Celebration of the Subarctic

The Horrors: Terrifying Tales, Book Two (edited by Peter Carver)